The elevator came to a halt.

The doors slid open and the cool night air drifted in. With a blind foot, she searched behind her for the lip of the opening. Another step back brought her in contact with the cement garage floor. She took a quick look over her shoulder to make sure no one was around, then instantly turned back to her adversary. Her arms were starting to stiffen from holding the gun so tightly, but her aim never wavered. Her eyes held his steadily as she reached over and repositioned the key into the slot labeled ROOF, then withdrew it. Pocketing the keys, she said, "It's been a pleasure."

She slapped her palm against the Up button, and the door began to close. She could feel relief rising and, as her adrenaline slowed, she relaxed.

A mistake.

He launched himself at the door. Her panicked scream blended with the two quick bursts she squeezed from the gun.

Myk felt the hot lead explode in his shoulder and the resulting pain spun him back against the elevator's wall. Her dark and frightened eyes were the last he saw of her as the door slid shut. . . .

BEVERLY JENKINS

THE EDGE OF MIDNIGHT

HarperTorch
An Imprint of HarperCollinsPublishers

This is a work of fiction. Names, characters, places, and incidents are products of the author's imagination or are used fictitiously and are not to be construed as real. Any resemblance to actual events, locales, organizations, or persons, living or dead, is entirely coincidental.

❦

HARPERTORCH
An Imprint of HarperCollins*Publishers*
10 East 53rd Street
New York, New York 10022-5299

Copyright © 2004 by Beverly Jenkins
ISBN: 0-06-054066-4

First HarperTorch paperback printing: February 2004

HarperCollins ®, HarperTorch™, and ❦™ are trademarks of Harper-Collins Publishers Inc.

Printed in the United States of America

Visit HarperTorch on the World Wide Web at www.harpercollins.com

10 9 8 7 6 5 4 3

In 1985,
Mary Henson, Joyce Puckett,
Sharon Lehman, and Monica Ninteman
read a draft of this book and loved it.
Many years have passed,
but I've never forgotten them
or their help and encouragement.
Here's your book, ladies. Thanks.

Prologue

Oakland County, Michigan
May 2003

At midnight, wealthy industrialist, Marvin Rand lay asleep in his Oakland County mansion dreaming of his long-legged mistress. In bed beside him, Rand's wife Marilyn, dreamed of divorce. Neither was aware that outside, five men dressed in black were overriding the mansion's state-of-the-art security system. The estate's six guard dogs had alerted no one. The animal tranq slipped into their dinner had the fierce Dobermans sleeping as soundly as their owners.

The men outside waited expectantly while their leader quickly attached the wires of a small device to the base works of the alarm box the Rands had been guaranteed no one could access. He then used a gloved finger to punch a coded number into the palm-sized computer in his hand and waited. When its tiny red light flashed, he waved his men on in.

They entered the house through the deck's huge

screen door. Senses alert, they moved through the shadowy rooms on steps silent as heartbeats. Their handheld penlights traveled over priceless antiques, expensive state-of-the-art electronics, and the wall vault that held Marilyn Rand's famous gems. The contents of the Rands' million-dollar home would be Paradise Found to an ordinary gang of thieves, but these men were extraordinary.

The information provided to the intruders on the house's layout proved accurate; the mansion was huge, and more than a few of the Rands' guests had gotten themselves lost in its vastness during the couple's many well-attended dinner parties. Tonight's uninvited guests had no such difficulties. At the expansive staircase that led to the upper regions of the house, the leader peeled off from the main group. He had business upstairs with Rand.

The rest of the men moved on. Their map led them down one level and directed them past the Olympic-sized pool, a billiard room, and a fifty-seat movie theater to their destination—the twelve-lane bowling alley. While one man knelt to spring the door's lock, the others used their penlights to sweep the surroundings for unwanted onlookers or surprises. The door was opened and once again the interior quickly swept with light. No one. Marvin Rand had an extensive stock of expensive liquor displayed behind the wall-long bar—he also had 5 million dollars' worth of blood diamonds in the bar's freezer. The stones were called blood diamonds because of the bloodshed surrounding their mining and illegal exportation.

The men made short work of the freezer's inadequate padlock and pulled up on the heavy door. The cold air swirled foglike around the thin beams of their lights. The seven packages were all wrapped in brown paper and placed exactly where the maid said they'd be. The men allowed themselves only a moment of satisfaction at the find. Then they lifted out the parcels and began to ready them for transport.

Upstairs, the leader silently entered the Rands' bedroom. He crossed the plush imported carpet over to the bed and stood above them for a moment while they slept. Although the couple was ignorant of his presence, he was certain that would change when Rand woke up in the morning and found the diamonds gone. To make sure he had a really bad day, the leader placed a parting gift on Mrs. Rand's pillow. It was a sealed mailer containing a videocassette detailing her husband's involvement with the diamonds and their links to international drug cartels and terrorist organizations, and, fifteen minutes of a fairly graphic encounter starring Rand and his long-legged mistress.

Satisfied, the tall man quietly moved around to the other side of the king-size bed so he could leave Rand a gift, too. It was a common, everyday playing card. A black ace of spades.

Three days later, noted architect Mykal Chandler sat in his expensive, riverfront home eating breakfast and reading the city's morning edition. The drapes on the wallwide windows had been pulled back to let in the still-rising sun. On page three, a small news item caught his eye: Industrialist Marvin Rand and his wife, Marilyn, were divorcing. Mrs. Rand's lawyer cited, "irreconcilable differences" as the cause of the action. Chandler turned the page and went back to his eggs.

One

Shivering with cold, thirty-three-year-old Sarita Grayson walked over to the worn pea coat hanging on a nail behind her desk and put it on. Even though it was only mid-October, the temperature inside her office in the old warehouse felt like below freezing. During the day, if the sun was out, being inside the drafty old eyesore wasn't too bad, but once evening rolled around, the temperature dropped like a stone, and cold ruled. The building's ancient heating system was kept running with duct tape, hairpins, and prayer. It was two-faced, however, and would cut off at a moment's notice, so Sarita and her staff didn't like turning it on until the weather outside made it absolutely necessary.

She blew on her hands to keep them warm, then dug through the mountain of papers atop her lop-sided desk looking for the notice from the city. She picked it up and read it again for maybe the fiftieth time since it had arrived in the mail three days earlier. The words had not changed. Block red letters, three inches high screamed EVICTION PROCEEDINGS across the top like a tabloid headline. The day it arrived the shock had paralyzed her. Even now, her hands shook a bit. She and her people had been using this abandoned warehouse for many years, working hard to transform the abandoned hulking structure into the hub of the struggling community surrounding it. The space offered the children a safe environment in which to learn and play and gave the senior citizens a place where they could meet and stay connected to life and the neighborhood.

But now, because the city wanted to auction off the property, they were being threatened with eviction.

The building had originally housed a food distribution company. After the owners moved the operation to the suburbs back in the early eighties, it sat empty, attracting gang graffiti, rats, and crackheads. One summer night in 1990, the local Baptist church down the street caught fire and burned to the ground. Having no place for the congregation to worship, Pastor Otis Washington and the elders approached the city about moving into the vacant building temporarily until money could be raised for a new church. The city gave its permission on the condition that if the building were sold, the church would move its services and neighborhood programs elsewhere. Washington and the congregation agreed. The new church was built, but the outreach programs dedicated to kids, seniors, and unwed mothers remained housed in the old warehouse. Because of all the neighborhood crack and crime, neither the city nor the congregation envisioned anyone's buying the place.

Obviously, times had changed; the city received a bid for the property two weeks ago. Sarita had taken over the running of the William Lambert Community Center after Pastor Washington's death in 1998, and if she could come up with the money to match the seventeen-thousand-dollar offer, then she and her people could stay—if not, they were on the street. How in the world the city expected her to come up with that much cash, and in six days no less, was beyond her.

Her thoughts were interrupted by the sight of Silas Devine sticking his gray head in the doorway. After the death of Sarita's grandmother and great-uncles, Silas had become the elder in her life. She loved him dearly.

"Afternoon, General," he said to her.

It was his pet name for her, and she gave him a smile. "Afternoon, Silas. How are you?"

"I'm okay. Any luck?"

She knew he was talking about the seventeen-thousand-dollar dilemma. She shook her head. "So far, nothing."

Silas was her right-hand man. He looked after the plumbing, mowed the grass, helped out with driving the homebound seniors wherever they needed to go; anything Sarita needed, Silas did. He was also the only person she'd told about the eviction notice.

"Something will come up," he said confidently. "This place is too important to shut down. You'll see."

Sarita agreed with him on the Lambert Center's importance to the neighborhood, but wasn't sure the city officials who'd sent the eviction notice felt the same way. "How's the van this morning?"

Their donated van was fifteen years old and on its last legs. It needed a new engine, muffler, and struts, and the floor was almost rusted through; but, somehow, Silas kept it running.

"It woke up in a pretty good mood," he told her. "Started right up."

They shared a grin, and Silas added, "I'm on my way to take Mrs. Black over to the train station so she can get to Chicago for her brother's funeral."

"Okay. I'll see you when you get back."

He nodded, then studied her silently for a moment, before saying, "Don't give up. Somewhere up in heaven, Pastor Washington and that grand-mamma of yours are all pulling strings. We'll get through this, I know we will."

She shook her head in agreement, but in reality, didn't share his optimism.

After his departure, Sarita got up from her cluttered desk and walked over to look out of her small, wire-screened window. The center's uncertain future filled her with a sense of helplessness that was totally out of character. In the years she'd been in charge, she'd always, always been able to effect some change in a seemingly unsolvable situation—able to do a fast shuffle here, call in a favor there to keep the ship afloat, but this time she wasn't so sure. School had let out about an hour ago, and out of her office window she could see the children playing down below on the cracked, broken pavement of the building's parking lot, which served as the yard. None of the kids were dressed for the weather. They were in the thin jackets, threadbare jeans, and cheap athletic shoes most would still be wearing during the *hawk*-raging months of January and February, but like most children blessed by love and life, they didn't seem to mind. Small knots of boys and girls played tag, twirled rope for double dutch and shot hoop at the leaning, no-net backboard.

So far, she hadn't told anyone but Silas about the city's notice—not the senior citizens who depended on the center for food and services—not the parents of the children whose only option for recreation might now be the streets. Sarita had kept the information on the down low, hoping beyond hope something would happen, but so far, nothing had.

She went back over to her desk and sat down. There had to be a way out of this mess. It wasn't like her to go down without a fight. To that end she picked up the phone. Her very last hope lay with the Mayor's Office. The newly elected mayor, Drake Randolph, had been in office less than a year. She and everyone else she knew had voted for him because of his vision for the future. The promises he'd made during the campaign were actually being kept in the form of working streetlights, more police patrols, and safer public transportation. Randolph's administration had begun freeing the city from the stagnation of the old regime, and the residents loved him. Sarita was sure that if he were made aware of the situation she and her people were facing, something could be worked out. However, for the last three days she'd been unable to get through to him or any of his people. Her calls to his office, answered by a snippy receptionist, hadn't been put through. According to the receptionist, the people Sarita needed to speak with were either out of town, in a meeting, or unavailable, and no, the woman had no idea when they might return Sarita's calls. All this unavailability made Sarita wonder if there were anyone in charge of the city at all because every time she called, she got the same runaround.

But she was determined not to give up. She vowed not to throw in the towel until she'd spoken with someone in the city administration. So to keep that vow (and adding a further vow to be polite and not curse at the receptionist as she'd done that morning), Sarita dialed the number of City Hall. In response, she got the same old song. No, the parties Sarita needed to speak with were still unavailable. And no, no one knew when they were expected to return. Angry, Sarita hung up.

Mykal Chandler waited until the nine men and women who made up the ruling council of the task force took their seats before passing out the folders. They called themselves NIA. In Swahili, the word, *Nia*, means, purpose, and the purpose of the group was to stop the flow of drugs into the city, *by any means necessary*.

Some of the people seated around the table in Myk's finely furnished dining room represented various law enforcement agencies, both federal and local. They were individuals Myk and his half brother Drake Randolph, who also happened to be Detroit's newly elected mayor, had personally recruited. Tonight's meeting was only one of the many that would be necessary if NIA were to be as successful as everyone hoped.

Myk had already read the initial reports; NIA's guerrilla tactics were having an effect. The midnight strikes against known crack houses, coupled with the outing of white-collar, corporate-executive types who handled the distribution and supply were beginning to be felt. NIA had been operating less than six months, and the Marvin Rand episode had been their biggest mission so far. The Blue squad oversaw the city's west side, while the Green squad operated on the east side. Both teams had included in their reports photos of some of the more well-known dealers, their houses, and their crews. The pictures would be added to NIA photo files and cross-referenced with the Feds' national and international databases.

Myk waited until the reports were all read, before asking, "Well, what do you think?"

"Everything seems to be going just fine, so far," a representative from one of the Federal agencies replied.

Others nodded their agreement.

The mayor tossed the folder he'd been reading back into the center of the table. "If we keep up the heat, maybe we'll make some progress."

They discussed some other issues pertinent to the group's mission, and, an hour later, the meeting ended. Drake stayed behind so he and Myk could talk privately.

Mayor Drake Randolph had been in office for almost a year. He'd been a highly respected orthopedic surgeon before taking on the challenges of running the nation's sixth largest city, and Myk, owner and CEO of Chandler Works, a multinational architectural firm, had amassed enough wealth through construction and investments to be named one of the most successful Black businessmen in the nation. Each brother had worked hard to make it to the top of his field. They both loved the city. Making it safe and viable once again was proving to be the most challenging undertaking of their lives.

Myk poured them both a small shot of cognac from the crystal decanter he'd purchased in Spain the year before and handed one to Drake. As they each took a small sip, Myk went over to the windows facing the river and looked out at the silent night. "You know, Drake," he said after a few moments of silence, "we have to be pretty arrogant to believe we can do this. The government has spent how many millions fighting the war on drugs?"

Drake tossed back, "Probably more than even they can count, but since you're the most arrogant brother I know, who better to be in charge?"

Myk gave his brother a small smile.

Drake grinned in response, "See, you won't even deny it. Besides, it's too late to have second thoughts now. The genie is already out of the bottle."

"But will we get our wish is the question?"

"We will. Wishes always come true when you're on the side of right, my brother. I don't know how much longer we're going to be able to keep this out of the media, though. We're busting crack houses pretty regularly now. Some of the investigative reporters in this town are very good. Sooner or later, one of them is going to start connecting the dots."

"So, they do a story on a mysterious force taking down drug houses. I don't think Detroiters are going to mind that. Probably sell a few papers, too."

"You're right, but we're breaking all kinds of civil rights laws."

"Dealers don't have civil rights. They lost them

the moment they decided selling death to people was okay. Besides, the government has always broken the law when it's to its advantage. Remember the Chicago Black Panthers back in the sixties? The government didn't care about their civil rights, and those brothers stood for truth. I personally have no problem with this."

"Well, if this task force idea of mine comes back to bite us, I doubt any grand jury will convict us for trying to stop drugs and guns from killing our kids."

Myk studied his brother closely. They'd discussed the political ramifications of Drake's being a part of NIA and how he might be negatively impacted should a stink arise over the task force's strong-arm tactics. Myk could honestly say his brother was a mayor who genuinely cared about the welfare of the city and its residents; Myk didn't want Drake's good intentions derailed by scandal. "You can always pull out, you know."

"I know, but why would I? This is my fight, and, besides, who would keep you in line? You need me to be your conscience."

Myk chuckled softly. Drake was right. Without him to temper Myk's intense nature, the NIA project might never have gotten off the ground. Drake's counsel, though not always appreciated, kept Myk sane. "When you met with the Feds yesterday did they say they how long the NIA funding would continue?"

Myk and Drake were both fairly wealthy, but not even they could afford to keep the NIA ship afloat without government help.

"No. It's been hard getting a straight answer.

Maybe they're waiting to see how much bang they're going to get for their buck."

Although forming NIA had been Drake's idea, Myk had been the one to approach the Feds about covertly supporting Project NIA because he had the contacts to do so. His four years of command with the Army's Special Forces had been a major key to opening the Fed vault, but his connections overseas had proven even more valuable. When Myk left the Army and began his company, young Black contractors were rarely hired in the US for big municipal projects, so he'd taken his then-small operation overseas and made his reputation in the third world countries of Central America, Africa, and Asia, building bridges, roads, and office complexes. During that time, he'd met a myriad of eccentric characters, some on the right side of the law, some not. Many of the Americans, like his half brother Saint, were agents of various United States intelligence agencies tracking the flow of illegal drugs, laundered money, and the movements of cartel kingpins. These agencies had scratched Myk's back by clearing the way for international work permits and introducing him to the local *patrons* he'd needed to pacify to keep the Chandler construction sites free of sabotage. Myk returned the favors by supplying the agents with any information he or his workers came across that might prove relevant to an ongoing operation. When the third world had enriched Chandler Works enough to move the bulk of his business back to the States, Myk no longer needed the government connections, but by then he knew the ins and outs of America's shadowy agencies better than most. "Well, I just wish they'd let us know how long the tap is going to flow. I hate working in the dark on this."

"It's going to take some time. This is the United States of America. You know the Feds can't be overtly associated with a group of Black and Brown vigilantes like us."

"Spoken like a true politician."

Drake inclined his head. "Thank you."

Myk's housekeeper, Lily, stuck her head in the door. "Myk, that woman from Saginaw is on the phone, again. She wants to know if you'll reconsider doing her television show?"

Myk's loud sigh told all. He'd turned down the request three different times. The woman was persistent if nothing else. "Tell her I haven't changed my mind."

Lily smiled over at Drake. "Maybe you want to take his place, Drake? She's doing a show on: *Michigan's Most Eligible Hunks.*"

Drake grinned, "Really? I couldn't possibly fill big brother's shoes on that one."

Myk shot Drake a look.

Lily left the room laughing.

When they were again alone, Drake continued his teasing. "Why don't you do the show?"

"Because I don't need the hassle. How many of those women do you still have to write to from that magazine thing you did last year?"

Drake grinned sheepishly. "Probably fifteen, twenty thousand."

"See what I'm saying? A hassle."

During last year's mayoral campaign, Drake had agreed to be featured in a national magazine spread titled, "The Most Eligible Black Men on the Planet."

For Drake, it had been a silly and fun way to blow off the stress of the upcoming election. He'd taken the day off, done the photo shoot, and thought no more about it. Three months later when the article ran, the responses began trickling in, first in twos and threes. Like most brothers, Drake had been happy as a kid in a candy store as he eyed the beauties in the pictures and read the letters they'd sent. The trickle soon became a river, and the river, a flood. Over the next six months he received close to thirty-five thousand letters from women of all races, from all over the world. "That was more mail than I've ever received in my life."

"And you're still determined to answer them all," Myk asked doubtfully.

"All of them. A good brother would do no less. Besides, it's been fun."

While Myk shook his head with wonder, Drake cracked, "Hey, I can't help it if your idea of fun is brooding in a dark room."

Before the smiling Myk could give the mayor a terse, two-word response, Drake warned prophetically, "Watch your language. I'm a servant of the people."

Both men grinned.

Drake brought the subject back to the television interview. "So, this woman's show comes out of Saginaw?"

"Yes, and I have no idea how these people find me. I'm not in the phone book. My office secretaries know better than to give out my home number."

"I wouldn't worry about it, man. If people want to find you, they will. That's the price you pay for being a rich, handsome, eligible brother. If you were still living in the Andes, maybe you could be a hermit. But this is the new millennium—nobody has any privacy."

"Well, I'm tired of being in the public eye. I almost missed that meeting with the Feds last week because when I walked out of my inner office, I found Dot Dexter sitting in the reception area with four of the homeliest young women I've seen, ever."

Dot Dexter had been a member of the City Council for many many years and wielded a tremendous amount of power. Unfortunately, that power did not extend to finding husbands for her four, plain-as-paper-plates daughters.

Drake felt compelled to reply out of fairness. "Her girls are quite nice, actually. They can't help it if they all look like their mother."

Myk took a swallow of his cognac, then observed, "Well, next time they can visit you. I didn't want them in my office, and I especially didn't like missing that meeting because of having to take them out to lunch."

Drake's handsome face registered surprise. "You took them to lunch? I do believe you are mellowing in your old age."

"No, I'm not. I took them to lunch because I knew you needed Dot's support for the upcoming bond vote. In fact, you owe me $112.65."

"They ate that much?"

"I felt like the trainer at the zoo."

Drake burst out laughing. "That's cold, Myk. Truly cold."

Myk grinned. "Yeah, well, you'll be getting my bill."

Drake shook his head and chuckled. "Had you met the daughters before?"

"No. I've only met Mama Dot once before. When she asked me to join them for lunch, I told her I had a meeting to attend in an hour and that I'd have to take a rain check. So she says, 'An hour? Then you have plenty of time to have lunch and hear my concerns on the bond vote.' "

"So you took them to lunch."

"I took them to lunch."

"I'm proud of you, man. Five years ago, you'd've turned your back on her and walked out."

"Five years ago, you were a surgeon, not mayor. Like I said, you'll get my bill."

"Okay." Drake chuckled. "So what were Dot's concerns?"

"Besides whether to have three glasses of the best wine in the house, or four, it was my being impressed by those frogs she calls daughters."

"Oh, Myk."

"I believe she actually drank herself into believing I was interested in hooking up with one of them. I heard all about their degrees in Home Ec., which one liked horseback riding, and which one wanted six kids. Go ahead and laugh; you weren't there."

Given permission, Drake did just that, out loud. When he calmed himself, he asked, "She didn't say anything about the vote?"

"Not a word, and it isn't funny. Since you got me involved in politics my life's been hell. Rallies, balls, community meetings. Everywhere I go, I'm beating off panting, salivating women."

"Some men consider that heaven."

"Feeling like meat on a rack is not my idea of heaven."

"Having Faye on your arm isn't deterring the hordes?"

Myk ran his hands over his head in distress. "Faye, why did I ever start seeing her? I'm so glad to have her out of my life."

"Because you needed dates for all those ceremonial functions, and you seem to be a slow learner."

"What's that supposed to mean?"

"Myk, you never learn. You date these beautiful, fine women, and not one of them has any substance. They bore you to death after six weeks. Now, granted, some, like Faye, even last six months, but in the end, you wind up paying them off so they'll go away."

Myk had to admit Drake was right, even if Myk didn't like hearing it. Myk stayed away from long-term relationships because his work came first, and that made it difficult to conform to the usual standards women expected. Some women, especially those with brains, had expectations about conduct and treatment. Others had expectations that once they finished planing, sanding, and painting him, he'd be their fantasy model of a perfect mate. Myk, on the other hand, didn't think he needed any polish or paint; he liked himself just the way he was. So, by choice, he kept to those women who didn't care if he were working in São Paulo and hadn't called them in weeks, just as long as he sent them a fur coat or a pair of diamond studs to beg their pardon. Expensive? Sometimes. But infinitely easier on the psyche of everyone involved.

Drake brought the conversation back. "You know,

you might enjoy being with a woman who can do more than figure the interest on a T-bill?"

Myk shrugged, "The women I date know the rules going in. No ties. No expectations."

"So why'd you dump Faye?"

"Because her greed was wearing me out. Every time I turned around she had her hand out. When she demanded I give her a key to the house, I knew it was time for adios."

"She wanted a key?"

"Demanded a key."

Drake spoke sagely, "Well, at least now you won't have to worry about her accidentally stumbling into NIA business."

"True. Now, if I could just shake the rest of the females on my tail, I'd be home free. Dot invited me to dinner next week after the bond vote. Connie makes excellent macaroni and cheese."

A laughing Drake asked, "Did you accept?"

Myk didn't even dignify that ridiculous question with an answer. "Drake, if I'm going to head up NIA, I can't spend my time being hounded by the Dot Dexters of this world."

"So what do you want to do about it?"

"I don't know, but something you said a minute ago got me to thinking. Remember when you asked me if Faye had been able to keep the women away from me when she and I went out?"

Drake nodded and took a small draw on the Remy VSOP in his glass.

"Well, wouldn't a wife be more effective than, say, a lady friend?"

"Sure. A wife has a tendency to quash stuff like that, especially when she's on her husband's arm.

So?" Drake knew Myk well enough to recognize when the computer Myk called a brain was booting up. Drake stared at him a moment, trying to figure out where this line of thinking might be heading. When the lightbulb finally came on, Drake's eyes widened.

"Yep," Myk said, "I need a wife."

Drake began to choke.

"No, wait," Myk cautioned. "Think about it. I could marry, drop off the set, and run the NIA missions in peace because no one would question my absence. I'm married. I'm settled down. And when it does become necessary to attend some function or other—a wife on my arm would deter the wanna-bes."

"So, am I hearing you correctly? You want to get married?"

"Yep, it's the perfect solution."

"When was the last time you had a full night's sleep?"

"Can't remember, but I'm serious, Drake."

"When do you want to do this?"

"As soon as possible."

Drake rubbed his eyes. The man mouthing such an outrageous proposal had to be an impostor. Mykal Chandler talking about marriage? Mykal Chandler, bachelor forever? "I take it you have a woman in mind?"

"The idea is only a minute old, Drake. Give me time to work out the details."

"Okay, here's a detail: Have you lost your mind?"

"You don't think it will work?"

"On paper, yes. In reality, too many holes."

"Such as?"

"Such as, you don't even have anyone picked out. Do you plan to stay married?"

"Of course not."

"How long then?"

"I don't know. Long as it takes for my life to settle down. NIA will be officially funded for what, eighteen months, two years, max?"

Drake shook his head in amazement. "Where are you going to find a woman who will agree to a proposal like that?"

"No idea, but for the right price, I'll bet it won't be hard."

Drake thought Myk was probably correct. However—"How are you going to keep her from finding out about your work with NIA? Not even you can live with a woman for two years and not leave some clue lying around."

"Hey, I'll buy her her own place. She only has to be around when I need her on my arm."

Drake thought Myk's attitude would go over real well with a prospective bride, but the more he mulled over the outrageous idea, the more possibilities he began to see. Myk hadn't been lying about all the attention he'd received since joining the mayoral campaign last year as financial chair. The women had been giving him fits, and he did need to keep a low profile if he were to continue to head up NIA. But where would he find such a woman? She couldn't be just anyone. Myk traveled in the highest social circles and rubbed shoulders with society's elite. This mythical wife would need to know deportment and proper etiquette. She would need to know how to conduct herself in public so as to not embarrass herself or her spouse, and, she would have to be a stunner. No one would believe the marriage ruse if the woman Mykal Chandler married had a face like one of Dot Dexter's daughters. "Do you really think you can pull this off?"

Myk shrugged. "Won't know until I try. We can talk about it at the next NIA meeting. Maybe someone knows a woman who'll fit the bill."

"I can't believe you're serious about this."

"I need my life back, Drake. We have a lot of work to do, and I need the freedom to do it right."

"Okay, but I still think you've lost your mind."

"Your support is noted."

Two nights later, the other NIA leaders echoed Drake's skepticism. Everyone agreed Myk needed to free himself in order to continue to be an effective leader, but a wife? No one thought the idea would work, but since Myk had already made up his mind, he let them toss the idea around for another twenty minutes, then moved the discussion on to the next item on the agenda—a report from NIA's intelligence wing.

Myk brought everyone back to attention. "Our Federal friends would like us to pick up a man named Barney Fishbein."

He passed around pictures of the lumpish, blue-eyed, glasses-wearing accountant.

"Mr. Fishbein likes to bet sports so much he owes his bookies fifty grand."

Someone at the table whistled.

"I know," Myk acknowledged. "Fish has agreed to be a courier for his bookies, so his wife and kids don't wind up wearing cement shoes at the bottom of Lake Michigan."

Drake asked, "What's he carrying?"

"Blood diamonds."

In the silence that followed, Myk added, "With all the emphasis on homeland security, the Feds are spread pretty thin, so they've asked if we'd be their legs on this one. They're confident taking Fish and his contact down will be a no-brainer."

"Are these diamonds connected to Rand?"

Myk shrugged. "No one's sure right now. We pick up the Fish, we find out."

"Who's the contact?"

"We don't know that either. We do know that the diamonds are worth—best guestimate—three-quarters of a mil."

One of the female members at the table asked, "When is all of this supposed to go down?"

"According to the tap on Fishbein's phone, 2 A.M. Day after tomorrow."

They spent a few more moments discussing the logistics of the operation, then moved on to the next item on the agenda.

Two

Sarita slammed down the phone. She'd spent the past two days calling every charitable agency in the county hoping for a bailout, but hadn't been able to raise a dime. As a result, she decided the time had come. Tomorrow she would call a neighborhood meeting and give everyone the bad news. It would take a miracle to keep from being evicted, but Sarita had stopped believing in fairy tales a long time ago. Putting on her coat, she picked up her purse and headed out of her closet-sized office.

Before going home, she stopped off at the kitchen. As she said good-bye to the kids cutting up carrots and apples to snack on for their late-evening tutoring session and the senior ladies playing bridge at the table, she hid her blue mood behind a fake smile. She reminded them all to be careful going home. They told her the same. Sarita left with a wave.

Sarita's small two-bedroom flat was only a few short blocks away. Even though by the clock it was early evening, outside, it was already dark. It still surprised her to come out at night and find the streetlights on. The last city administration had grown so negligent during its final years, basic city services such as trash collection and night lighting had been nonexistent in the poorer areas. But these days, thanks to the new mayor, you could see your way home. Now, if he could just get the vermin off the streets, maybe the city could really recover.

Speaking of vermin, she spied two lounging casually against the columns of her front porch as she turned up her walk. She was uneasy at first, but when they stepped out of the porch's shadows and into the arch of the streetlight, she recognized them and relaxed a bit. They were gang members, but both had younger siblings who played at the center. "Can I help you?" she asked.

"Yeah. Fletcher wants to see you."

Fletcher Harris owned many of the flats in their area of the city. He considered himself Donald Trump. Sarita considered him a thug. "Why?"

"He just said come and get you."

"And if I don't want to come?"

"We're supposed to bring you anyway. Understand?" He patted his coat.

Sarita studied them for a moment. The implication was that they were packing. Although she knew them, she didn't put it past them to force her to go, and since there was only one of her and two of them, the odds were not in her favor. Sighing her frustration, she said, "Okay. Let's go."

They led her to the car.

Seated in the backseat of the expensive European import, Sarita tried to close her ears to the deafening beat of the rap blaring from the speakers. She enjoyed some rap artists, but could do without the groups dissing women, and that's what the kids had on the CD. As the rapper began dogging out his mama, Sarita shook her head with disgust and turned her thoughts to Fletcher and his summons. Over the years she and Fletcher had come to an agreement of sorts—he stayed away from her center with his questionable dealings and thug hangers-on, and she stayed out of his business. Ironically, his sister, Alva had been one of Sarita's best friends growing up. Back then, although Fletcher had been five years older and had his own set of friends, he'd always been welcome in the Grayson home, because as Sarita's grandmother once said, "Fletcher Harris was a nice, polite boy."

Not anymore.

He was now thirty-five and a legend in his own mind. He sent his days lording over a real-estate empire that included most of the houses around the center. In reality, his holdings were strictly small-time, but he had his fingers in other pies, too. Most of them illegal. He didn't deal drugs as far as she knew but he didn't mind renting flats to people who did. She and Fletcher hadn't spoken directly since last summer when two of his tenants' crack houses burned to the ground. He'd accused her of setting the torch. She'd denied it, but he didn't believe her. She wondered what he wanted with her tonight?

The car stopped, and Sarita got out. This area, no more than eight blocks from her flat, seemed to be stubbornly resisting the mayor's efforts to improve conditions. The newly installed streetlamps were dark, apparently shot out by those whose business dealings fared better under the faceless night. The newly nailed-up plywood on the busted windows of abandoned houses were sprayed with the tags of the local gang.

Sarita followed her escorts up onto the porch of the small flat, which had at one time housed her best friend. Alva had been dead for years, a victim of a car accident. Alva's parents moved south the day after her funeral. The elder Harrises left their son Fletcher the house. Two weeks later, he too was in an accident when his car was smashed into by a city police car in hot pursuit of a seventeen-year-old carjacker. The crash put Fletcher in the hospital for more than a month. When his suit against the city was finally settled, he took the big cash payout and began buying up houses in their decaying neighborhood.

Guarding Fletcher's door were two more kids no more than fifteen years of age. Sarita wondered what Fletcher was so mixed up in now that he needed all this so called security. Both doormen tried to come off as gorillas but their short statures placed them more in the chimpanzee range. However, Sarita was wise enough to know that even chimps could be dangerous if armed with semiautomatics.

While one chimp patted her down for weapons, the other leered at her with his version of a sexy come-on. When chimp number two slid his hand across her breast, calling himself searching, she slapped his paw away and stuck an angry finger in his face. "That's enough!"

The simians laughed, of course, then opened the door so she could enter.

Inside, Fletcher Harris was dressed in a dark brown kimono and seated on a red velvet sectional. A young woman dressed in a matching brown teddy slid off his lap and disappeared into what was once Alva's bedroom.

Fletcher turned his attention to Sarita. Fletcher, with his pocked skin, had been an ugly child, but now, he was an even uglier man.

"Glad you could make it," he said cordially.

A tired Sarita was in no mood for chitchat. "What do you want?"

"To talk," he responded simply as he stood and walked over to the small bar. "After all, we are old friends."

He motioned her over to the red-velvet sectional. "Can I get you something to drink? Champagne? Cognac?"

"You can get to the point," she said, taking a seat.

He took a moment to pour himself a glass of cognac, took a swallow, then spent a moment or two observing her. She got the impression she was being measured for something but had no idea what.

Fletcher took another swallow to drain the glass, then asked, "So, how've you been, little sister? Things going okay over at the mission?"

Sarita thought about all the problems she faced, and lied. "Things are fine."

He held her eyes. "You know, you do good work

over there. It would be a shame if the place closed down."

Sarita viewed him cautiously. "As far as I know, we aren't closing."

"You lie so well," he returned smoothly. "Seventeen thousand dollars is a lot of money for a girl living off pension checks, wouldn't you say?"

She hesitated before answering, wondering how much he really knew. "Fletcher, get to the point. Why am I here?"

"Okay," he said with a smile that showed off his gold incisors, "let's cut to the chase. I know you need $17,000 to keep the city from closing your stuff down. How I know is my business. I can give you the money."

Sarita was unimpressed. "Fletcher, you don't *give* anybody anything."

"True, but in this case, I will."

"In exchange for what?"

He smiled again. "A small job."

"No."

"Sarita, you disappoint me. You've always liked adventure. Remember the time you and Alva liberated mama's car from the police impound lot? Or last summer when those two houses of mine burned down—"

"I didn't start those fires. I did cheer like everybody else, though."

Anger flared briefly across his ugly face before he regained his composure. "Whatever you say, but before you turn down my offer, hear me out. It doesn't involve dope."

"I don't care. No."

His voice remained even as he stated quite

bluntly, "Sarita, by this time next week your center will be closed, and you and your people will have no place to go. Think about all those old people and kids. What's going to happen to the widows and shut-ins if they don't have Saint Sarita and her Army to help 'em out? How're you going to live with yourself knowing you could have made it all better by just doing me a quick favor?"

"No."

He smiled sadly, "Well, stick to your guns. Tomorrow, I start eviction proceedings for some of your folks who are behind in their rent. How much trouble do you think old Mrs. Robinson is going to have finding a new place to live with winter coming on? Isn't she on disability for her sugar?"

Sarita was outraged. "Fletcher, that woman was a friend of your mama's. She's in her eighties."

"So."

"And you want to put her out on the street?"

"Hey, she's four months behind. I've got families on my waiting list ready to take that place the moment I give the word. Let's see. Who else is behind in their rent?"

While Sarita listened, he ran off the names of six other families who owed him money. All had family members with some sort of permanent ailment, or were young single mothers with small children in the home. She said angrily, "You're a bastard, you know that?"

He ignored her description and raised his glass to her in mock salute. "Man, I wish I had your principles. You're so high-and-mighty, you're willing to let your people be evicted rather than help a brother out. Bet you'll sleep real good tonight."

She knew he was baiting her. She also knew he'd evict the families first thing in the morning. He wasn't the type to threaten, then back down. This was blackmail, pure and simple, and they both knew it. Sarita looked into his mocking eyes and knew she had no choice. In order to keep her people in their homes and out of the reach of this predator, she had to deal. "What do you want me to do?"

"There's a package I want you to pick up."

"Where?"

He spoke the name of one of the big downtown hotels. "A place you are very familiar with, right?"

She was indeed. Sarita sometimes cleaned rooms there when the head housekeeper, a woman she knew from the church needed extra help and Sarita needed extra cash. "What's in the package?"

"Diamonds."

She stared, and choked out, "Diamonds?"

"Yes, little sister, a girl's best friend, and I need you to bring them home to daddy."

"Why me?"

"Because you know your way around the place. This is going down tonight, and I don't have time to find someone who can go there, do the deal quickly, and get out without getting lost."

Sarita understood his thinking. The hotel in question could double as a maze for a mythical Minotaur. It was being renovated because tourists and city dwellers alike constantly found themselves lost in the vast confusing jumble of shops, restaurants, and office towers.

Fletcher added, "I also can't risk having any of my people stopped and searched by the hotel's security. Police types have a thing about young Black males being in places like that late at night."

"So, what am I supposed to do?"

"Go into a room, get the diamonds, and leave."

"Is this room occupied?"

"Yes."

She looked at him as if he'd lost his mind.

He sought to reassure her. "By the time you get there the man in the room should be asleep."

"What do you mean 'should be'? Isn't he expecting me?"

"In a way, yes. In a way, no."

She didn't particularly like that answer. "Why do I get the feeling that there's more going on than you're telling me?"

He waved away her concern. "Don't worry. I hooked him up with a couple of ladies earlier this evening, and they promised me he'll be in dreamland by midnight. Nothing like a spiked drink to help you get a good night's sleep." He chuckled at his cleverness.

Sarita didn't. "Why can't these party girls get the rocks?"

"Because I don't want them knowing *all* my business. They have their role, and you have yours."

"Were will the diamonds be?"

"In the room safe."

"And how am I supposed to open it?"

"With this." He showed her a slip of paper. "This is the combination to the safe."

Sarita didn't even want to know how he'd acquired that. "So, this man will hopefully stay asleep while I take his diamonds?"

"I'm going to give you $17,000, Mother Sarita. A little intrigue will make the money that much sweeter."

"And if I'm caught?"

"You're on your own."

Her eyes widened.

"No, I'm kidding." His grin flashed gold. "The job'll be easy, and there shouldn't be any problems as long as you do what you're supposed to do, then get out of Dodge. So, do we have a deal?"

Sarita knew her soul would burn in hell for making deals with the devil, but there were no other options. The money she'd be paid paled when compared to the misery the families would experience if he went though with the threatened evictions. Her back against the wall, Sarita begged silent forgiveness from the spirits of her late grandmother and great-uncles, then said, "Okay, Fletcher, we have a deal."

He rewarded her with golden smile. "Good. Now, this is what I want you to do."

Sarita felt decidedly paranoid walking across the well-lit lobby of the hotel. There were still quite a few people milling about, even though it was just past midnight, and she was certain everyone she passed knew exactly what she was up to. Fighting to remain calm and keep her body language nonchalant, she managed to keep putting one foot in front of the other. Although Sarita didn't know anybody who worked the hotel's night shift, Fletcher had insisted on a disguise; so over her jeans and T-shirt she had on a nasty, oil-stained pair of coveralls, on her head an equally greasy baseball cap, and in her hand she carried a metal toolbox. On the cap and breast pocket of the coveralls were patches declaring her a worker for F&A Heating and Cooling. On her feet were well-worn work boots. Fletcher doubted anyone would challenge her right to be moving about the hotel because of all the renovations going on, and in a facility of its size something somewhere was always needing to be fixed. He'd boasted no one would look at her twice. For the moment, he appeared to be right. She passed a couple of uniformed security men leaning against their desk talking to a couple of honeys. The guards didn't even blink when she stepped over to the bank of elevators and got on. When the door closed, Sarita sagged with relief against the car's inner wall.

The elevator took her to the fifteenth floor, and she stepped out into the silence of the carpeted hallway. She waited a tense moment to make sure the hall was deserted. She saw no one. It was a good start, but it didn't slow her furiously pumping heart or banish the guilt over what she was about to do. The guilt she set aside, but her pumping heart wouldn't quit. Her familiarity with the hotel's layout sent her immediately to the left and down the corridor that led to the designated room. Most of the rooms along the route were silent, but a few had TVs blaring or music playing. She scooted by them quickly, not wanting to be surprised by some drunk heading to the ice machine. Room 1533 was the last room on the left.

When she reached her destination, Sarita took a deep breath and looked around. She didn't hear any noise coming from the rooms nearby. No televi-

sions. No music. She very gently placed her ear
against the door of 1533. Silence. She pulled the
black gloves from the side pocket of her dirty coveralls and put them on. She looked up and down the
hall once more, took the purloined pass card
Fletcher had also provided, and ran it down the
edges of the box-shaped lock. The small green light
came on just as it had been designed to do upon receiving the correct code. She slowly tried the handle. It swung all the way over, and when it did, she
pushed the door open just enough to see in. A quick
look up and down the hall reassured her the entry
wouldn't be seen, so she slid the door open a sliver
wider and slipped inside.

The first sounds she heard in the dark suite were
the loud, labored snores of the man asleep on the
bed. She sent up a silent hallelujah. The first smells
were of stale cigarette smoke and the loud, cheap
perfume probably worn by Fletcher's party girls.
Sarita quickly reached into the pocket of the coveralls and took out her small flashlight. A light tour
showed the framed landscape painting on the wall
across from the bed. The safe. She took another
deep breath to steady her screaming nerves, then
tiptoed past the bed. The man's snores were loud
enough to muffle a jet taking off, but she didn't care
as long as he kept it up.

Sarita worked quickly but quietly in the small circle of light provided by her flashlight. She'd had no
trouble taking down the landscape or opening the
safe. She tried not to think about the safe being tied
into the hotel's security camera and what might
happen if she were on a screen downstairs in the
guard room. She also tried not to think about her

grandmother and her great-uncles spinning in their graves over her actions here tonight. Instead, she concentrated on placing the beautiful gems in the pouch and thinking how the end justified the means. Yes, she'd crossed the line into Fletcher's slimy little world, but only because she'd had no other options. Legal channels had gotten her nowhere. In a few more minutes she would be out of there, and it would be all over.

Upstairs in his penthouse office, Myk was putting the last-minute touches on the plan for tonight's rendezvous with Fishbein and the diamonds, when he stopped and stared curiously at the light blinking on the computer screen. The light indicated the safe in 1533 had been opened. Surprised, he picked up the nearby headset and pulled it on. A sound device had been placed in the room that morning before Fishbein checked in so that the diamond transaction could be monitored and taped. According to the Feds, the deal wasn't supposed to go down until two. His watch said it was just twelve-thirty. Through the earphones, he listened for sounds in the room. Snoring, lots of it filled his ears. If those snores were coming from Fishbein, who was opening the safe?

With a curse, Myk snatched off the headset. He had to get down there. The others in the surveillance team wouldn't begin arriving for at least another twenty minutes. He knew he should wait for backup, but by then who knew what might happen. Myk grabbed his gun. After checking the chamber, he stuck the weapon into the small of his back and ran to the penthouse's private elevator.

Sarita placed the last of the sparklers into the small velvet pouch and drew the drawstrings closed. From the open toolbox at her feet she took out a roll of black electrical tape, then unzipped the front of the dirty overalls. She undid the top button of her jeans and pulled her T-shirt free. Using two long pieces of the tape, she fastened the pouch to the skin of her waist inside her jeans. Because the bag added bulk to her waistline, she had to suck in her stomach in order for the jeans to close again. They did, finally, but not without the sticky black tape pulling painfully against her skin. Removing the tape later would be no fun, but the slight discomfort would be forgotten once she received her money from Fletcher.

The man on the bed continued to snore, making her wonder what the women had given him, but she didn't dwell upon the question. She was just thankful they had. Just a few more minutes she prayed. She took a quick glance at the small luminous face of her watch—12:38.

She closed the safe, spun the dial, and rehung the painting. As she made a slight adjustment to the frame's positioning, she heard a noise and froze. Her eyes went immediately to the man on the bed, but his snoring hadn't changed. The noise came again. Her attention shot to the door, and her eyes widened with alarm. Someone was trying the knob!

With no time to spare, she snapped off the light. Her hands were shaking, her heart pounding. The toolbox lay open at her feet, but she doubted she had time to gather it up. Instead, she hoped it would remain hidden by the darkness while she frantically searched the shadows for a place to hide. She ducked down next to the dresser positioned beside the bed. Her mind whirled with the awful possibilities: security, the police, a friend of the man on the bed come to awaken him for some unknown reason. She prayed that whoever it was had somehow come to the wrong room and would realize the mistake and move on, but her prayers went unanswered.

The person entered the room cautiously, carefully, as if judging the interior in much the same way she'd done earlier. She listened to the barely audible footsteps, her heart beating wildly, her stomach in knots. She tried to make herself smaller, but the wall at her back kept her from cringing any farther.

The footsteps crossed the carpet like a whisper, and from where they halted she judged the intruder to be just on the other side of the bed. She heard the sound of the bed shaking. The intruder seemed to be trying to awaken the sleeping man, but the snores continued.

Sarita waited for the next move. The following seconds dragged by like years. The clock on top of the dresser ticked in the silence. The soft brittle sound, amazingly loud in the darkness, came to her ears like a death count. She debated what to do. The longer the person hung around, the higher were her chances of being discovered. She toyed with the idea of dashing across the room to the door, but if the person were armed she didn't want to chance catching a bullet in the back. Once again she had no options. All she could do was hide, stay calm, and keep praying the uninvited guest would leave.

No such luck.

She watched a small flashlight beam moving slowly over the walls. When it snaked menacingly over the rehung landscape, she tensed with renewed alarm. She could hear the footsteps crossing the room, then saw the shadowy figure of a tall, well-built man. She didn't dare even breathe. He stood in front of the painting and directly across from where she huddled. She tried to make herself invisible and watched with horror and fascination as he carefully took down the painting. Was he after the diamonds, too? Evidently yes. It took him only a few minutes to open the safe, but she felt a momentary sense of satisfaction knowing he wouldn't find anything. She wondered what he would do?

He answered her unspoken question by uttering a muttered curse. He slapped the door of the safe closed, a further show of his displeasure. He stood motionless then as if trying to decipher the dilemma. After a few long moments he bent to retrieve the painting he'd placed by his feet. When he didn't straighten up right away, Sarita's stomach turned sick from fear. She knew he'd discovered the open toolbox. As he turned the beam on the area, she waited, horrified. When he finally straightened to his full height, he had the flashlight in one hand and a gun in the other.

The light began a swift search of the premises, first over by the door, then the dresser, then she was onstage.

"Stand up!" he commanded.

Sarita uncurled herself and reluctantly stood, her legs shaking.

"Raise your hands. Slowly."

She didn't argue.

Myk stared curiously at the person caught like a deer in his light. A repairman? "Take off the hat."

Sarita hesitated but, using one hand, slowly complied. Her nerves were shot. Because of the light in her eyes, she couldn't make out the man's features, but not even the glare could mask his height, or the power in his large, muscular frame. She was shaking so badly, she couldn't think.

Myk watched the hat come off, then swung the light up to the intruder's face. Not a repairman, Myk thought testily. He had here a bandanna-wearing kid! Myk set the flashlight on the edge of the table. Gun in hand, he stepped over to the kid and began to pat him down for weapons. When his hands brushed the soft swells of female breasts, she jumped away, and he drew back as if he'd touched something hot. His eyes widened. He was so shocked, his first instinct was to pat her down again in order to verify this startling turn of events, but he held off. He shot the light back to her face instead. A woman! He reached up and snatched the bandanna from her head to reveal her sleek, short-cut hair. He cursed to himself. He patted her waist and felt the bulge. "Give me the diamonds."

Tiny rivulets of fear-fed sweat were running down the rigid, shaking column of Sarita's spine. She wanted to say she'd rather not, but he obviously didn't care to be kept waiting because he stuck the barrel of the gun between her eyebrows and hissed dangerously, "Now!"

When she hesitated, he mistook her shock for noncompliance and increased the pressure of the cold barrel against her skin. Sarita took in a deep, shuddering breath. "Okay, okay."

He and the gun backed up to give her some room. She slid the straps off of her shoulders then eased the front down to reveal her T-shirt. Stiff with anger and reaction she worked the coverall down to her waist and raised the shirt.

Myk could see the tops of her black panties but was more intent upon the package taped to her waist. Once he got her back upstairs to the penthouse he'd find out who she was and who she worked for. He sensed she didn't like him ordering her around because she didn't bother masking the angry flash of her eyes or the defiant set of her chin as she stripped off the tape and slapped the small bag into his outstretched palm. Looking at her more closely, he couldn't believe he'd mistaken her for a male. Now, he could see the face was too finely carved, the mouth too ripe to be anything but female. "Fix your clothes and let's go."

"Where?" she asked defiantly.

No answer.

"Are you hotel security?"

The look he gave her said no more questions.

Sarita took the hint, wondering if she'd live to see the sun rise. He had the diamonds, and she, well, she was probably expendable. Scared, but determined not to fall apart, she bent to get the toolbox while her mind whirled with alternatives to whatever he had in store. She could think of none.

"Let's go," he growled.

She preceded him to the door.

Sarita willed someone to be in the hall to see them leaving Room 1533, but as he eased the door open and peered out, she knew the chances were less than slim. She'd seen no one on the way in and now, with the hour even later, she doubted she would see anyone. Her guess proved correct. No one.

He steered her down the hall with a viselike grip on her arm and partially propelled, partially dragged her in his wake. She hazarded a look up at this face. It was mustached, dark brown, and cold. The stern eyes were fixed straight ahead.

To her surprise he took her to the penthouse elevator. The doors opened as if at his command. Was he a guest? If not, how had he gained access to the "limo" as it was called by the housekeeping staff.

He shoved her roughly inside. Once the doors closed, he pulled a ring of keys from his back pocket. He pushed one into a slot in the rectangular panel housing the floor buttons, but his large build prevented her from seeing which slot he'd used. When he withdrew the key the car began to rise. The limo led not only to the penthouse suite offices of various corporations, but also to the roof. Was that where they were headed? She looked up at him towering over her so malevolently. The vision of him killing her and tossing her body from the roof to the pavement forty-five floors below almost set her to screaming. She was certain he could feel her trembling under his painful hold on her arm, so she took a deep breath to steady herself against her rising fears—to panic would be to let go of the little bit of sanity she had left.

The limo was notorious for its slow climb. So far, it had reached the twentieth floor. Twenty-five more to go. The deliberate pace of the elevator would give her more than ample time to berate herself for getting mixed up in this scheme of Fletcher's in the first place. She wouldn't put it past him to have set her up this way just so he wouldn't have to pay her off.

The man beside her hadn't said a word since leaving 1533. She wondered if he could be convinced to let her go? She doubted it—that was a serious piece of firepower in his hand. He looked more likely to shoot her than to listen. She had to figure out something, though, because she dearly wanted to come out of this escapade alive. She also made a vow to never, ever, do anything like this again.

But how to escape him? She had no weapon. The only thing in her possession was the toolbox with a few generic tools inside to make her appear reasonably legit if stopped by a hotel employee. Neither the toolbox nor its contents was designed to stop a bullet.

The light for the thirtieth floor winked on and then off.

Fifteen floors to go.

Sarita turned her eyes away from the panel and went back to her dilemma. An idea came to mind, and from it a very raggedy-filled-with-holes plan began to take shape. Maybe the toolbox wouldn't have to stop a bullet. If she could distract him long enough to . . .

Myk underestimated his captive's determination. He thought her too intimidated by his gun and his size to do anything but submit meekly. Consequently, when she smashed the toolbox into the side of his face, he reacted a split second too late. The pain exploded in his head like shards of glass. His arm instinctively rose to ward off the next blow, but pain exploded again, this time from the vicious knee she planted firmly in his groin. The double agonies made him bend over. He almost retched as he slid uselessly to the floor. He didn't care that the gun rolled away.

The terrified Sarita snatched up the weapon. She slammed her hand against the down button on the elevator panel, praying the ascent would halt, but it didn't. Her would-be captor lay in the corner, eyes closed, breathing harshly. She leveled the gun on him. "Give me the key to this thing!"

Myk ignored her, more intent upon the fire raging in his genitals. The blow to the head had rendered him groggy and disoriented.

"I said, give me the damn key!"

In response, she received a glare that promised havoc once he got back on his feet, but a shaking yet amazingly calm Sarita didn't care. "I will shoot you."

Floor 38.

Myk touched the bleeding gash on his head. A few more inches, and she'd've cost him an eye. He surveyed his bloodstained fingers. "You fire that gun in here, and we'll both wind up dead." But she didn't appear to be in the mood for logic, he noted. Her well-balanced stance and the shaking yet steady hold upon the gun told Myk she just might know what she was about, and since he needed more time to recover before he could get up and strangle her with his bare hands, he ignored the hurtful throbbing of his injuries, fished around in his pocket, and produced the ring of keys. "Come and get it."

"Do I look like a fool?" she snapped sarcastically. "Slide them over here. Along with the diamonds. Easy now."

Myk, growing less groggy and more angry with each breath, complied.

A very wary Sarita kept the gun trained on him as she knelt to retrieve the big ring of keys and the bag. She pushed the diamonds into the pocket of her coveralls.

Myk thought he'd add to her stress by saying, "There's a lot of keys on that ring, little girl. Which one is the right one?"

She ignored him. She stuck the familiar key into the slot marked GARAGE, then said sweetly, "All elevator keys look alike."

The elevator was headed down to the underground garage. Its slow descent matched its slow ascent. She toyed with the idea of stopping it at a random floor and jumping off, but ruled it out. He had a key to the penthouse elevator. Who knew how he'd gotten hold of it. He could be connected to the hotel's security force, the police, or to a competitor of Fletcher's. She didn't want to spend the next hour ducking and dodging her way through this vast place trying to find a bolt-hole. No, the underground parking structure would be a better choice. From there she could go right to the city streets. Fletcher promised to have a ride waiting. She hoped she hadn't missed it. Fletcher. She didn't even want to think about having to explain this mess to him, but if she managed to escape, he wouldn't have to know.

Floor 27.

The descent was taking entirely too long for her liking, but she had both the gun and the diamonds, and that gave her a measure of confidence. However, she knew he would do everything in his power to keep her from leaving once the elevator car stopped. He didn't seem to be a man who enjoyed being bested, and being bested by a "little girl" probably made his defeat worse.

Finally, the light panel began to show floor levels in the teens once again, then single digits. Sarita did not lower the gun. Although the man hadn't moved, she could feel the heat of vengeance simmering in his eyes. Every second of the descent gave him back his strength, strength that could undoubtedly snap her like a twig. She'd have to say good-bye quickly when the elevator stopped.

The elevator came to a halt. The doors slid open, and the cool night air drifted in. With a blind foot, she searched behind her for the lip of the opening. Another step back brought her feet in contact with the cement garage floor. She took a quick look over her shoulder to make sure no one was around, then instantly turned back to her adversary. Her arms were starting to stiffen from holding the gun so tightly, but her aim never wavered. Her eyes held his steadily as she reached over and repositioned the key into the slot labeled ROOF then withdrew it. Pocketing the keys, she said, "It's been a pleasure."

She slapped her palm against the UP button, and the door began to close. She could feel relief rising and as her adrenaline slowed she relaxed.

A mistake.

He launched himself at the door. Her panicked scream blended with the two quick bursts she squeezed from the gun.

Myk felt the hot lead explode in his shoulder, and the resulting pain spun him back against the elevator's wall. Her dark and frightened eyes were the last he saw of her as the door slid shut. The elevator began to climb, and his howl of frustration echoed through the darkness.

Later, back in the safety of her little flat, Sarita took a long hot shower to try and wash away the fright and anxiety. It didn't work. She emerged from the water cleaner, but just as near hysteria as she'd been two hours ago. Fletcher's crew hadn't been there with the promised ride, so she'd had to take a city bus. Thanks to the new mayor, the buses now ran on time again even at such a late hour. No more than five minutes after leaving the man on the elevator, she'd hopped the first one heading up Jefferson Avenue.

She got into bed and pulled the covers up high on herself. She'd been trying not to contemplate his fate, but she hadn't been able to set aside those thoughts either. How seriously had she wounded him with those two bullets? Had he bled to death? And why had he looked so familiar? Back in the elevator, she'd been too freaked out at the time to give his face much thought, but now, as she replayed his features in her mind she swore she'd seen him somewhere before. She just didn't know where. Then again, maybe it was simply her imagination. In reality his identity didn't matter. Her life had been in danger. She'd done the necessary thing to ensure her own survival. Still, it bothered her on a moral level to have shot someone. Before tonight, she'd never shot anything other than the targets on the range operated by the local police precinct.

Sarita snapped off the lamp and darkness overtook her tiny bedroom. Shivering from the delayed reaction of the dangerous night, and from the steady draft that invaded the flat like an unwanted relative every fall and winter, she slid deeper beneath the quilts and blankets. She lay awake a very long time.

Sleep finally came, bringing with it dreams of guns, diamonds, and the howls of a furious, dark-eyed man.

"Hold still, Myk!"

"Dammit, Drake, hurry up! I have to find her!"

"It won't be tonight, so hold still," Drake demanded. The surgeon-mayor finally managed to bandage the wound on Myk's upper arm. In a way, he'd been lucky. The one bullet that caught him sliced through muscle, not bone. A few inches to the left, and it would have been a lot more serious than stitches, gauze, and bandages. "She give you this gash on your head, too?"

Myk's boiling glare skewered the mayor, but Drake, accustomed to his brother's temper, smiled and cleaned up the head wound, too. "She must have been an Amazon to inflict this kind of damage."

Myk didn't think any of this was remotely funny. He wasn't about to confess that the woman barely reached his shoulder; he'd endured enough tonight.

Drake asked, "How are you going to find her?"

"How the hell do I know!" Myk snapped. "But I will, and when I get my hands on that little—thief, she'll pay."

Although Drake did find some humor in Myk's plight, in reality this woman, whoever she was, could present quite a problem. She would probably recognize Myk if she saw him again, and that might put NIA and all its participants and projects in jeopardy if she were to let it be known that Myk had the diamonds.

Once Myk's wounds were tended to Drake's satisfaction, Drake put away his supplies, sat back, and watched Myk pace.

"Drake, I want every available person on this. She could've killed me."

"I know, man. We'll find her."

"Were there any prints on the toolbox?"

"Not any we can use."

Myk's mood became more grim. "She could be anywhere."

Drake agreed. Finding her in city of over a million people would not be easy—providing she was still inside the city limits. "You need to get some sleep. It's been a long night. We're watching all the known jewel fences, just in case she tries to dump them."

"I'm not sleeping until I find that little—*girl*. She not only has the diamonds, but my gun, too. That's all the city needs—one more weapon on the streets. Dammit, I want her found."

The mayor shook his head at his brother's single-mindedness. "Okay, don't sleep. I'll go home and sleep for both of us. I'll call you in the morning."

Drake showed himself out. He doubted Myk even noticed.

Three

When Sarita awakened the next morning, the clock on her bedside table read 6:30 A.M. The sun seemed to be sleeping in, but she didn't have that luxury. The sooner she met with Fletcher, the sooner she could get it all over with. Thinking about him made the memories of the previous night's close call surface again. She pushed them away. Her conscience could have its pound of flesh later—right now, she had business to attend to. Throwing back the quilts brought the predawn chill against her warm skin. Shivering, she lifted her robe from the bedpost and quickly drew it on.

To safeguard her bare feet from the cold kiss of the wood floor, she pulled on the socks she always kept by the clock. This particular pair didn't match, but they were warm. A yawn escaped her and she stretched in response. In midstretch, the sight of a man in the rocker on the far side of the room made her tighten and gasp with fear, but recognition immediately calmed her down. Seeing the familiar face did not calm the urge to strangle him for scaring her so badly though. "I won't ask how you got in here."

Number one, she knew he wouldn't tell her, and two, he had a habit of appearing out of nowhere. She'd grown accustomed to his magical appearances; almost.

"Good morning to you, too," Saint tossed back with a crooked smile.

Sarita had known him most of her life. Her was her foster brother; Sarita's late grandmother had raised them both, and they were close as siblings. Lately, though, he seemed to get a real kick out of freaking folks out with his silent-as-smoke entrances and exits. Rumor had it he'd learned the tricks working for military intelligence in the Middle East, South America, and Johannesburg. Many swore Saint still worked for some entity's intelligence arm because he seemed to know everything about everything. After being gone for three years, he'd returned to the neighborhood eighteen months ago. During his first few months back he gave the local dope peddlers fits by tipping off the police to deliveries, showing up unexpectedly in rooms during big transactions, and threatening the lives of gangbangers trolling for recruits at the nearby middle school. Word was, some eastside crews had placed a five-thousand-dollar bounty on Saint's head. Far as she knew, no one had been stupid enough to try and collect.

Sarita dearly hoped he hadn't gotten wind of her little escapade last night because if he ever found out, there'd be hell to pay. "I thought you vampires had to be in by dawn," she cracked. He might be legendary to some, but to her he was plain old, Anthony St. Martin.

Her gruff response made him smile, and ask, "Slept that well, huh, Sarie?"

She wanted to growl but didn't. She didn't want to give him any reason to inquire about her mood or her evening. To distract him, she got off the bed and went into the kitchen. He followed. She flicked on the overhead light, then set the old coffeemaker to earning its keep. She didn't drink the stuff, but knew he lived on little else. When it was ready, she poured him a cup, then led the way back out to the front room.

She sat down on the sofa that had been her granduncles' favorite, pulled her feet up, then said, "At this time of the morning, I assume you're here for more than chitchat."

He'd taken a seat on her grandmother's old recliner. Sarita waited while he took a few cautious sips from the steaming cup. She didn't rush him— he'd answer eventually.

While she waited, she looked him over with sisterly concern. There were deep circles beneath his eyes, and he'd stopped shaving. He looked tired, making her wonder what he was mixed up in now. His attire offered no hint because Saint's clothes were always the same: dark jeans, dark turtleneck, and on top, an old, once-green, Army-issue bush coat that brushed the ankles of his scuffed boots. He once told her he could live for weeks on the contents hidden in the coat's many pockets, and she didn't doubt it for a minute. In the nineteenth century he would have made a great cowboy. His attire and sexy, unshaven face made him look as if he'd just stepped out of a spaghetti Western. Here, in the twenty-first, women drooled over him like Häagen-Dazs.

Saint set his cup aside, and finally spoke. "First, some news: Fletcher's dead."

Her eyes widened. "What? When?"

"Last night about three."

Sarita was speechless. *Dead!* Good lord! What would she do about the eviction notice now; more importantly, what would she do with the diamonds? She knew she shouldn't've done gotten involved with Fletcher. Fate had a cruel, warped sense of humor. "What happened to him?"

"Had his door kicked in. Seems he was trying to cut into the business of a westside crew who didn't want to share. Sent him to hell along with some of his boys and a lady friend."

A chilled Sarita felt someone walking over her grave. Did the diamonds belong to this westside crew? She'd never heard of any local crews moving gems before. "Do the police know who the shooters were?"

"Not yet. Folks are saying the rest of Fletcher's crew flew down south."

Sarita was having trouble breathing.

Saint quipped, "So I guess you'll be burning down some other crew's houses now. The buzzards are already circling over Fletcher's old turf."

She cut him a look. "I didn't burn those houses."

"Yeah, right." He took a draw from the cup.

Sarita didn't bother arguing. No matter how

many times they had this discussion, he never believed her claims of innocence.

He asked her then, "So, have you found the money to stop the eviction?"

She shook herself free from the problems caused by Fletcher's death. "Nope."

Silence.

Saint set his cup down. "Well, I have this friend who just might be willing to offer you the cash you need."

An excited Sarita sat up straight. "Really?" Then she narrowed her eyes. Dealing with Fletcher made her decidedly wary of out-of-the-blue "gifts." "In exchange for what?"

"A year or so of your time."

"Oh, is that all?"

Saint smiled. "Always did like your dry wit. Like your mind, too. I'm sitting here wondering if I've anticipated all your questions."

Sarita grinned. "Probably not. You always did underestimate me. Remember that Christmas Gram gave us the Monopoly game?"

He did.

"I was only nine, and you were twelve, but I whipped you with one Boardwalk arm tied behind my back."

He hung his head at the memory.

"And then, your twelve-year-old male ego wouldn't give up, so I had to beat you again and again and again."

He looked up. "I remember you bragged for weeks."

"I remember you never played me again."

They shared a smile of mutual affection, before she asked, "So, who is this friend?"

"Technically, he's my half brother."

Once again, she stared speechless, then echoed, "Your half brother? Since when?"

"Since a few years ago."

"And you never said anything?"

Their gazes met.

He looked away. "When I got the letter from the lawyer, I tossed it. I never knew my father, so why should I care if folks claiming to be my family wanted to meet me." He turned to her. "I already had family. You."

Her heart swelled, "But Saint—"

He held up his hand. "Wait, let me finish. They tracked me down. Usually, that's pretty hard to do, but they did it. I have two half brothers."

"That's wonderful."

"Why?"

"Because they're your family."

He went silent for a moment, then said, "What's funny is, I met one of them about ten years ago in Thailand. Had no idea we were blood."

"Did you get along?"

"Sure. He wasn't a bad brother. In fact, I came to respect him a lot."

"So why the issues with him being family?"

"I don't know. Maybe because I've always been the lone wolf. Now I find out that not only am I not alone, but I'm the baby wolf."

She smiled. "You're the youngest?"

"Far as we know."

"What are your brothers like?"

"Rich. One's a doctor, the other's an architect. They live right here in the city."

"And one of these brothers wants a year of my time. What's his name?"

"Can't tell you that right now."

She looked at him for a moment then asked, "Oh, you're supposed to lure me in with this heart-tugging story first?"

His eyes sparkled with amusement. "He needs a woman."

"To do what?"

"Pose as his wife."

"Excuse me?"

"You heard me. Pose as his wife."

"Why?"

"Let's just say, he wants to settle down for a while, and a wife will help with that."

Sarita decided that her inability to understand Saint's explanation had to do with her being shell-shocked by his startling news about Fletcher and the long lost half brothers. "Start over."

He obliged. "He's a well-known wealthy brother, and because of his status, the women won't leave him alone. He figures if he gets married, the babes will go after other prey."

"And that's the only reason he's doing this is because the babes won't leave him alone? Since when does any man find that a problem?"

"Well, he does. All the attention is keeping him from his work."

"Is this the doc or the architect?"

"The architect."

"Uh-huh. Well, since I don't claim to know anything about the minds of the rich and famous, explain why you think *I'd* do this?"

"Because in exchange, he'll buy your building from the city and hand it over to you free and clear."

Sarita searched his face for hints that he might be joking. His bottle green eyes stared back innocently, or as innocently as a man like Saint could appear. "Free and clear?"

He nodded.

Sarita's imagination began to mine the possibilities. If the building came to her unencumbered, she'd find a way to keep it open. Somehow. But the exchange? Could she really play some rich man's wife? Her brain kept echoing, *"Free and Clear."* She had to admit the proposal sounded awfully tempting. She looked over at her foster brother's handsome golden face. "Now, tell me the real deal on this."

"You've heard the real deal. He just wants to get married."

She didn't believe him for a minute. She trusted him enough to know he would never involve her in anything dangerous—she hoped. He usually saved those roles for himself.

"Tempted aren't you?" he said knowingly.

She didn't answer at first, too immersed in thought, then, "Why does he have to hire someone to do this? Why can't he pick from all the ladies on his tail?"

"He doesn't know anyone who'll simply walk away when the job's done. He doesn't want to end up in court with some woman trying to get more than her due."

Sarita supposed that made sense.

Saint dropped the last shoe. "He's willing to pay all your living expenses, clothing bills, whatever. He'll also give you $50,000 when the year's up."

"Fifty thousand? *Dollars?*"

"In cash, or deposited in the financial institution of your choice."

She had to be still asleep. This couldn't be true. "But why me, Saint?"

"Because I think you're discreet enough and smart enough to pull it off, and you could use the cash."

That she could. But a year of her life? "Okay, suppose—just suppose I'm interested, what's he expect from me?"

"The usual—be on his arm—go to fancy benefits, dinners, that sort of thing."

"No—um, romance?"

He shrugged. "That's something for the two of you to work out. He's not the type of brother who'll force a situation if that's what you're worried about."

She added all of his answers to the mix. "When do you need an answer?"

"Right now. I want you to meet him tonight."

Sarita held his eyes and tried to see what lay behind them. She thought about the center, the fifty thousand, and the good it could do, if she agreed. But—"Okay. I'll meet him, but that's all. If we can work it out, fine—if not, he'll have to find someone else."

"Sarita—"

"Saint, as much as I would love to say yes, I have to meet him first. It's the best I can do."

He didn't press. "I'll pick you up tonight around seven."

* * *

True to his word, Saint knocked on the door at ten to seven. Sarita let him in and went to get her coat.

"That's what you're wearing?" he asked with a laugh.

Sarita looked down at her jeans and T-shirt. "Yes, Saint. This is what I'm wearing, or am I supposed to have on a ball gown?"

"Don't you have something a bit more ladyish?"

Sarita ignored his implication. "You're no representative of the fashion police yourself." She shrugged into her leather jacket. "Let's go before I lose my nerve."

Seated next to Saint in the front seat of the car he affectionately called Freedom, Sarita decided only an insane person would agree to something as crazy as this. But then she'd lost her sanity the moment the eviction notice arrived in the mail; her deal with Fletcher was proof of that. Had she become so desperate she'd accept this stranger's outlandish request? Yes, came the answer again and again. She had no choice. Simply to stand by and watch everything Pastor Washington had worked so hard to establish be turned into a vacant lot would be to succumb and surrender whole families, children, single teen mothers, and the elderly to a public assistance system stretched so thin it could hardly keep itself afloat. The governor, in his zeal to reduce the welfare budget, had swung his ax into the backs of innocents. Small children whose only sin lay in being born to a seventeen-year-old dropout were suffering from the dismantling of parenting classes, preschool programs, and education services for their mothers. The elderly, whose only sin lay in being just that, elderly, were threatened with the loss of visiting health aides, delivered meals, and supplemental funding that helped with winter heating bills. She refused to abandon them. She knew in the scheme of things her efforts were nothing but a drop in the bucket, but the center provided a rallying point for their community. If it closed, there would be nothing.

Sarita had been so deep in thought, she'd paid little attention during the drive. She came out of her reverie just as Saint cut the struggling engine. She looked around at the shadows draped over the large old homes. They were in one of the city's most historic areas. The houses, lovingly restored by their committed owners, were originally the homes of the city's nineteenth- and early twentieth-century movers and shakers. The integrated area was as beautiful now as it had been one hundred years ago.

Saint's voice brought her back. "You coming?"

Gathering herself, she nodded and got out of the car.

A pleasant-faced, brown-skinned woman met them at the door. She was dressed in a pair of gray slacks and a white sweatshirt embroidered across the front with the word, GRANDMA. She gave Saint a welcoming smile as she stepped back to let them enter. "Hello," she said to Sarita.

"I'm Lily, the housekeeper here. Please come in."

Sarita offered a polite hello in return and looked around. The grand entranceway, with its dark woods and elegant masonry, could only be described as a foyer. The high-arched ceiling, fitted with lead-bordered panels of beautiful stained glass gave the space a cathedral-like feel.

The woman noticed Sarita's interest in the glass, and said, "You should see it when the sun shines. Right now, the dragons are asleep. This way please. He's been expecting you."

Sarita's face showed her confusion. *Dragons?* She threw Saint a look. He smiled but didn't reply aloud.

They were shown into an elegantly furnished room filled with black leather furniture and sparkling wood end tables. It appeared to be a den. Books lined one wall, while a large stone fireplace, roaring with life, dominated another. The room was cozy and warm.

The woman asked, "Can I bring either of you something to eat or drink?"

Saint requested coffee, but Sarita, fighting off nervousness, declined the offer.

After the woman's exit, Saint looked over at Sarita, and asked, "Are you okay?"

Sarita confessed, "Not really."

"Just relax, everything'll be fine."

Sarita stared around. She could smell the money. "Maybe a ball gown wouldn't have been such a bad idea. I haven't been inside a house this large since Gram retired."

"He lives well, but he's worked hard for it."

Their hostess returned with a silver coffee service atop a beautiful sterling tray. She set the tray on the end table positioned in front of the luxurious leather couch and poured Saint a cup. The woman exited once more, and Saint sat back with his cup. He looked over at the now-pacing Sarita, and asked, "Well?"

"Well, what?"

She never received a reply because at that moment a tall, dark-skinned man entered the room. He was dressed in a charcoal-colored turtlenecked sweater and matching pants. Sarita recognized him immediately. Her panicked eyes darted around the room for the closest exit. Good Lord!

In that same instant, their eyes locked. He must have recognized her, too, because he roared, "You!"

Sarita ran. She made it back to the foyer, but the unfamiliar locks on the door defeated her plans for a quick exit. A strong arm snatched her up, and she screamed as she was lifted from the ground. Her kicking, arm swinging, and cursing at the top of her lungs did not prevent him from carrying her back. She landed on the couch with so much force she bounced, and when she came to rest, the dark eyes from her nightmares were an angry inch away. "So, we meet again," he purred in a voice that sounded all the world like a wolf's. Sarita couldn't stop her trembling. He was so close she could smell the subtle scents of his cologne and see the big black stone ring on his right hand.

Sarita's eyes flew to Saint, who stared back in amazement, asking, "What the hell—"

Myk replied in a pleased voice, "I should've known you be the one to track her down, Saint. You could spot a dime in the jungle. Where'd you find her?"

Saint's confusion was great. "Find her? Man, what are you babbling about? This is Sarita Grayson, the lady I wanted you to meet."

Myk stared thunderstruck at Saint, and then back down at Sarita, before saying, "Well, well, well."

Sarita couldn't have spoken, even if she'd wanted to.

The man gave her that slow, pleased, wolf's grin again, then asked her quietly. "He doesn't know about last night, does he?"

Sarita shook her head. *And don't tell him*, she wanted to yell.

Saint demanded, "What don't I know? Will somebody please tell me what the hell is going on?"

Myk couldn't tear his eyes away from her small brown face. Since last night, he'd been obsessed with finding her, only to have her drop right into his lap. The gods were kind, he thought, chuckling to himself. Ironic, but kind. "Remember the woman I had the run-in with last night?"

Saint nodded.

"Well, thanks for bringing her back to me."

Saint's eyes widened.

Sarita tried not to look guilty, but failed.

In a blink of an eye Saint was in her face bellowing, "*Have you lost your mind?*"

Sarita prayed for lightning to strike and put her out of her misery. She'd never seen Saint so furious.

He barked, "What the hell were you doing in that room last night?"

"A favor for someone."

"Who?"

Silence.

"Sarita?" his voice warned.

She had a few question of her own. "*This* is your half brother?" she asked tossing her chin toward the scowling man with the tight jaw.

"My questions first. Who?"

Sarita knew he would probably take a switch to her when she told him the truth. "The favor was for Fletcher."

"Fletcher?" Saint yelled. He stared at her as if amazed. "You have lost your mind!"

"Maybe," she snapped coming to her own defense. "But he was threatening to evict Mrs. Robinson and everyone else on the block behind in their rent if I didn't help him. I had to deal. In exchange I'd get the seventeen grand I needed."

"How'd you get into the room?"

"Fletcher gave me a room pass and the numbers for the safe."

Sarita sensed the vibrant presence of Saint's brother. He probably wanted a piece of her, too, but for now he seemed content to let Saint handle the interrogation. Sarita declared, "I was doing fine until *he* showed up."

Saint came back sharply. "You should be glad *he* did. Do you have any idea what you've set off?"

"Obviously not."

"This is as bad as those crack houses you burned last summer. You don't think of the consequences."

"I did not—"

"Yes, you did. I know you, Sarie. You probably poured the gasoline, personally."

Myk drawled sarcastically, "Oh, she's an arsonist, too? You're right, Saint. She'd make a perfect wife. What other qualifications does she have?"

At that moment Sarita almost wished she were married to him just so she could feed him rat poison for breakfast. "You're not exactly my idea of prime rib, either."

"Ah—and smart-mouthed to boot."

"Smartest mouth in the West," Saint concurred, before asking her, "So, do you still have the diamonds?"

She nodded.

"And my gun?" Myk added.

"Yes."

Saint was pacing. "What did you plan to do with the rocks now that Fletcher's dead?"

Sarita knew if she confessed, she would not see the sun rise ever again. However, since she and Saint were just like siblings, she trusted him to give her a decent burial. "I—was going to have you fence them for me."

"Me?"

Sarita and Saint had always been straight with one another, and so she sought to explain, "Look, Saint. Fletcher offered me the money. The job didn't involve any drugs. I couldn't let the center close. You know how much that place means. Maybe my methods were a bit outside the box, but I'd hit the wall, and there was no other way out. And like I said, everything would've been fine if *he* hadn't shown up."

"Sarie, I love you as much as I love breathing, but I can't believe you did this."

Sarita felt guilty for a moment, but when she weighed it against her hopes for the center, the guilt vanished. "So, if I turn over the diamonds and the gun, are we square?"

Saint's reply was blunt. "No."

"Why not?" she wanted to know. "I shot him, but he didn't bleed to death, or die."

"Because this has everything and nothing to do with the return of the gun and the gems."

"Try that in English."

When she received no reply, she turned her attention to the man across the room. He held her eyes emotionlessly. He knew the answers, she was certain. She turned back to Saint. "What are you mixed up in, Saint? What's this really about?"

"Something not even I can fix."

Saint turned to Myk, and said solemnly to him, "You and I need to talk, man."

They were gone for nearly an hour. Sarita paced angrily the whole time. The nice woman who'd initially met Sarita and Saint at the door came in after the men left on the pretext of keeping her company, but Sarita sensed the woman's real purpose was to make sure she stayed put until Saint and his brother returned.

When they finally did, neither face revealed what had been discussed.

The woman sitting with Sarita left quietly, leaving the three of them alone once more. Saint came over to where Sarita stood by the fireplace. The expression of sadness in his eyes gave her a bad feeling.

"Sarie, remember the proposal we talked about this morning?"

She did. She looked over at his brother. "He doesn't want to go through with the marriage. I understand. Neither do I."

Saint sighed, "If it were only that simple. Do you believe I would never do anything to harm you, or place you in harm's way?"

She did.

"Then don't fight me on this, okay?"

Sarita didn't commit, but his serious manner raised the hairs on the back of her neck. The other man was watching intently, silently.

Saint said, "The bottom line is this: You've set off some dangerous ripples doing Fletcher's deal. You may need protection."

"From whom, him?" she asked skeptically, indicating Saint's brother.

"No, from whoever owns those rocks."

Sarita had been thinking about that ever since learning of Fletcher's death. "But if I give them to you, I won't have them."

"No, but you *had* them. Not everybody in Fletcher's crew got popped in the hit. Remember I said some headed south?"

She did.

"Well, they're going to be found eventually, and they're going to be made to spill their guts. When that happens, depending on how much they knew about last night's deal, your name is going to come up, and then all hell's going to break loose. Those are blood diamonds—mined in Africa by enslaved kids whose hands are cut off when they don't fill their daily quota. These are very dangerous people, Sarie."

She wondered if he were trying to scare her; if so, he was doing a bang-up job. "So what am I looking at?"

"I want you to stay here," he replied softly.

"Why?"

Saint's half brother drawled, "Because he wants you to stay alive. Me, I'm still undecided."

Sarita took immediate offense. "I'll take my chances on the streets. I'm not staying here. Not with him."

Determination firing every step, she walked over to the door and took hold of the exotic brass handles. Locked. Willing herself to remain calm, she turned back. Her adversary stood across the room, his arms folded. She glanced over to Saint to ask him to do something about the locked door, but he wasn't there. A hasty survey of the room showed him to be no longer anywhere. Gone. He'd disappeared! She'd kill him!

Her host answered her unspoken question. "Saint had other plans. Have a seat."

"You can't keep me here against my will." Her bravado sounded hollow even to her own ears.

"Have a seat."

For a moment she stood her ground. He waited. Snarling inwardly, she complied. It was the last concession she planned on giving until she got some answers.

"Now, how old are you?"

"Why were you after the diamonds?"

"Just answer the question."

Sarita thought him entirely too arrogant. Since he was neither her parent nor her employer, she didn't respond.

He had thunderclouds in his eyes as he crossed to her. He leaned down into her face and spoke coldly. "You are about two seconds away from a plane ride to a place that not even Saint can find unless I receive some answers. And believe me, little girl, I can make you disappear"—he snapped his fingers—"just like that!"

Sarita jumped in reaction, hating her loss of control, but his sinister promise had her full attention.

He straightened to his full height, then slowly repeated the question. "How old are you?"

"Thirty-three." She met his eyes squarely. "And you?"

"Forty."

"Why were you after the diamonds?" she asked, but suddenly, the answer became irrelevant. For the first time Sarita actually looked at the distinct features of his face—the cut of his jaw, the dark eyes, the mustached framing his full lips. She knew him, knew his true identity and it scared her to death. "You're the mayor's brother! Mykal Chandler. You helped bankroll his campaign!" During the mayoral election, Chandler's face had been plastered all over the papers and TV. *Good Lord*, she thought to herself. Saint was kin to two of the most powerful men in the city.

Myk cursed inwardly. His worst fears were realized.

Sarita studied him for a moment, then came to a conclusion. "This isn't about my safety. You don't want me to leave because you're afraid I'll tell somebody, aren't you?"

It all made perfect sense to her now. Wow! What a story this would make: Half brother of mayor accused of possessing illegal diamonds. Oh yeah. The media would eat it up. There might be a way out of this after all, she crowed inwardly. "Does the mayor know his brother has a night job?"

He glared.

She smiled. "I'll tell you what. I promise to keep my mouth shut, and you let me walk out of here. I'll give Saint the diamonds and your gun, and we can both forget this little meeting ever took place."

"You're in no position to be bargaining."

The housekeeper entered the room to interrupt. "Your guests are here."

Myk acknowledged her without looking away from Sarita. "Thanks, Lily. Miss Grayson is going to be staying with us for a while. Will you get a room ready for her, please?"

"Certainly."

Sarita said, "Lily, don't bother. I won't be staying."

Myk's jaw tightened. "Go ahead, Lily."

Lily looked to the two of them, then, with a mysterious smile on her face, left the room.

He said to Sarita, "Come. It shouldn't take Lily long."

"You're not listening. I'm not staying. You are going to let me out of here. Now."

"Or what?" he asked, finding her continued defiance both amusing and unbelievable.

"Or I'm going to scream this place down, and your guests are going to hear me."

"They'll understand. Let's go."

Sarita knew that if she willingly followed him out of the room, her life would be changed forever. "No."

Before she could blink, he had her over his shoulder like a sack of cement and began walking. "Put me down!" she snapped

She did her best to wriggle free, but the carpet continued to bounce below her as he carried her upside down. *"Put me down!"*

Her angry demands, threats, and curses fell on deaf ears. He kept moving. Gathering her strength, she kicked him as hard as one could upside down. The toe of her boot caught him in his injured arm. He groaned with pain. Her satisfaction died quickly. He retaliated by tightening his injured arm across the backs of her thighs and swatting her hard across her conveniently positioned backside with the flat of his hand, not once but twice.

Her outrage filled the hallway.

He was now ascending a wide, rose-carpeted stairway. The furious Sarita could see a small knot of men and women grimly watching the show from the base of the staircase. She yelled for someone to call 911, but no one moved.

The NIA members who'd come for the night's meeting finished the agenda quickly. They knew Myk had other business to handle that evening, very vocal business that could be heard shouting for him at the top of her lungs.

After the meeting, Drake and Myk sat in the den listening to the ominous silence now coming from the upper floor. Drake, in the process of repairing the stitches Myk had torn loose wrestling with her, said, "Sounds like she's finally burned out."

Myk cocked an ear to the silence. "Let's hope."

Drake finished up and stepped back. "It looks fine, but no more combat or it will never heal."

Myk drawled, "Tell that to Ms. Grayson."

Drake waited while Myk shrugged back into his shirt, then said seriously, "You really ought to let her go."

"She knows too much," Myk countered.

"So, we get with Saint and work something out. Wiping out the bill on her building and handing her the title should be worth her silence."

"She stays."

Drake paused. He tried to understand Myk's logic, but couldn't. "Okay, let's leave that for a moment. What are you going to do about that marriage business?"

"It's still on."

The mayor shook his head. "That doesn't make sense. No man in his right mind would marry her."

Silence.

Because he'd known Mykal Chandler most of his life, Drake quipped, "You know, big brother, this is your Type A personality at work here."

Myk turned his attention from the silence that drifted down from above. "And that means what, exactly?"

"It means all you Type A's are alike. You hate to lose. I'll bet you've never had a woman beat you at anything."

"No, Drake, I haven't. Unlike you, I wasn't raised in a house filled with women."

It was a reference to Drake's three stepsisters. Drake could've taken offense at Myk's tone, but did not. "You're punishing her, man, for not only shooting you but for getting away with those rocks, too."

"Give the politician a prize."

Drake rubbed at his weary eyes. What a night. "Look, why don't you let me go up and talk to her—"

"No," Myk voiced quietly.

Drake stared. "What do you mean, no?"

"Just what I said, no. She already knows who I am. We let her see you now, and who knows what type of conclusions she'll draw. Nobody talks to her until I say so."

Drake viewed him strangely. The sequestered woman upstairs seemed to be affecting his judgment. "I still say you should let her go."

"And what about the reprisals for the diamonds? If you want to risk having one of the city's better-known neighborhood activists gunned down in a drive-by, just say the word, and I'll send her home."

Checkmate. Drake raised his glass of fruit juice in tribute. "That's why you're in charge, and I'm a politician."

"Exactly," Myk said, glad to feel the tension fading. He had enough problems on his plate. He didn't need to get into a fight with Drake, too. Taming the wildcat upstairs was going to take a lot more energy than he cared to think about. "Lord knows, I don't want to do this, but Saint will stake me out on a scorpion's nest if anything happens to her while he's gone."

"Where's he headed?"

"South, to try and get a line on the Fletcher Harris hit."

"You're really going to marry her?"

"I don't have a choice. I can't marry somebody else and keep the Grayson woman here, too. It'll be bad enough having one woman around. I can't handle two."

Drake shrugged. "Well, if Saint brought her to you as a legitimate candidate, maybe it will work out."

Myk cracked, "Right. I'll bet she doesn't know a soup bowl from a dinner fork. You know what scares me the most, though?"

Drake shook his head, no.

"The way she's dressed. What kind of woman comes to meet a prospective husband wearing jeans, an old leather jacket, and a black T-shirt that

SAYS, IF A MAN'S HOUSE IS HIS CASTLE—LET HIM CLEAN IT!!"

Drake grinned. "No idea, but if you marry her, you get to find out. Sounds like an African-American Pygmalion to me."

Myk didn't think any of this was funny.

Drake picked up his doctor's bag. "It's getting late. I'm going home. Good night Professor Higgins."

"Night." Myk smiled, finally succumbing to his brother's whacko humor. "I'll call you in the morning."

Drake flashed a grin and headed for the door.

Myk sat in the silence for a while longer, wondering about the woman upstairs.

Four

It was raining in the city of Chicago; a gray raw day that made the residents hunch forward as they hurried into their places of business. In an office on the top floor of one of the city's high-rises, wealthy businessman Clark Nelson reached into the bottom drawer of his imported teak desk and took out the vial of pills prescribed for the pain in his withered left leg. He'd contracted an infection in it during a forced stay in a Honduran prison many years ago, and the leg had been useless ever since.

Clark removed the brown vial's white plastic top, then washed down the two large green pills with the still-warm coffee in his cup. It would take the medication at least forty minutes to kick in. While he waited for the relief he turned his attention to a more troublesome matter.

To the city's movers and shakers, the short, thirty-eight-year-old Nelson was a successful entrepreneur. His import-export business supplied exotic and expensive objets d'art to high-toned interior designers from Toronto to Beverly Hills. He lived within the law, paid his taxes, and gave back to the community, but to men like Marvin Rand, Nelson was a drug dealer, pimp, predator, ruthless in his dealings with the people living on the dark underbelly of society, and chairman of the board of one of the largest drug syndicates in the nation.

The syndicate had been operating for nearly a decade without a hitch, but now there were problems. Clark reached across his neatly arranged desk top and picked up the small Ziploc bag. He studied the contents, a black ace of spades, through the clear plastic. The card had been sent to him by Marvin Rand a few days after his product had been stolen right from under his large Afrikaner nose last May. Nelson was still furious about the incident. The fact that Rand's dogs had been drugged and his mansion's fancy alarm system overridden electronically hadn't mattered at all to Clark. What did matter was that Rand had been robbed, and he had no idea who the thief or thieves were.

Clark visually scanned the card. Every time he looked at it, a chill ran down his spine. Old people called that tingle someone walking over your grave; a warning of bad times ahead, but Clark was an educated man. He didn't deal in the superstitions of ignorant country folk. Yet this card, found on Marvin Rand's pillow the night the diamonds disappeared, left Clark with an unsettling feeling he couldn't deny. He slowly turned it over. It was a standard, everyday playing card. There were literally millions of them in stores, bars, and homes all over the world. There'd be no way to trace it, and of course, there were no fingerprints on the one left for Rand. The card's surface had been spotless, just like the other three in his possession. Clark reached over and picked up the small clear bags that held the others. He shook the cards out, then lined them up. Four black aces of spades. All were from different decks and told him nothing. Rand had been the first hit, since then, three others at the top of the food chain had also been robbed, and now, the Fishbein mess. In his attempt to find a clean route to send the diamonds to Toronto, then on to his connect in Antwerp, Clark enlisted the help of a few Russian gambling friends, who in turn picked Fishbein to be the courier because of his anonymity. No one imagined Fishbein would go to Detroit and disappear, but he had, and so had another shipment of diamonds. Clark was furious; the people in Antwerp were furious, and so were the Russians, whom Clark placated by paying off Fishbein's debt anyway per the original agreement.

Clark paused for a moment in his thoughts in order to massage the ache in his left leg. He reached over and grabbed the ivory, snake-headed cane with which he could not maneuver. Using it for balance, he left the chair and limped the few steps to the window. He put the pain out of his mind and looked out over the rain and the Chicago skyline. Somewhere out there were people plotting the demise of his empire; people capable of striking at him from anywhere, if all four thefts were related, and he sensed they were. At first, he thought the government might be involved in the thefts, and he still hadn't ruled out the possibility; however, it didn't feel like a government operation. For one thing, the hits had been clean, no mistakes, no traces of anything left behind that might point to their identity or the ultimate goal. Except for those damn cards. If the whole matter weren't so serious, he'd have laughed at the ridiculous trademark. The cards were like something out of an old movie, but neither he nor his people were laughing. The cash flow problems resulting from all the thefts of product were affecting the bottom line. Having to hire additional security for houses and shipments, coupled with the diamonds not reaching market, exacerbated the problems. Some of his big investors in the syndicate were running scared, especially after the hit at Rand's estate.

The sound of the soft knock on his closed office door made him turn. His secretary apologized for disturbing him, then gave him a quiet reminder about the speech he was scheduled to deliver at that afternoon's Chamber of Commerce luncheon. He took the prompt silently, his gaze back on the rainy skyline. He then asked her to clear his calendar for the next two weeks. It was time to take matters into his own hands. The thief or thieves had to be found. Later, he would put in a call to the pilot of his private jet to prepare for a midnight flight to Detroit. The diamonds and Fishbein had disappeared there, and that's where he'd begin the search.

The bedroom Sarita had been given looked like something out of an upscale home furnishings magazine. Snow-white curtains covered the floor-to-ceiling windows. A huge stone fireplace was built into one wall. In front of it were two elegant chairs and a love seat, both covered with a soft emerald green fabric. Tall torchere lamps with Tiffany shades stood like sentinels on either side of the fireplace. The place reeked of money, but Sarita didn't want to smell anything but freedom.

She'd been locked in here for three days. True, she'd always dreamed about taking a long, lazy vacation with no phones, newspapers, or TV, but this was more of a nightmare. That first night, after Chandler dumped her in here, she'd pounded on the door until her hands were red and sore. She'd also screamed herself hoarse, but it hadn't mattered. He never returned. In the end, she'd given up. She'd fallen across the room's big sleigh-shaped bed, angry, frustrated, and admittedly a bit scared. At some point, she'd fallen asleep only to awaken in the middle of the night to find herself covered by a soft warm blanket. Her shoes had also been removed. Sarita guessed Lily; Chandler didn't impress her as the solicitous type.

So for three days, she'd been in this fashion plate of a room with no way out. The windows were locked—she'd tried them, and room's door, too. The only person capable of engineering her escape would be Harry Houdini, or Saint, and him she planned to strangle on sight. She then thought about Silas and the rest of her people. Her sudden disappearance probably had them worried sick. Had they gone to the police? She pushed those disquieting thoughts away. She was already on her way to being a basket case. Worrying about the folks at the center wouldn't help.

Sarita pushed the bedcovers aside and got up.

She wondered if today would be any different. All of this solitary confinement wasn't working for her. She wasn't accustomed to being the bird in a gilded cage.

Barefoot, she padded across the plush green carpet and into the adjoining bathroom. Although this was her third morning of captivity, the enormous space still filled her with awe. Above her head was an etched-glass dome that gave her a peek at the gray October sky. Surrounding her were gleaming wall-size mirrors and a veritable jungle of healthy, leafy green plants. There was a large stand-up shower housed in smoke gray glass; a closet stuffed with soft fluffy towels, and, dominating the room, an onyx sunken tub so large her high school swim team could have done laps in it. The tub's gold-and-crystal appointments gleamed like jewels.

So far, Sarita had successfully fought off the urge to bask in the big tub, mainly because she knew just how much she would enjoy it. Since she wasn't there to enjoy herself, she walked over to the shower and used it instead.

The shower and the rest of her morning needs didn't take long. She wrapped her wet body in one of the sumptuous towels and padded back into the main room.

She was not surprised to find Lily waiting for her return. The housekeeper had made similarly timed appearances the past two mornings, usually to bring in breakfast and clothing. In a way, Lily's seemingly magical appearances reminded Sarita of Saint. That snake! Sarita hadn't seen Chandler at all.

The ever-cheery Lily asked, "How are you this morning, Miss Grayson?"

"I'd be doing a whole lot better if I could leave here, but other than that?" She shrugged as if that were explanation enough. "How are you?"

"Fine. I'm a little worried about my daughter April, down in Atlanta though. She's due to make me a grandma any day."

"Your first grand?"

Lily looked proud. "Yep. April's a lawyer. She's been working on her career, so I've been waiting a long time to be a gran."

Sarita could not help but smile at the housekeeper's beaming face. "Congratulations," she offered genuinely, then asked, "What's he got planned for me today?" Sarita hoped the plans included clothes. Her own had "mysteriously" disappeared while she was taking a shower the first morning of her captivity. She hadn't a clue as to why they'd been confiscated, and, no matter how many times she asked about them, Lily always said they were in the wash.

That had been three days ago. What she'd been given to wear instead were gowns. The most recent version, in keeping with the others, looked like a long silk slip. It was pearl gray, had spaghetti straps that left her arms and shoulders bare, and had a toe-brushing hem edged with lace scallops the same color as the gown. The first day's set had been the color of midnight, the second, a dark emerald green. Each had come with a matching robe. The ensembles had a slinky rich elegance that made her feel like she'd just stepped out of an old Dorothy Dandridge movie.

Sarita ducked into the bathroom and slipped on the gown and collared robe. She tied the silk belt and wondered who these gowns really belonged to.

When she stepped out again, Lily smiled. "You look lovely as always."

Sarita shrugged. "Thanks." Although Lily had firmly refused to answer any of Sarita's questions about Chandler's plans, the woman had been kind. Over the past few days, she'd brought Sarita her meals, a deck of cards, and some magazines to pass the time.

Sarita glanced over at the small end table by the fireplace. Usually Lily placed the breakfast tray there, but this morning the tray was missing. "No breakfast this morning, Lily? He planning on starving me now, too?"

"No, dear. You're having breakfast together."

Sarita stiffened. "He's coming here?"

"No. He asked that I bring you to him when you're ready."

This was the confrontation Sarita had been waiting for, or had she? She didn't know whether to jump for joy or head for the hills. Her clothing added to her dilemma. She could hardly negotiate from a position of strength dressed like Diahann Carroll playing Dominique Devereaux.

"Lily, I need my clothes back."

"Miss Grayson, believe me, it won't matter what you're wearing."

Tight-lipped, Sarita stuck her bare feet into the gown-matching low-heeled mules and grimly followed Lily out of the door.

The last time Sarita had been in the hallway she'd been hanging upside down and yelling at the top of her lungs. Now, as she trailed Lily through the beautifully restored old house, she could see the walls held art pieces from myriad cultures: African fetishes, Mexican oils, and pre-Columbian masks. She wanted to stop Lily and ask about a few of the more outstanding pieces—especially the Olmec head that drew her particular interest, but the housekeeper didn't act like this was a pleasure trip, so Sarita kept her questions to herself. She'd ask her later; surely Chandler wouldn't mind Lily talking about the house's art.

Sarita's thoughts on the subject were set aside as they descended the staircase and she was shown into a small room on the first floor. A beautifully set table for two sat waiting. She had a clear view of the sky for the first time in three days. Sarita took up a position before the windows and looked out at the Detroit River. There was a barge slowly churning downriver. She was admittedly nervous about the whole situation, but Saint had promised her things would be all right; she just hoped he knew what he was talking about.

Lily asked quietly, "Are you ready?"

Sarita replied truthfully, "No, but let's not keep him waiting."

"Then I'll get him."

"Thank you," Sarita said softly.

It didn't take him long. When he entered the room, Sarita's first thoughts were just how gorgeous a man Chandler was—the deep rich skin, the lip-framing mustache. He had the features and build of a dark god. During the mayoral campaign, she remembered seeing a few of the city's TV anchorwomen reduced to giggling teenagers while interviewing him.

He was wearing a soft brown turtleneck topped by a matching suede jacket. The black wool slacks were perfectly tailored. His only jewelry was a small gold hoop in his ear and the silver black stone ring on the third finger of his right hand. He appeared confident, distant, and rich.

Dressed as she was, Sarita felt at a distinct disadvantage.

"Have a seat, please," he told her, gesturing to one of the chairs at the table.

Sarita was determined to brazen this out, so she took a deep breath and, with her head held high, walked to the table. She sat stiffly, then startled a bit as he moved to help her with her chair. The heat of his body wafted over her like a hot July day. The nearness of him set her insides to shaking, but outwardly she was cool.

Myk took his seat on the opposite side of the table. Her attitude surprised him. By all rights she should be crying and hysterical after being locked up for three days; but there she sat, regal and calm as a queen. Mad, too, by the look of her tightly set brown jaw.

She broke the silence. "When are you letting me out of here?"

Myk unfolded his linen napkin and placed it across his lap. "Right now, I'm going to eat. You might want to do the same."

Sarita watched him begin to fill his plate from the covered silver dishes. She wanted to argue, but didn't. It made more sense to let him show his hand first.

But she was so tense and so nervous, she couldn't eat. Her stomach knotted up the moment Lily had informed her of this little breakfast meeting. As a result Sarita could only swallow a bit of toast and a few bites of the bacon. She noted that he seemed to be having no such difficulties however. He ate his breakfast and read his morning paper as if the world were his.

When he finished, he set the paper beside his cleaned plate, and she felt her spine tighten in response.

Myk scanned the challenge and defiance simmering in her dark eyes and thought to himself, *This will not be easy.*

He gently tossed the packet of legal documents to her side of the table. "Your new lease," he pointed out, then poured himself more coffee. "As of nine yesterday morning, I own your warehouse."

Alarmed, Sarita picked up the packet and tried to read the legalese swimming before her eyes. What she found at the bottom of page two stopped her heart. He held title not only to the building, but to the land surrounding it, too, giving him legal dominion over everything she held dear. The included lease, drawn up on Chandler Works letterhead, had a bottom line of twelve thousand dollars a year! "You don't really expect me to pay you twelve thousand a year?"

"I expect agreement to all my terms."

The deadly calm in his words sent a chill through her soul. "And if I don't agree?"

"Then I evict your people at noon today." He took a moment to check the face of the expensive-looking watch on his wrist. "Right now, it's eight-thirty."

She wondered what type of man could talk so casually about forcing seniors and children out onto the streets. In that regard, he was no better than Fletcher. "And if I do agree?"

"Then they get to stay, and I'll pump enough money into your programs to run them they way they should be run."

That statement totally surprised her. "Why?"

He shrugged his brown suede shoulders. "One, it will look good at tax time. Two, my foundation's always willing to support well-run programs. And yours," he added, eyes straying to her mouth, "is reportedly one of the best."

Sarita knew it had to be her imagination, but she sensed something emanating from his dark presence that had nothing to do with what they were discussing. She shook herself free. "I know you aren't adopting us out of the goodness of your heart, so what's the real reason?"

Myk didn't find her skepticism surprising. The reports he'd gotten on her said she was very bright. "The real reason? The control I gain over you."

Her eyes narrowed. "Over me?"

He nodded. "According to Saint and everyone else I've talked to, that center and its people are your whole life. You'd do anything for them—even make a stupid deal with someone like Fletcher."

Sarita still considered Saint a traitor of the worst kind, but she couldn't deny the statement. She would and had moved heaven and earth to keep the Lambert Center open. When the furnace died the previous winter, she'd gotten out the phone book and called every furnace company in the county until she found one willing to do the work for free. It had taken her two days, but she'd found someone. When she was informed in the spring that her small programs would no longer be funded by the state, she'd taken a three-hour bus ride to the state capital and personally knocked on the doors of any legislators who'd give her a minute of their time. It turned out to be a futile trip, her center had been given the ax anyway, but she'd tried. Her people and the center meant a lot to her, but how did her commitment to them give him control over her?

He made it clearer. "By owning the building, I own you."

She wondered if he'd been born that arrogant, or if the attitude had come with his wealth. "And that works, how?"

"Simple. I could decide to level that block and put up, say, a parking lot."

She was really not liking this man. "And how do I keep you from putting up this—parking lot?"

"By agreeing to the original proposal to marry me."

She stated the obvious. "You don't want to marry me."

"No, I don't, but I can't just let you walk out of here."

"Why not? I don't care what you do in your spare time."

"Someone else might though."

She leaned in and promised earnestly, "Look, I won't say anything."

Myk steeled himself against the honesty in her eyes. "It doesn't matter. Either agree, or the building's padlocked."

Sarita wanted to leap across the table and shake him until sundown, but instead she made herself stay calm. "Why in the world do you still want to do this?"

Myk had asked himself the same question many times over the past few days. The answer he kept coming back to was that he could kill two birds with one stone. He definitely needed a wife, and at this point, because of the problems she presented, the very unsuitable, Sarita Kathleen Grayson would have to do. He could hardly marry another woman and have this firecracker locked up in the house, too. "I'm trying to keep you alive. Don't look a gift horse in the mouth."

"Gift?" she echoed throwing up her hands. "You lock me up for three days, take my clothes, threaten my people, and I'm supposed to be grateful? What planet are you from?"

"As rich as I am, most women would kill to wear my name. Here"—He tossed her another sheaf of papers—"your prenuptial agreement."

Caught totally off guard, again, Sarita croaked, "Prenuptial agreement?" She tried to focus in on the terms, but the words on the paper swam before her eyes just as the lease had done a minute earlier.

He told her emotionlessly, "It says that all you will receive after the divorce is the fifty thousand Saint told you about initially."

Sarita felt as if she were on a runaway roller coaster, and she wanted off. "You still haven't explained to me why you want to go through with the marriage."

"Because I need a wife, and you're it."

"That doesn't make sense. You have all this money, and you can't find anybody else willing to play your wife?"

"I don't want anyone else."

The power in his eyes pulsed through her like the low hum of an electrical current. She studied him. There had to be a way to make him reconsider. "The rich are supposed to marry the rich. Do you know how poor I am?"

"I do. I know all about you." He picked up a folder from the floor, opened it, and began to read aloud. "Sarita Kathleen Grayson. Born February 19, 1970. Both parents killed in a bus accident in 1976. Raised thereafter by Pearl Watson, maternal grandmother. Also in the home were two great granduncles—Nathan and Victor Grayson. They were twins?"

She nodded tightly.

He read on. "It says they were locksmiths."

Again, she nodded. So he knew a few biographical details. So what? He'd read nothing so far that indicated he knew *all* about her.

"You had your first brush with the law at age fourteen."

Her startled eyes flew to his face.

He continued, "You picked the padlock on a police impound lot and stole a car."

"Wrong. I picked the lock, yes, but the car belonged to a friend's mother. And we didn't steal it. It was stolen from her first. The police recovered it on the westside with the thieves still in it and impounded the car as evidence."

"Why didn't you and your friend just wait until the police released it?"

"Do you know how long it takes to go to trial in this city, even back then? Alva's mother needed the car to get to work. The city had it in the impound for six weeks."

He paused a moment to study her defiant face. He thought she must have been a handful growing up. "The court put you on probation."

"Yes. The judge said he understood why I took the car, but he couldn't condone my methods. He gave me a year's probation. He also told me my court record would be sealed. How'd you get your hands on it?"

The handsome face across the table offered no clues and not a hint of guilt or shame.

An angry Sarita turned away. How had he gotten information that was supposed to be legally inaccessible? She knew he was related to the mayor, but did Chandler's money and influence extend even to sealed court documents? Apparently so.

"I assume your guardians punished you for this prank?"

She gave him a withering look, and asked sarcastically, "What's it say in your report?" She'd no intention of telling him she'd received the last and worst whipping of her then-fourteen-year-old life. Her uncles were solid, taxpaying citizens, and they'd been furious that she'd broken the law.

Myk couldn't help but admire her spirit, even if she had tried to kill him. He also noted that not even her anger could mar the brown sugar beauty of her face. Her skin appeared to be as soft and blemish-free as the fabric of the gown she was wearing. Her small but fully ripe lips drew his attention again and again, and the fire-breathing mahogany eyes only enhanced her features. Anyone seeing her would never doubt her ability to attract and hold the attention of a man like him, and that, too, fit right into his plan.

"So," he asked, "what have you decided? Do you want the wedding ring or the padlock?"

Sarita weighed the matter but saw guillotines everywhere she looked. She now understood what he'd meant about owning the center and, as a result, her. She couldn't let her neighborhood be leveled. What would happen to the people? She supposed she could do worse than find herself married to this rich and powerful man, but what would be the cost? What danger would she be placing herself in by being his wife? Saint promised she'd be safe, but she wasn't so sure. She wasn't sure about anything right now, except Chandler's promise to padlock her center. That she believed. Her decision made, she looked across the table at him. She hated being so powerless. "I agree."

"I heard you were bright."

She could have done without the sarcasm.

"As I said, your center is well run. While you're here, I'll appoint an administrator to oversee things."

"Wait a minute. You can't do that."

"Yes, I can."

"No, you can't."

"Did you just agree to my terms or not?"

"Yes," she replied coolly. "I agreed to be your wife. I didn't agree to some suit-wearing bean counter sitting in my chair."

"If I want to put a suit-wearing *chimpanzee* in your chair, it's my business, not yours."

Sarita was furious. "That's my place and my people."

"Not anymore." Myk noted the blaze in her eyes, the angry face, and the gap in her robe offering him a slight view of the valley between her breasts as she leaned in to make her point.

Sarita swore, "I will fight you on this, Chandler. I mean it! I'll agree to whatever else you want, but you will not take my center from me."

"I already have."

Sarita slammed her fist on the table.

Myk had no intentions of changing his mind. No one knew when Fletcher's scattered crew members would be found or what tune they'd sing to keep from winding up in a grave. And Saint didn't want her name mentioned in any of the verses. Letting her have free run of her neighborhood might place her in jeopardy. It also might result in an information leak NIA could ill afford. Too many lives and careers hung in the balance. "I'll have Lily take you back to your room now."

"This discussion is not over, Chandler!"

"Yes, it is. Later today we'll go shopping. That should cheer you up. It works for most women."

"I'm not most women."

He stood. "Sarita, you'd be surprised just how common you are."

She felt slapped.

As if cued, Lily appeared.

Myk looked down into Sarita's furious face. Her arms were crossed so firmly, the tight pull on the silk plainly showed the buttons of her nipples. He redirected his attention to her sullen features. "I'll see you later."

She gave him her best, go-to-hell face, then followed Lily back to the gilded cage.

Five

At noon Sarita was still simmering over the outcome of her breakfast meeting with Chandler. Pacing the floor in her cage, she replayed the encounter in her mind again and again, trying to find a way out of the net he'd thrown over her; but he had her, lock, stock, and barrel, and there wasn't a thing she could do. A knock on the door slowed her pacing. She called come in, and in came Lily struggling under a stack of boxes and bags that all but dwarfed her short stature.

While Sarita stared confused, Lily set everything on the bed, and said, "I had to guess at the sizes, you're such a tiny thing, but I think everything should fit."

Sarita walked over and saw boxes and shopping bags bearing the names of some of the most expensive stores around; stores she only window-shopped in on her way to the discount mart.

"You should find everything you need," Lily said, heading back to the door. "Hurry and dress now. He's waiting."

Sarita had a million and one questions, but Lily left without a further word. Had Chandler been serious about this shopping trip? Apparently so, because in the boxes and bags Sarita found a complete set of clothes—everything from a suit and camisole, to undies, to stockings and heels. There was even makeup. For a moment she debated what to do. Did she get dressed, or did she sit in the room and play the martyr queen. She didn't care about shopping; she didn't care about him, but she had been cooped up in one room entirely too long. Any reason to leave it was a good one, she concluded, so she got dressed.

Afterward, she stood before the large mirror of the low-slung vanity table. The beautiful navy blue suit had a straight slim skirt and a tailored jacket. The blouse beneath was snow-white silk and easily the softest garment she'd ever worn. Everything fit, just as Lily had hoped; in fact, the clothes fit so well they could have been purchased by Sarita personally. However, on the small pension check Sarita received each month as her granduncles' beneficiary, she would have trouble affording even the stockings.

In the bottom of one of the bags, she found a small velvet jeweler's box. Inside were a pair of small sapphire studs. For many many years, Sarita's grandmother had been the housekeeper for Mr. Samuel Aronson, then one of the country's most famous jewelry designers. During the summers, Sarita would often help her grandmother at the Aronson house. Sometimes Mr. Aronson would invite Sarita into his workshop to show her his latest creations. Thanks to him, she learned quite a bit about stones, and as a result knew the difference between the real McCoy and paste. Her trained eye said the small brilliant sparklers mounted in the velvet box were as real as old Mr. Aronson's smile.

Sarita fit the studs in her ears, noting that a girl could get swept away by all this if she weren't careful, but she planned on having no such reaction. Fancy jewelry or no, Chandler's wealth would not make her any more comfortable with the mess she'd gotten herself into, or with him.

Downstairs, Myk expected Sarita to be intimidated by the expensive clothes. But when she entered the room, she literally knocked his socks off. For a woman whom reports said didn't own a dress or a skirt, she exuded an aura of sophistication and elegance that seemed natural. She was wearing his sapphires in her ears and a familiar, chin-raised iciness on her perfectly made-up face. To his surprise and satisfaction, she looked as if she'd been bred for the role he wanted her to play. The straight skirt emphasized the firm and surprisingly long brown legs. The heels added height to her five-foot-one frame. The color on her lips made them even more lush. He approved of how well she'd cleaned up.

Sarita read neither approval nor disapproval on his dark face. All she saw for sure was him motioning her in the direction he wanted her to go, so she did. The small expensive handbag on her shoulder matched her blue suit and shoes. The purse had nothing in it, but it gave her hands something to hold on to.

He led her out through the kitchen to the house's attached garage and over to a beautiful black sports car. Sarita shivered from the chilly October temperature. He opened the door, and she got in.

He got in on the driver's side. Myk couldn't help but notice her shivering. "The heat will be up in a minute," he told her, adjusting levers and dials before putting the car into gear.

She didn't acknowledge his statement, she was too busy hugging herself and praying that the promised heat would soon start pounding her sheer-hosed legs. She'd kill for a pair of jeans.

"Do you want my coat?" he asked backing the sleek, French import out of the garage and down the driveway.

She shook her head. "No." The day was as gray as her mood.

He stopped the car at the foot of the drive and paused a moment to take in her averted profile. He and Lily had forgotten about adding a coat to the items purchased for her to wear. The oversight would be remedied first. The last thing he needed was for her to get sick; he wouldn't put it past her to induce pneumonia intentionally just to pay him back. He slid the stick into gear and drove away from the house.

The car roared down into the city's belowground expressway system, merging easily with the fast-paced Detroit traffic. To Myk, the silence in the car was like a third passenger. "There're some CDs in the glove box. Help yourself."

"I'm okay."

Myk mentally shrugged. He supposed there'd be no pleasing her, at least no time soon. He really wished Saint had hooked him up with a nice docile woman instead of this fire ant. According to the reports compiled on her, she was a true crusader, a relic, a throwback to the days when people actually cared about the less fortunate and committed their lives to making a difference. He wondered if she knew she was about thirty years too late, and that those who'd battled in the trenches back then no longer seemed to care. Most of the activists of that day were now more concerned with tax cuts, private schools, and whether to buy one German sports car or two; the less fortunate no longer fit their lifestyle. He supposed the men and women of NIA were relics, too, probably the only thing he and Sarita had in common.

When he pulled the car into the mall's valet parking lane, Sarita tried not to gape at the surroundings. This was *the* mall. It opened last summer with much media pomp and circumstance, and catered to the area's wealthiest citizens. Inside were stores with branches in Palm Springs and on Rodeo Drive, stores where you could get massaged after a long day of flashing your gold card, or easily spend enough in a day to feed a family of four for a year. It was a mall where people like Sarita had about as much business being as a goat had being in school, as her uncles used to say; but as the uniformed valet came to her door and opened it, she stepped out as if she'd been shopping in such places all her life.

Stop number one turned out to be the small, exclusive shop of a highly distinguished furrier. While

Myk walked over to greet the owner, a Nigerian named Andrew Obari, Sarita waited a few feet away. She wondered why Chandler had come there, but was sure if she asked him, he'd tell her to mind her own business, so while the two men continued to talk, she took a slow, disinterested walk around the mirror-filled salon. Her hand trailed over the fine array of light and dark furs, and not even her bad mood could deny their beauty. Her eyes lingered over a full-length number the color of a chocolate night. Beneath her hand it felt soft and luxurious. It was plush enough to take on any Michigan winter. A coat dreams were made of, she thought wistfully, but not for a woman like herself.

"Do you like this one?"

She startled at Chandler's voice. He'd come up behind her so silently.

"It's nice," she replied.

He startled her even more by taking the coat from the rack, removing the hanger, and handing her the fur. "Here, try it on."

"No."

If this was his idea of humor, Sarita didn't find it very funny; she didn't need to be reminded how poor she was, and in angry whispers told him just that.

The few customers in the shop were discreet enough not to stare openly at the beautiful young woman in blue and the tall handsome man in the black suit, arguing over the coat.

Sarita soon sensed the interest of the other customers, so to halt the show and shut Chandler up, she put on the coat. He made her turn and face the mirror.

Draped in the elegant sable, Sarita viewed herself in the mirror. She had the eerie sensation of looking at someone she didn't recognize. The rich dark color matched her eyes. She'd never tried on anything this fabulous, ever.

"Well?" Myk asked.

His voice brought her back to the present, and she looked up. "Well, what?"

"Well, do you want it?"

She took off the coat and handed it back. She wondered what his problem was? "Of course not. I can't afford anything like this."

"But I can."

It took a moment for the words to register. A speechless Sarita stared into his unreadable eyes, and asked, "You are seriously talking about buying this?"

He nodded.

"For *me*?"

Again, the nod.

Sarita found this very hard to process. "But—"

Myk realized they'd be there all day if he had to wait for her to set aside her social worker values and decide. So he decided for her. He handed the coat to the hovering Obari and asked that the purchase be added to his account.

Sarita stated firmly, "Chandler, I don't need that coat."

He didn't acknowledge her attempt to make him see sense. He strolled over to join Obari at the register, leaving her standing there openmouthed. *This is insane*, she thought wildly. What could he possibly be thinking of?

Whatever he had in mind he didn't share. He

simply handed her the coat, waved good-bye to the Nigerian proprietor, and politely escorted her out of the salon.

He shopped for her for the rest of the day. She forgot to be distant and uncooperative—she was too busy being amazed by the man's buying power. Everywhere they went he spent money as if he had a personal pipeline to the national treasury. He signed for evening gowns, shoes, hairbrushes, beautiful sweaters, jeans, blouses, and expensive silk hose, along with everything else a woman could possibly need. And through it all, Sarita's eyes kept straying to the sable coat folded oh so nonchalantly across her arm. *How much money does this man have?*

She attempted to draw the line when she saw where they were headed next. The store, a branch of a famous British franchise, offered items both scandalous and demure.

To keep him from going inside, she latched on to his arm. He looked down at her small hand, and asked, "Problems?"

"Yes," she stated. "You are not buying my underwear."

Myk nodded a greeting to an older woman passing by them in the nearly deserted mall, then asked Sarita, "Why not?"

"Because." No man had ever bought underwear for her in her life. Well, her uncles had when she was young, but not since she'd become a young lady.

He searched her eyes. "Because, why?"

"Because you don't know me that well."

Myk studied her. "I see." He'd concede her that point. "Then I'll let you pick out what you want."

"Good," she said, glad this hadn't turned into a major argument. "Let's go down to Sears. They have better prices."

Her frugality almost made him show a smile. "We're not going to Sears."

"Why not? Sears has nice things."

"I'm sure they do, but this is where I want to shop."

"And if I insist on Sears?"

He told her quietly, "You can insist all you want, but I'm the one paying, remember?"

"I remember that I didn't ask to come along."

"Then I get to spend my money where I want."

He started toward the door. "You coming or not?"

Snarling, Sarita followed him inside.

The store was tasteful, she had to admit. Headless, mannequin torsos sported beautiful jewel-toned bras and scanty little nightgowns. Color was everywhere, and fragrance scented the air. She spotted Chandler in the back. He was surrounded by salesgirls who seemed to sense that the tall handsome man was a no-credit-limit customer and were tripping over each other trying to gain his attention.

"What about this one, baby?"

Sarita realized he was talking to her. The endearment fell on her ears, softly, possessively, and he had a look in his eyes that mirrored his voice. The intensity she saw there threw her even as it touched her. What was he up to?

He explained. "I was just telling the salesladies that you want to replace everything in your underwear drawers. Ladies, my wife, Sarita."

That threw her as well. "Hello," she managed to say. The girls grinned back.

Gathering herself, Sarita stepped close to his side and told herself she wasn't affected by the bone-melting sound of his voice or the vivid touch of his eyes, but it was a lie.

What he wanted her to see was the item he was holding up for her approval. It was a sexy sequined black bustier elegant enough to wear to the White House. She'd never worn anything even remotely like it before, but, seeing the salesgirls watching so eagerly, she cleared her throat, and croaked out, "Sure. I like that."

"See anything else you like?"

His dark eyes had turned playful. She knew he was only flirting with her for the benefit of the crowd, so to cover her rising reaction to him, she tossed back in a knowing saucy voice, "Yes, I do. And you? See anything you like?"

Myk gave her a slow grin. *Who'd have thought this female hornet had a sultry side.* "I see plenty, but there are children in the room, so let's get this shopping done."

Sarita swayed on her new high heels. She turned her attention back to the salesgirls who were now watching the interplay as if it were a movie. Her heart was racing like the Indy 500, but they didn't know that. "Can I see some nightgowns, ladies?"

So, for the next forty minutes, Sarita looked at nightgowns, bras, and panties. The salesgirls brought out silk pajamas with matching wrappers, scented soaps, slips, and camisoles by the score. Sarita picked out what she wanted and turned down what she didn't.

Sarita didn't pay Chandler much attention during all of this. He'd drifted away from her at one point, but now returned with one hand filled with what appeared to be bits of lace and silk. Sarita eyed him curiously. As she watched his hand open and saw the small cache of thongs float down to the counter as if they were made from angel wings, curiosity morphed into shock. Her eyes flew from the thongs to his face. He had the nerve to be smiling like a very pleased wolf.

"Thought you might like them," he told her.

She blinked, then said with a false brightness, "I do. Thank you."

"So," he asked her then, "are we done here?"

They were only a few inches apart, and Sarita hadn't a clue as to how to answer that double-edged question.

Myk felt oddly spellbound by her nearness. For that tiny moment he ceased to be the head of NIA and became a man filled with the urge to find out just how close to the surface her sultriness was. Under the watchful eyes of the salesgirls, he slid a slow caressing finger down her cheek. "Let's pay for this stuff and get out of here. . . ."

Sarita was sure the unexpected gesture was nothing more than an act on his part, but his touch left her dazzled and vibrating like a five-string guitar.

The girls ran his credit card, he signed the slip and escorted Sarita out.

In the car, Sarita sat in the passenger seat reeling from her first outing with the man she'd made a deal to marry. A treasure trove of boxes, bags, and packages filled both the trunk and the import's small interior. The haul accounted for only about a third of the spree. The rest would be delivered later in the week. She glanced over at his serious face. All traces of the playful sensual man in the lingerie store had vanished the moment they exited the store. She told herself it didn't matter. "You didn't have to buy me all this stuff."

"It isn't for you. It's for the image."

He took his eyes off the road a moment and held hers. "I can't have my wife running around in faded T-shirts and ripped jeans, even if she is temporary."

"Oh," she said, feeling more than a bit put down, then turned back to the window. "And what if I prefer faded T-shirts and ripped jeans?"

"Wear what you want at home. Out in the street, you'll wear—stuff."

She looked over at him to see if he were intentionally trying to lighten the mood, but the face appeared to be as serious as ever.

When they got back to the house, Lily had a message for Myk to call his office at Chandler Works. While he went off to take care of that, Lily asked Sarita, "How'd the shopping go?"

Sarita shrugged. "Fine I guess. I watched mostly."

Lily smiled. "Lunch in ten minutes."

Sarita carried as many bags as she could up to her room and took off the beautiful sable coat. Seeing it, touching it, still filled her with awe.

Back downstairs, Sarita stood by the windows and watched the gray waters of the river while she waited for Chandler to return. Her thoughts drifted to Silas and how worried he must be over her disappearance. She had to convince Chandler to let her call the center so Silas and the rest of her people would at least know she was alive.

When Lily came in pushing a cart filled with covered dishes and silverware, Sarita's first impulse was to help. Sarita's grandmother had been a day worker for almost fifty years, and because she was, Sarita felt a bit uncomfortable being waited upon.

Lily seemed to sense Sarita's urge, and said, "You stay right where you are, young lady, and let me do my job. If I need help, I'll call."

A chastened Sarita dropped her head and nodded.

Chandler returned right on the heels of the conversation, and said to Lily, "No, let her help, she'll need to know these kinds of things."

His mocking tone grabbed Sarita's attention, and she slowly turned to face him. She realized he didn't believe she knew how to set a table. He'd called her *common* this morning at breakfast, and her pride was still stung. Was this his attempt to prove himself right? "You don't think I know anything about this, do you?"

He shrugged those magnificent shoulders and crossed his arms.

Sarita walked over to the cart and picked up the china plates. She set each fragile blue-and-white plate down with a ring. "Your reports must have missed something, Chandler. My grandmother was setting tables for rich folks before you were even born. *I* started helping her as soon as I could see over the tops of the tables."

Sarita knew not only where to place the plates, salad plates, and water goblets, she asked that Lily go back to the china cabinet and bring out dessert plates and forks.

When the housekeeper returned, a seething Sarita

was in the middle of interrogating Chandler while she went around the table. "Do you know how many inches should be between the dessert fork and the plate?" she asked him, "or how far the plate should be from the edge of the table?"

Silence

"You don't know?" she asked mockingly. "What about the water glass and the tip of the fork?"

Myk knew better than to say a word to the furious woman in the blue suit. He'd underestimated her again, and had apparently insulted her pretty badly if this demonstration were any indication.

Once Sarita finished setting the table to her grandmother's exacting standards, she took a seat and drawled, "Have a seat, Chandler, or can't you do that with both feet stuck in your mouth?"

Lily coughed behind her hand to cover her surprised laughter.

The stone-faced Mykal took his seat.

Lily stayed around only long enough to thank Sarita for her help with the table, then left the two alone to fight it out.

Myk didn't like being shown up, but was honest enough to admit it had been his own fault. He conceded her the round by raising his water glass and saying with sincerity, "My apologies for insulting you."

She stated flatly, "Fifty thousand is not going to be enough."

He picked up his fork, and in spite of his mood, chuckled inwardly. *What a woman.*

After they finished the meal, Sarita stood up to leave.

His voice stopped her, "There are some papers here you need to sign."

"What kind of papers?"

"The ones I showed you this morning."

"I don't need to sign a prenup. I don't want anything from you."

Myk wondered if she'd ever met a situation she hadn't challenged? Even with her back against the wall, she still insisted upon having her way. Saint had warned Myk it would be easier to pull nails from cement than to get her to go along with something she didn't like, and he'd been right. Never in Myk's whole life had he ever had a woman say no to a sable coat, but this one had. He told her, "Humor me then, and just sign it, please."

"I need to call my people at the center. They're probably worried sick."

"We'll discuss it after you sign." He set the papers on the table and held out a pen.

Knowing she had no leverage, Sarita took the pen and grudgingly signed in all the places he indicated. "Can I call now?"

"I'll bring you a phone."

He left a moment, then returned with a white cordless. It was the first phone she'd seen since her arrival.

Before she punched in the number, she asked pointedly, "Can I have some privacy?"

He retook his seat. "No. Make your call and keep it short."

Sarita punched in the numbers. She supposed she should be happy he let her call, but his attitude didn't make her feel real grateful.

She got Silas on the other end. As soon as she said hello, he lit into her. Seconds passed before she could find a space in his tirade to say anything else. "Silas—"

More tirade.

"Silas, I know I made everybody worry. Silas—"

Although she loved him, he was the bane of her existence sometimes. "Silas—"

He kept going on and on about how worried everybody had been, and how could she go off on her honeymoon and not let anybody know she was getting married?

For a moment she was speechless. "Who told you I was getting married?" she asked, meeting Chandler's eyes across the table. When Silas gave her the name, she yelled, "Saint!"

Before she could react to that, she had to reply to another question. "Yes, Silas. I'm sure Saint's right, you will like this brother much better than Greg."

She turned away from Chandler's curious face. "I know, you never liked Greg. Silas—Silas, I have to go. Silas I'll see you in a few days. Okay. I know. Silas, I'm hanging up now."

And she did. She put the phone down and ran her hands wearily over her eyes.

Myk asked, "Who's Silas?"

"One of the seniors over at the center. They all think I'm in Arizona on my honeymoon. Wait until I get my hands on Saint."

"Who's Greg?"

Sarita looked up. "An old boyfriend."

"How old?"

"Old enough." She thought back to the lingerie

store and the feel of his hand caressing her cheek. She shook it off. "I have a question for you."

He nodded.

"Saint told me you won't be expecting sex, is that true?"

Myk held her eyes. If nothing else, she was blunt. "Yes. When we're traveling we'll have to share a room, but we can work that out."

"So what will I do as your wife?"

"Other than be on my arm, not much."

She wanted to know if he would define the role of a real wife in such limited terms? His response made her realize that it had never crossed her mind when she was swallowing Saint's baited hook that she might not click with the man involved. As she'd stated earlier, fifty thousand would probably not be enough. "Saint said you'd need me for about a year?"

"Right. If it has to be longer, I'll let you know. By the way, I found the gun and the diamonds in your flat, but not the bullets. Where are they?"

She added one more sin to Saint's litany of offenses. The hidey-hole behind the electrical plate in her bedroom had been her secret spot for buried treasure since she was eight years old. No one had known about it—not her grandmother who had a Ph.D. in nosy, not her granduncles, only Saint, and he'd had to sign his name in blood before she would let him in on the location. She was certain it was the first place he'd told Chandler to look. She supposed under the circumstances, pacts made between siblings could not be honored, but she still felt betrayed.

"Sarita, where are the bullets?"

"What?" she came out of her reverie.

"The bullets, where are they? We searched the flat from top to bottom."

She debated using her reply as a lever to get Chandler to make a few more concessions but knew it wouldn't fly. He held all the cards, and besides, he could always go out and buy more bullets; in this town they were as easy to find as used tires. "Your bullets are in the river. I flushed them."

Myk noted the smug smile of satisfaction on her face as she said this. He then watched as she eased off one navy pump, then the other, before she reached down to massage her liberated feet. Her soft sigh of relief sounded so much like a sigh of pleasure, his manhood responded instantly. She'd done nothing more than remove her shoes, and he was as hard as a beam.

Sarita happened to look up. In response to his piercing gaze she slowed her actions. "I'm not used to being in heels all day."

"I've work to do."

To her surprise, he got up and left the room. No other words, just gone. *Now what*, she thought to herself, but there was no answer.

Myk didn't go upstairs to his home office. Instead, he went outside and stood on the planked walk that led down to his small dock. In an effort to calm down his manhood, he drew in a few long breaths of the chilly October air. He absently rubbed at the discomfort in his still-healing shoulder. He was not supposed to be attracted to her. As he'd noted before, she'd done nothing but take off her shoes. He blamed it on the lingerie store; all that sexy silk had done something to his brain. Stroking her cheek hadn't helped. He'd no idea her skin would be so soft or that that softness would still be echoing within him more than an hour later. The plan he and Saint had concocted was not following the script.

The next morning, Lily awakened Sarita early. Chandler had a business appointment at nine, and he wanted her to accompany him. A quick glance at the clock showed it to be almost a quarter of eight. Sarita showered, grabbed a piece of toast from the breakfast tray, did her hair, then dressed quickly in the clothes Lily laid out on the bed.

Sarita, wearing a dove gray suit beneath her fur, sat beside Chandler in the car but had no idea where they were headed. When they reached their destination and he parked the car, she at least knew where they were: the underground garage that handled the parking for the city's main administration building. The lot was nearly full. People with business to conduct in the courts and offices above walked through the cement cavern toward the door and elevators. She glanced over to see if his face held some clue as to why they'd come here, but as usual his features didn't reveal a thing.

Because of downtown's close proximity to the river, the garage was a wind tunnel. She pulled the sable closer for warmth. Dressed in the expensive coat and heels, and wearing the dark glasses he'd insisted she put on, she once again had trouble recognizing herself. When they reached the door, he opened it solicitously.

Inside, the building was teeming with people. She wondered if she would see anyone she knew. If she did, they'd probably have as much of a problem recognizing her as she did herself.

Still, she discreetly searched the faces of the multitudes swarming over the interior. And she did see one. Saint's! Her breathing stopped. He stood propped against a water fountain, framed yet hidden by the comings and goings of the thick crowd like a man hidden in a picture. Their eyes met across the crowded lobby and held. The smile he sent her was bittersweet. She glanced up to see if Chandler had noticed his presence, but Chandler gave no indication he had. When she swung her eyes back to Saint he was no longer there. Gone. Her quick, almost frantic, scan of the surroundings proved futile. It was as if she'd imagined him. Had she? A stunned Sarita followed Chandler into a crowded elevator.

They exited on the fourteenth floor. The hush of the carpeted hallway was in marked contrast to the din in the lobby. The name of one of the city's most prominent judges was etched on the small brass plate on the closed door Chandler stopped in front of. Sarita's recognition of the famous name and her having seen Saint downstairs only added to her nervousness.

A secretary showed them into an inner office, where a smiling gray-haired man came out from behind his desk and greeted them with a smile. "Morning, Mykal. This the lucky young lady?"

Myk nodded. "Morning, Your Honor. Yes, this is Sarita Grayson."

"Good morning, young woman."

"Your Honor," Sarita said, shaking his outstretched hand. In spite of the mysterious reason for the visit, it was indeed an honor to meet him. Judge Wade Morgan's work with the Civil Rights movement and other nation-changing issues were well known. He was in his seventies, and his age had slowed his roll a bit, but he was still one of the most respected jurists in the country.

Judge Morgan eyed her, and said, "Been trying to get this rascal to marry for years. Glad to see he's ready to make the plunge."

Sarita stiffened. She knew she'd agreed to marry him, but today? Like this? With no warning? Didn't she need a blood test first?

The judge said, "Are you both ready?"

Myk looked down at his soon to be bride and hoped the ceremony would go smoothly. "You ready?"

Truthfully, Sarita wanted to say, no. She was no more ready to marry him than she was to walk barefoot on the moon, but they'd made a deal, and she would honor it. "Yes."

So the judge began reciting the words and a silent Sarita willed herself not to shake.

The judge stopped at one point, and asked, "Is there a ring?"

"Yes," Myk hadn't had time to buy her a true ring, but did have one that would do until he made a visit to the jeweler's. He withdrew the black-stone ring from his finger. "I know it's too big," he told her. "I'll get you one that fits in a couple of days. Until then let's do this. . . ."

He undid the catch on the thin silver chain around his neck and lifted it free, then threaded the chain through the ring.

Sarita was shaking; her cool gone. When he gently placed the chain around her neck his eyes were as brilliant as the ring's stone. For just a moment, the chain retained the heat of his body, and that warmth against her skin touched her with a strange sense of something she couldn't name.

Judge Morgan said with a kindly smile, "I now pronounce you man and wife. You may kiss your bride, Myk."

Sarita didn't want to be kissed; she was having enough trouble keeping herself together as it was.

Myk looked down at that lush mouth and wondered what it might be like to kiss her slowly and fully, but to satisfy that curiosity there in front of the judge would be to take advantage of the situation and of her. Myk was more of a man than that. Holding her eyes he said instead, "Sarita's a bit shy. I'll save that kiss for a more private place, if you don't mind, sir. . . ."

The judge chuckled. "Oh, of course not."

Sarita just knew she was going to shake apart.

Now that the civil ceremony was over, the new Mr. and Mrs. Mykal Chandler signed all the papers in all the spots indicated by the judge's clerk, and a few minutes later were back on the elevator to the underground garage that held his car. If someone had told Sarita that by today she'd be married to the man she'd shot in the elevator, she'd have said they were nuts.

That evening, a somewhat blue Sarita sat in her room. She hadn't seen Chandler since the return from the judge's office that morning, but that wasn't what had her so down. What had her down was her out-of-control life. Lily had come up a few times to check on her and bring lunch, but Sarita felt too blah to eat.

Instead, she was seated cross-legged on the floor in front of the roaring fireplace, brooding. She'd drawn the drapes long ago but not turned on any lights. The big spacious room echoed silently around her, the crackling fire the only sound. She knew feeling sorry for herself would not help things. Seeing Saint downtown that morning only generated more questions for which she had no answers. *What the hell have I stumbled into?* she asked herself for the hundredth time. Why in the world would a man like Mykal Chandler be stealing diamonds in the middle of the night? Did he know Fletcher? Did he and Saint know more about Fletcher's shooting than they'd revealed to her? She put her hands to her eyes. No more questions. Any more, and she'd go insane.

A knock on the door sounded, and she tensed as the door slowly opened. The light from the hallway framed Lily against the dark. Sarita relaxed. It wasn't Chandler.

Lily's voice sounded concerned, "Are you okay, dear?"

"I'm fine. It's just been a long day."

Lily came over and stood near where Sarita sat on the floor. Lily knew the circumstances around the young woman's coming there to live, and the housekeeper had to admit to being totally surprised by Myk's solution, especially knowing he could have sent Sarita to any number of places around the country where she would be safe until things became clearer. It never occurred to Lily that he might have other reasons for keeping Sarita under his wing until she witnessed the small fortune he'd spent on this particular young woman in the past few days. Lily had known Mykal a long time, and in the past he always preferred the painted, flashy type, like that Faye he'd finally gotten rid of. This small, solemn one fit neither category. "I wanted to come up and say good-bye."

Sarita didn't remember Lily ever coming up and saying good-bye on previous nights, but tonight Sarita appreciated the sentiment. Sarita stood up against the fire's light and showed Lily a pleasant face. Lily had been nothing but kind through this whole craziness. "Okay, I'll see you tomorrow."

"No, honey. I'm leaving for good. I won't be back tomorrow."

Sarita stiffened, "For good?"

Lily nodded. The distress on Sarita's face almost made Lily wish she hadn't stopped in.

Sarita jumped to her own conclusions. "Did he fire you?" she asked, her hand on her hip.

Lily chuckled. "No, nothing like that. My daughter finally had her baby, and I'm going home to Atlanta. Now that Myk has a wife, I get to go play grandma. My ride to the airport will be here in a little while."

"Congratulations," Sarita offered sincerely. Although the two women could not be considered friends, they had gotten along. For Sarita it had been nice having someone in the house besides Mr. Personality. For Lily it had become a pleasure watching Sarita put Myk through his paces, and she doubted she would ever forget the performance the young woman put on at lunch yesterday. She guessed neither would Mykal. Lily believed it would do him a world of good to be challenged so fearlessly. Those who loved Mykal had a tendency to let him have his own way most of the time because most of the time he was correct. Lily did not see Sarita deferring to him so easily, correct or not.

Sarita asked, "Did he mention that we were married today?"

"Yes," she replied gently, then added, "Sarita, things are not always the way they seem. The man you married today is hard, yes, and tough—but beneath all that he's fine and caring. He has a lot on his mind right now. Give him some time, and I think you'll be surprised."

Sarita thought she'd be surprised if Lily's predictions came true. "You won't be offended if I reserve judgment?"

"No."

"Good. Did your daughter have a boy or girl?"

"Girl. Named her Alexis Lily." Lily's beaming face told all.

"Well, you have a good time with little Lily and kiss her for me. Maybe you and I will meet again."

"I'm sure we will. Take care now."

"You too," Sarita responded softly.

Lily exited, closing the door gently. Sarita stared over at the closed door. She'd never felt so alone in her life.

Six

When the taillights of the car taking Lily to the airport faded into the darkness, the watching Myk sighed and closed his front door. He'd miss her. She was not only a valued friend, but a member of the NIA board as well. In fact, it had been her idea to enlist a few of her trusted day worker friends to surveil the estates of the wealthy suburbanite dealers on NIA's initial hit list. At first, many on the task force had been cool to the idea, but Lily's corps of maids, cooks, gardeners, and chauffeurs soon proved their worth. The night NIA hit Marvin Rand, it had been one of Lily's cooks who'd secretly mixed the tranq in with the Dobermans' dinners. Lily's arm of the organization had become a vital part of the operation.

As of today though, Lily was no longer on the board. She'd resigned. The birth of Alexis Lily meant more to her than being a crime fighter, so her duties as chair of her wing would be given to someone else.

Myk headed upstairs to the office he maintained at home. He had work to do, but Lily lingered in his mind. How was he supposed to get along without her? For the past six years, she'd not only fed him and kept his house; she'd put up with his moods. He could talk to her, confide in her, and most of all, trust her to tell him the truth whether he cared to hear it or not. Yes, he would miss Lily Sanders, very much.

Myk's home office was located down an inner hallway that led from his bedroom. Inside, he flicked on the light and closed the door behind him. Drake had dubbed the space, the War Room. From there Myk ran NIA. Stretched out on the wall above the computers hung a big map of the city and surrounding suburbs. Multicolored pins were stuck into areas where operations were under way. The number had grown in the past few months, representing the rising strength of the organization and the resolve of the men and women who'd committed to the fight. NIA's successes were just a drop in the bucket when compared to the hundreds of drug-infested cities across the nation, but it was a start.

An hour passed before he finally finished the reports on everything from the names of the legal owners of the crack houses NIA's squads would be hitting the following week to profiles of the dealers squatting in them.

Stretching for a moment to ease the strain in his neck and shoulders, he swiveled his chair around and pointed a remote at the bank of video monitors built into the back wall. He'd had the display installed as part of the house's security system. At the punch of a button he could see into every room in the house. He brought up Sarita's bedroom. The screen showed his new bride seated on the floor in front of the fireplace. He supposed he should offer to take her to dinner someplace. It was her wedding night, and some women expected traditional treatment regardless of the circumstances. He doubted that would apply to her though; convention didn't seem to be her strong suit. However, they needed to talk. If he took her to a public place, he hoped she would be less likely to go off once the discussion began. Undoubtedly she would hit the ceiling when he told her about the wedding reception they were going to have in two days. In reality, Myk wasn't thrilled with the idea either; but after hearing Drake's explanation as to why the reception would be necessary, he'd grudgingly agreed with the logic. In order for people to accept the marriage as real and not a facade, he and Sarita would have to have the traditional dog-and-pony-show celebration. Everyone would be expecting it.

Once the reception was over and the hoopla died down, Myk could cut his ties to the limelight. Maybe he'd move the entire operation up to his house on Lake Michigan and really put some miles between himself and all the distractions. He especially hoped the reception would send the female pack after other meat. The invitations had gone out yesterday, and he could already feel his ears burning. The announcement of his marriage would definitely give folks something to talk about. He hoped so, because with everybody speculating on that topic, no one would be interested in his other life.

He walked around to her end of the house and rapped at her door. When he didn't get a response, he pushed his master key into the lock and walked into the firelit room. No one. On her vanity table lay the chain laced with his ring. He supposed she'd taken it off the minute she'd returned. He set aside how that scenario made him feel and concentrated instead on where she might be. He wouldn't put it past her to have somehow managed to smuggle herself out in Lily's luggage. On the heels of that thought, she stepped out of the bathroom, and he relaxed.

Sarita hid her surprise at seeing him and hastily wiped away the tears in her eyes. They were the last thing he needed to see. "I assumed you knocked first?"

The sight of her tear-bright eyes surprised him to say the least. "I did. No answer. I wanted to make sure you hadn't snuck out in Lily's suitcase."

"I should be so lucky," she drawled drolly. "Did you want something?"

"I came to invite you to dinner. There are loose ends we need to tie up."

"What are they?"

"Over dinner," he repeated.

She studied him for a moment. "Is this going to be another one of your surprises?"

Myk saw the challenge in her eyes. "You have a bone to pick with me about something?"

"Yes," she stated plainly. "I do. It would have been nice to have known ahead of time that I was going to be married this morning."

"It wouldn't have changed things."

"But I would have been prepared."

"I thought doing it my way would cut down on the drama."

"In other words, you expected me to cause a scene?"

He shrugged. "Yes."

She looked him in the eye. "Why?"

"Why?" he asked with humorous astonishment. "Why shouldn't I?"

Sarita felt as if her head were spinning.

Myk added, "So, we are legally married, whether you want to be or not."

"Oh, I want to be because I can't wait to collect my fifty grand."

He ran his eyes over her bewitching mouth. "And I can't wait to pay it."

On the ride over to the restaurant, Sarita sat silently, watching the city lights roll by the window. She told him softly. "I want to go back to work, Chandler." Being separated from her work and the people she loved was also fueling her blue mood. She added, "I understand I might be in danger from the owners of those rocks, but I'm a stand-and-fight kinda lady. I don't like all this sneaking and hiding."

Myk noted her serious tone. "Suppose I let you return to work and something happens?"

"You could shop for a new wife," she said lightly.

He smiled in spite of himself, "That's not what I meant. Suppose you're threatened?"

"I've been threatened before. Saint may not believe this, but there are other people around capable of helping me protect myself."

"Such as?"

"Well, there's Mr. Fukiya."

"Who's he?"

"An Asian man who lives a few blocks from the center. You'll have to meet him. He moved into the neighborhood about four years ago. The kids are convinced he's a Ninja just because he teaches them martial arts. I told them they'd been watching too many movies until the night Fletcher's houses burned down last summer."

"What happened?"

"A few hours after the fire department and the police left, Fukiya knocked on my door. I was surprised to see him because he'd never come to the house before. He told me not to worry about the threats Fletcher had made and to sleep peacefully. And he left."

"When did Fletcher threaten you?"

"While his houses were burning down and the folks from the neighborhood and I were standing across the street cheering on the flames. He just knew I'd lit the match, and told me they'd find my body in the river in the morning. He was *too* angry."

"Did the police hear him?"

"No, they were gone by then. The people in the crowd heard him though."

"So what made you change your mind about Fukiya being a Ninja?"

"Because Fletcher came to my office the next morning and apologized profusely for the threats. Told me he was only kidding about hurting me, went on and on. Then he said, tell the Ninja he'd apologized, just like he promised. I looked at him like he was crazy. Then he said again, tell the Ninja he apologized. I figured Fletcher had been sampling his tenants' products, so I said to him, okay, and he left. I didn't think any more about it until Mr. Fukiya came in later that same afternoon and said he'd heard Fletcher had come over and apologized. I was surprised because I hadn't told anyone about Fletcher's visit, or at least I didn't remember telling anyone. When I told Mr. Fukiya what he'd heard was true, he nodded good-bye, and left. He and I have never had a conversation about it since."

Myk took a hand off the steering wheel and ran the hand over his eyes, then down his face. Good Lord, a Ninja. Now they were going have to contend with a self-appointed guardian angel who might or might not be a trained martial arts master.

Sarita saw the gesture, and asked, "What's the matter?"

"Nothing, just a little tired," he lied. "So, if I let you run your center and let you go back to work, will you settle down?"

"Probably."

"Probably?"

"Okay, I will."

"And cooperate a little more?"

"I've been cooperative. You're the one saying no all the time."

"And cooperate a little more?"

"Okay, okay, and cooperate a little more. When can I go?"

Myk didn't believe her for a minute, but he was pleased he'd at least convinced her to unball her fist. For now. "We'll see how things look in a few days."

"A few days? But—"

"I want to test the wind in the neighborhood first."

"What's that mean?"

"Just waiting for some additional info."

Her voice mirrored her confusion. "Info? I thought you were an architect?"

"I am."

"I'm going to assume that's just your day job. Saint sneaks around a lot, too. Are you his boss?"

"Saint isn't an architect."

She could tell by his manner that the conversation was closed, but she was certain she'd find out what was going on; hey, she had a year.

The restaurant he chose turned out to be one of the most exclusive eateries in town. Of course, she'd never been there before, but the maître d' greeted Chandler by name and gushed and fussed over their arrival.

They were immediately shown to one of the small private rooms glassed off from the main dining area. Each of the compartments had wooden blinds that could be rolled down to ensure privacy. As Chandler helped her with her seat, she wondered if he received the royal treatment everywhere he went.

Once the maître d' withdrew, and they were alone, she asked, "Now what about these loose ends?"

Myk ran his eyes over her. She had on a white cashmere turtleneck sweater tucked into a killer pair of dark green leather pants. She was easily the finest woman in the place, and he had to force himself not to stare at his ring hanging against her breasts because the ring was not the real focus of his interest. "Let's order first, then we'll talk."

Sarita conceded. "Sure."

A young male server entered their room carrying a tray topped with glasses of ice water, a coffeepot, and two cups. He set everything down, then placed two menus on the table before silently departing.

Sarita picked up the menu. As she scanned the choices, her eyes widened. She knew this was a fancy place, but *thirty-five dollars for fish? Are they crazy?* She looked over at him.

"Something wrong?" he asked.

"No," she lied, and dropped her gaze. Of course she knew people like him ate better than folks like her, but she still found the astronomical prices stunning.

"Order whatever you want," he told her.

Having helped her grandmother in the kitchens of rich folks most of her life, Sarita was quite familiar with the dishes offered, but the prices were making her head spin. "I'll just have the lobster bisque."

He set his menu aside. "That it?"

She nodded tightly.

"According to Lily you haven't been eating much."

"I haven't been hungry."

When his eyes probed her, she stared back emotionlessly.

"What's really wrong with you?" Myk asked quietly. The memories of the tears in her eyes earlier this evening suddenly resurfaced. Thinking about them bothered him, though he couldn't pinpoint exactly why.

"I'm just trying to adjust to all this," she replied. "Sable coats, fancy clothes, thirty-five dollars for fish."

"You'll get used to it."

"That's the problem, I don't know if I want to. When this is all over I don't want to go back to my life thinking I'm somebody else."

"Does that mean you've finally accepted this arrangement?"

"No, it just means I'm not used to being around someone who spends like you do."

"I can afford it," he countered bluntly.

"That's all well and good, but the panties on my behind cost more than we spend on food at the center in two weeks. Do you have any idea how uncomfortable that makes me feel?"

He didn't blink. "Being rich is a whole lot better than being poor. I know, I've been both. I worked hard to get where I am."

"I'm not questioning what you have, it's what you do with it that bothers me. I do not need five dresser drawers of nightgowns."

He shrugged. "Maybe I went a little overboard."

"Maybe? Chandler, if I lived to be a hundred years old, I couldn't wear all those clothes."

"What would you prefer I spend my money on?"

His eye were focused on her, and his voice had softened as if he really wanted her opinion. It gave her insides the oddest sensation. "I don't know. You said you have a foundation. Do you give away a lot of money?"

"I do."

"To whom?"

"Children, mostly."

She was impressed. "Then you're doing your part."

"Yes, I am, so it doesn't really matter what I pay for the panties on your behind, does it?"

Sarita didn't know what she was supposed to say to that, and so was very glad to see the waiter make his return. She picked up her menu and quietly ordered a cup of the lobster bisque.

When she was done, Chandler gave his order, then told the waiter, "Ask Andre if he'd send out some scallops for my wife. She's hungrier than she'll admit."

His presumptious attitude made Sarita's irritation rise, but she held her tongue until the waiter exited. Once they were alone again, she said, "I don't need you ordering for me. I told him what I wanted."

"You need to eat. Starving yourself is not going to make me turn you loose."

Frustrated, she folded her arms across her chest, and sank back against the seat. She didn't bother hiding her displeasure.

"Quit pouting," he said with quiet amusement.

She shot him a look that would have silenced a less confident brother, but it didn't seem to bother him at all. "I'm not pouting."

"Yes, you are."

"How do you know I even like scallops?"

"Saint e-mailed me a list of your likes and dislikes."

"And were Arrogant Brothers on the top of my dislike list?" she asked drolly.

"Didn't notice."

"You wouldn't."

He smiled at that. "Now let's talk about the reception."

She blinked. "What reception?"

"The one the mayor's throwing for us."

Considering this was the first time Chandler had mentioned such an event, she gave herself credit for keeping her voice even. "Why is the mayor giving us a reception?"

"So people can get a good look at you."

Sarita studied him. "What people?"

"The people you're going to be spending the next year being around—you know, the society types. Folks will want to see the woman who finally got me."

Sarita supposed he was a prize. Rich, handsome, articulate—the body and face of a dark god. Well dressed. Good manners. If you overlooked the arrogance, a sister could call him heaven-sent. Sarita had called him many things since they hooked up but none suitable for the ears of angels. "So when is this supposed to take place?"

"Saturday night."

Her dark eyes widened. "That's the day after tomorrow."

"Yep."

"How many people is he inviting?"

"Two, three hundred."

Sarita eyes went wide as saucers.

He poured himself a cup of coffee. "This is going to be *the* social event of the year."

As she watched him raise his cup to drink, she wondered how in the world she was going to pretend to be his wife in front of three hundred strangers? She could barely handle herself in this restaurant. She'd seen the curious looks they'd gotten when they arrived. Were there really going to be that many people interested in his bride? She supposed he was right. He and the mayor were the two most eligible bachelors in the city. The society section in the city's newspapers always had pictures of them at some fancy gathering or another, and they were always surrounded by a bunch of grinning, well-dressed women.

The waiter returned with their plates. Although the food smelled and looked delicious, she had no appetite. As usual Chandler seemed to have no such trouble.

"I can have Andre fix you something else if you'd like."

Sarita had been so preoccupied with her own thoughts it took her a moment to realize he'd spoken.

She shook her head and put down her fork. "The food's fine. I'm just not very hungry."

Myk wondered about the bleakness in her eyes as she looked away. Was the fight finally going out of her? He sensed her hovering near the edge. Although she appeared composed, her shoulders were tensed beneath the soft white sweater she was wearing, and that luscious mouth was tight and unhappy.

Sarita had to ask, "What about the people at my center? Will they be invited to the reception?"

"I think we'll limit it to the fur-and-diamond set. We can have something at the center later, if you want."

"I'd like for them to come."

"No."

"Why not?"

"How do you think three hundred people who consider themselves upper-class are going to treat a bunch of senior citizens, unwed mothers, and kids dressed in hand-me-downs? If you want to put your people through that, then fine, invite them."

She didn't like admitting he was right. The rich folks in his social circle would probably not want to rub shoulders with the city's poor, and they most certainly wouldn't be kind. She felt herself sinking deeper and deeper into a funk.

He asked, "You ready to talk about the rest of the details?"

She didn't respond.

"I'll take that as a yes."

But, as he began to speak, Sarita heard only his voice, not his words. Mentions of the mayor, champagne, gifts, and guests went in one ear and out the other. Sinking further beneath the weight of her mood, she scanned the patrons on the other side of the glass. There were intimately whispering couples seated around the room. Other couples were engaged in laugher and soft conversations. The sight only added to her melancholy. What right did they have to be happily going about their lives while she was forced to play mouse to Chandler's cat? Yes, he was handsome, polished, and apparently rich as Midas, but she preferred to be elsewhere. She picked up her fork and slowly forced herself to eat.

After taking the first few bites, she realized just how great a chef Andre really was. The lightly sauced scallops were so succulent they practically melted in her mouth.

Over his coffee cup, Myk smiled inwardly watching her beautiful face be transformed by Andre's scallops. One minute she'd been angry and sullen, now, she looked as if she'd died and gone to heaven. "Good, aren't they?" he asked.

Sarita paused in midbite. She'd been relishing the scallops so much she'd forgotten she wasn't supposed to be enjoying herself.

He added, "I've finally done something right, admit it."

She looked over at him across the table and wondered how long she'd be able to maintain her distance. Part of the problem was that he was too damn fine for his own good. The dark chocolate skin, the matching eyes, the mustache. Women had probably been chasing him since kindergarten. Call her a fool, but as fine and as rich as he was, Sarita had no intentions of being another link in his chain. "You do get points for this. Thank you."

"You're welcome."

She finished the scallops, sautéed veggies, and bread, and gently set her plate aside.

He asked, "Full, or do you want dessert?"

"Maybe. What did Saint's list say about dessert?"

"Hot fudge sundaes."

She smiled at him for the first time.

So Myk had the waiter bring her a hot fudge sundae. When it arrived it was so decadently prepared she could only stare at the mounds of ice cream topped with hot fudge, whipped cream, and a cherry. "Now that's a sundae."

"Yes, it is."

She waded in with her spoon. Bringing a small portion to her mouth, she tasted the warm dark chocolate and the slightly melted ice cream, then moaned softly with pleasure.

"That good?" he asked.

Sarita was in heaven. "Many points for this, Chandler. Many points."

"Glad I could help." Myk watched her over the rim of his cup. The tiny licks that she gave the spoon as she tasted some of the fudge were teasingly erotic. She slid a small finger over the piled-high whipped cream, and when she gracefully sucked the finger into her mouth he hardened like a pipe. Innocent as her actions were, Myk knew that in the future he'd never be able to see another hot fudge sundae without thinking of her. He couldn't remember ever being aroused by a woman eating ice cream before, but then he'd never been around a woman like Sarita before.

Sarita looked up. "I can't eat all this. Do you want some?"

He again picked up his coffee cup. "No." He wanted to kiss that sassy mouth of hers so he could taste the chocolate and the cream, but chastised himself for even thinking such a thing.

Sarita sensed he'd retreated behind his walls again. She set aside her spoon. "We can leave if you're ready to go."

"No. Go ahead. Eat as much as you want."

Sarita wasn't sure he was telling her the truth, but she went back to the sundae. Finally, she'd had enough. "I can't eat another bite." The sundae had to be the best one she'd had in a long time. "Thanks again."

"No problem. Are you done?"

She nodded.

"Then let's head out."

At the door, she waited for him to sign the bill

and to retrieve their coats from the checkroom. She would've preferred to put on her leather jacket without his assistance, but knowing they were being casually observed by the other diners, she made herself stand still for his assistance. As he helped her on with the coat, his fingers accidentally brushed the back of her neck, and she leapt as if burned.

To those observing, his leaning forward to whisper in her ear had the look of an intimacy shared. Only Sarita heard his real words.

"You'd better do something about that before the reception. Nobody's going to believe our little game if you jump to the ceiling when I touch you."

His nearness and the soft rush of his breath against her ear increased her heartbeat. She knew he was right, but what did he expect?

Once they reached his house, he pulled the car into the garage and cut the engine. Turning to her, he said, "Are you really going to be able to go through with this?"

She knew he was talking about the reception. "If I say no, will you call it off?"

He shook his head.

"Then I'll be able to do it."

"Can you dance?"

"Of course I can dance."

"With me."

She went silent. The guests would be expecting them to act like newlyweds, and newlyweds danced. *Good Lord!* She really hadn't thought this all out. "I don't think that'll be a problem," she bluffed.

He didn't look like he believed her for a minute.

"I've got a few drawings to go over, but in about an hour—you and me—dancing."

"But—"

"No, buts, Sarita." He opened the car door and got out.

Since she had no real wish to spend the night in the cold garage, she got out, too, and followed him inside.

Sarita went up and took a shower. When she was done, she wrapped herself in a towel and waded through the dresser drawers in hopes of finding something comfortable to wear. As she pawed through the soft piles of silk and lace, she wished she'd paid more attention when Lily was putting all this stuff away. She swore she'd seen some sweats somewhere. Closing yet another drawer stuffed with camisoles and spaghetti-strapped nightgowns, she headed to the huge walk-in closet. The interior could have held her whole bedroom at home. It was filled with suits hanging from padded hangers, shoes, handbags, and boxes and bags still waiting to be opened. Shaking her head at what she considered to be a waste of good money, she tightened the towel and dived in. After a few minutes of intense searching she unearthed a boxed set of sweats. She didn't bother wondering where you could buy sweats that needed to be boxed, but instead finished drying off, found a suitable pair of panties, and slipped into the expensive sweats. Picking up a magazine from the pile on the coffee table in front of the fireplace, she stretched herself out on the green velvet Cleopatra divan and flipped through the monthly's pages, hoping it would distract her from thinking about having to dance with Chandler in an hour. It didn't.

In his office, Myk rolled up the drawings for the bridge his company was putting up in one of the neighboring suburbs and stuck them back in the tube. In spite of his mind's objections, he found his interest in his new wife growing. He couldn't help wondering how things might have been different had he met her at a party or happened to run into her at a bank or a concert. No doubt he would've been attracted to her, any man in his right mind would, but this way? This way was crazy. He headed to her room.

He knocked, and when she called come in, Myk opened the door and stepped inside. He looked at her standing by the fireplace in her sweats, and said, "You're going to have to change clothes."

Confused, she looked down at what she had on. "Why?"

"Because you'll be wearing a dress, not sweats."

"And?"

"And, remember how you jumped in the restaurant when I was helping you on with your coat?"

She didn't want to, but she did.

"Well, we can't have that Saturday."

"I know."

He then turned and began going through her drawers, searching for what, she had no idea. "What are you looking for?"

"Something that'll substitute for the dress you'll be wearing."

"You already have the dress?"

"Yes."

Sarita had a thousand questions, but he was focused on his search. He closed the drawer and opened another. She watched him consider and discard nightgown after nightgown. He then went to the closet. Shaking her head at his intensity, she strolled to the edge of the closet and leaned against the jamb to watch. He pulled another nightgown down from the rack, studied it for a moment, then handed it to her.

Sarita looked skeptically at the slinky, navy silk gown, or was it a slip? Suffice it to say it was more forties diva wear. It had spaghetti straps, a triangle-cut bodice, and a very low back. The discreet slit up the side would run from her ankle to midthigh. Surely he didn't believe she was going to wear it to dance in. "Why do you want me to wear this?"

"Because it's something like the dress you'll be wearing to the reception."

"I think I'll stick to the sweats," she declared, holding out the gown so he could take it back.

He ignored the offering. Walking past her, he said instead, "Get dressed. I'll be back in ten minutes."

"Chandler—"

"Ten minutes," he repeated quietly at the door. He opened it and stepped out. As it closed, Sarita let out a soft, irritated sigh.

True to his word, he came back ten minutes later. Sarita had put on the gown, but she wasn't at all happy about it.

Myk on the other hand was standing in the doorway, trying not to stare openly at the midnight blue silk flowing smoothly around the delicate lines and curves of her body as only silk can. Her bare shoulders were bisected by the thin straps. His ring hung from her throat, and the soft swells of her breasts rose provocatively above the unadorned bodice. The issues Myk had with her faded into the distance. Right there, right then, the only thing that mattered was feasting his eyes on the brown sugar beauty across the room. From the queenly sweep of her short-cut hair to the slim ankles above her bare feet in the short strappy black sandals, she was luscious, ripe, and damned if he didn't want her. In light of the circumstances forcing them together, desiring her made no sense, but the male in Myk didn't care. She piqued his interest the very first time he'd laid eyes on her.

Because he'd been staring at her for so long Sarita felt compelled to ask, "Is this better?"

Myk ran his eyes over her hungrily. "Yes." In reality it was way more than better. Lord, she was lovely.

Sarita was very conscious of everything; the feel of the silk against her skin; the way his eyes traveled over the bareness of her shoulders and throat. Even though she didn't know what he was thinking, his intense gaze touched her like a flame. "Are we going to dance in here?" she asked, needing to say something, anything.

"No. Let's go downstairs."

He led her to a shadow-filled room she'd not been in before. It was long and wide and had huge floor-to-ceiling windows running the length of one wall. The thick pulled-back drapes with their soft pleats were graceful and elegant. The flames in the fireplace lit the room with a soft hush.

He walked over to a large wooden armoire and opened its double doors to reveal the impressive display of audio and video components inside. "The original owner of the house used this room as a ballroom," he explained to her while looking through the CDs. "When my brother forces me to have dinner parties, it becomes my dining room. The table's over there beneath the tarp."

Her eyes brushed the long green tarp shrouding the table. Other than a pool table down at the far end of the room and the huge flat-screen TV on the wall, the room had few other furnishings. "What do you use it for in the meantime?"

"Recreation."

Music drifted into the room then, a quiet hypnotic sax, and Sarita's nervousness returned full force. He walked over to her and held out his arms. "Well, let's try this." Sarita didn't really want to, but, gathering her courage, she walked to where he stood, then stopped a short step away. He wordlessly took her hand in his, then raised it slightly while his other arm circled her waist, coming to rest just above the crown of her hips. Even though the room was awash in shadows, his eyes were brilliant as the sun. There was a reasonable amount of space between their bodies, but she was trembling just the same.

On the beat, they began to slow dance—old-school style; he led, and she was supposed to follow, but she was so nervous she couldn't relax enough to let herself be guided by the music's languid notes, and so her steps were awkward and clumsy. When she stumbled over his foot, his skeptical eyes met hers, and she winced in embarrassment.

"Relax," he whispered.

She tried, but she was so overwhelmed by his closeness, a few steps later, she tripped again.

"I thought you said you could dance?"

"I can."

"My feet think otherwise."

"It's not like I can hurt you in these thin shoes, Chandler."

He gazed down at the painted toes peeking out of the expensive little sandals, but didn't comment.

Sarita was determined to get through this. "Okay, I'm ready now."

He looked skeptical, but began again. She concentrated on matching his short steps and flowing movement, willing herself to take deep breaths. His hand holding hers was warm; the arm around her waist gentle but firm. Sarita made it to the end of the song without any further stumbling, but just barely.

When the music faded away, she backed out of his arms so she could regain her composure. Her reprieve was short. The beautiful and familiar strains of "Creepin'"—Luther's version—came out of the speakers. The song, about a woman creeping into a man's dreams, was originally written and recorded by Stevie Wonder, and was one of Sarita's all-time favorites. She was quite surprised to hear the tune coming out of Chandler's speakers, though.

Her reaction must have shown on her face because he asked, "What, I'm not supposed to listen to Luther?"

She was embarrassed. "I'm sorry. I just didn't think a man like you . . ."

"Liked music?"

Her embarrassment soared. "Maybe it's because I associate jazz with men your age."

Myk's eyebrow rose. "Men my age? I'm forty, Sarita, not seventy-five."

Sarita decided she'd said enough. To keep the

hole from becoming any deeper, she told him apologetically, "It's not as if I know a lot about you."

Myk searched her face in the shadows and said quietly, "Well, now you know that I like Luther." He held out his arms, "Let's try again."

With Luther's sweet voice singing softly, Myk eased her close and let the music guide his feet. In spite of the need to keep her at arm's length, he found himself savoring her scent, her nearness, and the tantalizing feel of her body moving in tandem with his own. He was careful to keep a respectful distance between them though. He didn't want to alarm her or have her think this was just a cheap way for him to take advantage of her, but the perfumed heat of her leaping across the gap was undermining his control.

Sarita didn't know if the spell of Luther's voice was responsible, but she felt more relaxed, more comfortable. Her shaking had all but subsided, and she was actually enjoying dancing with him. She followed his steps as if they'd been partners for years.

In a tone that matched the hush in the room, he said to her, "For a lady under forty, you slow dance well."

The words pleased her. "Thanks."

"You're welcome." His eyes drank her in, and the soft smile she offered up made his heart clang in his chest. The uncharacteristic reaction caught him by surprise. Suppressing the contradictory emotions, he redirected his attention to the matter at hand. "If we're going to be convincing newlyweds, we should be dancing closer," he pointed out.

Sarita knew he was right, but having just gotten

comfortable enough to stop trembling, she wasn't sure she could handle it. "Closer is fine," she tossed back, more bravely than she felt.

Wordlessly, he eased them closer and when his hard frame met her soft skin, she was sure her clothes were going to catch fire. His body touched her everywhere it seemed; hardening her nipples, making her feel the warm male pressure of his thighs against her own. She wanted to swoon but pretended she wasn't affected.

She sensed he was pretending, too. The blaze in his eyes made her heart do tiny flip-flops. Their steps slowed, then stopped.

"The groom will be expected to kiss the bride."

Sarita swallowed dryly.

"Think you can handle that?" His voice was as dark as his gaze.

She tried to form words, but no sound emerged.

He cocked his head at her. "Speechless?" He smiled softly. "That's different, coming from you. May I?"

She nodded.

With his finger he coaxed her chin up, then lowered his lips to hers. She drew back nervously. He paused, gave her a moment to collect herself, then resumed his journey to her lips. He found the target closed tight as a childproof bottle.

Myk drew himself back up to his full height and chuckled sarcastically, "Oh, yeah. You're going to do just fine at the reception."

Sarita's eyes fled. Truthfully, she was afraid to kiss him because she knew how good it was going to be. To him, this was a game, but she'd never played at love before and didn't know the rules.

He asked, "Is it me or just inexperience?"

Silence.

"Sarita?" He gently raised her chin so their eyes could meet. "Talk to me."

"This is just so strange, that's all. I'm okay now."

He studied her for a moment. "You sure?"

"Yes," she lied.

Myk's reports on her said that she had no special male friend, but he wanted to hear it from her lips. "Am I going to have an irate boyfriend on my hands because of this marriage?"

The question elicited a soft bitter chuckle. "No."

"Not one?"

"Would it make a difference it there were?" she asked quietly, feeling the attraction between them beginning to sweep her away like a flood.

"No," Myk replied. It wouldn't. She was *his* wife, pretend or not. "Why no man?"

"I don't have time for a man." It was the truth; the few boyfriends in her past would all testify to that.

He asked, "All work and no play make Jill a dull girl?"

She gave him a small smile in response. "Something like that."

The CD player had switched to another cut. Teddy. "Turn Out the Lights." Sarita took in a deep breath.

He said, "Suppose we forget the kiss for now and just go back to dancing?"

Sarita nodded, glad he wasn't going to force the issue.

He said to her then, "Okay, all I want you to do is relax. Lean in . . . let's see if we can't thaw you out, ice princess."

She shot him a look of warning.

"Don't worry, I won't touch any parts that will get me slapped. Just dance."

They began to move again, but as Teddy began to sing so seductively, and the music slid into her bones, Sarita became less concerned with what Chandler meant by "thawing her out" and just danced. His sweater felt soft beneath her cheek, his chest hard yet cushioning. His heart sounded strong and rhythmic against her ear, and the faint scent of his expensive cologne whispered to her nose.

Even though she was more relaxed, and they were moving easily together, her trembling returned, a normal reaction under the circumstances, she guessed, but she wanted to show him her control; show him that it didn't matter that he was holding her close enough to meld their heartbeats or that she could feel his strong thighs through the thin silk of her gown. She very much wanted to be the ice princess he'd alluded to earlier—but it was hard to maintain that front.

He whispered against her forehead, "I'm going to touch you, now . . ."

True to his word, his hand came up and slowly began to move up and over the skin of her back. The flaring sensations that resulted closed her eyes.

"Keep dancing . . ." he instructed heatedly.

His finger traced the sensitive flesh on the back of her neck, then slid down to trail across her bare shoulder blades. As he brushed a fingertip over the soft small bone of her jaw, she knew she was one degree away from melting into a puddle on the floor. Even a woman with Sarita's limited sexual experience knew expertise when she encountered it, and this man was no amateur. She could feel her shakes fading only to be replaced by a response far more complex. Next, he bent to brush his lips ever so gently against her jaw, and her breathing sounded jet-engine loud in her ears. She wanted to back away for a moment so she could catch her breath, but the urge dissolved under the caresses murmuring their way to the shell of her ear.

He whispered, "Now . . ."

This time, when his lips found hers, they were soft, yielding. Sparks flared. In fact, Myk found the experience so blood firing, he had to draw away or drown. He stared down into her passion-lidded eyes and knew this woman was capable of making him lose sight of all he was supposed to be; NIA be damned. That truth made him mentally shake himself. He'd thawed her out. He'd have to settle for that. "I think you'll be okay tomorrow," he said, turning her loose. "Good night."

He exited, leaving Sarita breathless and alone.

Back in his room, Myk poured him a shot of Remy XO and took a seat on his love seat. He sipped at the fine cognac and thought about his new wife. He couldn't remember the last time he'd run from a woman, but he had just now. Had the kiss lasted one second longer, he would've been looking for a place to lay her down so he could coax her into letting him make slow, sweet love to her. He'd wanted her from the top of his head to the soles of his feet. She'd softened beneath his kiss so completely he could still taste her. Myk took another draw of the cognac. *This is not good.*

* * *

Lying in bed in the dark, Sarita stared at the ceiling. She touched her lips. They were still tingling. Was this really only a game for him, or was their marriage of convenience morphing into something more? Because of this night, she would forever link "Creepin'" with Chandler. But how could she keep him from creeping into her dreams?

Seven

The next morning, Sarita headed out of her
bedroom intent upon breakfast when the
smell of something burning made her
pause on the steps. She sniffed the air curiously. A
second later the wail of an activated smoke detector
filled the house. Alarmed, she hustled down the
stairs and ran to investigate.

In the kitchen she found Chandler walking a
smoke-filled skillet to the sink. He'd protected his
hand with a pot holder, but nothing had protected
whatever he'd burned in the skillet.

Over the sound of the still-screaming alarm, she
yelled drolly, "Cook often?"

He turned and glared.

"It was a joke, Chandler, goodness."

Ignoring his mood, she grabbed a dish towel from
the island counter and began to fan it up under the
smoke detector. She shouted, "You might want

to open those doors," and pointed to the curtain-covered French doors that led to the deck outside.

Once he complied, the wind off the river floated in and thinned the smoke somewhat. The mess in the skillet was no longer a threat, but the scent of burned bacon permeated the air.

A frowning Myk looked over at her standing against the counter and decided she was sass person-ified. He wondered if she brought that spiritedness to a brother's bed. "Good morning," he said coolly.

"Didn't look that good a morning when I first got here," she tossed back with a straight face. "We have cooking classes at the center you know."

He shot her a look that let her know she was on the edge, so she cut the jokes. "All right, I'll stop. It's just nice knowing you're human like the rest of us."

She walked over to the fridge and opened the door. The interior shelves and niches were stocked well enough to feed twenty Chandlers. "How do you like your eggs?"

"Why?"

She looked his way. "I assume you want some-thing to eat, and since it looks like I'm the only cook available . . ."

"Scrambled."

She smiled inwardly and took out the container of eggs.

They shared a breakfast of scrambled eggs, grits, toast, and unburned bacon. Myk had to admit she was a much better cook than he, but then so was most of the free world. Myk couldn't boil water. When he'd eaten his fill, he said to her genuinely, "Thanks."

"You're welcome."

A silence fell between them then, and soon both were remembering last night's dance. She remembered the way he'd kissed her, and he could still taste the sweetness of her lips.

Myk turned his thoughts to saner issues. "We have bank business at ten."

She looked at her watch. It was eight-forty. "When do you want to leave?"

"How soon can you be ready?"

"Twenty, thirty minutes. Let me clean up in here first."

"Don't worry about it. You go and get dressed."

The skillet and the pot that had held the grits were still sitting on the stove. Sarita knew Lily would want everything cleaned up and put away, but since Lily was in Atlanta and this was Chandler's house, Sarita excused herself from the table and went back up to her room.

When she returned twenty-five minutes later, dressed in a new pair of jeans, a red cardigan sweater set, and a pair of low-heeled black boots, the kitchen was deserted. It was clean, however, and the dishwasher was running quietly. Since she was sure he hadn't hired a housekeeper in her absence, she assumed he'd done the work himself. She was impressed. As she'd told him earlier, she was pleased to learn he was human. The way he carried himself gave the impression that he was bigger than life and that there was nothing he could not do. Well, he couldn't fry bacon. Smiling to herself, she went to find him.

Across town, tall red-haired Faye Riley returned to her expensively furnished town house apartment after her weekly workout at the local gun range and set her duffel bag on the floor by the armoire that served as her gun cabinet. Target shooting was an unlikely hobby for a former debutante from Virginia, but Faye's mother, one of the nation's first female cops, had insisted her daughter learn. She wanted her daughter to grow up independent and strong; Faye just wanted to be kept by a man who was independently wealthy.

Faye put away her gear, locked her piece in the armoire, then shuffled through the envelopes left by the mailman. She scanned them all with a jaundiced eye. Bills, bills, and more bills. She would just have to talk to Myk again. She still didn't believe their relationship was over—after all, hadn't that little Nigerian, Obari, let her charge the blue fox stole the other day? If Myk had been serious about breaking up, her account would have been closed, but since it hadn't been . . .

What's this? she wondered, coming across a small ivory envelope at the back of the stack. She turned it over. It was addressed to her but curiously there was no return address. Using an ivory-handled letter opener, she slit the flap and found another envelope inside and lifted it free. The original name and delivery address had been heavily blacked out, but in the left corner she spotted the Chandler Works logo. Had Myk finally come to his senses? Maybe he was throwing a party, she thought excitedly. If so, the glorious blue fox would make for a grand entrance.

She opened the second envelope and inside was an elegantly engraved card. The florid gold words read: *"Mr. and Mrs. Mykal Chandler respectfully re-*

quest your presence at a reception honoring their recent marriage. . . ." The card went on to announce the date, time, and place, and an enraged Faye hit the roof. "He can't do this to me!"

That Myk Chandler hadn't been man enough to tell her to her face made it even more galling and humiliating, having to find out like this—and she shook the card furiously for emphasis—like everyone else, was the lowest slap of all. She threw the invitation across her pink-and-gold living room. Once word of his marriage got out on the vine, Faye's friends would laugh themselves sick. They'd warned her not to count her chickens too soon; a man with Chandler's wealth and power would not be hooked by just a pretty face, but Faye had been confident that her beauty and Southern belle ways would get her what she wanted because it had always been that way. So in response to the warnings from her friends, Faye had turned up her nose and continued to plan and build upon the likelihood of becoming Mrs. Mykal Chandler, even though he refused to grovel at her feet like all the other men in her past or put up with her *shit* as he so eloquently phrased it. She wanted to marry him because he was fine, rich, and had a lifestyle she felt born to. She had no intentions of working herself to death like her mother, only to retire on a pension that was never enough.

But *this*, she raged inwardly while pacing the plush carpeted floor, this marriage of his changed everything: the jewelry she'd been itching to buy, the full-length sable she'd been coveting at Obari's, the dinner parties, she'd planned on throwing. Everything had changed, and she didn't even know the gold digger's name. "Well, I'm sure as hell going to find out!"

She snatched up her cordless. Using a sculpted bloodred nail, she angrily tapped in a number. Somebody somewhere had to know the details, but an hour of calling proved her wrong. No one she talked to—and she'd talked to everyone she could think of—knew anything more than the information stated on the invitation.

Faye went over and picked it up off the carpet. She had no idea if the person who'd mailed it to her was friend or foe, nor did she care. All that mattered to Faye was that she had an invitation, and whether Myk wanted her to attend or not, she was going to his reception Saturday, and she was wearing her new blue fox.

On Saturday morning, Myk clicked off his cell phone and put it back in his shirt pocket. He'd been talking with Drake about the details for that night's reception and about Sarita. Sarita. Her name was as lyrical and sensual as she. If Myk weren't careful, his attraction to her was going to roar past his defenses, and all hell was going to break loose. Admitting that she'd gotten under his skin didn't help matters, nor had dreaming about her last night.

He got up from his desk. Deciding he needed a walk outside to clear his head, Myk left his room and headed for the kitchen.

He assumed she was in her bedroom, but found her outside, seated on the long bench built into the plank walk leading down to the small dock. The October wind was blustery and cold, but she wasn't wearing a coat.

He walked up, and asked, "Trying to catch pneumonia so you won't have to dance with me tonight?"

Her eyes flashed with amusement. "No, but it's worth considering."

He wanted to sit beside her but chose to stand. "You should go get a jacket or something."

"I'm okay. I was on my way back inside in a minute anyway. Just wanted some fresh air. I'll bet it's real peaceful out here in the summer."

"It is." He watched her look around at the setting. "Lily put in the rosebushes behind you, and she picked out all the shrubs and trees."

In the spring the walk down to the water was alive with the pale blossoms of the flowering trees Lily had insisted he plant, and each year the area grew more lush. The hypnotic call of the river and the shade offered by the trees made the spot a perfect place to sit and relax.

She stood. "I'll head back so you can be out here alone."

"You don't have to leave."

Their eyes met.

He removed his jacket and handed it to her. "If you stay, you have to put this on."

Sarita took the jacket from his hand and silently shrugged into it. It was way too big, but it still held his warmth and scent.

Seeing her in his coat gave Myk a thrill, but he kept his face free of any emotion. He looked out toward the river. "Tell me something about Sarita Grayson I don't know."

She answered, "That first morning we had breakfast together you said you knew all there was to know about me."

"I was wrong."

The blunt statement made her go still. He glanced over his shoulder at her, held her eyes for a long moment, then turned back to the water.

Sarita's eyes scanned his back. What could she tell him? Her eyes strayed back to the trees fading in anticipation of winter. "I'd like to plant a bunch of trees and flowers around the center."

He turned to her. "Is that what you wanted me to know?"

She shrugged. "I don't know what you want me to say, but that's what came to mind." A memory rose, and it colored her voice. "My grandmother did day work for a rich man named Mr. Aronson, and he had flowering cherry trees on his property. When I was little I always begged my grandmother to take me to work with her in the spring so I could see the trees."

"So did she?"

"Yes. At least once every year."

Myk smiled inside. Faye would never have pined for trees or flowers; diamonds and furs were more up her alley.

"Will I ever know what this thing you and Saint are mixed up in is all about?"

That caught him a bit off guard. His eyes swept her face for a moment, then he told her the truth. "No."

Sarita sighed her frustration. "Chandler, I—"

"Let it go," he replied quietly.

Sarita sighed again. "Well, did you at least get a good price for my diamonds?"

"Your diamonds?"

"Yes, *my* diamonds."

Myk shook his head. Would this woman ever give up? "*Your* diamonds are gone, so you should forget about them. Have you eaten this morning?"

"Yes, why?"

"Don't want you to look starved for the pictures."

"Pictures? What pictures?"

"You and I have an appointment with the brothers and sisters of the Black press this afternoon at two."

Sarita's shock was all over her face.

His eyes showed his amusement. "Go put on something classy but dazzling, and I'll meet you at the door in say, an hour?"

Sarita still hadn't found her voice.

"Welcome to the society pages, Mrs. Chandler." That said, he walked back to the French doors and went inside.

By early evening, the veneer over Sarita's nerves felt as thin as the delicate white tissue paper wrapped around the dress she would be wearing to the reception. After the afternoon's whirlwind photo op, she wondered how body and soul still managed to be in one piece.

As far as she was concerned, Chandler had taken full advantage of the situation, knowing she couldn't protest. Admittedly, by the time the shoot was over, she hadn't really wanted to, but it was the principle of the thing. The pictures were going to be used by myriad magazines and news outlets. Some were small heads-only shots destined for the local papers' Recently Married columns; others were for larger spreads in national magazines like the famous Black monthly, *Spectrum*. When one of the photographers asked that she and Chandler pose for a kiss, she hadn't wanted to and hoped Chandler would ignore the request, but instead, he gently raised her chin and stared down into her eyes. The look she saw reflected there made her heart race, and she trembled with anticipation. His lips met hers gently at first, coaxing her to let him taste her fully. Sarita's initial nervousness made her pull back slightly, but he pursued her, wooed her, his arm closing ever so slightly across her back until the kiss blended their bodies into one. The room exploded with the flashes and clicks of cameras. The photographers apparently felt the heat and began calling out encouragement. Sarita barely heard them. When Chandler finally, sluggishly, pulled his lips away, her legs and knees were weak as spring rain. Her eyes refused to open, and she swore she had the brain of a shoe box.

After the kiss, she'd tried to pull herself together and appear cool and unfazed, but that only lasted for a few moments; the press wanted more.

By the time the photographers packed up their gear, she and Chandler had shared more kisses than she could remember; each more fiery than the last.

Now, in her room, her emotions in a confused uproar, her lips still kiss-swollen, Sarita laid the tissue-wrapped dress on her bed. Remembering Chandler's kisses and the way she'd responded to them made her want to question her sanity. She'd thought herself way past the age of being overwhelmed by a man. The wild, careening sensations churning through her body were reserved for a sixteen-year-old, not someone her age. She'd left Chandler's arms reeling like she'd been sideswiped by a truck.

The paper wrapped around the dress would have done a mummy proud, but it finally came free. The stunning creation inside made Sarita voice a small, dejected, "Aw man . . ."

Like everything else he'd given her, the dress was expensive and gorgeous. Made out of what looked like yards of brocaded indigo silk, it was strapless and full-skirted, with a skinny straight-line bodice cut a lot lower than anything she'd ever worn before. There was no ornamentation. It didn't need any. This was a rich woman's version of a smoking gun, and just looking at it made Sarita know it would fit like a glove. Why was he doing this to her? He was like the proverbial snake in the garden, tempting her with wealth, kisses, and his no-limit credit cards. The dress hadn't been intended for a neighborhood activist scraping out a living on the little bit of pension left to her by her deceased uncles. It had been designed for a woman a whole lot more worldly and sophisticated. Not that she couldn't pull it off, but she didn't want to. Her life lay on the other side of town.

She very carefully lifted the dress free of the paper and raised it so she could see it better. Chandler had been almost right about its resemblance to the gown she'd worn the night before to dance with him, although her arms, shoulders, and neck would be even more bare. She would be expected to act as if she dressed this way all the time. She would also be expected to be butter in Chandler's arms. For a moment, she let herself contemplate just how it might feel to give in and enjoy the warmth of his mouth trailing hot across the bare planes of her shoulders, the edges of her throat. Scandalized by the daydreaming, she shook herself back to reality and decided to get ready.

Downstairs, Myk, dressed in a black-and-white evening tux, checked his watch. His driver and friend, Walter McGhee would be there with the car in about forty minutes. It was six-thirty, and the festivities were supposed to jump off at eight. It gave them plenty of time to get to the reception. He was so anxious to see her, however, he had to force himself not to go up to her room to see if she was dressed.

He took a deep breath and tried to calm down. Why he was so uncharacteristically nervous was beyond him. He was acting as if this reception was the real McCoy instead of just a way to cover his ass. He hoped the ruse worked. The sooner he could get her settled in and return to his NIA duties, the happier he'd be. He had tonight to get through though.

A half an hour later, the sound of rustling silk broke the silence. He turned, and there she stood in the doorway. She was so breathtakingly beautiful he didn't know where to settle his eyes first. The gleaming roundness of her bare shoulders; the soft brown breasts rising above the low neckline; the way the indigo silk hugged her torso; all of it made him granite hard, and he had to take a deep breath to bring himself back under control. "Wow . . ."

It was all he could say. Once again, Sarita Kathleen Grayson-Chandler had knocked his socks off. "You look fantastic. . . ."

"Thanks." Sarita was trying to act cool and nonchalant, but she was so nervous it was a wonder she hadn't shaken to pieces. She knew she looked good, though, and it pleased her that he thought so, too, but she had the rest of the evening to get through, and she already knew how unpredictable he could be.

"I opened some champagne."

She shook her head and declined. "No thanks. I'm not much of a drinker."

"No problem," he replied quietly. He poured himself a flute and nursed it alone while she perched hesitantly on the edge of the leather sofa. He lingered over the drink in much the same way his eyes lingered over her in the beautiful dress.

After a few more moments of heated silence, Myk set the flute down, then said, "Excuse me for a minute."

When he left the room, Sarita let out her breath. All she could think about was his vivid gaze. How in the world was she going to keep him at arm's length tonight when deep down inside parts of herself didn't want to? A woman would have to be dead not to be affected by all that he was, and Sarita was very much alive. She'd been celibate by choice for the last year, and Chandler's raw sexiness was making her realize just how long it had been; but sleeping with him would only make this mess even more complicated, so she planned to follow her grandmother's age-old advice: *Keep your panties up and your dress down!*

Chandler came back into the room a few moments later. He had a small, thin, black velvet box in his hand. When he unceremoniously sat down beside her, she jumped nervously, earning a disapproving glance.

"Sorry," she whispered in response.

Opening the box, he told her, "Take that off."

Sarita's heart skipped, and her hand moved protectively to the bodice of her dress. Not sure what he was intending, she backed away warily. *Did he want her to take off her dress?*

When Myk looked up, that was the position he found her in. He searched her eyes for the reason for her stance. It then occurred to him what the problem might be. "Not your dress. The chain around your neck."

He made her turn, and it took him only a few seconds to release the chain's clasp. Once he did, he lifted the chain clear and set it aside.

"Now, hold still . . ." he murmured.

His warm fingers returned, accompanied by the feathery weight of an ornate necklace. The painted tips of her fingers touched the circlet questioningly while he did up the delicate clasp.

Sarita rose from the couch and went over to mirror hanging over the fireplace mantel to see. The sheer beauty of it left her speechless.

Myk came up behind her. "I should record this."

Sarita was so focused on the blue-and-gold jewels reflected in the mirror that she didn't hear him. "What?"

"Your silence," he explained. "I said, I should record it. It's rare, coming from you."

Sarita was so overcome, she missed the point of his teasing entirely. "You can't record silence." Then, in a voice burning with wonder, she asked, "Are these sapphires?"

"Yes, they are." Myk's eyes traveled hungrily over the reflection of the blue stones nestled against her unmarred skin. "Sapphires, diamonds, and gold."

Sarita had never worn anything so exquisite. The necklace looked like a string of small golden snowflakes. The centers were gleaming blue, the points around them sparkling diamonds. "These are real, aren't they?"

"Of course they're real," Myk countered. The question might have offended him were it not for the pure awe in her voice. He added, "You know, you're never supposed to ask a man if the jewelry's real."

Sarita turned slowly and looked up into his mustached face. "Says who? That's a man you're quoting, right?"

Myk chuckled at her dead-serious manner. "How'd you guess?"

Sarita turned back to the glass. "A woman would never say anything so ridiculous." Once again the necklace around her neck grabbed her attention. "Do you have any idea how much these are worth on the street?"

"I'm sure you could tell me."

His cold tone brought her up short. Of course he knew how much they were worth.

He told her quietly, "I bought those sapphires to hang above your sweet little breasts, not for you to give to your neighborhood fence."

"You bought these for my—for me?"

"Of course they're for you." Myk was getting real tired of her country girl act. "Who else would they be for?"

Sarita didn't trust the mirror to give her a true read, so she turned to face him. "Why do you keep doing this?"

He didn't hesitate. "If I had a *real* wife, she would expect me to keep her in the best style my money can afford. And that"—he nodded nonchalantly at the sapphire-centered snowflakes—"is part of that style."

A silent Sarita peered down her chin to the gold at her throat, then up to his unfathomable eyes. "Believe me when I say I would never, ever, pawn something this beautiful. Never." She wanted that fact to be clear, but the mask over his features made it difficult for her to gauge whether he believed her or not.

The silence that followed made her so uncomfortable she turned back to their reflections in the mirror. "Thank you, whatever the reason."

Their gazes met in the glass and held. The crackling of the wood burning in the fireplace was the room's only sound. Time seemed to stretch and suspend. His dark eyes searched and probed hers, making her remember the kisses they'd shared. Had they affected him as much as they had her?

He turned away to retrieve something else from the table. It broke the spell. She struggled to regain her composure.

He came back to her holding earrings to match the necklace. He waited silently while she removed the gold studs she had in her lobes. When they were replaced, she turned to face him once more.

Myk's attention moved from ear to ear, then down to the sapphires circling her smooth brown throat. The thought that she was everything he didn't want in a woman surfaced in his mind again. She was mouthy, stubborn, and opinionated enough to drive a brother out of his mind, but he found himself wanting to cancel the evening activities. He suddenly had no desire to share her with anyone else. He had a stronger need to pull her into his arms and taste that lightly painted mouth, then run his lips over the bare edge of her throat and smell her perfume. At that moment he could well identify with those eccentric collectors of rare art who never let their treasures be seen. Standing before him was a black porcelain masterpiece. "You make me want to keep you home."

Sarita swallowed. She thought he meant to punish her for bringing up the street value of the jewels. "Look, I didn't mean to imply I would fence the gems. When I said I wouldn't, I was serious."

"That's not what I meant."

Sarita read his blazing meaning, and her breath stacked up in her throat. He wanted her, no apologies. The implications were so staggering, she had to look away.

Myk placed a finger against her jaw, and with a gentle insistence brought her ebony eyes back to his. Her skin trembled beneath his touch; a trembling he'd felt before, tasted before; a trembling he wanted to soothe away with his lips and his touch. That afternoon's kisses at the photo op had been the appetizer to a dish he wanted to order double helpings of, even though she wasn't supposed to be on the menu. "I'll try and make this evening as easy on you as possible. Considering this will probably be the only wedding reception I'll ever have, I'd like the memories to be good ones."

His finger traced the satin skin of Sarita's cheekbone with a tenderness he'd never exhibited before. "No fighting tonight, okay?"

He seemed to be addressing himself as well.

"Okay," came her softly spoken reply.

For a moment neither spoke. In the silence, he absently continued to stroke her cheek, making the heat and trembling gripping her that much more intense. She took a hesitant step back. "Um, shouldn't we be going?" She slipped past him, feeling like a rabbit.

His eyes continued to pursue her. "One last thing."

Out of his pocket he extracted another small, black velvet box. The princess-cut diamond inside wasn't the largest she'd ever seen, but its beauty and detail rivaled the necklace. "I knew you would probably fuss if I got you a large stone, so . . ."

Sarita met his eyes.

"Hold out your hand."

She complied, and he pushed the sparkler onto the third finger of her left hand.

"Now, we can go."

Without further word, he pulled out his phone and dialed Walter to see if he had the car out front, then escorted her to foyer closet to get their coats.

Eight

Faye Riley hated Sarita the moment she laid eyes on her—one, because Sarita was obviously younger and, two, by all rights Faye should be the one standing by Myk's side in this crush of a party. Faye wished the people ahead of her in the receiving line would hurry the hell up so she could get a good look at the nappy-headed heifer up close, but people were taking their time, lingering over their congratulations as if Myk's marriage was really something to celebrate. Because of all the guests and their chitchatting with the bride and groom about nothing, the line behind Faye stretched out into the hallway. It was almost as long as the line of people in front of her. Faye wanted to scream, *Hurry up, dammit!* when she saw one of the members of the City Council and his loudly dressed, skinny wife going on and on with the newlyweds. Someone behind Faye bumped her accidentally and she turned on the offender with a glare. She pulled her new fox stole tighter around her designer-gowned shoulder as if trying to protect herself from a disease. She felt like a princess in a cattle car, and she would never ever forgive Myk for putting her through this.

Drake, on the other hand, was standing in the receiving line and thought Sarita an absolute delight. After having watched Myk carry her screaming and cussing up the stairs that night, Drake had worried how she'd fit in; but his fears had been laid to rest by her smile, her patience with the people in line, and the way she looked in that stunning dress. Who knew she would morph into this brown-shouldered fox. He peered down at his tall, immaculately dressed brother stoically accepting congratulations from the guests. For someone who hated this sort of thing, Myk seemed relatively relaxed, but who wouldn't be with a woman like Sarita by his side? Leave it to big brother to pull a dark-eyed rose from the ashes of that diamonds fiasco. Anyone else in the organization would probably have discovered an armed opponent in Fishbein's room that night instead of this satin doll, but once again, the Chandler luck held. *The legend lives on*, Drake thought wryly.

Standing between Chandler and Mayor Randolph, Sarita wasn't sure what kind of impression she was making. There were so many people! She was quite sure she wouldn't remember half of the names, and she was very conscious of saying the wrong thing or embarrassing herself. Although Chandler seemed relaxed beside her, she knew better than to use him as a barometer. The line of well-wishers seemed endless, and no matter how many hands she shook, or how many gracious smiles she gave, the guests kept coming.

Myk asked her between greetings, "How're you doing?"

Terrible, she wanted to whine. Her feet hurt from the heels she was wearing, her face hurt from all the smiling, and her hands hurt from all the pumping. Grown Black women didn't whine, however, especially in the presence of the mayor and a ballroom packed with people, so she lied, "I'm okay." They'd only been at it an hour.

Myk ran his eyes over the sapphires hanging around her neck. The sight aroused him as much as it had back at the house. He raised his eyes to her face. "We'll get a seat in a few minutes."

Taking him at his word, she turned away. As the next group of well-wishers approached, she plastered on her smile

The few minutes he'd promised turned into another half an hour. By the time Sarita finally got a seat, she didn't want to shake another hand, smile into another face, or stand on her feet for the rest of the night.

The head table had been placed on a horizontal riser that lifted them a few feet above the floor, making the bride and groom visible from most points in the big ballroom. From her vantage point, Sarita could see everyone and everything. The room had been tastefully decorated with trimmings of ivory and gold. She'd never been the main show for so many people. Politicians, auto execs, television personalities, athletes and their owners—the well-known and the unknown had all turned out to help celebrate the marriage of a man they obviously thought they knew. Many came up to the table and offered their congratulations. She wondered how they'd react if the truth about Chandler's extracurricular activities suddenly showed up on the front page of the paper.

There was a small orchestra setting up near the back of the room. Ringing the dance floor were at least a hundred small tables set for dining with white tablecloths, polished silverware, gleaming china, and gold-edged linen napkins. To Sarita it looked like a giant cabaret, but it was not your typical Friday night BYOB. She hoped there were enough seats to go around; but that didn't seem to be a problem, even though newcomers continued to file in. The orchestra started up, but the music had a hard time competing with the din of clinking glasses and the low buzz of a hundred conversations.

Many of the guests had brought gifts. Surprised, Sarita watched the beautifully wrapped items being placed in a steadily growing pile by a crew of tux-wearing young men. She didn't need gifts. Chandler already owned everything! Maybe he'd let her donate the presents. There had to be a lot of items that could be put to good use by the families at her center. She made a mental note to talk to him about it later.

Thinking about him made her look for him in the crowd. He'd left their table to speak to the musicians and promised to be right back. That had been over twenty minutes ago. She scanned the room hoping to spot him, but became distracted by the sheer size of the crowd. Everyone was dressed so elegantly. There wasn't a pair of gym shoes in the house. The men were in tuxedos. The women were draped in furs. She wished her kids at the center could be here to witness this. None of them had ever been invited to such an elegant affair. Thinking about them made her realize that she missed her people very much. She just hoped she'd be able to convince Chandler to let her return to work soon. Problems needing her attention were probably stacking up like rush-hour traffic on the freeway.

She finally spotted Chandler in his classic tux standing just to the left of the musicians. He was talking with a tall, fair-skinned sister with red hair. The two were too far away for Sarita to hear their conversation, but she could see the woman's angry gestures, the agitation in her face, and the fluffy blue fur draped over one arm. Sarita assumed the woman was upset about something. In fact she looked furious.

"Faye," Drake said beside her.

Sarita turned.

"Faye Riley," he said explaining further. "Myk's old lady friend."

"Oh." Sarita turned back to check the woman out. By any standards, Faye was beautiful—tall, thin, and shapely. And well aware of it, it seemed, because the dress Faye had on was so thin and transparent it would have made the church ladies at home break out their fans. The pale dress shimmered over her body like pink stars, but in this setting, she caused not a ripple.

The mayor cracked, "She came dressed to kill though, didn't she?"

Sarita got the impression that Drake didn't think much of Miss Faye.

The meeting broke off abruptly, and an unruffled Chandler walked back toward the head table. His ex appeared less than satisfied. Tight-faced, Faye threw the blue fur around her shoulders and made her way stiffly through the crowd. When she reached the exit, she kept going.

"Uhp, she's leaving," the mayor said with a mocking sadness. He then lifted his glass in a sarcastic toast.

Sarita couldn't suppress her grin. "Not one of your favorite people, I take it?"

"You take it right."

When Myk returned to the table, he set a glass of cola with ice in front of Sarita, then shared a loaded look with his brother.

Drake quipped, "How's Faye?"

Myk didn't answer. He was certain Faye was going to cause trouble somewhere down the line, he could feel it; but he planned to cut her off at the pass. He told Sarita, "I think everybody's waiting for us to start the dancing. Let's go."

Sarita had never heard a less gracious request in her life, but she held her tongue and stood. He took her cold hand in his. She assumed his thoughts were elsewhere because as he led her out onto the floor he didn't look at her once. Sarita put her bet on Faye. Why the idea of him thinking about another woman bothered her, Sarita didn't want to deal with. However, when Chandler escorted her to the center of the ballroom floor, and the guests broke into thunderous applause, the searing eyes said Sarita was the only woman on his mind.

The music began, and they moved together like true lovers. His hold on her waist was light but possessive. The swell of applause faded away, replaced by the sweet drifting notes of a saxophone. Where he led, Sarita followed instinctively. They were the only couple on the floor, and they might as well have been the only couple in the world. She could feel the curve of his arm burning across her back, and she was unable to tear her eyes away from the commanding power in his. They danced silently, assuredly, steps blending naturally while the crowd looked on enthralled.

No one knew anything about the woman Mykal Chandler had married, but the passionate look in his eyes as he gazed down at his bride made even Faye's friends envious. In fantasy, they were the subject of Chandler's hot stare. The palm he was now turning to his lips belonged not to Sarita, but to them; and it was their hand not hers touching his face so softly in response. When he stopped dancing altogether and lowered his head, their lips parted to receive his kiss. The whole room felt the heat.

When Chandler finally broke the kiss, Sarita could hardly stand. She had the vague sense of wall-shaking applause coming from the guests, but she couldn't be sure. He still held her in the circle of his arms, and she clung to him for balance. Her head was on his chest, and her senses were spinning. He gave her no time to recover though. Placing a finger beneath her chin, he gently raised her eyes back to his burning ones, then bent and kissed her again, whispering his lips across the parted corners of her mouth, plunging her back into the abyss.

"Mykal, stop, please . . ."

Reluctantly, he pulled away, but his finger traced her lips. "Is this all I have to do to get you to call me by my first name . . . just kiss this sweet mouth of yours?"

To test his theory, he kissed her again, deeper this time.

The guests were delighted. It was quite plain to everyone in attendance that Mykal Chandler had finally lost his heart to a chocolate-shouldered sparkler with flashing eyes who looked every bit as in love as he.

Sarita wasn't sure how she made it back to the table, but dinner was served immediately after, and for that she gave thanks; having to concentrate on eating helped distract her from her overwrought nerves. Chandler, on the other hand, didn't seem affected at all. That was the part that threw her. A few moments ago, he'd drawn her soul from between her lips and made her such a mental wreck she'd had to plead for him to stop, but he was sitting and talking with his brother as if nothing had happened. Could he possibly be that good an actor? Had he really felt nothing? She'd melted out there, literally. Desire was thundering so loudly between her celibate thighs it was a wonder everyone in the room didn't hear it. How in the world was she going to be with this man for a year? If he could put her body in such an uproar after only a few days, what would she be like in three months' time?

"How's your food?" Myk asked. He wondered if she knew how kiss-swollen her lips looked.

Still trying to gather herself, she said. "Fine." The salmon fillet was grilled and flavorful, just the way she liked it.

Myk forced himself to turn away and concentrate on his meal. As he ate, though, he couldn't get the taste of her kiss and the sound of her voice whispering his name out of his mind. Thinking back on it made him hard all over again. He wasn't supposed to be wanting her; he'd told himself that a thousand times in the past few days. He also knew that sleeping with her would make this mess even more complicated, but he wasn't accustomed to denying himself a woman whose desire seemed to match his own.

At that moment, the ballroom filled with the sound of tinkling glass. Sarita scanned the seated dining guests for the source. The diners were being waited on by a crew of white-jacketed young men and women who were weaving in and out of the tables with unobtrusive efficiency, but the sounds, rising now to a musical crescendo, came from the guests. Each and every one was happily tapping a piece of silverware: knives, forks, spoons, lightly against the side of their water glasses. Sarita had no idea what it meant.

Myk saw the confusion on her face. "Never seen this before?"

"No."

"It's a wedding tradition that's not so common in our communities, but the glass tapping is a signal. The guests want a kiss from the bride and groom."

The explanation only added to her bewilderment. "I am not kissing everyone in this room, Chandler. Forget it."

The sound had risen to a high-pitched roar.

Myk chuckled at her stance. "That's not what they want. They want this . . ." And he kissed her, silencing all of her confusion with the warm pressure of his lips. Once again, he left her spinning and breathless, and when she opened her eyes, he was leaning above her, looking very pleased and very male indeed.

The guests applauded their approval.

The mayor then proposed a toast to the newly-weds. In response, Chandler entwined his black-coated arm with her bare one. Their eyes locked. She drank from his cup, and he followed with a sip from hers. He leaned over then and sealed the matter with another, slow-as-molasses kiss. She could taste the champagne on his lips and he could taste the same on hers. When he pulled back, she was dizzy. The guests responded with more applause.

The glass chimers interrupted the meal three more times before the dinner plates were finally whisked away. Each time Chandler responded, his kiss became more and more potent, and her senses became more and more aroused. Although Sarita tried to play it off by smiling and looking calm, she was a basket case. Every inch of her body was on fire. Her nipples were hard, her lips were parted, and she didn't even want to talk about what was happening in all those places that made her a woman. She wanted to hike up her dress and run out of the ballroom like Cinderella, but doubted that would go over real well.

After dinner, the orchestra slid into a thumping old-school set, and folks took to the dance floor as if they really were at a cabaret. Sarita loved to dance, and her shoulders began to move in response to the music's call. She turned to ask Chandler if he would dance with her, but, at that moment, a phone began to beep. He automatically reached into the pocket of his coat and placed the phone to his ear. "Yeah."

Sarita sighed. Next she knew, he was saying to her, "I need to take this."

He and the mayor shared a look, and the mayor replied, "Have one of the officers take you to my office. You'll have some privacy there."

Myk told the person on the other end, "Okay, give me the number and I'll call you back in five minutes." After committing the number to memory, he hung up, then said to Sarita, "I'll be back as soon as I can."

A real bride would have given her groom hell for leaving the reception to answer a phone call, but Sarita knew Chandler would take the call regardless of how she felt, so in response, she nodded her approval distantly, then turned back to the dancers.

Myk could tell by the tightness in her jaw that she wasn't real happy about him leaving, but it couldn't be helped.

While the party continued, he discreetly left the ballroom. With escort in tow, he headed upstairs to Drake's office. He knew better than to conduct NIA business on a cell phone. They were notoriously susceptible to all kinds of electronic eavesdropping, but the line in Drake's office was clean and secure, and it was swept every few days to make sure it stayed that way.

Myk thanked the officer for the escort, then slipped into Drake's office and closed the door behind him. The small Tiffany lamp on the desk gave the shadowy room a soft glow and enough light for Myk to see by. He picked up the desk phone and punched in the memorized number he'd been given by Saint.

When the band segued into its next tune—one

that everyone knew called for the Electric Slide, Sarita grabbed the mayor's hand, and said, "Come on, Your Honor. It's hustle time."

The beauty of the Electric Slide is that partners aren't needed, so Sarita and Drake joined the four horizontal lines of dancers who, once they got the rhythm synced up, stepped through the familiar moves in unison. Sarita grinned. This was the first real fun she'd had in days. The mayor grinned back. When the line turned, neither of them missed a beat. As always, there were a few people in the way; stepping to the left when they should've been going to the right, or vice versa, but the dancers flowed around them as best they could. Soon, most of the people in the ballroom were in line, and in step, and everyone, including Sarita and the mayor, were hustling up a storm.

When the music ended, everyone on the floor happily applauded the musicians and themselves. It had never crossed Sarita's mind that rich people would throw down like this, but they had. Little gray-haired ladies dressed in diamonds and gold had rocked next to news anchors and athletes decked out in their own versions of diamonds and gold. Even the waitstaff had joined the lines, and no one seemed to mind.

"So," mayor asked as he escorted the smiling Sarita back to the table, "what do you think of the reception?"

"Mr. Mayor, you throw a hell of a party."

When they reached their seats, Sarita didn't want to admit it, but she was a bit disappointed to see that Chandler hadn't returned. It must have shown on her face, though, because the mayor said, "The call had to have been important; otherwise, he wouldn't've left."

Sarita shrugged nonchalantly. "A brother has to do what a brother has to do."

"Myk's a good man."

Sarita didn't respond.

When Chandler still hadn't returned after thirty minutes, Sarita could tell by the whispering behind hands and the questioning looks that the groom's absence hadn't gone unnoticed by the guests. She had no idea how long the event was supposed to last, and as more and more faces began turning her way for guidance, she leaned over to the mayor.

"He'll be back," was all he had to say.

Sarita tried to keep the frustration from coloring her voice, "Do you know who he's talking to, then?"

He didn't respond.

Sarita had seen the speaking look the brothers had exchanged when the call came in, and it made her believe Drake knew way more about what was happening than he was willing to admit, but she didn't pursue the matter any further.

Sarita shared a few more dances with Drake, some up tempo, one slow, then was approached by some of the men in attendance who wanted to dance with the bride, too. She gladly accepted, and allowed them to escort her out to the floor. Whatever Chandler was up to: good, bad, or ugly, Sarita knew she had to make things appear as innocent and normal as possible. Her fate was too intertwined with Chandler's to do otherwise.

By the time she stepped onto the floor with her fourth partner, a player for the local NFL team,

Sarita was having a ball. She'd danced a waltz with Judge Wade Morgan, ballroomed with the next two men, and now she and her fourth partner, a cute star receiver for the local NFL franchise, were doing a mean Harlem Shake on the crowded dance floor.

When it was over, Sarita gave him a smile and thanked him for the fun. He smiled back, and they joined the crowd in applauding the musicians. That done, Sarita turned to have him lead her back to her seat. In the same motion her eyes strayed innocently to the head table. Seeing the standing Chandler watching her with eyes that seemed to burn the distance between them, caught her so off guard she stumbled. Her partner reached out to catch her. Luckily, she didn't hit the floor. Apologizing to him, she steadied herself. When she looked toward the table again, Chandler had taken a seat and was talking to the mayor. She fumed inwardly. How dare he be able to reduce her to a stumbling idiot with just a look from across the room!

"You're sure you're okay?" the athlete asked.

"I'm fine."

She reached the table without any further mishaps. After she took her seat beside Chandler, her dance partner commented, "Quite a lady you got there, Mr. Chandler."

Myk's eyes grazed over her lightly. "I think so." In reality, he wanted to punch the brother in the nose. Myk was jealous, a new experience for him.

In response to the coolness she saw in Chandler's eyes, Sarita's chin rose defensively. She had the distinct impression that in spite of his easygoing exterior, he wasn't as pleased with her as he would like the athlete to believe. Knowing she had nothing to apologize for, she ignored Chandler for the moment, and said to her partner, "Thanks for the dance."

"Anytime."

He and Myk shared a look, then the man disappeared into the crowd.

Myk watched him walk away, then said to Sarita. "We've time for one last dance, then we should get going."

Sarita almost asked where they were going, but decided it didn't matter. She took his offered hand and stood. It also didn't matter what he'd been doing for the last forty minutes, but she was sure people would certainly talk if the bride and groom left so soon after his return, at least folks would in her world. "Don't you think that'd be pretty rude, us leaving right now?"

"Nope. They'll party without us. They'll assume we have other plans—if you know what I mean."

She did. Hot embarrassment washed over her cheeks. She couldn't look him or the mayor in the face, so she let herself be led back out onto the dance floor.

As he took her into his arms her silence continued. Other couples dancing by to the slow song smiled, and Sarita smiled politely in reply, but that was all.

Myk said quietly, "Did I embarrass you by referring to something that brides and grooms have been doing for thousands of years?"

"Yes, because you and I haven't been doing anything for thousands of years."

He whispered softly into her ear, "With reincarnation, hey, you never know what we might have done in the past. I could've made love to you a thousand years ago on the banks of the Nile—or sampled your nakedness in the mountain grasses of China . . . or—"

"Would you stop?" she whispered, scandalized. She quickly looked around to see if he'd been overheard.

He lowered his head until his lips brushed her ear. "What's wrong? Don't you want to hear about the love we made on the steps of the temples in Peru . . . or the times I took you twisting under the stars?"

Sarita couldn't breathe.

"Some nights you came to my tent in the Sudan dressed in nothing but your hair and my jewels, and the heat we made was hotter than the desert wind . . ."

Sarita's legs were jelly. "Mykal, stop . . ."

His lips against her ear were like a hurricane. "I haven't even started."

His lips found hers, and she totally lost control. The deep possessive kiss singed her, burned her; made her wrap her arms around him and respond with passionate surrender in spite of her mind's warnings. For the moment, she just wanted to drink him in as deeply as he was drinking from her, and when he finally released her lips, the world was spinning.

"We aren't supposed to be doing this . . ." she murmured.

"I know. You're everything I've never wanted in a woman. You're uncontrollable, you're hostile." His lips teased her ear and jaw. "You're hardheaded, stubborn. Not to mention where and how we met. But your mouth is as sweet as an island mango, and making love to you could become one of the biggest challenges in my life."

When she found her voice it came out ragged and soft. "This isn't a game we're playing."

"You're wrong, baby. It's the oldest game in town."

He took her by the hand and escorted her off the floor.

Nine

Needless to say, Mykal Chandler was a lot more man than Sarita was accustomed to handling. As she settled into the backseat of the limo for the ride to his house, her heart was still racing. She'd never had a man whisper so erotically to her before. Every inch of her body was pulsing and open. No sense in lying, he was turning her inside out. It was strictly physical. Chandler wasn't her type. The few men she'd been with in the past had been dreamers, artists, men with fine-boned hands who gave her paintings and poems. She'd bet Chandler had never written a poem in his life.

But his words on the dance floor could have melted steel, and she could either deal with her attraction to him head-on or spend the next year running from it.

His voice interrupted her thoughts. "Warm

enough?" The jazz from the limo's CD player floated melodically over the shadow-filled interior.

"Yes," Sarita answered.

Silence settled between them for a moment, then he said, "Just so you'll know, that phone call was from Saint."

That caught her by surprise. "How is he?"

"Fine. He called to let me know Fletcher's two party girls were found dead in St. Louis last night. Murdered."

Sarita shuddered.

Because of the shadows, Myk couldn't see her reaction, but he'd found news of the deaths disturbing, mostly because NIA had no idea who killed the women or why. Saint had been concerned too, and he and Myk debated whether to let her in on the deaths.

"So, how does this all affect me?" Sarita asked.

"Depends."

"On what?"

"On who killed them, and why."

Sarita supposed that made sense.

Myk added, "So far, Saint hasn't been able to connect their deaths to Fletcher. Some local thugs could've capped them, but—"

"You don't know for sure."

"No."

Sarita sat back against the seat, her mind working. If Fletcher's girls were killed in connection with the diamonds, her first question was: Did they drop a dime on Fletcher's plan before their deaths? Was someone after *her* now? She wished she knew how many other people, if any, Fletcher had let in on the deal they'd made that fateful night. She didn't like not knowing. "Did Saint say when he'd be coming back this way?"

"No."

"But he'll be okay?" Sarita asked. Even though Saint was still on the top of her shit list, it was hard not to worry about family.

"Yes." Myk heard her concern. Saint meant a lot to her and she to him. Their bond bothered Myk for reasons he couldn't explain. An inner voice mocked that it was because she'd never have the same concern for him, but Myk dismissed the voice as not knowing what the hell it was talking about.

He looked over at her sitting near the door. He wanted to take her to bed, though, that he freely admitted. Setting aside what such an encounter might cost, he wanted to hear her whisper his name again, feel his hand sliding over her satin skin, and kiss her when she came. There was a physical attraction between the two of them that no amount of denial could hide. He felt it; so did she. When all this drama began—could it really be less than a week ago?—he'd no idea of the stubborn, rock-hard brain that whirled behind those raven black eyes of hers. He'd naturally lumped her in with all the other women he'd known socially, beautiful but unable to ignite more than a passing interest. He'd been so wrong. Just finding her in Fishbein's room with the diamonds had been intriguing enough; but then for her to shoot him and escape? The women in his past were all too willing to do his bidding. Sarita was different. She didn't have a submissive bone in her body, and that backtalking mouth of hers had no trouble telling him where to go. Tonight though, that mouth had parted under his kisses, and damn her if he didn't want another taste. "You held up your end real well tonight."

"Is that a compliment?" she asked, facing him.

He could see flashes of her features in the passing streetlights. "Yes."

"Then, thank you," she replied. Sarita could feel the air between them thickening, and she forced herself to be as casual about it as he seemed to be. "What are you going to do with all the wedding presents?"

He shrugged. "No idea."

"Can I have them? For the center, I mean."

He didn't answer.

"If I'm out of line for asking, tell me so."

"You aren't."

"So, can I have them?"

He chuckled. "Don't you ever stop?" Before she could respond, he boldly scooped her up and set her on his lap.

"Chandler?" she scolded. The heat of his thighs burned through her clothing like hot coals from a barbecue grill.

"Just sit still. We need to talk."

"We were talking fine the way we were."

They were facing each other, no more than a few inches apart.

"This is better," he quoted, holding her eyes in the dark.

The tone of his voice in tandem with his nearness made Sarita's lips part unconsciously.

"So," he asked, "what should we do about what we're both feeling?"

She didn't speak.

"Oh, you're going to deny it?"

"No." How could she after all he'd made her feel tonight. "I just—"

"Just what?"

"I shouldn't be attracted to you."

"Why not?"

"Because this sounds like something out of the tabloids. Kidnapped woman sleeps with captor— has his baby."

He didn't like hearing himself described that way. "You haven't been kidnapped."

"What do you call it?"

"Safekeeping."

"No," she disagreed, shaking her head. "It's you taking away my freedom."

"It's more complicated than that."

"Then explain it to me."

"I can't."

Frustrated, she trained her vision on the darkness passing by the windows.

"You're pouting again," he pointed out in hushed amusement.

"I am not, but if I was, I have a right to." Sarita put as much earnestness in her voice as she could. "I really need to see what's going on back at home, Chandler. The center needs me. You said I could go, but when?"

He sighed. After his phone conversation with Saint, her going home was probably not a good idea, but Myk found himself wanting to please her. "Suppose we stop by there Monday morning, and I scope the place out?"

Without thought, she threw her arms around his neck in gratitude. She gushed with delight, "Thank you, thank you, thank you!" In the middle of the celebration, she caught herself. Her arms slowly dropped. "Sorry."

"Nothing to apologize for." Frankly, he'd enjoyed it. Having her on his lap felt natural. Her hot little hips made him feel something else. "I'm not making any promises about your being able to stay, though."

"That's okay," It wasn't really, but Sarita was convinced once he visited the center and saw the work being done there, he'd have no choice but to leave her in charge. After that, she'd work on convincing him to let her return permanently.

He asked, "Happy now?"

"Yes." Although the repercussions radiating from Fletcher's death loomed over her life like a storm on the horizon, Chandler's acquiescence was the best news she'd had in days. "Thanks, again."

"You're welcome."

A yawn escaped Sarita. Being a rich bitch was work.

"Tired?"

"It's been a long day."

"Then lean back," he said softly. "We'll be home in a minute."

Sarita searched his face in the dark. "I don't think so."

"Why not?"

"Because this is a game to you, and it doesn't make sense for me to pretend that it's not."

Myk knew she was correct, again. It was a game but not on the level she assumed. Over the past few days something about her had wormed its way under his skin, and his attempts to use his legendary discipline to counteract it weren't working. In the past, he'd always been able to place logic ahead of emotion, especially where women were concerned—Myk Chandler could always fall back on his control; but tonight, the words he'd whispered to her on the dance floor had risen out of places inside of himself that he hadn't even known existed. Hot feverish scenarios of lovemaking had been vivid enough to make him want to drag her into the closest private space and wear her out.

Because Chandler had gone quiet, Sarita assumed he'd been thinking, and she had been doing the same. First thought: to get off of his lap before she gave in to his invitation to ride the rest of the way back in his arms. Second thought: If she did give in, how much harm could there really be in pretending just for a moment that this was her life and that he was the man she'd married? Her mind floated back to the memories of his hot words on the dance floor. She had her answer. Chandler was probably dangerous in ways she couldn't even imagine. "I think I want to sit back over there."

"We're both adults, Sarita."

"I know," she admitted, but left his lap anyway. Sarita was battling herself. She didn't consider herself a prude. No sister in her right mind would kick a man like him to the curb, but sleeping with him would make her a coconspirator in her own captivity. Her strong sense of self refused to support such an illogical choice, and there was no sense in pretending she enjoyed being kept under his lock and key. There was something she had to know though. "What you said to me while we were dancing—have you used that with other women?"

Myk wanted to lie; male consensus was: Never tell a lady the depths of your feelings, but telling her the truth felt right. "No," he confessed softly. "You're the only one."

The implications resonated through Sarita with such power she drew in a shaky breath.

"Which is why we need to talk," he added. Without asking permission, he scooped her up again and set her back on his lap.

"Chandler!"

"When we were dancing, you called me, Mykal."

She went red-light still.

He added, "You've only called me Mykal twice since we met."

She couldn't deny that, or that both times had been because his kisses had turned her brain into oatmeal.

"Lean in," he invited softly again. "Like I said earlier, this wedding reception will probably be my one and only. I'd like to end the evening by holding my wife, even if she isn't real."

Sarita knew she was fighting a losing battle. Being with him was like being buffeted by high winds. She was rattled, torn, and yes, seduced by all that he was. His words had been spoken honestly, though, and hadn't she agreed to play this role? Swallowing her misgivings, she leaned in and placed her head against his chest.

As she settled in, Myk gently tightened his arms around her. The contact of her softness fired his blood. The sensations seared him so badly, he had to close his eyes against the sweet pain.

Sarita asked quietly, "You are going to behave, right?"

"Probably not."

She rose.

. He responded with a soft shrug. "I'm telling the truth."

She shook her head. "What am I going to do with you?"

"You tell me. . . ."

For a moment neither seemed able to speak. The heat of their attraction rose like steam. He traced the skin of her cheek. She trembled with sensual response.

"I'm waiting for an answer," he whispered, then grazed his lips across her jaw.

It took Sarita a moment to form words. "You're making it hard for me to think. . . ."

"Good . . ." he murmured, brushing his mouth against the perfumed warmth of the skin beneath her ear. "If we think, we may have to come to our senses."

Sarita could feel every inch of her body beginning to sing. *This is crazy,* she thought, but his lips were nearing hers, and what little sense she had left took flight.

The kiss was long, welcomed. The passion they'd been playing around with all evening rose up and opened the door to something they both knew was a bad idea but let consume them anyway. They fed slowly—inviting, learning, feeding each other. As happens, this initial taste was not enough, so he cuddled her tighter, closer. When his tongue moved enchantingly against the sensitive corners of her mouth, she groaned with pleasure. She didn't know her coat had fallen open until she felt his lips traveling down her arched throat to pay dizzying torrid tribute to the skin above the sapphire necklace.

Myk wanted her, her lips, her throat, the jeweled lobe of her ear. His hand slid into her coat and lazily began to explore the curves and valleys of her silk-encased body; he wanted to touch more. He husked out against her ear, "Baby, if you don't want me doing this, you need to say something, right now . . ."

Sarita was floating in a pleasure-filled fog. Her vision was hazy, her lips parted with passion. His big hands were lazily sliding all over her—tempting her, inviting her to experience a bliss intended solely for her delight. She was halfway to orgasm, and he hadn't even touched her inside of her clothes. The anticipation of that made her moan.

He teased a very expert finger over one nipple. "Tell me something . . ." he coaxed.

Speaking was the farthest thing from Sarita's mind. She was so hot and throbbing everywhere she didn't know how much more her body could take.

He eased down the zipper on the side of her dress, then without a word undid the front hook on her strapless ivory bra and freed her breasts. When he took one candy-hard nipple into his mouth, her orgasm broke, and she cried out.

Myk knew an orgasm when he heard one. He was surprised that she'd come so quickly, but the knowledge made him hard as hell.

Sarita came back to herself, shimmering. The echoes of her release pulsed between her thighs like the faint fading beats of a drum. She noted the warmth of his embrace and the sound of her own breathing. When she could speak again, she confessed quietly, "You probably don't think I'm very good at this."

"Good at what?"

"Sex."

Myk decided then and there that she had to be the fiercest, most honest woman he'd ever met. He squeezed her gently. "Why would I think that?"

"Because I came so quickly."

"There's nothing wrong with that." He reached down and teased his finger over her still-exposed pebble-hard nipple. "Are you always so—quick?"

Under his expert coaxing, Sarita felt the heat spring to life again. "Not usually, no, but with you—"

Their eyes met and held. Myk wanted more of her. No sense in lying. Like all males, though, he was pleased to hear that he was affecting her as much as she'd been affecting him.

"Don't get a big head," she chastised lightly. Even though she couldn't see him clearly, she was sure he was pleased with himself. "I've been celibate for the last year. I'm blaming my quickness on that."

He chuckled.

She smiled.

"Why celibacy?"

She shrugged. "After my last relationship ended, I decided it was easier. I—"

Suddenly the limo's door was open, and cold night wind came swirling inside. A panicked Sarita snatched her coat closed over her bare breasts, then shrank back against the shelter of Myk's broad chest.

"Dammit, Gee! Close that door!" Myk barked at his driver, Walter McGhee. The order was immediately followed, but Sarita was mortified. She and Chandler had been so much into each other that neither noticed that the car had stopped. They were home.

Myk said, "I guess we're here."

"Guess so."

He patted her on the butt. "Up. Let's go outside so I can kill Gee."

Sarita hastily tried to fix her clothes. Her nervous fingers couldn't rehook the bra, though, and as a result it wouldn't go back down beneath the top of her dress. Although he didn't say a word in response to her fumbling, she sensed his silent amusement. "Laugh, and I will punch you."

"Laughing never crossed my mind," he lied.

In the end, a frustrated Sarita gave up and had to settle for holding her coat tightly closed over her nakedness. How in the world she would ever be able to look Walter McGhee in the face was beyond her. She was sure he'd gotten an eyeful. She blamed it all on Chandler.

Sarita's plan to run straight to the house and avoid Walter didn't happen. The moment she and Myk stepped out of the limo, a female voice came out of the night, and called cheerily, "Myk, over here. I know you told me to come by your office Monday morning, but I thought I'd come tonight instead."

Faye.

Sarita rounded on him. The driveway's floodlights clearly showed his irritation.

The coolness Myk saw in Sarita's eyes made his mouth tighten. "It's business," he told her. "Strictly."

He then turned to Walter. "Take Sarita on into the house before she catches cold. You can head home after that."

Holding on to her coat and not caring whether Walter followed or not, Sarita turned and went inside.

Myk was so mad at Faye for showing up like this he wanted to chase her away with a stick. His plan had been to whisk Sarita inside, strip off that dress, and slowly begin again. Instead, he was standing out in the cold knowing Faye was there to cause trouble. Well, he'd deal with her now because after tonight he wouldn't have to deal with her ever again.

When she reached his side, she said, "I hope my showing up like this won't cause trouble in paradise."

Myk noted that she didn't bother hiding the bitterness in her voice. "Let's just go in and get this over with."

Faye raised her chin and headed to the door.

Upstairs in her room, Sarita tossed her coat onto the bed. She knew she had no reason being upset over Miss Faye's showing up, but it didn't matter. She was. Sarita slid the zipper down on her dress just far enough to strip off the offending bra. She sent it sailing onto the bed, too. On her way to the closet, she happened to catch a glimpse of herself in the mirror of the vanity table. She stopped. Her bared breasts had spilled over the partially opened gown. The sapphires sparkled like blue stars against her brown skin. She paused and studied the reflection. She looked like an erotic painting. Her nipples were hard, her lips parted. She could still feel Chandler's lips on her breasts, and the heat of that white-hot orgasm. *Lord!* She raised wondrous fingers to her lips. *What a man!*

Putting him out of her mind—after all he was downstairs with Faye—Sarita turned away from her reflection and slid the zipper the rest of the way down. She was just getting ready to step out of the dress when a rap on the door froze her in motion. Before she could say anything it swung open and a surprised Sarita watched Chandler walk in. The way his hot eyes traveled over her made her slowly drag the dress up to cover herself. "Whatever happened to 'May I come in'?" she asked coolly.

Myk had never been with a woman who made him hard each and every time he saw her. "I apologize. I—"

"Turn around."

He didn't want to, she could see it in his eyes, but for the first time, he actually did what she asked. She used the moment to slip back into the dress. She didn't bother retrieving her bra because that would take time. Yes, he had touched her, and yes, he'd made her orgasm in the backseat of his limo, but that didn't mean she was going to be parading around like a stripper in a video.

"Now you can turn back."

When he did, his disappointment was plain.

She ignored the glimmer of mischief in his eyes. "Done with the Faye business?"

"No. She's waiting downstairs."

"Then why are you up here?"

"Making sure you're okay."

Sarita found that heartwarming. "I am."

"Want to meet Faye?"

"No," she said shaking her head and chuckling, "Maybe another time."

"Too bad."

"Why?"

"Trying to see how much madder I can make her."

"Why is she so mad?"

"Because I married you."

Sarita wondered if clothes made out of lead would keep her from feeling the heat of his desire on her skin. The silk gown she was wearing was way too thin to offer any protection. "Oh."

"She brought me her bills."

"Why?"

"So I can pay them."

That surprised Sarita. "Are you going to?"

"Yes."

"Why?"

"Because it'll get her out of my life for good."

"Is it a lot—the total bills I mean?" The sum he quoted made Sarita's jaw drop. "And you're going to pay it!"

He nodded.

"You're crazy," she said. "No way in the world would I pay off some hoochie's bills."

Myk smiled inwardly. If he could bottle her energy and sell it, he'd be the richest man in the world by far. "I think Faye would prefer to be called a gold digger."

Sarita said sarcastically, "Right."

Myk couldn't contain his laughter.

Sarita noted the rare sound and smiled. "You probably shouldn't keep her waiting."

"You're right." But Faye was the farthest thing from his mind. He hadn't meant to burst in on Sarita unannounced as he had, but the memory of her nude in his hands had been permanently burned into his mind. He could see her bra on the bed, which meant her breasts were bare beneath the silk gown. "Sure you don't want to join me?"

The soft-spoken invitation coupled with his own unique magnetism played havoc with Sarita's hold on herself. Nothing was sure where he was concerned.

He asked, "Will you come if I promise to behave myself?"

His sultry tone stoked Sarita's desire like wood thrown on a fire. She'd never been around a man who could verbally seduce so well. The double entendre of the word, *come*, turned up the heat even higher. "Women don't tell you no, do they."

"Not often."

"They should," she stated, even as she felt her nipples hardening shamelessly. "You're way too good at this."

Myk smiled. "Glad you're having a good time."

And she was, strangely enough. A few days ago they had been at each other's throats, and on the ride back to his house, she'd called him a kidnapper, but now? Now, she began to tremble as he approached her slowly.

Standing in front of her, Myk reached out and traced her soft mouth. "All of your lipstick's gone. . . ."

"Talk to the man who's been kissing me," she whispered. "It's his fault. . . ."

The kiss that came next was inevitable. Neither had gotten enough on the short ride home, and they passionately corrected that. He nibbled her bottom lip, and she teased her tongue lazily against his. Hands roamed, and the sounds of heightened breathing floated in the silence.

"I thought you were going back downstairs . . . ?" she asked him in between his now lazy kisses.

"In a minute."

He captured her mouth again; wanting nothing more out of life than the tastes, scents and feel of her, just like this. Every inch of his being wanted to carry her over to the bed and feast. To that end, he began to slide her zipper down.

Loving his kisses, Sarita clamped her hands on top of his to stop their progress. "You have to go . . ."

He mumbled something that sounded like agreement, but she couldn't be sure because her hearing was being overridden by the feel of his hot lips meandering over the skin of her throat and the soft tops of her breasts. Her hold on his hands melted away, freeing them to tease her nipples until they were hard in vibrant response. "Mykal . . ."

He raised his mouth to hers, "What?" he asked. "I'm trying to stop . . ."

He slid the zipper down so he could fill his palms with her silk-soft breasts. Giving in to a purely male need, he dropped his head and pleasured her until she was gasping. His manhood was roaring like a jet engine. If he didn't get a full taste of her soon, he was going to burst.

He breathed huskily, "Okay. I'm stopping . . . We can go downstairs, now." Holding her in the circle of his arms, Myk looked down into her beautiful face and couldn't ever remember going to such lengths to seduce a woman before.

Sarita wasn't ready to go anywhere; she could just about imagine how she looked with her lips all swollen and her eyes half-closed. "I can't go down there looking like this. She's going to know what we've been doing."

He didn't respond.

Sarita leaned back to study his face for a moment. Then it came to her. "That's what you want her to see."

She had to hand it to him; he didn't look away when she hit the nail on the head. "This really is a game with you, isn't it?" Sarita could feel anger replacing everything she'd felt up to that point. Why did she keep forgetting. She tried to back out of his arms, but he wouldn't let her go.

Myk didn't lie. "Yes, it's a game, but you and I are the only players. Faye has nothing to do with us. Period."

She eyed him a moment, then asked, "Does paying off her bills and getting her out of your life have anything to do with the way we met?"

Myk went still at the accuracy of her guess. Faye was trouble all the way around. With her out of his life, NIA would have one less security concern. "Yes," he replied finally.

"Took you a while to answer," Sarita pointed out.

"Wanted to say the right thing."

"Uh-huh." Sarita didn't believe him for a minute. More than likely he was deciding how much of the truth he needed to share. She backed out of his arms and zipped her dress again. "You know, if you told me what this is all about—"

"Not tonight, okay."

Sarita saw the seriousness in his face. "Okay." She supposed tonight was not a night for such a discussion. They hadn't argued all day, and she wanted that record to continue. In reality, Sarita did want to see Faye up close, if only to see the kind of woman he'd been attracted to once upon a time. "I suppose it won't hurt to meet her. Should I go down and clown? Put my hands on my hips and tell her ghetto style to stay away from my man?"

He grinned. "Let's save the stereotypes for another time."

She grinned back. "Let me brush my hair right quick, and we can go."

Myk had asked Faye to take a seat in the big sitting room off the foyer. When he finally returned with Sarita in tow, her flashing hazel eyes told him exactly what she thought of being kept waiting. He ignored her displeasure and made the introductions. "Faye Riley. My wife, Sarita."

"Ah, I finally get to meet your little wife," Faye stood, and the rose pink dress shimmered like a starry night. Her striking five-foot-ten-inch height matched Chandler's height well.

Sarita took instant offense at the condescending tone, and responded coolly, "Pleased to meet you." Sarita then told Chandler, "I'll leave you two alone."

"No, stay," he responded. "This won't take long."

Faye's chin rose, and her eyes darkened, but she

composed herself just as quickly. "Shall we sit?" she asked, as if this were her home. "I want to hear all about how you got him to the altar."

Sarita wasn't buying Faye's fakey-jakey smile. The anger radiating from behind Faye's light brown eyes made it clear she hated Sarita's guts.

Ten

Faye resettled herself elegantly in the big recliner, while Myk and Sarita sat side by side on the soft black leather couch. Sarita drew up her shoeless feet, as if wearing sweats instead of a designer gown, and cuddled close to Chandler's side. He swung an arm out to surround her, and she made herself comfortable.

Myk smiled down at Sarita's unexpected show of docility. To demonstrate his pleasure he placed a soft kiss on her lips. Afterward, he reluctantly returned his attention to Faye. "Now, where were we?"

Faye was furious. She wanted to reach over and snatch Sarita out of his arms, but Faye was above such ghetto drama. "You know," she told Sarita, "Myk's marriage surprised everyone. How long have you known him?"

"A while." Sarita had no intention of telling this woman any more than that.

Faye wasn't satisfied. "How long is a while? A week, a month, a year?"

Myk answered, "It doesn't matter, Faye. That's not why you're here."

Anger flashed across her beautiful face, then faded. "I'm not trying to be nosy, Myk," she reassured him with a deep-throated laugh. "I mean after all, a month ago you and I were shall I say, quite tight, so a little curiosity is natural on my part—wouldn't you think?"

Sarita rolled her eyes.

Myk wasn't in the mood for prolonging her visit. Back at the reception he'd told Faye that his relationship with Sarita was none of her business. The only reason he hadn't shown Faye the door already was the knowledge that he'd have to deal with her all over again on Monday. At least when Sarita defied him it was over a principle. Faye's only principle was a dollar sign.

Faye had to admit the meeting was not going the way she'd planned. In spite of the angry words she and Myk exchanged at the reception, she still refused to believe it was over between them. It suddenly crossed her mind that maybe he was just pretending to do this in order to keep his little ghetto queen from learning the truth. That had to be it. She decided to overlook the way he kept rubbing his finger idly against the edge of her jaw as if he'd been doing it for a lifetime. "Well, Myk. Now that I've met Shaniqua, I really think we should conduct our business in private."

Myk could hear Sarita growl softly in response to being called out of her name. He leaned down and brushed his lips against her ear, "Settle down, warrior princess."

She smiled up at him, but whispered back, "If she calls me that again, it will be on."

Chuckling in response to the threat, Myk told Faye, "We aren't going to be discussing anything she can't hear so hurry up. I want to take my wife to bed."

Faye's responding voice was cold, "Fine." Faye hated the way the bride's eyes slowly slid closed as he continued his innocent stroking. It brought back the memories of those same sure hands on her own skin: Not that she'd enjoyed doing the *wild thang*. Faye only tolerated sex; it mussed her hair and made men sweat all over her, but she put up with it because it usually got her what she wanted. "These have to be paid," she stated. The *these* referred to the fat stack of bills in her manicured hand.

As the two former lovers discussed Faye's financial obligations, Sarita looked on silently, amazed. Furriers, jewelers, rent, car notes, hairdressers, florists, and credit card statements. You name it, Faye owed it.

Faye added finally, "And if they can all be paid by the end of the month, I'd much appreciate it."

Myk replied emotionlessly, "Leave them on the table."

Sarita wondered how he could be so calm. Granted, he probably had the money to take care of the bills, but goodness. And Faye sat there as if she had every right to have them paid.

Faye was careful not to show her reaction but she found Myk's acceptance of the situation surprising. Maybe she'd been right after all about his not wanting their relationship to end. As far as she knew, no brother in his right mind would agree to cover so much debt without an argument, unless he was planning keep the lady around—or paying her off. She turned to Myk with panic-stricken eyes.

Myk read the final understanding in her alarmed face, and in response explained smoothly, "From now on your bills are all your own, Faye. I've turned off your all your credit cards and closed down your charge accounts."

"But—" She caught herself; she wouldn't beg. A month ago, she'd been so sure of her hold on him. Now? She picked up her beaded clutch, and the blue fox stole, and rose to her feet. "Then, I suppose, this is good-bye, Myk. Thanks for everything. I would say I hope you and Shaniqua will be very happy, but I'd be a hypocrite."

Myk didn't feel sorry for her. She'd cost him a pretty penny during the time they'd been together, plus, she'd known the ground rules from the get.

Faye looked over at the happy couple, not sure which one she hated most. "Don't get up. I'll see myself out."

In the silence left behind after Faye's huffy exit, Sarita cracked, "Well, that was a nice way to end the evening. Do you always pay the bills of the women you kick to the curb?"

"No."

"Then she must have been special?"

"Not really. She's classy and looks good on a brother's arm, but that's about it."

"Is that all you want, is for your lady to be classy and look good on your arm?"

Myk was certain he'd said the wrong thing, but wasn't sure what. "Is that a trick question?"

"No," she said shrugging. "It just speaks to the kind of person you are, that's all."

"And that means?"

She could hear the undertone in his voice but she ignored it. "Have you ever loved any of your girlfriends?"

Myk couldn't lie. "No."

"Were they all classy and pretty like Faye?"

"Yeah."

"So you just have them around for show?"

"Mostly."

"That's a pretty cold statement."

He supposed it did sound that way, but he didn't apologize. "With my work schedule, I don't have time for commitment, and the women I hook up with know that up front."

"And they don't mind those rules?"

"Not when I buy them fur coats for their birthdays or take them to Antigua for Christmas."

Sarita studied him. "This may sound stupid and corny, but I want my man to love me for me," she said, pointing to herself for emphasis. "Not because I look good on his arm or because I know how to toss my hair."

He ran a slow finger down the sleek short hair that she wore so well. "Not much to toss."

"You know what I mean."

He nodded, then said, "I do."

"Besides, the women in my family have always had strong marriages. My great-great, oh I don't know how many greats, grandmother came to Michigan from California in the 1870s to be a doctor, and fell in love with my many-greats-grandfather even though she had to shoot his hat off his head to get his attention."

Myk snorted a laugh. "What?"

"She shot his hat off."

"Why?"

"He wouldn't let her practice medicine in his town."

"Why not?"

"Because she was female."

"So, she shot his hat off?"

"Yep."

"So, you come from a long line of out-of-control women then."

"Yes," she replied with pride. "We Grayson women do not play."

She went suddenly silent, and Myk looked down to see her eyes focused on something he couldn't see. "What's the matter?" he asked quietly.

His words made her look up. "Nothing. Just realizing that I'm probably going to be the last of those out-of-control women. As far as I know, I'm the only Grayson left."

"You don't want children?"

"Yes, but I'd like a husband first. I'm old-school that way."

Why Myk found her confession pleasing he didn't know. He and Drake had talked about kids a few times in the past, but having kids had always been Drake's dream, not Myk's. Myk was content to be Uncle Myk. "And if you don't find one?"

She shrugged. "Adoption maybe. I don't know, but the biological line will stop with me."

Myk could just about imagine her daughter; she would be just as fine and sassy as her mama. "If you want to get married, I'm sure some brother will come along."

She snorted. "I doubt it. The men I hook up with always wind up wanting me to be somebody else— their mama, sister, cousin. I just want to be me, Sarita. They can't seem to handle that though. One brother told me I was too much of a crusader to be his lady. He said I spent more time at the center than I did with him."

"And did you?"

"Well, yes." When she heard herself she quieted, then said, "I won't apologize for helping people who need it."

"And you never should."

Sarita was glad he understood. Few men did, or so it seemed. Her goals and aspirations were always looked upon as little more than a hobby that she would grow out of eventually.

His cell phone rang suddenly, and he grimaced. Reaching into his pocket he extracted it, and said to her, "Sorry. Excuse me a minute."

Sarita got up from the couch to give him some privacy. She walked over to the fireplace and stood looking into the flames. From behind her she heard him say into the phone. "Okay, hold on." Then, "Sarita?"

She turned.

"I'm sorry. I need to take this. I'll see you in the morning."

Sarita was quite taken aback by such an abrupt ending to the evening, but kept the reaction out of her face. "Sure. Good night."

Tight-lipped, Myk watched her leave. As she closed the double doors behind her, he sighed regretfully, then turned his attention to the voice on the phone.

Surrounded by the dark, Sarita lay in bed thinking about the man downstairs. Truth be told, she was glad the phone had rung when it did. Who knew what might have happened had they not been interrupted. Would he have invited her to his bed? Maybe. If he had, would she have said yes? Parts of herself answered, *yes*, while other parts screamed, *no!* In a way, she wished she could have met him under normal circumstances because then she'd have no reason to be wary of who he was. But in reality, she really knew no more about him than she had the night she shot him in the elevator. Well, she did know that he could arouse the woman inside herself with just the sound of his voice, and that he had a seductiveness about him that bordered on the magical. The only other thing she knew about him for sure was that he and Saint were mixed up in something that had cost her her freedom.

On one level she appreciated their concerns for her safety; she didn't necessarily agree with their temporary solution, but that was water under the bridge. On another level she wanted to know what was going on, just in case there was no cavalry around when the time came for her to fight her way out of the

Alamo. Maybe if she explained her concerns to Chandler that way, he'd be more forthcoming about whatever she was embroiled in. She didn't think so, but made a note to give it a shot anyway.

She turned over and snuggled deeper into the bedding. When the time came for her to return to her former life, she'd miss this bed a lot. It was big enough to swim in, and the sheets and blankets were luxurious. At home, her mattress was so old and battered that the ground in her backyard was more comfortable; this, however, was heaven.

She glanced over at the clock on the nightstand. The lighted dial read ten after one. A yawn escaped her. She had no idea how she and Chandler would act toward each other in the morning, but right now, she was too sleepy to care. Her eyes closed, and as she drifted into sleep, her last thoughts were of him and his whispered promises to make love to her beneath the stars.

At 2 A.M., a uniformed policeman knocked on the door of the Detroit hotel room occupied by Clark Nelson. Nelson's bodyguard let the cop in, then disappeared into one of the back bedrooms so Clark and the cop could meet privately.

The cop didn't waste any time. "Fishbein's party girls were sent over by a small-time player named Fletcher Harris. He was popped the same night. Here's the report." He passed Clark a manila folder.

Clark asked, "Do the cops know the girls are dead?"

"Word just came down this afternoon."

"The St. Louis detectives have any leads on the shooters?"

"No and they won't. My crew and I made sure the hits were clean."

Clark was pleased to be working with someone who knew their job and did it well. The girls were dead, and that was one less issue. He reached into the pocket of his smoking jacket and pulled out a sealed envelope stuffed with the hundred-dollar bills the cop was owed for his services.

The man took the envelope and stuffed it into the pocket of his blue pants. "You need anything else, you know how to get in touch."

Clark nodded, and the policeman left the room.

For the first time in days, Clark allowed himself a smile. There were advantages to having cops on the payroll. Here in Detroit the number of policemen willing to do business on Clark's behalf was small, but the few who were were good. He pulled the reports out of the file and skimmed over the details.

Apparently the girls had talked up a storm before their demise. They'd given Clark's man answers to all of his questions about this Fletcher Harris except how he'd known about the diamonds. Clark wasn't really concerned about that now; his concern lay with the scattered surviving members of the Harris crew. They probably held the key to the diamonds, which is why Clark's people were out looking for them. He didn't think it would take long.

At 3 A.M., Myk was still up and working. The phone call that ended his evening with Sarita had been from one of NIA's down South government contacts. She'd called to relay the latest information on Fletcher's two dead party girls. The autopsy had turned up some interesting but gruesome facts. The women had been worked over pretty good. Fingers were broken; some in more than one place. A large-caliber bullet was found in the kneecap of one, and both earlobes had been severed on the other. Someone had tracked them down, then gone to great pains to hurt them before eventually taking their lives.

Myk had the contact fax him the full autopsy report. When it arrived about an hour before, the reading of if left him grim. What had begun as a side operation into the tracking of illegal African diamonds had evolved into something far more life-threatening; especially now that the next life being threatened might be that of the woman he called his wife. He thought back on the evening. Just the memories of her sitting on his lap made him hard all over again. He pushed aside the distracting remembrances and concentrated on the matter at hand. Since the night he met Sarita, NIA had been quietly trying to discover who Fishbein's bookies had gotten the diamonds from and who Fishbein's connection in Detroit would have been had Fletcher not sent Sarita in to mess everything up. The Chicago bookies, Russian emigrants, had been hauled in by the Feds for questioning, but the men were only talking through their lawyer, so progress was slow. At first, Fishbein hadn't been very cooperative about describing the women either, mostly out of fear that the bookies would harm his family, but after the Federal agents promised Fishbein protection for them, he'd loosened up enough to give the sketch artist detailed descriptions. The pictures were shown to the hotel's security people and a make was made right away. The women worked for a local escort service and were in and out of the hotel all the time. Their names:

Candy Shaw and Iris Pierce, both nineteen. The escort service's owner swore he knew nothing about the Fishbein date, claiming the girls were freelancing that night as they did sometimes. Now, they were dead.

It came to Myk then, that since Sarita knew Fletcher, she might also know the women. She hadn't been questioned since the night Saint brought her there. How to ask her without revealing the essence of his own involvement was the problem, however. The lady in question was no dummy; sexy and smart, yes; dummy, no. He wouldn't be surprised if she already knew what was going on. He ran his hand over his hair. This was not the way his plan was supposed to work. He was supposed to get a beautiful but empty-headed woman to pose as his wife, not one who seemed to grow more fascinating by the day. The phone call that ended the evening had been a godsend. Who knew where they might have wound up. More than likely his bed. Even now, he couldn't turn off sweet taste of her mouth or the remembered feel of her soft breasts against the palms of his hands. He walked over to the bank of monitors mounted on the wall and looked in on her. The room was dark. She was sleeping. He imagined what it might be like to wake up next to her and run his hand slowly over her sleep-warmed skin. He quickly cut the picture. The reception and all its hoopla was over. He needed to go to bed. Thinking about her was becoming a habit he couldn't afford to have no matter how much he wanted her.

Eleven

Sarita came downstairs unsure where she and Chandler stood after last night, but her plan was to follow his lead. She hoped seeing him wouldn't remind her of the orgasm he'd brought her to, but the moment she walked into the breakfast room, and he turned from the windows to face her, the memories came roaring back so ferociously, she had to draw in a shaky breath to steady herself. "Good morning," she said with a flippancy she didn't feel. "Did you sleep well?"

Myk wanted to whisk her back upstairs, undress her, and slowly finish what they had left unfinished. "Good morning. I did," he lied. Only he knew that he'd dreamed about her in such hot and wicked ways that he'd awakened this morning hard as a concrete beam.

Sarita could feel the heat in his eyes licking over

her, but she forced herself to not to show it. "Are we going for breakfast?"

"Yes, the St. Regis, if that's okay?"

"That's fine." Even a poor girl like Sarita knew about the St. Regis Hotel's fabulous Sunday Brunch. She'd never experienced it, but she'd heard about it.

Myk couldn't take his eyes off her in her hot black leather pants. The red cashmere sweater unwittingly emphasized the soft roundness of her breasts. The hoops in her ears made him remember the warm scents he'd discovered there the previous night. "I eat there pretty regularly on Sundays."

"No church?"

He shook his head, "No. You?"

"Yes. Most Sundays in fact. St. Mary's on Canfield and Van Dyke."

"Catholic?"

"Episcopalian."

The simple conversation was nothing more than small talk to cover the volatile undercurrents flowing between them. She sensed it wouldn't be much longer before everything exploded. "I'll get my coat."

When she went out into the foyer, it was if she'd stepped into a kaleidoscope. The sun was shining through the stained-glass atrium above her head, casting rays of tinted light onto the dark wood below. For the first time she could see the patterns in the leaded glass clearly, and her mouth dropped in awe. Dragons. Beautifully entwined dragons, some purple, others gold. The night of Sarita's first visit, Lily had mentioned something about the dragons being asleep, and Sarita hadn't a clue as to what the

housekeeper meant. At last, Sarita understood. The
dragons looked as if they were playing in the sun-
shine.

"Is this the first time you've seen them?" Myk
asked.

Sarita had been so fascinated she hadn't noticed
him walk out to join her. "Yes."

He pointed up. "The indigo-colored ones are the
females. The gold ones, the males. This glass has
been in my family over a hundred years."

Sarita had never seen anything like it before.
"Why dragons?"

"My many-greats-grandfather had a thing for
them. The purple ones represent his wife Hester, the
gold ones, himself. His name was Galeno Vachon."

Sarita met his eyes. "He must have loved her very
much to commission something this beautiful."

"He did. She was a conductor on the underground railroad, and he was a slave stealer."

"He owned slaves?"

"No, he helped slaves escape and led them north.
That's how they met. He was pretty famous in his
day, according to my grandmother. They lived here
in Detroit after they married."

Sarita thought she could stare up at the dragons
all day. "They're beautiful. He must have been
pretty well-off to be able to afford this back then."

"He was."

"Is that where you get your extravagant ways?"

He shrugged and smiled wryly. "I suppose."

Their eyes met, and once again Sarita could feel
her body responding to his unspoken call. "Did Faye
like the dragons?"

"No, she thought the stained glass was old-fashioned. Wanted me to replace it with something clear and modern."

"I'd never take it down."

That pleased Myk. "My grandmother would be happy to hear you say that."

"Is she still alive?"

"Yep. Eighty years old and still kickin'. She loves the dragons."

Sarita wondered if she would ever get to meet this grandmother. "This can't be your grandfather Galen's original house, can it?"

"No. The original house stood about where the mayor's mansion is now. When Galen's descendants moved back to his home in Louisiana in 1900, they dismantled the glass and took it with them. The dragons were part of a huge door back then."

"Well, they're fabulous. Very cool."

In her own way, she's fabulous too, Myk thought to himself.

The brunch at the St. Regis Hotel turned out to be just as wonderful as Sarita had imagined. There was an endless array of breakfast and lunch fare, with everything from the standard eggs Benedict and sausage, to waffles, fried catfish, grits, and four different varieties of cheesecake. There were so many mouth-watering dishes to choose from she had a difficult time deciding, but she managed to build a plate to her liking. Once she was done, she walked over to join Chandler in the small booth, and took her seat.

He surveyed her plate, and said with amusement, "You don't eat enough to keep a ladybug alive."

Sarita looked down at what she considered a

piled-high plate. "I may go back for more later, but a buffet is all you can eat, Chandler. Not all you can *carry*," she cracked, indicating his bulging plate.

"Hey, I'm a growing boy," he explained.

Grinning, she shook her head, then started in on her food.

"I didn't get the chance to ask you last night, but did you have a good time?"

Sarita raised her eyes to his. "I did. It'll probably be my only wedding reception, too, so thanks for the memories."

"You're welcome."

Sarita didn't want to discuss the more sensual details of the evening, so she concentrated on cutting her waffle into manageable pieces. "Where does your grandmother live?"

"Outside Baton Rouge."

"I've never been to Louisiana."

"I try and get down there once or twice a season. She fusses if I don't."

"You sound like you care for her a lot?"

"I do. She's a real firecracker."

"Are your parents still alive?"

"No."

The terse response made her think he didn't want to discuss his parents, so she left it alone.

Myk sensed he'd spoken more harshly than he'd intended. "Sorry, if I snapped."

"Apology accepted. I didn't mean to pry."

They ate in silence for a few moments more, then Myk said, "I never knew my father. My mother abandoned me at the hospital the day after I was born."

Sarita felt her heart break.

"My father's mother raised me."

"Drake, too?"

"No. Drake's mother was a widow with four daughters when our father blew into her life. He left her with a broken heart and a son."

"You two seem to get along well."

"Yes, we do, strangely enough. We're pretty different though."

"You think so?"

He nodded, "Drake's pretty laid-back. Me, I'm more—"

"Intense?"

He chuckled. "I'll take that. Yeah, intense."

They ate in silence for a few more moments, then Sarita said, "You didn't have to tell me all that."

"I know. I wanted you to know."

"I was raised by my grandmother, too. It's something we have in common."

Myk realized she was right. "Did your grandmother make you take piano lessons?"

"No, did yours?"

"Yes, from age four."

Sarita stared. "You play the piano?"

"Yes. Hated it at first. Loved it after I learned to appreciate it. Only music she allowed in the house was Duke Ellington. By the time I was twelve, I could play all of his standards and many of the not so standard."

"Like what? I've heard of the 'A Train' and 'Satin Doll,' but that's about it. What would be a nonstandard to someone like me?"

"Ever heard of a tune called 'Passion Flower'?"

"No."

"Written by Duke's boy, Billy Strayhorn. It has

more horns than piano, but it's one of my grand-mother's favorites."

"I'd like to hear it sometime."

"Okay."

Sarita couldn't imagine him as a little boy practic-ing chords while his grandmother looked on. Only hours earlier she'd bemoaned the fact that she knew very little about him, but now? She knew he'd been abandoned as an infant and had a thing for Elling-ton. There was more to him than she'd imagined.

His voice interrupted her thoughts, "I know I promised you we'd go to the center tomorrow, but I've meetings, until three. It'll have to be after that. Sorry."

She sighed. She'd wanted to go first thing in the morning.

"If I could dump the meetings, I would, but I can't."

"It's okay," she lied. At least it would be tomor-row and not next week sometime.

He asked then, "I've a question for you."

"Shoot."

"Do you know a Candy Shaw or an Iris Pierce?"

"Nope. Should I?"

"They're the dead women I told you about last night. Thought since you knew Fletcher Harris, you might know them, too."

Sarita shook her head, saying, "No, I don't. What are you trying to find out?"

"Just trying to fit all the pieces into the puzzle."

When he didn't say anything else, she knew the conversation was closed but decided to press a point anyway, "Suppose you're not around when whatever is going on reaches out and grabs me? Don't you think I could maybe defend myself better if I knew what was going on?"

Myk did, but he was torn. The night before, on the phone, he and Saint had toyed with the idea of telling her everything, but Myk wanted to run it by the others before making a decision.

When he didn't respond, she said, "I can't fight what I can't see, Chandler."

"I know."

But it was all he said. Sarita sighed her frustration.

He told her frankly, "I won't let anybody hurt you."

"Thanks, and I mean that genuinely, but sometimes a damsel in distress doesn't need a knight. Sometimes she just needs a map of the castle so she can get out on her own."

He grinned softly. "I hear you."

"Does that mean I get a map?"

"I'll let you know."

"When?"

"Soon."

"I'm holding you to that."

"I know."

They went back to their meals.

When they returned to the house, Myk walked her back into the den. "I have some work I need to catch up on, and it's going to take me most of the day. So I'm going to apologize up front for leaving you on your own."

Sarita told herself she wasn't disappointed, but she was lying. "Don't worry about me. I'll be fine."

"Are you sure?"

"Positive."

"You won't try and leave the minute my back's turned?"

She studied him for a moment, then smiled ruefully. "Worried, are you?"

"Maybe."

"Good. I don't want you taking me for granted."

"Never."

His husky tone made her heart beat fast. "Go to work, Chandler. I promise to be here when you come up for air."

Myk had never met a woman like her. She was playful, sexy, and cockier than any female had a right to be. He wanted to kiss her until she pleaded his name. "I'll see you for dinner."

"Is there anything in your freezer?"

He eyed her curiously. "Probably. Why?"

"Because I'm cooking dinner."

He raised an eyebrow. "Oh, really?"

"You have a problem with that?"

"No. As long as my kitchen is still standing when you're done."

Her hand went to her hip. "I'm not the one who set off the smoke detector."

He had the decency to look embarrassed. "What time's dinner?"

"Six or so okay with you?"

"That's fine. The fire extinguisher's under the sink there."

Sarita cut him a playful look of warning. "I'll see you later."

Myk watched her head upstairs to her room. Who knew having a woman in the house would be so delightful.

* * *

Later that afternoon, Sarita went to start dinner in a kitchen she considered a cook's heaven. She'd only had a brief encounter with the space the morning she'd cooked breakfast, but now had the time to check out the place at her leisure. Every modern appliance known to woman was either built in or hidden inside the banks of buffed-wood cabinets covering the walls. In the middle of the room was a large black marble island complete with double sink and a gas cooktop. There was a big walk-in pantry and a stand-up freezer filled with meat. Sarita found everything she needed from measuring spoons to baking powder.

Sarita spent a moment just taking in the kitchen's beauty. She liked the soft yellow paint on the walls; the old-fashioned sheer white curtains on the French doors; the many many cupboards. After washing her hands in the other double sink near the dishwasher, she went to work.

Sarita was standing over the stove stirring the sausage in a skillet for the jambalaya when the back door opened. In walked Walter McGhee. Seeing him made her remember last night, and she was embarrassed all over again.

He didn't appear comfortable either, but he nodded politely, "Afternoon, Mrs. Chandler."

"Hi. Call me, Sarita, please."

"I'll do that."

There was an awkward silence, then he asked, "Where's the man?"

"Working." Sarita had no idea where his room was, or if he worked in a separate office area, or what. Much of the big house was still a mystery to her.

Walter said quietly, "I didn't mean to embarrass you last night."

Sarita tried to concentrate on the browning meat. "I know."

"I didn't expect—"

"It's okay. You had no way of knowing—" Sarita really wanted this conversation to be over. She felt as if her face was beet red.

Walter added with sincerity, "Myk and I spend a lot of time together and—I don't want you to be uncomfortable around me."

Sarita faced him. "We're fine, Walter. Really we are."

"You sure?"

"Yes."

He smiled, "Good." He then added, "So, what's in the pot?"

She grinned. "Sausage for jambalaya."

"Jambalaya? You can cook?"

"Stay for dinner and find out."

He smiled. "I'll do that. Now, though, I need to see the boss."

"Before you go? Do you know if there's a small TV somewhere I can put in here?"

"Yeah. Use Lily's."

Before she could ask where it was kept, Walter picked up a remote from the island top and pointed it. Out of the edge of the island a TV rose.

Sarita stared in amazement.

Walter smiled at the awe on her face. "Lily had Myk install it last year so she could watch her stories in here."

"Now that is cool."

He grinned. "Yeah, it is, isn't it?"

"Punch up the game. Let's see how bad the home team's going to get whipped this week."

"A fan?"

" 'Til I die. My great-uncles started taking me to games when I was eight. Loved football with a passion ever since."

"Well, all right," he said with approval. "You're a lady after my own heart."

That said, they put Saturday's embarrassing event behind them and started anew.

Walter watched the game for a few minutes, then headed off to find Chandler.

Upstairs, Walter knocked softly on the door to the War Room, identified himself, and walked inside.

Myk was going over reports. He looked up. "Hey, is my kitchen on fire yet?"

Walter grinned, "Not so far. She's making jambalaya."

Myk's surprise etched his face. "You're kidding."

"Nope. She invited me to stay and eat. If that's okay with you, of course."

"That's fine with me. Jambalaya, huh?"

Walter nodded, then said, "I apologized for embarrassing her last night."

"Good. I wanted you dead."

"I figured that. What're you doing?"

"Looking over the numbers from our charm school."

Walter chuckled, "How are the debs doing?"

"Called out there earlier this morning and talked to Blue. He said things are going well. Considering."

Blue Reynolds was an ex-Marine. He and his handpicked staff ran the NIA rehab camp. "He says the gangbangers weren't too happy finding out they were now living in the middle of nowhere. Ninety percent of them don't even know where Wyoming is. The first group we sent spent the first morning cursing and threatening the staff—until the instructors came in."

"Nothing like fifteen or twenty retired drill sergeants to change your attitude," Walter put in with a grin.

Myk smiled. "After a few days of doing laps and push-ups, he says everybody's starting to settle down."

The rehab camps were parts of Drake's vision. He wanted to take those kids who were the hardest core and try to mold them into productive, contributing members of society by physically removing them from their home environment and plunging them into one filled with hard work, strict discipline, and education. Since there was not a gang member in the city who would willingly go along with such an idea, given the choice, the mayor's program eliminated choice with the help of the juveniles' parents, child social services, and the courts. At present there were thirty-five enrolled, aged twelve to fifteen. The camp, set on a ranch in Wyoming, began operations less than a month earlier. Drake had no doubts the program would succeed; Myk hoped his brother was right.

"Saint call back?" Walter asked.

"Not today, so far. He's trying to run down Fletcher's boys."

"The ones who went south after Fletcher got popped?"

"Yeah. Our friends at the FBI think whoever

killed the ladies may now know about Fletcher's role, and, if so, we need to find his boys first."

"And we still don't know who gave the bookies the diamonds?"

"No, and so far, they aren't telling."

Walter and Myk spent the next hour sifting through faxes, reports, and notes sent in by NIA operatives on various projects. There were photos of snitches to ID, names of dealers that needed cross-referencing in Federal law enforcement data banks, budget requests to consider, and a lot of other issues demanding attention that would have overwhelmed someone lacking Myk's organizational expertise; but he had an eye for detail, and a calm about his leadership that kept everything and everybody up to speed.

Myk lifted his head and sniffed the air in his office a few times. "Is that chicken frying?"

Walter lifted his nose to the wind. "Smells like it to me."

Myk went over to the monitors and brought up the kitchen. There she stood, frying fork in one hand, yelling at the game on TV. "Why is she watching football?"

"Says she's a fan."

Myk turned and stared. "Really?"

"Said her uncles started taking her to games when she was eight."

They could see her banging her fork on the counter. Myk hit the button to bring up the room's sound just in time to hear her yell, "Catch the damn ball! A squirrel with one arm could've caught that pass!"

Myk looked over at Walter, who asked with a

slow grin, "I take it, Saint didn't tell you about this part?"

As they continued to watch her berate the home team for its inability to score on fourth and goal, Myk answered, "I think Saint didn't tell me about a lot of things."

Dinner consisted of jambalaya, fried chicken wings, and the lightest corn bread Myk had ever tasted. "I knew you could cook breakfast, but you can *cook*, can't you?"

Sarita smiled mockingly. "No kidding."

Walter was too busying savoring his jambalaya to state an opinion, but his silence said it all. "Mmmm," was all anyone heard.

After dinner, Myk and Walter helped with the cleanup, and soon, the dishwasher was loaded, the leftovers were put away, and the kitchen was as spotless as before.

Myk and Walter excused themselves to head back upstairs, and Sarita settled into the recliner in the den and clicked on the TV. The home team had lost, again, and the local news had just begun. The female reporter, one of the best in the city, was doing a special report on a rash of crack house busts. Sarita sat forward. This was her first real look at the news since her confinement, and she hadn't heard anything about the busts. According to the reporter, over the last eight weeks, there been sixteen similar incidents in various parts of the city. What made the busts unusual and, therefore, newsworthy was that they weren't being conducted by law enforcement. Witnesses to the raids talked of seeing masked men dressed all in black, hauling out dealers and throwing them into dark-colored vans with black-tinted windows, and driving away. Also unusual was the fact that once the houses were raided, they stayed closed down; the dealers didn't move back in the next day and set up operations again as often happened. When the reporter canvassed the people in the affected neighborhoods, most had nothing but praise for the mysterious men in black. A spokesman for the police department denied that the operations were theirs and said vigilantes weren't what the city needed. The citizens didn't agree. The folks interviewed on camera didn't care who the men were or where they came from, but expressed hope that they'd come back and clean out the rest. One elderly man was so happy that the house next door to him and his seventy-six-year-old wife had been raided, he had tears in his eyes. He told the reporter the masked men had been sent by God and that he hoped Judgment Day would come to every dope dealer in the city.

After the reporter signed off, Sarita made a note to ask Silas when she saw him tomorrow if the men had visited any of the dealers in their neighborhood. Like the people in the report, she was all for whoever these men were, vigilantes or not, and like the old man, she also hoped they paid a visit to every dope house in the city.

Sarita clicked over to the Sunday night football game and settled in to watch. She wondered how much longer Chandler and Walter would be working, but more importantly what they were working on. Was Walter tied in with Chandler and Saint? *Probably*, her inner voice answered. She thought about the report on the dope busters and thought it sounded like something Saint would be a part of. She went still. A chill ran over her skin. Sarita knew she was jumping to conclusions; she had absolutely no proof to link Saint and Chandler to anything but the diamonds, but what if? Sarita's grandmother had often chided Sarita for having a too-vivid imagination sometimes, and right now that imagination was working overtime trying to come up with a scenario that fit into what she'd seen on the news. Nothing came. Sarita knew her foster brother well, and all that masked man stuff really smelled like Saint. She'd rarely asked him for details on what he really did for a living because most of the time she didn't want to know, but now, suddenly she did.

Sarita ran her hands over her eyes. She needed to go home and get away from all this intrigue. Maybe the only reason she was trying to tie Saint to the masked vigilantes was because she was losing her mind from being locked up. She drew in a calming breath and forced her imagination to go away so she could watch the game.

At the end of the first quarter Chandler and Walter came into the den. Chandler had on his coat. "I need to go over and check on one of the construction sites. The security company called and said an alarm's going off."

"How long will you be?"

He shrugged. "Couple hours? No idea. Walter's going to stay with you until I get back."

Sarita's eyes strayed to Walter.

Chandler said, "I don't want you here by yourself."

"I'm not going to disappear."

"That's not the reason. It's a safety issue."

She eyed the men and thought about the two

dead women. "Okay. Well, if you're not back by the time I head to bed, I'll see you in the morning. We're still going to the center, right?"

"Right."

Their eyes held. He said, "I'll see you in the morning."

Without a further word, he headed to the door.

Sarita and Walter had a good time watching the game. He was amazed by her knowledge of the game's intricacies, and she found him a good game-watching companion. They popped popcorn, drank soft drinks, and second-guessed the coaches and officials.

It was after eleven when the game ended. Sarita said good night, and left Walter in the den watching the sports news.

Twelve

After school, the center's parking lot was usually packed with children, but when Chandler pulled the car up to the curb and cut the engine, Sarita didn't see anyone playing outside. She assumed they were all inside to avoid the midforties temperature.

Sarita stepped out of the car, and the moment her feet touched the ground, she felt home. Looking around at the familiar grayness of the neighborhood, she didn't see the run-down houses or the boarded-up stores; instead she saw the beautiful red and gold mums still blooming in Mrs. Kennedy's front yard; the familiar wooden rocking chair on Mr. Wilson's porch. He wasn't sitting in it, but would have been if the weather were warmer. She looked across the street, and seeing all the birds perched on the rim of Viola Boston's birdbath made her smile. During the winter Viola was known for coming out in her housecoat and pouring hot water into the birdbath so that her babies, as she called them, wouldn't freeze. Sarita had grown up here, buried her uncles and grandmother here with the help of the church. Her neighbors, of all ages, were her family. Being here meant she could step back into herself and live a true life once again.

Myk watched her look up and down the street. He could almost touch the emotion she was radiating. For a few moments, she simply stood there, silent, taking in first one house, then another. He stayed quiet and still; watching her. In less than two weeks he'd learned a bit about the Sarita who posed as his wife, but knew very little about the Sarita who ran this center. It was this woman that he needed to know the most. This was what defined her.

She finally looked his way. "Come on. Let's go in."

The perimeter of the old brick building was surrounded by a fifteen-foot-high, wire fence, so she and Chandler had to walk down the sidewalk to the only opening in the wire to enter. While the October wind whipped at their faces and blew up the edges of his black cashmere coat like a flag, they crossed the cracked asphalt parking lot that doubled as the playground, then over to the door.

Myk pulled the heavy industrial door open for her to enter first, and they were almost bowled over by the Cobb twins barreling outside. Ten-year-old Tracey and her sister Sally immediately stopped dead in their tracks. Both gave Sarita a curious look. "Miss Sarita?"

"Yep, it's me."

They checked her out in the expensive leather

coat and the high-heeled boots, and decided, "You look different."

"No kidding," she answered.

"You look rich," Sally added.

"I like your coat," said Tracey, Sally's mirror image, then asked, "Who's he?"

"My husband," Sarita answered. She was surprised to hear herself say the word so effortlessly.

"He's cute," the girls declared with a giggle. "See ya!" And off they ran.

Sarita made no comment on their assessment, but saw Myk's mustache twitch with amusement.

Sarita's assumption about the weather forcing everyone inside had been correct because the cavernous place was filled with children. The din was deafening. She wondered why they were all on the main floor though. As usual there was a basketball game going on, but as the players tried to keep themselves from tripping over the little kids gathered around for story time, knots of girls jumping double dutch, kids playing backgammon and chess, and a circle of girls throwing jacks, the makeshift court resembled more of an obstacle course. Why was everybody there instead of spread out around the building in the rest of the rooms?

With Chandler trailing behind, she walked farther into the chaos. She and the tall, well-dressed Chandler weren't noticed at first, but once they were, all noise and activity stopped. Just as with the twins, it took her children a minute or two to reconcile their old jeans-wearing Sarita with the fashion plate standing in front of them; but once they did, all hell broke loose.

She was mobbed by the little kids and circled by

grinning teenagers. Everybody competed for her attention and the privilege of talking to her first. She basked in their love, and tears of joy sprang to her eyes. She was home!

She gave out as many hugs and kisses as she could. Her vision was blurred when she finally ended the celebration by yelling, "Okay, hold up!"

They finally settled down, and she looked out over the smiling faces while she smiled teary-eyed in return. She had missed each and every one of them. "Yes, I'm back."

"For good?" little Corey Davis called from the back.

"Yes, Corey for good," she promised. *Chandler will just have to deal with it*, she thought to herself. "But tell me, why is everybody up here? Why aren't you using the basement?"

They all answered at once, telling her about pipes and water and the furnace and Silas said, until finally she threw up her hands and yelled out again, "Wait a minute! I can't hear everybody at once."

Grinning, they quieted.

"Now, I want one person, just one," she added quickly as a handful of kids opened their mouths at once, "to tell me what's going on."

In the back of the crowd she saw sixteen-year-old Keta Kennedy wearing his purple beret. "Keta?"

He made his way to the front. "The furnace died last Thursday, so there's no heat, then the pipes busted from something on Saturday. The Health Department is going to shut us down on Wednesday if everything isn't fixed. So, Silas said for all of us to use this floor until he came up with something. We didn't know where you were, and Silas wouldn't tell us anything, except you'd be back."

Keta then looked at the man standing so silently behind her. "Who's he?"

Although Keta was tall for his age, Myk looked down into the sixteen-year-old eyes and smiled. He knew a challenge when he heard one.

Sarita had forgotten all about Chandler. "Oh, this is Mykal Chandler, everybody," she offered absent-mindedly. Her brain was preoccupied with the tale of drama Keta had just told.

"Why's he here?" Keta asked. He checked out Myk's expensive suit and the cashmere coat thrown over his arm. "Is he somebody from downtown come to help us out?"

"No, he's my husband," Sarita answered still immersed in thought. "How much water is in the basement?"

When Keta didn't respond, she asked him again, "Keta?"

But Keta hadn't heard. His whole sixteen-year-old being was focused wholly on Chandler. Before Sarita could ask him about the water for the third time, he pushed his way back through the crowd and headed toward the exit.

Watching him striding away so angrily, Sarita murmured, "What in the world—" Had she missed something? Keta snatched up his coat and books, and Sarita turned puzzled eyes to Chandler. Then, it finally dawned on her what the problem must be. "Keta!" she called urgently, but he was already out the door. She was stricken over the pain she saw in his retreat, and she chided herself for forgetting how fragile sixteen-year-old-boy hearts could be.

Keta had considered himself "in love" with Sarita for quite some time. She, of course, had never encouraged his crush, but it hadn't mattered. She turned back to Chandler again and saw sympathy and understanding in his eyes. Apparently he'd figured out Keta's problem also.

"I was young once, too," he told her.

Sarita was going to have to have a talk with Keta as soon as possible, but right now there was work to do.

She and Chandler spent over an hour assessing the damage done by the busted pipes. There had to be at least four feet of water in the basement, and the furnace problems couldn't be dealt with until the water was gone. The two floors above the main floor didn't have the benefit of the body heat generated by all the playing kids, so it was almost see-your-breath cold as she gave Chandler a tour of the place.

Myk took the tour silently and listened carefully to her explanations about the programs run out of the building and in which area the programs were housed. All the while, he watched her intently. With so many items needing her immediate attention, it was clear she didn't want to spend the time showing him around, but she took the time, and he respected her for it.

When she showed him into her so-called office, he looked around and thought about the contrast between his many opulent offices and this cluttered, closet-sized space.

Going behind the desk, she offered solemnly, "Have a seat."

He had to move a stack of flyers announcing a

nearby church's sale of chicken dinners from the dilapidated folding chair underneath. It didn't look sturdy enough to hold him, so in the end, he said, "I'll stand."

"It looks bad, but it'll hold you."

Myk still had his doubts, but sat on it precariously. It immediately took a slow tilt to the side.

"You have to balance yourself in it. Yeah, like that."

Myk used the weight of his body as a counterweight. He felt like he was on the deck of a listing ship. He got to his feet. "I'll stand."

"Okay," she said, but her attention was focused on the stack of mail awaiting her return. She opened a few of the envelopes, then tossed them aside.

The grimness on her face, made Myk ask, "Problems?"

"Nope. Just more bills I can't pay—to add to a basement full of water and a furnace that's probably drowned by now—not that it really worked before."

She shook off her coat and instantly regretted it when the cold snapped at her, but she tossed the leather onto the desk and walked back over to the open office door. Sticking her head out into the frigid hallway, she yelled, "Messenger!"

A few moments later, a teenager wearing a purple beret entered the office. Myk watched silently as she gave the kid his instructions.

"Tell all the Guard captains, I need to see them, ASAP."

He nodded.

"And go by Silas's place and see if he's home."

"He went to the doctor. He said he'd be back before five."

Sarita checked the fancy white gold watch on her wrist. It was a little past four now. "Okay, that's fine. Who opened up after school today?"

"Keta."

Myk noted that the young man, who looked to be about fifteen, stood before Sarita like a private before his commanding officer.

The teenager asked, "Anything else?"

"Nope, that's it. Oh, Jerome, split up the job so you can get the word out quick. I'd like everybody here by five, if they can make it."

Jerome turned to exit, but risked a sideways glance at the tall man everybody was talking about.

Sarita saw his interest, and said to Jerome, "This is my husband, Mr. Chandler. Tell your mama that she and the ladies at the church can stop praying for me now," and she nodded meaningfully in Chandler's direction.

Jerome smiled. "Okay, I'll tell her." He gave Myk one quick parting look, then exited to carry out her orders.

Once Myk and Sarita were alone again, he couldn't keep the curiosity out of his voice, "Messengers?"

"We don't have a phone here, and many of our families don't either, so this is our communication system. By being a messenger, the children learn responsibility and to listen. Everything is a lesson. The Guards escort the seniors to the store, help with chores, run errands, mow lawns, tutor."

Myk could see the seriousness in her face.

"We're about education here. Any fool can open a neighborhood center and let the kids come in and play ball all day, but we do more than that. Our mission is to save this one small portion of the city and its children. We have rules and regs, and anybody not playing along has to leave, sometimes permanently, but most times not. The kids love coming here, and none of them want to be *banned*, which is what they call it when you can't come back."

"You're carrying a lot on your shoulders, aren't you?"

"No more than I can bear."

He eyed her silently. Her commitment to this place was as strong as she. "So, if you had a million dollars to spend here, what would you do?"

"Find another 1.5 mil to go with it, tear this sucker down, and start over."

Myk chuckled, "Another 1.5?"

"Yes, I've calced it all out. To fix everything and to put in place all the programs we need, it would cost 2.5 million, to start."

Myk studied her closely. Man she was something. "Someday, when you get the time, I'd like to see those numbers."

"Sure."

When he asked then to see the center's current books, Sarita found the old leather ledger hidden away beneath the piles on her desk and handed it to him. She didn't know why he wanted it, but she had nothing to hide. She did wonder if he planned to use the books further to justify his decision to appoint a new administrator, and that made her resentment rise all over again.

Myk could see by the columns of entries that the little money she'd gotten over the years had been well spent—food for the senior shut-ins, reimbursements for gas for people who'd provided transportation to health clinics and doctor appointments.

She'd stretched every penny until it screamed, and, according to the books, hadn't spent a cent on anything not directly related to her programs. "Do you pay yourself a salary?"

She shook her head. "Nope."

"The pension from your uncles is all you live on?"

Sarita told herself not to be offended. "Yes, Chandler, but I get by okay. Saint sends me cash when he can."

"Which you probably spend on the center, am I right?"

Her chin went up defensively. "Sometimes, not all the time."

In the listings in the ledger Myk came across a fifteen-hundred-dollar grant she'd gotten from one of his foundations three years ago. She purchased eyeglasses, child safety seats, and secondhand appliances for the building's kitchen. He also noted an entry for a scholarship fund. "How much is in your scholarship fund?"

"Not a dime. We ran out of money eighteen months ago." Sarita was starting to wonder where the interrogation was going. He couldn't possibly be questioning her spending decisions, too.

"It says here, you gave out," he looked up. "Five?"

"Yes, Chandler, five. Five graduating seniors got one hundred dollars each. The children couldn't go to college without clothes."

Myk tried to soothe away the challenge flashing in her eyes. "I'm not criticizing, Sarita." Not by any means, he only wished he had known of her plight earlier. He would have gladly given her ten times the amount. "Why didn't you apply for more grants?" he asked softly.

"Because the last city administration spent all the Federal neighborhood money fixing up downtown. Little groups like mine were left out."

A knock interrupted their conversation, and in walked the center's most prominent senior citizen, Silas Devine. Sarita made the introductions.

A grinning Silas leaned on his cane and pumped Myk's hand. "So you're the man behind Chandler Works. Glad to meet you, Mr. Chandler. Real glad!"

Sarita thought to herself, trust Silas to know all about Chandler.

"Call me, Mykal, sir."

Silas was nodding approvingly. "It's about time Miss Girl jumped the broom. Been telling her that for years," he pointed out, while continuing to look Myk straight in the eye. "Yeah, real glad to meet you."

And then as if Silas suddenly remembered where his loyalties were supposed to lie, he glanced Sarita's way. "Is he treating you all right?"

What else could she say, but, "Yes, Silas. He hasn't sent me to bed without dinner for at least three days."

Silas seemed so outdone meeting Chandler, the sarcasm sailed right over his gray head. "Good. You treat her right. Mind you, she's a little opinionated, and a whole lot bossy, but a man is just what she needs. A *man*," he emphasized, looking over at Sarita sternly. "Not that jelly-spined musician she was going out with last summer. She walked all over him."

Sarita loved Silas dearly, but right now, she wanted to strangle him. "Are you done?"

"Almost. You think your brother the mayor's at

home? We need him to call the water department about those busted pipes."

"Silas!" Sarita said appalled.

He waved her off. "Hush, girl. If you marry a rich and powerful man, you're supposed to take advantage of it."

Sarita couldn't believe her ears, well she could; Silas was always saying something outrageous.

The look on Sarita's face made Myk laugh, "Silas, you and I are going to get along fine." In Myk's opinion, anyone who could talk to Sarita like that and live to tell about it was someone Myk wanted as a friend. To further get Sarita's goat, Myk asked Silas, "Tell me about this musician."

Silas opened his mouth to respond, but Sarita was quicker. "Save it for later. Tell me about the basement."

As far as Silas could tell the water was from a broken main, but the city water department people refused to come and look at it.

Sarita asked, "Why?"

"They say they can't do anything about the main until the water level drops."

"How long will that be?"

"Soon as we get the water pumped out."

"What do you mean, *we*? It's their main."

"They only pump if it's city property; this is private."

Sarita had heard some asinine things in her life; this ranked right near the top. "So, in the meantime, we wait for what, typhoid, cholera before they get their butts out here. Don't they know we service children?"

"Sure they do, and so does the Health Department. Your buddy 'News' Bertram made sure of that. She called them and told them what was going on. They came out and told us get the place cleaned up by Wednesday or they'll shut us down for being a health menace."

Myk was lost. "Who or what is a News Bertram?"

Sarita answered, "She's an old biddy who if she doesn't stop sticking that nosy nose of hers in our business, I'm going to chop it off."

"Now, Sarita—" Silas warned.

"Now, nothing. She's been tap-dancing on our last nerve since the day she moved into the neighborhood. If she paid half as much attention to her crack-dealing son—"

The look of amusement on Chandler's face made her calm down. He probably thought she was crazy going on like she was. "Well, the woman's a menace."

Silas added, "Your 'Army' paid her a visit this morning to tell her just that."

Myk was lost again "Her army? Are you talking about the young men in the berets?"

"No, their mamas," Silas explained. "I call them the Army because they're the biggest bunch of order-giving women on the eastside. Of course, they get that from Little Touissant over there. She's the one organized them, and there's been hell to pay around here ever since."

"Silas," Sarita said warningly.

As was his habit when he was speaking the Silas Truth, he ignored Sarita and kept talking, "Anyway, that's why I asked about your brother. Grandson, if you have any pull downtown, we can really use it."

Sarita added, "And Chandler, you are the land-lord."

Myk looked from Silas to Sarita; the senior citizen had hope in his eyes; his wife appeared skeptical. He wondered if pumping the water out of her base-ment would impress her more than all the material things he'd been showering her with. Something told it him would, so he reached for his phone and punched in the number.

Because it was late afternoon and all of his men were on jobs, it took Myk almost an hour to line up a crew and borrow a couple of pumps from one of his construction sites. By the time all the arrange-ments were made and the men and equipment ar-rived, dusk had fallen.

The men went to work immediately. Wearing hip-high boots, they waded down into the murky depths of the unlighted basement. While they did their evaluations, Myk sent some of the assembled Guard captains out into the surrounding streets to make sure the sewer grates were free of leaves and debris. He knew Little Touissant would have a fit if they pumped out all of the water only to have the streets flood. When the patrol reported back to Myk, the pumps were fired up.

Although Sarita wanted to be in the basement helping the men, Myk convinced her that they knew their job, and she'd only be in the way. She eventually agreed, grudgingly, and concentrated on coordinating the cleanup efforts.

Throughout the evening, mothers and fathers drifted into the center with offers to help, and to bring over plates of good hot, home-cooked food for the men operating the pumps, and for Sarita and her new husband. It was the husband most came to see. Jerome's mother, Shirley for instance. Bearing a thermos of coffee in one hand and a freshly baked pound cake in the other, she made no bones about why she'd come. Shirley Lee was in her midthirties. She and Sarita had been friends for years. She, like Silas, declared the handsome, dark-skinned Chandler to be a much better choice than "that old musician you were walking all over."

The comments on Sarita's *choice* were echoed by all comers, and after a while, she just threw up her hands. Chandler, in the process of stuffing himself with peach cobbler, fried chicken, pound cake, green beans flavored with chunks of ham and onions, homemade rolls, coffee and everything else the Army had to offer, basked in all the attention, listened to it, and smiled.

At nine that evening, Myk shut down the basement's operation and sent the men home. They'd each find a bonus in their paychecks at the end of the week for helping out. Watching them leave, a confused Sarita pointed out to Chandler, "But there's still water down there."

"Sarita, those men started work this morning at 5 A.M. For a couple of them this was the sixth straight 5 A.M. start. They have families, and some just want to go home and take a shower. I know you're concerned about your place, but I can't ask them to stay any longer."

She knew she was being selfish and that she should be thankful to have gotten any help at all, but she'd wanted the job finished that night. "You're right. I get carried away sometimes."

They were back in her office, and she was standing with her back to him looking onto the dark streets below. He could see the weary slump in her shoulders. Even though he'd had to practically carry her out of the basement so the men could do their job, she'd still dragged hoses, hauled tools, and generally helped out when and where she could. Seeing her in action today showed him facets of Sarita he'd been unaware of. He knew she hadn't cared for all the cracks from her neighbors and friends about this whole marriage business, but it hadn't put a damper on the generosity of spirit shown to both young and old. And everyone loved her. Wherever he went people told him tales of Sarita's good deeds, and cautioned him to treat her right and treasure her for the precious individual that she was. More than a few men threatened to "kick his ass" if he caused her to shed even a tear. To them she was not Little Touissant but Little Queen, and they worshiped the ground she walked on.

"Ready to go home?" he asked quietly.

"I am home." She turned from the window, and he could see the unshed tears in her eyes. "If you take this away from me, Mykal, I will truly die."

Her unshielded emotions were there for him to see, and his heart swelled in response to her use of his given name. "I know, Sarita."

"I have never begged anyone for anything in my whole life, but I'm going to now. Let me keep my center. I will cook for you. I will clean for you. I will—"

"Don't say it. When we make love I don't want it to be tied to anything but passion."

She turned away to hide her tears.

He continued speaking, "I've seen how much these folks mean to you, Sarita. I might be a rich, arrogant bastard, but I'm not blind. I apologize for even thinking you could be replaced here."

His confession left her stunned. Mykal Chandler apologizing? Did the Army put something in his food?

"You look surprised." And he smiled.

"I just never expected to hear you say something like that, that's all."

"*Never* is a pretty strong word. Contrary to what some might think, I do have a heart." Then his voice changed. "Would you really cook for me?"

That caught her by surprise, too. She searched his face for some hint as to what he was really thinking, but she saw nothing reflected there but honesty. "Do you want me to cook for you?"

"Yes, I do. I don't expect three squares a day—but every now and then would be appreciated."

Again, honesty.

"You aren't lying about not replacing me here?"

He shook his head.

She looked away for a moment to gather her jumbled thoughts and emotions. He'd ridden to her rescue like the famous Tenth Cavalry. Granted, she and people might have eventually found a way to dry out the basement without his help, but his expertise and connections made the whole mess easier to manage. She owed him, and if he wanted her to cook for him, she would. Sarita always paid her debts. "First, I want to thank you for helping with all the water. You and your men were a blessing. Second, I will cook for you, if that's what you want."

"It's what I want."

His eyes seemed to be saying so much more, and Sarita's breathing became as erratic as her heartbeat. Her attraction to him had grown by leaps and bounds over the past few days, and his help today only made things worse.

"So, are you ready to go home, now?" he asked.

"Will I be coming back here tomorrow?"

"Yes, and if I can't come with you, I'll send Walter. I don't want you here alone."

She wanted to protest but decided it was a decent compromise. "Okay, then let's go home."

On the way out she stuck her head in the kitchen to say good night to the small group of Army members washing up the dinner dishes. "See you tomorrow," Shirley called back. "And take care of that man. He was good to us today."

Sarita smiled and let Chandler escort her out into the chilly night. "Before we go, can we stop by my place a minute? I just want to make sure everything's okay."

"Sure."

Following her directions he drove to her small upstairs flat and after parking the car, walked with her to the door. Inside, the place was cold. She turned on a lamp, and the soft light revealed a place that from Myk's point of view rivaled her small office in size. He ran his eyes over the worn but comfortable-looking furniture, the houseplants, and the old-fashioned lamps. In a way the interior reminded him of his grandmother's place, especially the big red roses decorating the fabric of the couch cover. While he took a seat on that same couch, she took a brief tour to make sure everything was where it should be. Once she assured herself that all was well, she watered the plants, grabbed some personal items and threw them in a plastic grocery bag, looked through the mail left on top of the TV by, she assumed, Saint, and proceeded with Chandler out of the door. After a quick turn of the locks, they headed back to the car.

Inside the car and surrounded by the warmth of the heat and the soft jazz from the CD player, Sarita began to relax. Her first order of business would be a long hot soak in that swimming pool bathtub in her room. She planned to follow that up with a nice long sleep.

"Still cold?" he asked. They'd both spent most of the evening sloshing through water in the chilly basement.

"No, this is much better. I didn't realize I was freezing until now."

He reached over and took her hand. Her fingers felt numb. "Wear gloves tomorrow. You can't work with frostbite."

She noted that his hand was as cold as her own, but he held on to hers until it warmed up. When he finally released it, she felt a strange sense of loss.

He said, "I've got a question."

"And, it is?"

"I want to help with the center's financial problems," Myk said to her, "but I need your input."

Sarita was a bit surprised.

He added, "I know what I said that morning about doing what I think is best, but I know now that you know better."

Sarita was impressed. "It takes a big person to admit they were wrong."

"So, can I help?"

"Whatever you can do, we'll appreciate."

When they entered the house, Drake and Walter were sitting in the den eating the largest subs Sarita had ever seen. Since she'd already eaten and wanted to take her bath, she waved good-bye to the men and left them alone. They all visually followed her exit, but one set of eyes lingered long after she'd disappeared.

Drake said, "You know, when this is all over, you're going to have a hard time giving her up."

Myk came out of his reverie. "No, I won't."

Walter chuckled. "Right. You're half in love with the girl already."

Myk took a seat and didn't respond.

Drake said, "Gee's right, and do you know how I know?"

"No," his brother answered coolly. "How?"

"Because we had an appointment tonight at eight-thirty. It's now after ten."

Myk's eyes widened, and he cursed. They were supposed to be meeting with some DEA agents. He'd totally forgotten.

"Not like you to be missing in action."

Myk had to admit his brother was right. The scheduled meeting hadn't even crossed his mind. "I got hung up over at Sarita's center. Some pipes burst, and the basement flooded."

Gee and Drake shared a look. Myk ignored them. "Did you reschedule?"

"Yes. Next week. Same time, same place."

"Thanks."

Drake said, "We were supposed to ride by those houses we took down over the weekend. You still want to go?"

"Yes." Myk got to his feet, and asked, "Gee, will you stay and keep an eye on the lady?"

"No problem."

Myk nodded. "Let me go up and see her a minute, then I'll be ready to ride."

Once he was gone, Drake shook his head. "He is so far gone."

Gee agreed. "Tell me about it."

Upstairs, Myk's soft knock on her door brought no response, so he went on in, moving quietly just in case she was already asleep. She wasn't. The bed was empty. In fact, he didn't see her anywhere in the shadow-filled room. Then the sound of lapping water floated to his ears. She was in the tub. Closing the door noiselessly, he quietly crossed the carpeted floor to the partially opened door that led to the attached bathroom. He looked in. The sight of her nude and sitting on the edge of the black marble tub dangling her toes in the water made him so hard it became difficult to breathe. Looking his fill, he realized he'd been a fool to turn down her offer back at the center. No brother in his right mind would take cooking over this. If he ever got her in the back of the limo again, all bets were off. Were Drake and Gee right? Was he really falling for a chocolate-nippled beauty with soft brown skin, flaring hips, and a riot of tempting hair between her gorgeous thighs? As he continued to feast his eyes, he couldn't answer the question, nor did he care that Drake was waiting for him downstairs. All Myk wanted to do was slowly tumble her into the bubble-filled tub and show her his own version of home cooking; take those dark nipples into his mouth and tease them until she moaned for more; much more—part her thighs and . . .

He dragged his mind back to saner territory. He had more serious matters to apply his mind to, and Sarita, as luscious as she was, couldn't be on the list tonight.

But the male in him refused to walk away, so he stole back over to the bedroom door and pretended to have just entered. "Sarita?" he called out. "Where are you?"

The sound of Chandler's voice made Sarita slide quickly into the tub and drop below the fluffy bubbles covering the scented water's surface. "I'm in the tub, Chandler. Go away."

He came on in anyway but stopped near the entrance. "My . . ." was all he said.

"Why can't you ever do what you're told," she scolded to hide her reaction to his tone and his eyes.

After seeing her nude, Myk found the sight of her hiding in the bubbles just as erotic. "I'll be gone in a minute."

The way he was looking her over made Sarita swear the temperature of the water was rising. "Can I help you?"

He reached behind him and closed the door. "Don't want you to lose your heat," he said softly.

Losing the heat in the room was the least of her problems, Sarita thought to herself while trying to pretend calm. The closer he walked to the tub, the farther down she retreated. When she couldn't submerge herself any lower, he hunkered down on the edge of the black marble and looked at her across the distance. If only he were old and ugly, she found herself thinking, maybe she could deal with him better.

"Drake and I are going out. Gee's going to stay with you until we get back."

Up close, Myk could smell the heady scents she'd put in the water. He reached out and lifted a finger full of bubbles, then softly blew the foam in her direction.

The sensual gesture, coupled with the maleness in his gaze, made Sarita's throat go dry and her nipples harden.

"Enjoy your bath," he whispered. Straightening, he turned and walked out.

Thirteen

When Walter McGhee came downstairs the next morning, he found Sarita already up and cooking. The sun was just throwing off the covers, but the kitchen smelled wonderful. "Good morning, my sister."

She grinned. "Morning, my brother. Did you spend the night?"

"Yep, got a space up in the attic Myk lets me call my own when I need it. Hizzoner stayed over, too. What's cooking?"

"Breakfast. There's coffee, biscuits—"

"Biscuits? From a can right?"

"No," she responded in a tone that suggested he should know better. "Biscuits. Scrambled eggs in that bowl over there. Sausage, grits, and bacon."

His eyes relayed his excitement. "Can I start?"

She laughed. "Dig in."

"Thank you!" he gushed, and grabbed a plate.

In the meantime Sarita placed generous portions of everything she'd cooked on a plate, then placed the plate on a tray. She added silverware, a large cup of coffee, and a glass of orange juice.

When Gee saw the tray's setup, he asked, "What, you don't like my company?"

Sarita was confused.

"The tray. Are you going to eat somewhere else?"

Finally understanding, Sarita said, "No, this isn't for me. It's Chandler's."

Gee stared. "You're taking him breakfast on a tray?"

"I—promised to cook for him."

"Since when?"

"Since none of your business. You just eat. I'll be back in a minute."

As she left the kitchen, she didn't see Walter's knowing smile.

At the foot of the stairs, Sarita realized she had no idea where his room was. She was just about to go back and ask Walter for directions, when she saw the sleepy-looking Drake come to the top of the stairs. He descended saying, "Good morning, lovely sister-in-law. I'm assuming that food is for my dragon brother and not for me."

Sarita enjoyed the mayor's lively humor. "You're right, but I don't know where his room is."

"Left at the top of the stairs. Follow the hall and take a right. You'll see the dragons on the doors."

"Thanks."

Going up, she called back to Drake, "There's breakfast in the kitchen, or at least there was when Walter started eating."

Drake took off at a run.

Gathering her courage, Sarita knocked on the massive double doors. They were made from a dark, glowing cherrywood, and each section had a large twisting dragon carved into the face.

She knocked again, harder. Nothing. She debated for a moment as to whether to go on in, then decided, why not. He was always walking in on her; maybe she'd give him a taste of his own medicine. Balancing the tray she turned the polished brass knob and stepped inside.

Silence reverberated around her. Reaching back she quietly closed the door. It looked to be a sitting room, and it was twice the size of her bedroom on the other side of the house. Floor-to-ceiling drapes ran the length of one wall but were closed against the early-morning light. Small tea candles flickering inside black metal wall sconces gave the room a soft glow. Once her eyes adjusted to the shadows, the oriental theme could be seen in the lush rugs on the polished wood floor, the low-slung, black-lacquered benches upholstered in a fine red velvet, and in the design and colors of the love seats, chests, and chairs positioned about the space.

Since Sarita had yet to see Chandler or anything resembling a bed, she assumed his bedroom was somewhere close. Common sense and a rapidly beating heart told her to put the tray down and leave, but she couldn't. The interior drew her as if she'd just entered the den of some mythical beast, and she had to find his lair. With that in mind, she quietly crossed the room and let instinct guide her steps.

Through a carved archway on the far side of the room, she found the mythical beast awake, fresh from his morning shower, and nude. Sarita whirled around so fast, she almost lost the tray, but her movements weren't fast enough to stop the image of him muscular, tall, and mahogany beautiful from being seared into her brain. Against the shadows, he'd resembled an African god of the dawn.

A smiling and yes, delighted Myk tossed aside the towel he'd been using to dry his hair. He didn't cover himself however. "Good morning."

"Good morning. Are you dressed yet?" she asked.

"Nope."

"Will you put something on, please."

It was a wail worthy of a romance novel virgin, so Myk, still smiling, reached over and dragged on a black silk robe. "You can turn around now."

Sarita did, and was glad to see he hadn't lied to her. The memory of his nakedness hovered on the edges of her consciousness, haunting her. "I— brought you breakfast."

"Thanks." He took the tray from her shaking hands and set it on a low table before the fireplace. Unlike the cold, silent grate in the outer room, this one was aglow with flames.

The bed dominated the room however. It was a magnificent four-poster made of wood so dark, it glowed black in the firelight. Flowing panels of black silk enclosed the bed. They were tied back, but Sarita could see the dragons embroidered on them in gold and red. The veiling gave the bed a mysterious sensuality that made Sarita imagine what it might be like to lie within all that silk while he made love to her.

Realizing he was watching her, she forced her attention away from the bed and back to him. "I should get back downstairs."

"You aren't going to join me?" he asked from over by the food.

"Your brother and Walter are waiting . . ."

"They're big boys. They can take care of themselves for an hour or two."

"An hour or two?" Her eyes flew to the bed.

"Just a figure of speech, relax."

Easier said than done. Whether by design or not, his robed manner oozed seduction. The shimmering light from the fireplace and the low glow from the wall sconces above the bed added to the lush exotic atmosphere.

She watched him remove the tops she'd placed over the dishes to keep them warm.

"Will you stay?" he asked.

She wanted to. Trying to ignore his allure was becoming an exercise in futility. "I should get ready to go to the center."

"You'll have time. Have you eaten?"

The lie almost left her lips, but she forced it back and told the truth, "No, I haven't."

"Good, then come and join me."

Sarita knew they were going to share more than the meal; it was in his eyes. The anticipation of the certainty made her nipples tighten and her lips part. "I only brought one plate."

"We'll share. Looks like there's more than enough food, too." Smiling inwardly at her hesitant manner, Myk unloaded the bounty from the tray. The piping hot biscuits running with butter made his mouth water. The idea that she'd boldy entered his domain to bring him the food she'd promised made his mouth water for her, too. Finding her standing there when he stepped out of the shower a moment ago had aroused him instantly. He was still thick and hard. "Come sit . . ."

She walked over and took a seat beside him on the love seat. She told herself she had no reason to be so nervous, after all, she'd experienced his touch and kisses before, but that was the problem; she knew how magical this man could be.

"Here . . ." His voice brought her back to the present and the fork he was directing toward her mouth. She accepted the small sampling of egg and sausage without thought. He slid the implement out very slowly, and while she chewed, his dark eyes glowed with approval. The sensuality of his actions made her heart do flip-flops and the gates to her core swell with awakening desire. He raised the fork to her lips again, tempting her with the well-seasoned grits. When he eased the tines out, she swallowed, then delicately licked the corner of her mouth.

Myk appeared to be calm and in control, but his manhood knew better. That she'd actually let him feed her this way made his blood roar. To stop himself from easing her back against the love seat and feeding on something more substantial, he reached instead for a biscuit. Breaking it open, he tore away a small portion and held it out. She ate it from his hands, then shocked him by darting her tongue against his finger as she moved back.

Through the haze of desire, Myk husked out, "You keep that up, and I'll be sampling more than your biscuits, little girl." But unable to stop himself, Myk leaned in and kissed her gently, fully. Her eyes closed, and he pressed her deeper into the love seat. He moved a hand to the porcelain-fine curve of her jaw. The skin felt like silk. "Better run before I find out how you taste with jelly. . . ."

"I dare you . . ." she challenged huskily, her eyes hot.

He pulled back for a moment. "Playful, are you?"

"With the right man," she whispered in response.

Myk's senses flared, and he pulled her onto his lap. He leaned in, and with tiny lazy licks of his tongue seduced the corner of the mouth. "Then come play with me. . . ."

Small shots of lightning exploded through Sarita's blood, but before the thunder could subside, he transferred his attention to the other corner of her mouth, making her lips part invitingly.

"Gorgeous . . ." She heard him breathe, then he kissed her so masterfully, her whole world reeled.

Myk fed sweetly, taking his time. With any other woman, he would've simply stripped away her black sweat suit and helped himself to the treasure, but Sarita he wanted to unveil slowly, languidly. He wanted to spend days arousing her, days kissing her, and days making her moan.

Sarita tasted the fullness of his lips, felt the strength of his desire beneath her hips, and wanted him closer. Raising her hand, she gently took hold of the back of his neck, letting him feel her need.

He eased down the zipper on the jacket of her sweats, then ran his hands over the loose silky camisole she was wearing underneath. He was delighted to find her braless and even more so when her warm breast trembled in his adoring hand. He had just enough light to see her face as his finger played and dallied. He watched her eyes close in response to the slow, deliberate manipulations, then he leaned in to to savor her mouth. As he slid kisses down her throat, he slipped down the top her camisole, then lowered his head and bit each nipple gently, making her suck in a shaky breath, increasing her agitation and elongating the stacked-up sighs of pleasure in her throat.

Sarita couldn't have left his lap if she'd wanted to; the feel of his circling tongue, the sweet, wicked sucking of his warm mouth set off a fever in her flesh that burned her everywhere. Because of his expert loving, her nipples were hard and damp, her core hot and alive. She felt ready to burst. For the first time in her life she wanted to bare herself completely and totally for a man so he could teach her every sensual secret there was to know about the heat between a man and a woman.

The relentless throbbing of Myk's manhood demanded he take her over to the bed and finish their unfinished business once and for all, but he didn't want to move. The scents and tastes of her were plunging him into a whirlwind of sensations so powerful his hands were moving over like a man reading Braille. Having her on his lap with her breasts bare and pleading, while his hands slowly mapped the outside curve of her hip, had him sensually rooted to the spot.

Besides, he reminded himself that he wanted to go slowly. He wanted to relish her, savor her; prolong each and every touch of his lips, every sweep of his hands, every taste of her skin. He felt compelled to memorize the porcelain weight of her breasts, the curve of her jaw, the line of her throat;

the way she sighed when he bit her nipples; the smells and heat of her hair. She was like a rare wine or a fine imported cigar. No, he would not rush this. She was too beautiful for this first time to be quick and unmemorable.

Raising his head, he recaptured her lips, then slipped his tongue into the honeyed cavern. When her tongue met his, he groaned his delight and joined her in a sweet duet. He moved his hand over her sweats-covered thighs, then slowly in between.

Sarita arched with the pleasure and wantonly parted her legs for more; she had no shame; she was as hot as a teenager in the backseat of a car. He rewarded her by intensifying the delicious touches. She moaned like the celibate woman she was.

"Let's take these off . . ." he whispered in a voice as hot as his exploring hand. He was referring to her sweats. She lifted her hips, and he gently dragged them down and off. The jacket came next.

Sitting on his lap in nothing but her navy blue bikini and matching camisole, she raised her lips to his and melted into him without a thought, returning his hot kisses, responding to the wanderings of his magical hands, demanding he give her more, and he did. He plied her until she melted back against him, her will gone.

Myk had no idea she'd be so uninhibited, so passionate. His semicelibate wife with her jewel-hard nipples and honey-filled thighs made his need flare like the Fourth of July. Spurred on by the sight of her arched and rising sensually to the melody he was playing at the gates of her soul, he eased the panel of her panties aside and ran his finger over lush wet flesh.

It was too much for Sarita. She climaxed, scream-ing his name. She didn't care if folks heard her downtown; the orgasm was glorious. It buffeted her like a tiny boat tossed about on a stormy sea.

Then a phone rang; insistent; jarring; interrupting.

"Dammit!" he growled angrily.

"Let it ring," she whispered. Still in the throes of her climax, she kissed him, hoping to distract him so the moment wouldn't be lost; so they could continue.

The ringing persisted.

He sighed and eased back. Lifting her, he gently set her aside. "Don't move."

Sarita sighed with frustration.

Myk picked up the cellular phone on the stand by the bed, and barked, "What?!"

Sarita waited, her body pulsing with the desire he'd unleashed. She hoped the caller would be quick.

Myk looked her way, then covered the phone's face with his hand. "This shouldn't be but a minute."

Turning back, he spoke into the phone, "Okay. Fax me the drawings. I'll compare them to what I have on my disk and fax them right back."

Still talking, he disappeared through an alcove on the far side of the room, and Sarita was left alone. She gave him ten minutes. When he didn't return, she pulled on her sweats, zipped the jacket, and left.

When Myk came downstairs forty-five minutes later, the house was empty. He was mad at Sarita for not waiting; mad at his engineer for a call that could have waited for later, but most of all he was mad at himself for not treating Sarita with more care. The call he'd promised would only take a few minutes had taken almost forty; not a problem for most of the women in his past. They would've waited for him to return until hell froze over, but he kept forgetting Sarita was different. He was neither her sun nor her moon; she didn't care about his money or how important he considered himself to be. She'd come to him offering him nothing but her spirited, beautiful self, and he'd chosen to answer the phone instead.

Brooding, he took a moment to grab a cup of coffee from the still-warm carafe and take a few sips. He knew Sarita would be expecting him at the center, but rather than subject her or her people to his foul mood, he drove to his office instead.

Clark Nelson sat in his plush hotel room looking at the newspaper. The photo of a man from his past froze him in place. Mykal Chandler. The age-old hate Clark felt for his former employer rose up from the depths of his psyche and manifested itself in the contempt twisting his face. Had it not been for Chandler, Clark would never have gone to prison and been crippled. The leg ached as in sympathy, but Clark ignored it and read on. It seemed Chandler had just gotten married. The picture of the couple was taken at a reception given by the mayor. Clark studied the bride. Even though the picture was black-and-white, her beauty radiated. Clark wondered how Chandler would feel if she were snatched and shipped to a man Clark knew in South Africa whose brothel specialized in Black beauties? Would the pain of losing her equal Clark's years of misery in the Honduran prison Chandler had been so instrumental in sending him to?

The charge had been rape. It hadn't been rape.

The girl had been coming on to him since his first day as an employee of Chandler's construction company, so he simply took what she'd been offering. She turned out to be the granddaughter of the local magistrate. During the trial, Chandler had offered no assistance, and when the guilty verdict was returned, Chandler washed his hands of the affair, and Clark never saw him again.

Now, their paths had crossed again. Did Clark really want to tangle with Chandler after all these years? The answer was yes. Even though the contacts he'd made in the Honduran prison had been instrumental in the building of his illegal empire, affording him a life he never could have imagined, he'd never been able to forget or forgive Myk Chandler. Even though Clark had come to Detroit for other purposes, he looked upon it as fate, and an opportunity for payback.

With that in mind, he picked up his cell phone and placed a call to the policeman who'd handled the party girls. Clark needed to know all there was to know about Mykal Chandler and his beautiful new bride, and once he did, the game would begin.

By evening, the men from Chandler Works had pumped out the center's remaining water, but it took Sarita and her Army another three days to rid the basement of the smelly sludge left behind. On the fourth morning, the mayor arrived, bringing with him the director of the Water Department, who assessed the broken main and promised his workers would be out to start repairs before the end of the day. The children were awed by the visit from the downtown dignitaries, and Sarita gave her brother-in-law, a big hug for his help.

Over the next several days, Sarita saw very little of Chandler. Walter became her daily companion, telling her only that Chandler was catching up on his work. Sarita assumed he was mad at her for leaving like she did, but frankly, she was tired of his phone ringing every time things started heating up. She told herself she didn't mind his absence, especially after the new furnace sent over by his foundation was delivered and installed, but she found herself thinking about him more often than not.

She threw herself back into the center's routine, and into getting the drafty old building ready for winter. Courtesy of the Chandler Foundation the center received new vinyl windows, roofing materials, carpeting for the bare cement floors in the upstairs rooms, computers for the library, two new phone lines, and, for the kitchen—a brand-new stove, fridge, and dishwasher. Thanks to his generosity, she and her people no longer had to pray over the ancient furnace, or heat cold water to make it hot, as there was a new hot water heater, too.

He even took care of her back bills, and had his foundation's financial officer, a young woman named Juanita Mason, set up an account for the center at Eastern Market, the city's largest, thus making it possible for the Army to purchase a fresher and wider variety of fruits and vegetables for the meals that were taken to the neighborhood's senior shut-ins. Having the account was fine, but when Sarita explained to Ms. Mason that the center had no reliable transportation to get to places like

Eastern Market, she promptly leased them a van.

To keep up her part of the bargain, Sarita cooked dinner for Chandler every night; she told herself she might as well since she and Walter had to eat, too, but inside it stung knowing Chandler never showed. The standard excuse from Walter remained the same: Chandler was working.

She did see him one morning. It was very early, and she and Walter were heading out of the door on their way to the center. Chandler walked into the kitchen just as she was grabbing her coat.

Sarita was so surprised to see him, it took her a moment to find her voice. "Morning," she finally said.

"Good morning."

He was dressed for work. Dark tailored suit, crisp white shirt, beautiful tie. To Sarita he looked like he'd just stepped off of the cover of a Fortune 500 business magazine. She was dressed in jeans, athletic shoes, and a Michigan State University sweatshirt.

He asked, "How are you?"

"I'm well. You?"

"Busy." Myk held himself at a distance by the sheer force of will. He wanted to apologize to her, but being who he was, he didn't know how. He'd never had the need or the desire to explain himself to anyone, yet deep inside an urge to make things right between them was gnawing at him. Being around her was changing him, and he wasn't sure how to handle that either. "Things going okay at the center?"

"Yes. Everything you've sent over has been well appreciated."

"Good."

Their eyes held, and Sarita got the impression that he wanted to say more, but all he said was, "I should get to work."

She nodded.

And he was gone.

By the second week, Myk's employees were starting to complain to each other about what a bear he'd become, growling at the secretaries, barking at his foremen, chewing out staff members for making honest mistakes. Dr. Drake diagnosed his half brother as bordering on crazy. Everyone else in Myk's sphere agreed and prayed the storm would blow over soon.

Faye paced her apartment nervously. Today was the day she'd meet her new secret admirer. She didn't have a clue as to mystery suitor's identity; but from all the flowers he'd been sending over, and the expensive little baubles that were arriving daily, she was sure he was rich. It had occurred to her that he might be a toad, but with all the problems she was having trying to make financial ends meet—thanks to that bastard Myk Chandler, Faye didn't care if he looked like a cartoon ogre as long as he let her spend his money.

When the doorbell buzzer went off, Faye looked over at the clock. Noon. He was right on time. Only discipline kept her from dashing to the door and flinging it open. It wouldn't do to appear too eager; she didn't want him to think she was desperate. She had an image to maintain. Instead of answering the door, she fussed over the beautiful lilies that he'd had delivered to her that morning. She always made her men ring twice; it was her way of telling them Faye Riley was worth the wait.

Still admiring her flowers, Faye prayed this new sugar daddy wasn't deformed or disfigured. Old and ugly she could handle, but not a freak. Intruding into her self-centered thoughts came the tingling sensation that something was wrong. She raised her eyes to the door. She didn't remember hearing another buzz from the bell. *Good Lord!*

She ran to the door and pressed her eye against the peephole, but saw no one. Throwing open the door she looked up and down the carpeted hallway. Nothing. She hurried out into the hall just in time to see a group of finely dressed brothers getting into the elevator, but before she could reach it, the doors slid closed. She hurried back to her apartment, but realized that in her haste to catch the men on the elevator, she hadn't set the lock, and it had locked behind her; a small problem compared to the anxiety roaring through her.

Being locked out meant she couldn't phone down to the lobby and have the doorman stop the men from leaving the building. Her only hope was the fire stairs, and her heart pounded not only with panic, but blanched at the prospect of running down fourteen flights of stairs to beat the elevator to the lobby.

She made it down as far as the tenth floor before disaster struck. The heel of one of her olive green Italian pumps slipped on the metal fire stairs. She stumbled and, with a scream, went sprawling. She hit the landing on floor nine, hard. For a moment, she thought she'd killed herself, but when she looked down at herself she wished she had. Her hands were all scraped up, the heel on her pump was only partially intact, her green skirt had a big streak of dirt across it, and she wanted to cry when she saw the huge hole in the knee of her twenty-five-dollar-a-pair imported, silk hose.

There was no time for pity though. She had a man to catch.

By the time Faye pushed her way through the door leading to the lobby she looked like hell. Never having been one to exercise, she could barely breathe after the fourteen-flight ordeal. She stood unsteadily on the one good olive pump, and only the grip she had on the doorknob kept her upright. She was too exhausted and outdone to care about the shocked looks from the people milling about. Her only concern was stopping the small entourage exiting the elevator and heading toward the large glass front doors. "Wait!" she yelled with what she knew had to be the last breath she'd ever draw. "Wait!"

Her call made everyone in the lobby look up.

Clark sent his bodyguards to retrieve the car, then turned around and viewed the obviously distressed Faye. She was tall, light-skinned, and even more beautiful than the pictures in the file his cop had compiled, but she already had one strike: She had not answered her door after he'd given her his standard fifteen-second wait. It was a trick most women of Faye's breed pulled or attempted to, but Clark Nelson played by his own rules. He had not gotten to the top of the food chain catering to the game-playing Fayes of the world. Where he came from, only a woman rang more than once, never a man.

He could see her moving toward him, and the closer she got, the more he smiled inside. She looked like a car wreck. The once carefully styled hair spilled crazily about her face. There were large rips beneath the armpits of her fancy green blouse. The darker green skirt was stained, and the front hem sagged as if it had been ripped free. The shoes and stockings were indescribable, yet she limped toward him like a queen.

When she faced him, she stuck out her hand, "I'm Faye Riley."

One of building's maintenance women passed by and cleared her throat to cover her laugh. Faye ignored her.

Clark did not clasp her scraped dirty hand. Because of his leg's susceptibility to infection, he avoided dirt whenever he could. "Miss Riley. I didn't think you were home." Taking a moment to visually assess her, he added, "You look like you had a small accident."

"I—I was in the back of the apartment."

"I see."

Faye ignored the strong sensation that he knew she was lying and tried not to break into tears over this ridiculous and, yes, humiliating situation. Should she explain why she looked so bad? She didn't think he'd want to go anywhere with her considering the way she looked, but she thought maybe he was as classy as he dressed and would be moved by her unfortunate chain of events. Faye tried to explain, "I came to the door just in time to see you and your friends getting back on the elevator. And then I was locked out of my apartment, so I had to take the stairs. Clumsy me, I tripped, tore my stockings . . ."

His dark eyes never wavered. A chill ran up Faye's spine. He didn't appear to care a bit about her humiliation or that she'd nearly killed herself trying to catch him. In fact, he acted like her mad dash was par for the course, expected.

"Well, Miss Riley, if you can be ready in say, fifteen minutes, we can still have lunch."

Faye felt slapped. She knew how bad she looked. It would take her twenty minutes just to fix her hair.

Without another word, he and the ivory cane headed toward the doors, leaving Faye alone to field the still-curious stares of the gawking lobby crowd.

But she did it. With the help of a spare key from the desk so she could get back into her place, twelve and a half minutes later, Faye was beside him in the long gray limo as it pulled away from the curb.

Over lunch in a quiet, expensive restaurant downtown, they toasted their new partnership. He'd told her about the raw deal he'd gotten at Chandler's hand in Central America, and Faye told him her own story of woe, so in exchange for twenty-five thousand dollars up front, Faye agreed to help him bring Myk Chandler down and be Clark's hostess for the duration of his stay in Detroit.

Fourteen

The weeks leading up to Thanksgiving were hectic ones at the William Lambert Center. Thanks to the Chandler Foundation, Sarita and her Army had for the first time ever the means to provide full holiday dinners for every homebound senior and needy family on their list. There'd be no turning people away because the money had run out. Turkeys and hams were purchased along with fresh veggies and canned foods. They spent a week filling baskets, and with the help of the new van and the teenagers of the Guard, got everything delivered. Sarita didn't even think about her own holiday plans until the Tuesday before Thanksgiving. She had no idea how or if Chandler celebrated the holiday, so she asked Walter about it on the way to the center that morning.

"He won't be here for Thanksgiving," Walter confessed solemnly.

For a moment, Sarita was confused. "Is he going to visit his grandmother?"

"No, he's out of town. He had a presentation to give for a hotel project Chandler Works is bidding on in Milwaukee."

"Oh."

Walter heard the dejection in the single word and wished he could make things better. Myk had flown to Milwaukee that morning, apparently without telling her his plans. He'd told Walter to expect him the day after the holiday.

"Well, then," Sarita declared with false brightness, "if you don't have any plans, would you like to come over and have dinner with me?"

"Just you and me, my lady?"

She smiled, "No. You, me. Silas probably, and Jerome and his mother, Shirley."

"Shirley's coming?"

Sarita heard his eagerness. "Yes, she is. So, should I set a place for you?" she asked innocently. Everyone knew how well he and Shirley were getting along.

"Oh, yes, ma'am."

They laughed and spent the balance of the ride discussing the menu and other possible invitees. By the time they reached the center, Sarita's bruised feelings were better.

On the Thanksgiving Eve flight back to Detroit, Myk had run out of excuses. Initially, he'd had no intentions of flying home until Friday, but once he learned that the dates for the bidding had been changed at the last minute, he had no reason to stay. He told himself he could spend freed-up days at the office catching up on some of the other proposals and bids he'd let lie the past few hectic weeks. In the end, however, he had to face the truth. He'd flown back for one reason, and one reason alone: Sarita.

Sarita and her crew were in Chandler's fancy kitchen having a good time working on the preparations for Thursday's Thanksgiving feast. Keta and Jerome were washing greens. Silas and Walter had decided to add chittlins to the table's bounty, and were cleaning 150 pounds of the innards in the counter sink. Shirley, famous for her sweet potato pie, had enlisted Drake as her assistant, and the two had enough of the golden, seasoned filling for a dozen of the traditional pastries.

Sarita's role was bread maker. She was wrist deep in dough for yeast rolls, and the front of her silver-and-blue Detroit Lions apron was covered with flour. The home team would be playing as they always did on Turkey Day. She doubted her beloved Lions would be able to do a thing with the juggernaut St. Louis Rams, but stranger things had happened in the world of football, so she was wearing her colors to show her support. Working on the far end of the marble island, Keta's grandmother, Mrs. Kennedy, cut up celery and onions for the dressing. The corn bread she needed for the base was in the oven, almost ready to come out, and its fragrance added to the rich aroma permeating the air.

The tantalizing smell of the food caught Myk's attention as soon he entered the house. *Why in the world is she up, cooking at this hour?* Pulling his key from the lock, he also wondered about all the voices and laughter he could hear. Puzzled, he closed the door, set his luggage down, then hung up his coat.

When Sarita glanced up and saw Chandler standing in the kitchen doorway, she dropped the small glass bowl of flour in her hand and it hit the tiled floor with a crash.

"Glad to see you, too," he told her, while watching her scramble to grab a broom and clean up the mess. He was greeted by smiles and hellos from everyone except Keta, but that was to be expected, so Myk ignored Keta for the moment and focused his attention back on the apron-wearing Little Touissant in her black leggings, bunny slippers, and too-big sweatshirt. His pulse leapt at the sight of her.

Chandler's vibrant eyes made Sarita remember everything that had gone before, and she had the urge to say something, anything, to cover her wild nervousness. "I—I thought you weren't going to be back for a couple more days."

"Change in plans."

As Sarita swept up the glass and flour, she couldn't help herself. She kept glancing at the long thin box in his hand. The box was wrapped with beautiful silver paper and sported a large, dark blue bow.

Myk noted her curiosity and her attempts not to appear so. Inwardly, he smiled. "Are we having a party?"

Sarita couldn't gauge his mood. He looked harmless enough, but she knew better than to assume anything. Was he going to be angry with her for inviting her friends to dinner without his permission? "I—well, yes. Thanksgiving dinner, tomorrow." She finally managed to get up all the glass, walked the dustpan to the trash container, and dumped it in.

He asked, "Think your troops could do without you for a few minutes?"

A hesitant Sarita looked around. They all gave her smiles of reassurance. She set the broom and dustpan back in the narrow closet and closed the door. "I suppose so."

They went into the small dining room where they sometimes ate breakfast. He closed the door, and Sarita took a seat at the polished table. Looking down at her hands, she realized the man had her so freaked out she hadn't even washed them. Drying flecks of white dough coated her palms and fingers.

Myk saw her dilemma but didn't want her to think he was bothered by it. "I'll only keep you a minute or two."

Being a lifelong football fan, Sarita knew that the best defense was a good offense, so she told him, "If you're mad about my inviting them to dinner—I—"

"Did I say that?"

"Well, no. But—I—"

"Give a brother a chance," he countered easily.

She stared down guiltily at her dough-caked hands.

"Here," he said then.

She looked up to see him holding the mysterious box out for her to accept, but the state of her hands made her hesitant. "Will you open it for me, please?"

A bit exasperated that his homecoming wasn't going the way he'd envisioned, he said tersely, "It's for you to open. Go wash your hands."

She retreated hastily.

Myk chastised himself for being short with her. He could have very easily honored her request and opened the box, but that would have deprived him of the pleasure of seeing her excitement. Admitting that he wanted to be a source of her happiness was difficult for the great Mykal Chandler. It was much easier to admit that he wanted everyone out of his house and gone, though. He wasn't pleased with having to share her. After all, he'd flown *coach* to get back to her, and the CEO of Chandler Works hadn't flown coach in ten years.

Her soft steps made him turn to watch her enter the room. Even covered with flour she was gorgeous. She mockingly held up her hands for his inspection. He nodded approvingly and gestured her to the box.

Sarita had no clue as to what the box held, but finding two dozen of the darkest red roses she'd ever seen in her life hadn't even been on the list. "Oh, Mykal . . ." she whispered. The emotions uncoiling within her were so strong tears burned her eyes.

Myk saw the tears and the small, shaking hand she'd placed against her lips. He forced his features to remain expressionless. Had she never received flowers before?

"No one's ever given me roses before . . ." she confessed in a soft, quivery voice.

"Well, if they're going to make you cry, I won't buy you any more."

Her stricken eyes made him want to cut out his own tongue. He crossed quickly to her side. "Baby, I was only teasing. Don't look like that. Please."

The remark had already done its damage. Sarita threw up her chin. "I'll try and be more sophisticated next time," she declared. "I'm sure Faye never blubbered over flowers."

"I wouldn't know. I never gave her any."

She stared surprised. "I don't believe that."

"Never. And I certainly wouldn't have sent her those."

"Why not?"

"She cost me enough money without flying in flowers from Brazil."

Sarita's mouth dropped open in astonishment. "*Brazil!* You had these flown in from *Brazil!*"

"You can't get roses that dark just anywhere. I ordered them before I left for Milwaukee. They were waiting in the fridge at the office when I stopped by on the way home."

Sarita wondered if she would ever be able to reconcile herself to being the beneficiary of his too-large lifestyle. She didn't think so, but because they'd had words about his extravagant spending before, she thought it best to leave it alone; she didn't want to start an argument. "Thanks for the roses." She picked up the box. "I—need to find a vase and get back to the kitchen."

Myk sensed the change in her mood. "I was only teasing, Sarita."

"I know."

"Is there something about the roses you don't like?" He gently captured her hand to keep her from walking out.

"There's nothing wrong with the roses, but suppose there were? Would you send off to Spain next time?"

"Maybe."

She snarled her frustration and snatched her

hand free. "See!" she accused plainly, then set the box firmly back down on the table.

Myk didn't see a damn thing. "Speak English, woman. Are you saying you're mad because you wanted roses from Spain?"

"Of course not," she snapped. "The problem is you probably would be dumb enough to buy some woman roses from Spain!"

Myk took in her angry pacing and didn't know whether to laugh or take offense.

"Don't you dare laugh at me," she warned prophetically.

"I'm not laughing, but are you still having issues with my money?"

"Yes," she said quietly. "Yes, I am."

Myk shook his head. He'd been home less than twenty minutes, and they were on the verge of battling already. "Do you need anything else for the center?"

"No."

"All the old windows replaced, the van's running, and the computers working?"

"Yes."

"How are the furnace and the new appliances?"

"Fine," she answered, but wondered where he was headed.

"So, how much do you think I've spent on the center since my first visit?"

She didn't have to think about the sum. "Thousands, I'm sure."

"Well, don't you think that after all that dogooding I should be allowed to spend a little speck of my money on you?"

She met his eyes, but couldn't hold the contact for

very long because of her guilt. "I suppose. Yes, but—"

"I'm not done," he interrupted her in a gentle voice.

"Okay."

"I also wanted to give you the roses as my way of saying I'm sorry."

She studied him. "For what?"

"For believing you were as common as the other women I've known."

He saw the frown of confusion between her eyes and attempted to explain, "Remember the day I called you common? I know you do."

She did. She remembered it as if it were yesterday. He'd tossed out the unfair comment the morning she learned he'd purchased her building. The remark stung as much then as the memory of it did now.

"Well, I was wrong," he said earnestly. "You are the rarest thing I've ever had in my life . . ."

Sarita's eyes flew to his.

"When the phone rang, I shouldn't have left you like that. I'm sorry."

Sarita searched his face. The honesty and sincerity reflected there set off emotions far stronger than the ones caused by the gift of the flowers. Before her was a man who over the past few weeks had made most of her dreams for her center come true. He'd provided for her in ways that continued to amaze, and she was certain that if she asked for the moon, he'd try and get it for her. Yes, he was arrogant, and really hard to get along with most of the time, but—
She knew she'd never forgive herself if she started bawling, but it was plain to her that she was ankle

deep in love with him already, and the tide seemed to be rising every day. She'd been so sure he'd put up a fence between them because he was angry at her for leaving; she'd been wrong.

He then confessed, "I've never said this to a lady before, but woman, you are turning me inside out."

Frankly, she felt the same way.

He looked into the water-filled eyes of the fire ant he'd flown hundreds of miles just to see and knew he had made the right decision to return home. "Come here . . ."

The softness of his voice was her undoing. She walked into the comfort of his outstretched arms, and he held her tight. "I'm sorry," he whispered again. "Forgive me."

Sarita would deal with the mind-blowing concept of Chandler apologizing later, right now, she just wanted him to hold her. "You don't have to buy me stuff to say you're sorry, Mykal. A simple apology is all I need."

The sound of his name on her lips always thrilled him and at that moment, he was even more moved. He raised her chin so he could see her small brown face. "I'll remember that, but in the future, when I want to buy you something. I will. Period. It's genetic. Humor me, okay?"

She supposed he had earned the right to indulge himself. "Okay."

"Good." With wonder and all of his feelings blazing in his eyes, he slowly traced the soft full mouth he'd been dreaming for weeks about kissing again. "I need to ask you something."

"Shoot."

"Can we put away all the barriers and just enjoy ourselves?"

"You mean act like we're really a real couple?"

"Yes, I guess that's what I'm asking."

She kept hearing him call her rare.

"I want you to share my table, my life, my bed. I want to wake up with you in the morning, hold you close at night."

Sarita drew in a shaky breath. She listened to his heart beating beneath her cheek and felt his arms tighten their hold tenderly.

"Legally, you're already my wife, but I want you to be my lady, too."

Their eyes met.

He asked her, "Yes? No?"

There were no doubts in Sarita's mind that he meant what he was saying, nor did she doubt that he had some feelings for her. He hadn't mentioned love, but she wasn't expecting that type of commitment. Theirs was a contracted marriage of convenience, and she knew the conditions going in, but could she keep her own feelings from blossoming into full-blown love? If she couldn't, would she be able to hide it from him? The last thing she wanted was for him to find out and think he owed her sentiments he didn't really have. She didn't need his pity. She hadn't forgotten the Fletcher Harris issue either, but that didn't figure into this equation. What he'd asked centered only on her and the impossible man holding her against his heart.

"Well?" he asked.

"My answer is yes, but only if you promise to patronize a local florist."

He smiled down. "Why do Black women always want to negotiate? This is nonnegotiable. Me and my checkbook come as a package."

Her eyes shining, she tossed back softly, "I suppose I could do worse."

He lightly swatted her on the behind. "Sassiest woman I've ever met, too."

"It's genetic. Humor me."

For Myk, being around her was like having the windows of his soul thrown open to the sun. She made him warm in places he'd shuttered years ago in order to have the discipline necessary to make his way in the world. He hadn't had time for feelings or softness. Mesmerized, he gently traced her lips again. "I want to kiss you, but if I do, I know I won't be able to stop, and those folks in the kitchen won't see you again until Saturday . . ."

The quiet certainty in his voice stroked her down to her toes. "Then how about we agree on just one?" she suggested in a sultry voice.

His dark eyes sparkled at her banter. "Sometime soon—real soon, I'm going to see just how playful you really are."

"I think you'll be pleased."

Her cocky answer fired Myk's blood. Growling sensually, he pulled her closer and kissed her so slowly, passionately, and possessively, Sarita didn't care if the dough waiting back in the kitchen rose as high as the roof, or if the turkey never made it into the oven. Nothing was as important as the heat he ignited in her.

"I'm warning you . . ." he said with his lips against her ear and his hand moving lazily over the hard tight buds of her breasts. "If you don't leave,

I'm going to lay you back on this table and make you scream, then—"

When he felt her hot hand exploring the hard root that made him male, his words died away uselessly.

Seeing his eyes close, she ran her hand up and down the proof of his desire before giving a soft lusty squeeze. "All threats and no action make Mykal a dull man. . . ."

A knock sounded on the closed door. Their heads snapped up, and they yelled angrily in unison. "What?" and shot daggers at whoever was on the other side.

Keta's voice came through the door. "Sarita, the dressing's made, and my gramma wants to know what dish you want to put it in?"

Myk rolled his eyes, and said to her, "You know his grandmother didn't send him."

"I know," she replied. She then spoke to the door. "Tell her I'll be there in just a minute."

"Okay."

Sarita listened. When she didn't hear Keta's retreating footsteps, she walked over to the door and snatched it open. The eavesdropping Keta all but fell inside. He looked highly embarrassed.

Sarita almost didn't care. "Do you want to lose your beret?"

"No," he said tightly.

"Then stay out of grown folks' business, Keta."

"But—" he started to say, his angry eyes on Myk.

"But nothing." Sarita took a deep breath and addressed him gently. "Look, baby, you know I love you—always have, always will, but not in that way. Keta, you're sixteen."

"I won't be sixteen all of my life."

"And what, I'm supposed to wait until you grow up?" she asked with a small smile. "Let's be logical here."

He looked down at his basketball shoes, then up at Myk and swore, "If you ever make her cry, I'll kill you."

"Keta!" Sarita shouted with wide eyes. This was a young man who had a fit if anyone stepped on a ladybug in the parking lot, and now, he was threatening to kill someone?

"I mean it," the teenager said. "Not one tear. You hear me?"

Myk nodded. "I hear you, man."

Sarita looked back at Myk to ask him why in the world he was encouraging this foolishness, but decided she'd take it up with him later.

"You promise?" Keta asked Myk.

Myk held out his hand. Keta stepped to him and, with a look of hard solemnness in his sixteen-year-old eyes, grasped Myk's hand. They went through a ritual handshake, and when they finished, Keta turned and left the room without another word.

A confused Sarita stared. "Did I just miss something?"

"It's a man thing, but he and I agreed to disagree."

"I see," she said slowly, but she didn't really at all.

Myk could still see the confusion in her face, but they could discuss Keta later. "Do you think I'm ever going to get to make love to you?"

Just the sound of the question made her senses flare to life once again. "Apparently not."

He held out his arms, and she went to him willingly. He enfolded her, and she placed her head on the soft black sweater over his chest and felt herself able to relax mentally for the first time in a long time. He kissed her hair. "Well, I'm telling you now, the next person that interrupts us is going to get staked out on an anthill."

"I'll bring the stakes and the rope."

He chuckled and kissed her softly. "Go finish in the kitchen. I'm going to go upstairs and change. You can put me to work when I get back."

"Unfortunately, it won't be the kind of work I'd really like for you to do."

Her sauciness made him swat her playfully on the behind. "Get, before I show you what a hard-working brother really looks like."

She slid her hand over him fleetingly, then cooed, "Can't wait for that."

Myk's eyes widened, and his face broke into a knowing grin. "Oh, yeah. Me and you. Soon."

She picked up her flowers, winked, then left him alone.

Watching her go, Myk shook his head and laughed.

On the way back to the kitchen, Sarita knew she'd never been so forward with a man before, but he seemed to enjoy her bold side, and, frankly, she did too. It was the new millennium, and Sarita felt women had a right to express their sexuality, as long as they weren't acting like the hoochies in those terrible rap videos.

Shirley met Sarita's eyes when she walked into the kitchen, and said, "Whoa, look at those roses. You two must have made up."

Laughing, Sarita put the roses down on the cluttered counter and searched the cabinets for a vase.

"You just worry about your pies, Miss Nosy."

Shirley tossed back. "Made up that good, huh?"

Sarita ignored the smiles on the faces of the others and went back to her dough. When she met Keta's eyes, he looked away.

Myk came into the kitchen a short while later after having changed into a pair of worn jeans and a sweatshirt with CHANDLER WORKS emblazoned across the front, and Sarita put him to work peeling apples for the brioche she planned on baking for breakfast. The apples combined with finely chopped walnuts and cinnamon made up the filling. The filling would sit in the refrigerator overnight along with the brioche dough and the dough for the rolls.

An hour later, everything that could be accomplished for the night had been. Over Sarita's protests, Walter and Shirley insisted upon cleaning up the kitchen, but the more Sarita tried to change their minds, the more stubborn they became, so, smiling, she threw up her hands and let them take on the monstrous job of returning the kitchen to its previously immaculate state. Drake, Silas, and Myk took Keta and Jerome down to the basement to play video games and shoot a little hoop. Sarita escorted Mrs. Kennedy into the den and gave her the remote so she could watch the Shopping Channel, one of her favorite pastimes. Walter would be taking everyone home once he and Shirley finished in the kitchen.

Sarita drifted back to the kitchen, but when she saw Shirley and Walter kissing passionately against the counter, she smiled and quietly backed away. She decided to go to the basement instead.

The basement was as nice as the rest of the house

in Sarita's opinion. She walked past the room with the minitheater, complete with curtains and a widescreen TV; the weight room filled with state-of-the-art equipment; the laundry room; and the room that sported a pool table, another large TV, and a fully stocked bar with black leather barstools. Turning a corner she heard the bounce of a basketball, which signaled where the men were. The gym was only large enough for half court, but when she walked in she saw Myk and Keta going at each other one-on-one like it was the NBA finals. Drake, Silas, and Jerome were sitting in folding chairs along the side.

"Foul!" she heard Keta yell.

"Quit being a baby," the winded Myk shot back. "You think those college boys are just going to let you slide your way to the hoop!" He tossed Keta the ball hard, and Keta took the ball out.

Sarita asked suspiciously, "What's going on?"

Drake said, "I think they're battling for the hand of yon fair maiden."

Silas laughed. "Grandson, you got a way with words."

Sarita's eyes watched the court. "Can I have that in English?"

Jerome's eyes never left the action as he explained, "Mr. Chandler told Keta that if Keta beat him to fifteen, he'd never show his face at the center again."

"What? Why?"

Silas said, "Because the center's Keta's turf, and you don't let another man rule your turf. It's a man thing. You wouldn't understand."

Sarita rolled her eyes.

Drake, watched Keta's swish push the score to

eight–five in Keta's favor, and said, "Yep. My brother, the old guy in the shorts and the cutoff sweatshirt, challenged a sixteen-year-old kid to a basketball game."

Sarita asked, "Does he know Keta's been All-City since the ninth grade?"

Silas said, "I think he's finding out."

Another swish—9–5—Keta.

Sarita didn't think Chandler stood a chance, even if he did look awfully fit in his shorts and sleeveless sweatshirt. In comparison, Keta looked like the man-child that he was, with his skinny arms and legs. However, Keta Kennedy had the sweetest, purest shot in the state and was being recruited by colleges all over the country. She hated to be the bearer of bad news, but Chandler was about to get his butt kicked.

In the end, it came down to experience versus youth. In his younger days, Myk had also been somewhat of a phenom on the courts, but that had been years ago, and time had taken its toll. He knew that if he didn't hurry up and end this game, and quick, he was going to keel over from exhaustion. So, he took Keta Kennedy, All-City, All-State, to school. The two combatants were fairly evenly matched in height, but Myk outweighed the young man by a good fifty pounds and used that strength to his advantage. By holding, elbowing, and sticking his adult male chest into Keta's skinnier one, Myk played him like a pro and scored point after point.

The contest ended at 15–9. Chandler.

The small crowd, which by then included Shirley and Walter, roared their approval and Keta and

Myk shook hands. Nobody had beaten Keta one-on-one in a long time. As both ballers bent over to catch their breath, Keta wondered what else Sarita's new husband could teach him.

Sarita hoped the game would finally put to rest all the drama between them. Both males were parts of her life now, and she'd much rather they get along.

Myk gave Keta one last congratulatory pat on the back, then walked over to stand before his wife.

"Did you win the hand of the fair maiden?" she asked him.

"Yep, and I'm going to need that hand to help me upstairs. Lord, what was I thinking? Don't anybody ever let me play ball against a young brother again."

Drake laughed. "Take him upstairs and put him in a hot tub, Sarita. Walter and I will lock up and take everybody home."

Myk draped his arm across Sarita's shoulders, and hobbled his way toward the door.

Keta yelled out, "Hey, old man!"

Myk turned and his eyes smiled across the distance. "What?"

"Next time, I'll be ready."

Myk chuckled. "Do I look like there's going to be a next time? Good night, Keta. See you tomorrow."

Once they were out of sight of the others, Myk scooped her up into her arms and her mouth opened wide with surprise. He carried her up the back stairway that led directly to his room.

A confused Sarita asked, "I thought you were hurt?"

"I was playing possum."

"Why?"

"Well, it made Keta feel good to think he'd worn me out, and it made everybody else go home."

She threw back her head and laughed out loud.

The hallway of his wing was quiet. The soft lighting along the walls seemed to add to the stillness. Even though she'd agreed to be his lady, the reality that they would probably make love tonight, filled her with both nervousness and anticipation. "I can walk, you know," she said, as they arrived at the massive doors that led to his inner sanctum.

"I know, but consider this our wedding night. The man always carries his lady over the threshold."

She wondered if this was how it felt to be in a fairy tale. "Mykal Chandler, you're a romantic."

"Don't tell anybody," he tossed back.

She chuckled, but it died as he lowered his head to place a soft kiss on her lips. Then he opened the doors, kicked them wide, and carried her inside.

Fifteen

The moment he set her on her feet, time seemed to stop. Sarita could feel every inch of her being connecting with him, and when he kissed her, she returned it ardently. The kissing soon deepened into a slow-as-molasses sonata, accented by exploring hands and rising desire. Long, humid moments passed as they learned the slopes and curves of each other; touching, cajoling, whispering. His wandering hand rucked up her sweatshirt and covered her bra-enclosed breast. The warm skin encased in the lacy satin increased his hunger. Still kissing her, he slid the demicup aside to free the soft treasure inside, then husked out against her lips, "After that game with Keta, I need to shower."

The fiery movements of his palm over Sarita's pebble hard breast, made her shudder lustily, but she somehow managed to say, "Me too . . ."

He bent to lazily circle the hot tip of his tongue around the pleading, aroused nipple, then took it into his mouth. An elongated groan of delight escaped her lips, and she arched her back to receive more. He shifted the other bra cup just far enough to free the nipple, then played with it while she dissolved.

When Myk was certain her nipples were his and his alone, he raised his head and let her sweatshirt fall back in place before reclaiming her mouth. He loved kissing her; could do it for a lifetime. Who knew she'd be so deliciously responsive? He wanted to eat her up. "Go get in the shower," he whispered. "I'll get the bed ready and find you something to wear . . ."

The anticipation sent heat echoing through Sarita's core, but his kisses now trailing lustfully over her arched neck were too tantalizing to walk away from. "I can't go if you keep kissing me, Mykal . . ."

As always, the sound of her whispering his name fired Myk like the kick of an aphrodisiac in a spiked drink. He was aroused and hard and couldn't seem to keep his hands or lips from sampling her sweetness. The last thing he wanted to do was turn her loose, but a few breathless moments later, he did.

Sarita could barely stand. Her world was rocked, and she didn't care who knew. Every inch of her body was pulsating and damp.

He led her into the bathroom. After placing a lingering kiss on her lips, he departed. Her eyes still closed, Sarita began removing her clothes.

The shower's hot water felt good. Turning and arching under the powerful spray, she let it add to the sensations searing her aroused flesh. Washing with the cloth and the vanilla soap he'd given her, she slid the suds over her skin while the drumbeat of passion continued to pound.

When she was done, she dried off, then wrapped herself in one of his man-sized towels and padded back into the bedroom to rejoin him. Candles had been lit. Flames danced in the fireplace. The warm bedroom glowed with a soft, wavering light.

He was standing by the bed. He'd stripped away the sweatshirt and was wearing only his shorts. Although he didn't utter a word, his call to her body was loud and clear.

Myk forced himself to stay where he was. Knowing she was nude beneath the towel, and that if he stripped it away his lips would find warm, shower-damp skin, swelled his need. He couldn't ever remember wanting one woman so much. "I'll be right back," he finally said, "Your nightgown's on the bed."

His reluctance to leave was very apparent, but he disappeared through the archway, and Sarita walked over to the bed. The black silk hangings co-cooning it were soft to the touch. Each was emblazoned with dragons. The sight made her shake her head. In her estimation he might be in too deep with all these dragons everywhere, but the needlework on the panels was exquisite.

Her eyes drifted down to the satin comforter covering the sheet and pillows and saw not dragons but the gown and matching robe he'd laid out for her. They were both a deep dark purple. The silk appeared to be as finely made as the panels shrouding his bed, and nearly as transparent. Moved by the beauty of the gown, she did feel as if this were her wedding night. Hands shaking, she held it up. It was long and flowing. No ornamentation, no lace. The short seams across the shoulders were softly gathered, and the circular bodice was designed to fall loosely across the breasts. There were no side seams however. Two small satin ribbons, one on each hip, were all that held it together. Its design made Sarita think of Egypt. The gown looked like something Cleopatra might have worn to please her lovers Marc Antony or Julius Caesar. Thinking about her own dragon lover releasing the ribbons stoked her own fires. The gown was hot, and it made her hot just looking at it.

She slipped it on and tied the ribbons. The sides of her ribs and thighs were left elegantly bare. Taking in a deep breath, she tried to slow herself down, but the sound of the shower turning off made her heart and breathing take off again. Calming herself, Sarita stood and waited.

With a towel cinched around his waist, Myk stepped back into the room. His eyes burned over her in the gown. "I see you found it."

"Yes, do you like it?" she twirled for him, nearly blinding him in the process with the flash of her breasts and thighs.

"I like it a lot."

Feeding on the arousal she saw glittering in his eyes, she asked, "Do you always dress your women before taking them to bed?"

"Nope. Just you. Been wanting to take that gown off of you for quite some time."

Sarita's senses rippled. He was so much better at this than she. Why did she even think she could best him in verbal foreplay. Just looking at him should make her know better. The flickering candlelight caught the lingering sheen of moisture in his hair and on the sculpted riches of his dark shoulders and forearms. She thought him the most gorgeously made man she'd ever seen. Emboldened by her wanting, she held out her hand, and he slowly came to meet her.

The feverish steamy kisses that followed melted them back onto the bed. This time there'd be no phone calls or nosy teenagers knocking on the door; tonight they planned on taking each other to the heights of love, and dared anyone or anything to intrude.

To that end, Myk slowly ran his large hands beneath her fine indigo gown and savored the feel of his flesh gliding purposefully over her own. Her nipples were ripe, her waist sleek. The firm thighs now parting so lusciously beneath his silent command held a dark warm treasure he'd been wanting to open all evening. First, however, he undid the ribbons at her waist, then with a lusty hand wantonly moved the rich purple silk over the heat he'd been coaxing to life all evening. Under his scandalous tutelage, her trembling legs widened shamelessly, while above her Myk watched with glowing eyes.

Continuing to tempt her with the silk, he circled and seduced her until the fabric became as wet as she. Only then did he replace the silk with his hand. He dallied there until her hips rose in glorious invitation, and her low answering moan floated against the silence.

Sarita didn't know such pleasure was possible.

His hands were magic, his technique bliss. When he lowered his head and placed his kiss against the inside of one thigh, then the other, she could feel her climax hovering on the horizon. "Mykal," she pleaded softly.

He bent to flick his tongue over the nook of her navel, "What baby?"

"I'm going to come. . . ."

"Then let's get this first one out of the way. . . ."

He slid his hand over the sweet ache between her thighs. She spread herself in surrender, and to reward her he lowered his head and paid her hot, carnal tribute.

"Oh," she cried out lustily. She'd never been loved this way before. It was erotic, raw, and then, she couldn't think anymore because the orgasm tearing through her made her buck and twist and scream out the name of the dragon who was eating her up.

Myk decided he'd found his real mission in life— making love to Sarita. He'd always been a considerate lover; the more pleasure he could make a woman feel, the more it fueled his own desire, but Sarita he could love all day long, all night long. He slid a finger over the slick pulsating vent and knew he'd never get enough, not even if she stayed with him a hundred years.

Sarita trembled when his fingers moved over her again. She couldn't help herself. As blown away as she was, she wanted more. He'd introduced her to something she'd often read about but never experienced, until now. She could honestly say the written word didn't even come close.

She opened her eyes and met his. He was

propped up on his elbow and stretched out beside her. She reached out and cupped his cheek. Leaning up she kissed him softly, whispering, "You're way too good at this, dragon man."

He smiled, and covered her hand. "You ain't seen nothin' yet."

And to her delight, he was right. He brought her to pleasure once more with his mouth and hands, and by the time his condom-sheathed manhood eased its way home, Sarita was so dazzled and breathless she would have let him make love to her on the front lawn of the City-County Building. She welcomed him into herself gladly and without inhibition. He loved her fully, scandalously. When he told her in a passion gruff voice to turn around and kneel up against the headboard, she did; when he lustily invited her to ride the dragon's horn, she impaled herself slowly, shamelessly, eagerly taking in his full glory while her eyes blazed down into his. It was a hot, steamy symphony of unbridled lust and intensity, and when they were done, they both fell away weak and unable to move.

"Lord, woman . . ." Myk said in surrender.

"Me?" she countered as she smiled contentedly in the now-very-disheveled bed. "You're the dragon. I'm just the captured maiden."

He dragged her over to him and nestled up against her back. "You certainly screamed like one."

She elbowed him playfully. "You roared a few times yourself, or was that some other man?"

He grinned and squeezed her soft behind. "You are something else."

Although nothing was said aloud, they both knew that this night was another turning point in their relationship. "I'm just glad I didn't mess this up," he told her softly.

She was confused. "What do you mean?"

He answered with a shrug. "Brothers worry. Will we somehow mess it up? Will we say the wrong thing? Will we answer the phone if it starts ringing?"

She found that hard to believe but smiled. "You? I figured you were all cool, calm, and collected as my grandmother used to say."

"With another woman, maybe. Not with you."

The honesty in his face made the love tide she'd identified downstairs rise from her ankles to her knees just like that. Regardless of what the future had in store, she knew she would carry the memory of this man in her heart for the rest of her days. "I couldn't possibly make you nervous."

"Why not?"

"Because I'm just me."

He traced his finger over her shoulder. "Any woman who would shoot a man with his own gun is a sister to be reckoned with."

She chuckled, then confessed truthfully, "You scared me to death."

"But you still had the presence of mind to squeeze off two shots."

"I hate guns," she told him, "but I had to protect myself. I didn't know you."

He kissed her shoulder. "No need to apologize. It's what you were supposed to do."

She turned over so she could look up at him. "I'm glad I didn't blow you away."

"Me too."

She touched his cheek, "When this is all over, I don't want anything from you."

He knew when the time came to let her go, it was going to be difficult indeed. "I know. You're probably the first woman who doesn't. Makes you special." He lowered himself to her lips. "Very special."

Sarita placed her arms around his neck and slowly drew him down so they could begin again.

Myk woke up to an empty bed and the sound of the shower running. In the darkness, he pawed at the clock to turn it around, then stared groggily at the numbers—5 A.M.! What in the hell was she doing up so early? It occurred to him then that she'd gotten up to shower so she'd be fresh and ready for more loving when he woke up. The erotic possibilities of that scenario made his manhood stretch appreciatively. Making love in the morning was one of Myk's favorite things, and he couldn't think of a better way to start the day than with his sexy little wife.

When she entered the room, however, she was dressed; fully dressed in a pair of bright red leggings, a black long-sleeved Detroit Lions T-shirt, and the same pink-and-white bunny slippers she'd had on last night.

"I'm sorry if I woke you. I went to my room and got my clothes while you were still asleep. I was trying to be quiet."

Just looking at her made him hard, Myk realized. "You didn't wake me, but why are you up and dressed?"

"I have a turkey to put into the oven and I have to start breakfast. Everybody will be here at eight."

Myk was confused. What happened to his erotic early-morning scenario. "Breakfast? For who?"

She then explained that she and her friends always spent the holiday together and that they began the day with breakfast.

"I thought they were just coming for dinner," he groused.

Sarita scanned his face. He didn't look happy. "If it's not okay, you need to say so, now."

"I'm not saying that."

"Then what are you saying?"

"That I'm not real good at sharing."

Sarita put her hand on her hip. "I am not letting you eat that whole brioche by yourself, Mykal Chandler."

His laughter rang out around the room.

"What's so funny?" she asked.

For a moment, he couldn't stop laughing, but when he finally managed to get a hold on himself, he spent a moment eyeing the woman who had single-handedly turned his world upside down. "I wasn't talking about the brioche. I was talking about not wanting to share you."

The tone of his voice gave rise to memories of the night, and Sarita found his possessiveness thrilling.

"I was hoping you were coming back to bed," he said frankly.

"I'd like to, but if I do, there won't be any breakfast, or dinner."

"I don't care."

It was her turn to laugh. "Are all dragons so insatiable?"

He shrugged. "Couldn't tell you. I'm the only one I know."

She shook her head. "Go back to sleep. You'll need your strength for later."

Silence.

The scowl on his face made Sarita say teasingly, "Why, Mykal Chandler, you're pouting."

"No, I'm not."

"You are, too."

Their eyes met and held. She said, "I would love to spend the morning with you, but—there's always tonight."

Myk felt like a kid deprived of his favorite dessert. "I suppose I can wait. Go cook. I'll be down to help soon as I shower and get dressed."

"You're sure, it's okay."

"No, it's not okay, but my grandmother raised me to be nice."

"She did?"

He gave her an amused glare. "You are about two seconds from having those red leggings pulled off so I can paddle your sassy little behind."

She giggled.

"I'm not kidding. March."

She gave him a crisply elaborate salute, turned sharply in her bunny slippers, and marched to the door.

The sound of his laughter followed her through the sitting room and out into the hall.

Sarita took the big roaster holding the seasoned turkey out of the fridge and placed it in one of the built-in ovens she'd preheated upon her arrival. The oven below was heating up for the brioche, but she had to put the filling together with the dough and let the whole thing rise again before it could bake.

She was in the process of doing that when he sauntered in. "Coffee's ready," she pointed out. Like Saint, Chandler lived on little else. Thoughts of

Saint made her wonder where he might be and if he'd turn up for dinner. He usually did, but she tried not to get her hopes up just in case he didn't show this year. Since his return to the neighborhood, she'd become accustomed to having him around, and she'd missed him the past few weeks.

Myk sipped on his coffee and watched her prepare the brioche. All he wanted to do was make love to her again. He hadn't gotten nearly enough last night, and frankly, the male in him was still not pleased that he'd had to play second fiddle to a damn turkey. Whatever happened to a woman being so overwhelmed by his expert loving that all she could think about was more of the same? he thought sarcastically. He'd never had a woman leave his bed to go and cook instead. Being around Sarita was an experience, and a humbling one at that. "So, what else is on the menu?"

She looked up from the rolling pin she was using on the dough. "Let's see. Eggs, grits, catfish, biscuits, fruit, and this brioche."

When she had the dough rolled out to a fourteen-inch rectangle, she added the filling of apples, chopped walnuts, and cinnamon. Once the filling was spread over the rectangle of dough, she slowly rolled it up jelly-roll style and placed it in the loaf pan. The recipe made two loaves, so she repeated the whole process with the second loaf, then covered both pans with a clean dish towel for the final rising.

She went over to the sink to wash her hands. They were sticky from working with the filling and floury from the dough. In the process he came up behind her, and she stilled when his body heat enveloped her. His first move was to brush his lips over the side of her ear. Next came his hands moving oh so lazily over her breasts—plucking, rolling. He whispered, "I have never been kicked to the curb for a turkey before."

She grinned and stretched sensually. Her leggings were coming down. "You are such a spoiled, dragon man."

Her panties followed and she rippled with anticipation. "Am I on punishment for choosing the turkey over you?"

"Yes," he breathed, as his hand traveled meaningfully and possessively over her bare behind. Myk thought she had the softest skin he'd ever caressed. Her hips and thighs were warm, and so was he. He moved his hands between her thighs and played lustily until she was panting, weak, and running with love.

"I like being on punishment," she breathed hotly.

Myk entered her just as she was, and as she took him in, he rasped out, "God, you're sweet."

He started out slow, letting her savor his length and strength, while he delighted in the feel of her sheathing him. The pace increased, and a purring Sarita braced herself against the sink so he could get it all. She soon had to hold on to the counter to keep herself steady. Each upward thrust made her gasp with pleasure, and as the pace increased and her answering movements met him stroke for stroke, she cried out hoarsely and surrendered to the climax that rolled over her like thunder.

Her cries set off his own completion. Growling, head thrown back, he stroked her as life itself were in the balance, then filled her with all that he had.

When they finally parted, Sarita had a hard time slowing her breathing and her thumping heart. Her inner thighs were damp from his essence, and her core swollen and tender from lusty use. "I'm supposed to be cooking . . ." she said, her back still to him.

He ran his hand up her spine. "Wasn't that what we were doing?"

She glanced up into his amused dark eyes. "I'm going to have to ban you from the kitchen."

He flicked his tongue over her ear, and countered thickly, "Every time you come in here, you're going to think of what we just did."

He was right, too right. Sarita knew that she'd never be able to stand in front of this sink again and not remember the feel of his thrusts and the sweep of his magical hands. How in the world she was going to be able to walk away from this man when their time together came to an end, she didn't know.

For the rest of the day, his eyes teased her. Awareness of him stroked her through the arrival of the guests and breakfast, during the watching of the game, and when they all sat down at his long dining room table to eat the well-prepared meal. Each time she looked his way, the memories floated back.

By the time everyone went home, Sarita was tired from the long day, but the promise of pleasure glowing in his eyes gave her more than enough energy for what he had in mind. "I'm going up and take a shower."

"Okay, and while you're gone I've a few phone calls to make."

She gave him a warning look.

He came to his own defense, "Don't worry, I'll be

here when you get back because I have a surprise for you."

She eyed him skeptically. "What kind of surprise?"

"If I tell you, it won't be a surprise," he told her with amusement in his voice. "So go take your shower."

"It's not something real expensive, is it?"

"Sarita, if you don't stop asking me questions, I'm going to write a check for the Taj Mahal and give it to you for Christmas."

She laughed. "Okay. I'm going."

When Sarita came back downstairs she felt refreshed and relaxed. The shower had been glorious. The blue cotton pjs and the terry-cloth robe she had on were soft and comfortable, and the clean pair of red socks kept her feet warm.

Myk glanced up at her entrance into the kitchen and, after checking out her attire, shook his head and smiled.

She looked down at herself. "What?"

He took a swallow of the papaya juice in the glass he was holding, then said, "Pretty sexy outfit."

She tossed back, "I knew you'd like it. Too tired for diva clothes tonight."

His mustache lifted with his smile.

"So, where's this surprise?"

"Be right back."

He returned a few moments later carrying a small bag emblazoned with the logo of one of the national phone companies. In his other hand he was carrying some papers. "Your new cell phone."

Sarita peered down into the bag. Sure enough there was a phone in it. She pulled it out. "Oh, wow." She'd wanted a cell phone, but had never been able to afford even the cheapest plan.

While she looked it over, he added, "If it's okay with you. I'd like to get a few more for the Guard to share when they're on duty. The foundation will pay the charges, of course."

The offer touched her. "That's very generous of you."

The sincerity of her tone made Myk's heart do strange things again. Were Drake and Walter right about his being in love? "The phone isn't the surprise, though."

He spread the papers on the table. She saw that they were architectural drawings of a building. "What are these?" she asked, looking up at him curiously.

"I took the liberty of working up some ideas for rehabbing your building."

She shot him a look of surprise, then trained her excited eyes back on the drawings.

There were three mock-ups. They were similar in ways and different in others. Doors were in different places; the landscaping varied, as did the positioning of the playgrounds. The detail and thought that had to have gone into the project took her breath away. "These are wonderful," she whispered with awe.

He pointed out the distinct features in each design, explaining size and dimensions, why he positioned rooms the way he had, and how long construction might take. They discussed the pros and cons of the three choices, estimated the costs of the renovation, and kicked around other ideas to incorporate into the final design. He brought out his laptop, and when the drawings came up on the screen, he incorporated her ideas into the design with a skill she found dazzling. "You're pretty good at this."

"Thanks."

They spent a few more minutes talking over the plans, then he shut down the computer and set it aside. Sarita didn't know what to say in the face of such generosity. "I'm speechless."

His mustache twitched. "Good."

He pulled her into his arms and looked down into the face that filled his dreams. "Too expensive?"

She dropped her head, "No. Thank you, so very much." Leaning up, she kissed him softly. His arm tightened across her waist and pulled her close. She placed her head against his chest and hugged him tight, relishing his strength and generous spirit. "You're the best sugar daddy a girl could have."

He chuckled. For the first time Myk had a woman he wouldn't mind sharing the rest of his life with. He had no idea how she felt, but he was willing to be at her side for as long as she wished.

They made love in his bed until the wee hours of the morning. When they were done, he pulled her up against him, covered them both with the blankets, and slept content.

Because it was the Friday after Thanksgiving, the kids in the neighborhood had no school. Sarita had scheduled a morning meeting with the Guard. Among other items, she wanted their input on the center's new design. However, before she could get started on the agenda, Jerome asked excitedly. "Did

you hear about the bust on Townsend last night?"
Townsend was three streets over.

Sarita set her big purse on top of one of the tables.
"No. What happened?"

"They dropped down on them dealers so hard!"

"The police?"

One of the girls cracked, "Didn't look like no police to me. They were driving a black van with the windows tinted up."

Sarita remembered the TV news report she'd seen recently and wondered if this was the same crew. "Are you sure they weren't the police. State police maybe?"

Jerome said, "The state police don't wear ski masks."

She had to agree. The kids then told her about other busts they'd heard about through friends at school and from cousins on the westside. Keta echoed what all the kids felt. "I don't care who they are as long as they keep jamming those dealers."

Sarita said, "Amen."

After the meeting ended, Sarita walked to her office with a cup of cocoa and the morning paper. She took a seat behind her messy desk and sat down to catch up on the day's news. On page one was a story on the Townsend street bust, and like the kids, the reporter who'd done the articles wondered who the men were. According to what Sarita read, there had been at least fifteen similar incidents in the past six weeks, and the police continued to deny any involvement. The Feds weren't talking, as usual, so if the government was somehow behind all the doors being kicked in, they weren't telling. *It must be Federal*, Sarita thought as she turned the page to see what else was going on in her city. *Only they have the balls to bust someone without a warrant.*

In his office, Myk glowered at the article on the front page of the paper. Drake had warned him it wouldn't take the city's reporters long to get wind of NIA's operations, and as always, the mayor had been right. Myk tossed the paper down. The last thing they needed were reporters sniffing around. He was confident no one in the organization would give out any information, but reporters made their living ferreting out folks' business, and Myk didn't want them sniffing around his. On the next outing, they'd have to make sure no unauthorized persons were lurking in the darkness with video cameras or some other way to record the goings-on. All bets would be off if the face of one of the operatives showed up in the next article.

His secretary's voice came over the intercom. "Mr. Chandler, there's a Mr. Kerry Fukiya here to see you. He doesn't have an appointment."

The name Fukiya sounded familiar to Myk, but for a moment he couldn't place it, then, suddenly, he knew. "Send him in, and hold my calls. Thanks."

Mr. Fukiya was Sarita's Ninja.

Myk was expecting an elderly man for some reason; stereotypes probably, but instead, the man entering his office appeared to be no older than Myk. He was of medium height and tightly built, and was dressed in jeans, a flannel shirt, and a winter parka.

They shook hands. "Have a seat," Myk said.

The man ignored the gesture and stepped to the window instead. "Nice view."

Myk studied him. "I like it." No, Fukiya was not what Myk had been expecting.

As if he'd read Myk's mind, Fukiya turned from the window, and said, "Not what you were expecting?"

"Frankly, no. Sarita described you as an Asian gentleman. I thought she was referring to age."

"No, she was referring to my charming nature."

Their eyes met. Myk saw a depth in Fukiya's dark brown eyes that contrasted with his flippant remark.

"How is she?" Fukiya asked.

"Well."

He turned back to the view. "The Empress Sarita is a very special woman. When I first moved into the neighborhood four years ago, the gangbangers covered my house with their tags. It was their way of saying, 'Move out,' but I stayed, and do you know why?"

"No."

"Because Sarita and her Army were at my door first thing the next morning, paintbrushes in hand. They wanted me to know that the bangers didn't represent everyone in the neighborhood. She, and those women—and their kids—painted my place, had me over to dinner, and introduced me around."

He looked Myk's way. "The donated paint they used was a god-ugly gray, but to me, it was as beautiful as gold."

Myk smiled. "She is something."

"That she is. Which is why I am here. I wanted to meet the man she married."

Myk met the man's eyes squarely.

"I would think a woman like our Empress would

find it hard being married to a man as rich as you are Mr. Chandler."

"Are you trying to offend me?"

"No. Just stating fact."

"Why are you here?"

"As I said, to meet you, to introduce myself, and to say, that like you I will protect her with my life."

Myk tried to read Fukiya's intent. "Sarita thinks you're a Ninja."

He didn't blink. "She's seen too many Hollywood movies."

Myk didn't press the matter. Now that he'd met the mysterious Mr. Fukiya, he planned to run his name through the databases and see what they turned up.

Fukiya said then, "I'll let you get back to your work. Welcome to the neighborhood, Mr. Chandler. I hope you will treat her like the jewel that she is."

Myk could see in Fukiya's eyes that this wasn't just friendly chitchat. The man meant for Myk to hear his words. "Don't worry," Myk told him.

Fukiya walked over to the door and exited, leaving a very thoughtful Myk alone.

Sixteen

At the end of the business day, Myk swung by the center to pick up Sarita. He wanted to tell her about his encounter with Fukiya and see if her lips were still as sweet as they had been that morning when he'd kissed her good-bye.

Sarita wasn't at the center however.

In her office sat Silas, who told Myk, "She went by her place to water her plants. She'll be back in a few minutes."

Myk hid his alarm. "By herself?"

"Yep."

Carefully keeping his voice and manner even, Myk said, "Think I'll go and see if she needs a ride back."

Myk left the office and quickly went to his car.

Sarita had just watered the last plant when a knock sounded on her front door. She checked the peephole. A very tall, well-dressed man was on the porch. She opened the door but didn't undo the lock on the screen door. He was easily six feet, eight inches tall, clean-shaven, and bald. *Nice suit*, she thought to herself. "Can I help you?" she asked.

"Looking for Sarita Grayson."

Sarita stilled. "Why?"

He responded with a smile so sinister, she felt the hairs dance on the back of her neck.

"Need to give her a message."

Sarita waited.

"Tell her, my boss wants his diamonds back."

Sarita buckled inside.

The big man studied her for a moment longer, then said, "Think you can remember that?"

When she didn't respond, he smiled again. "You have a nice day."

He walked back down to his car and drove away. Sarita closed the door. Her heart was beating so fast she thought she might be sick. Bending over she drew in a few deep breaths, willing herself to calm down so she could think. It came to her then that she should've gotten the license plate, but she was too busy freaking out. Lord. The chickens were coming home to roost. On shaky legs, she walked over to her purse and pulled out her phone. Standing by the window to make sure the man was gone, she was just punching in Myk's number when she saw him drive up. Snatching up her coat, she went out to meet him.

Driving her back to the center, Myk listened to her story, then asked, "That's all he said?"

"Yep. His boss wants his diamonds back."

She met his eyes. "Now what?"

Myk knew she was scared and was doing her best

to put it aside. It angered him that she'd had to face the threat alone. "I won't let anybody hurt you."

Sarita sighed. "Mykal, that man could have blown me away in my living room, and you'd be making my funeral arrangements right now. What the hell am I involved in?"

His jaw tightened. "I can't tell you. We've had this discussion before."

"And you said, you'd tell me eventually—that I'd get a map, remember?"

Myk did, but didn't respond.

She studied him. "Well, put on my headstone. *I couldn't tell her why.*"

He took his eyes off the road for a second and looked over at her tight-set face. There was nothing he could say, so he didn't say anything. He refocused his attention on driving, knowing he had a hard decision to make, but she had a right to know what was going on. "Do you want to have dinner with me?"

"Sure."

Myk felt blessed that she was even talking to him. "Your friend Fukiya came by my office today."

Sarita's mind kept replaying the encounter with the menacing hulk on her porch. "What did he want?"

"Just to check me out, I think."

"I hope you were nice to him."

"I was."

"Kerry Fukiya is a friend. Keeps to himself mostly, but he has a good heart, has to, to put up with those kids," she added with a smile. "The Army loves taking care of him. They say he's cute."

Myk had no way of judging a man's cute quotient, so he left that alone. "He's very protective of you."

"No more than anyone else he cares for in the neighborhood. It's the way he is."

"He called you the Empress."

"Yes. That a problem?"

"No." Myk admitted to a bit of jealousy, even though there was nothing in her relationship with Fukiya that warranted such an illogical and possessive response. "Do you know where he lived before moving here?"

"Nope. Did tell me one time that he came to Detroit for his health, though."

Myk's brow knitted in puzzlement. "His health?"

"Whatever that means. Why are you so interested in Kerry?"

"Just interested in all the players, that's all."

"Because of whatever this is you can't tell me about?"

His mustache thinned. "You're persistent, if nothing else."

She responded by turning her eyes to the passing cityscape.

He turned off of Gratiot and onto Van Dyke. While they waited for the light to turn green, her eyes scanned the decaying neighborhood that had been so vibrant when she was young, but it, too, had aged under the weight of time of crime and drugs. "What do you think about these dope busters, as the kids are calling them?"

He shrugged. "I've been so busy, haven't really had time to check it out."

"Well, I think it's about time. No, we can't have vigilantes taking over the streets, but this is different."

Myk kept an eye on the light. "Why?"

"It just is. We have a whole generation of city kids who've never walked into a store or a burger place that didn't have bulletproof screens. A couple of years ago we took some of our kids on a field trip to a suburban museum, and when we stopped to have lunch, all the kids asked me, 'How come there's no glass?'"

She met his eyes. "Life wasn't locked down like this when I was growing up. The drugs breed crime, which breeds more crime, carjackings, B and Es, prostitution. It's a circle that needs to be broken."

The light turned green, and he made the right onto Van Dyke. "So, you think dropping down on the dealers is a good idea?"

"As long as they're busting the big white-collar fish too, I'm all for it."

A silent Myk drove on.

The restaurant was in the rising and falling neighborhood near Agnes and Van Dyke, where trendy refurbished brownstones stood next to windowless hulks. The block was dotted with weed-filled vacant lots that had once held stately Victorian homes. The building he pulled up to had a green-and-gray-striped awning over the door that read simply: ANDRE'S.

A young brother neatly dressed in black slacks, white shirt, and a black leather jacket walked around to Sarita's door and helped her out. She thanked him. Myk handed over his valet key, then escorted Sarita inside.

The place was small and very crowded. There could have been more than fifteen tables tops, and all were full. Myk and Sarita stood behind three other couples, one of whom turned out to be Faye Riley and her date.

"Well, hello there," Faye said with a false smile. "Fancy meeting you two here. How are you Shanika?"

Sarita's jaw tightened, but she smiled, "I'm well, and how are you, Fake. I mean, Faye. Sorry. It's been a long day."

Faye turned away and set her cool eyes on Myk, "Mykal, I want you to meet my new friend. He says you two know each other."

Myk studied the face. "We do?"

"Yes," the man replied, moving closer into the light. He had on an all red outfit; suit, coat, hat, shirt, shoes. A snow-white cane aided the left side of his body. "I worked for you once down in Central America. Name's Clark Nelson."

Myk went still.

Clark directed his attention to the woman on Chandler's arm. The woman who'd taken his diamonds. "Is this your wife? Faye said you just got married. Congratulations."

"Thank you," Myk said. He didn't make any introductions however. He didn't want Sarita anywhere near Nelson.

With that in mind, Myk caught the eye of the returning maître d' who came over, and said with a smile, "Ah, Mr. Chandler. This way please."

Faye took immediate offense. "Excuse me, but we were here first."

The maître d', a short thin brother with a thick mustache, looked her up and down critically, then said, coolly, "Mr. Chandler owns this restaurant, ma'am. Now, if you'll excuse us?"

Myk gave Nelson one last look, then gently steered Sarita to follow the maître d'. Sarita didn't have to turn around to see the hate in Faye's eyes; she could feel it.

They were taken to an upstairs dining area that was just as intimate as the main floor. The candlelit room with its blazing fireplaces, one on each wall, had a very romantic feel. There were tables spread about, but there were no other diners. Sarita wondered if they would have the entire space to themselves.

Chandler helped her with her seat. His body heat shimmered over her, and she fought off the instinctive reaction to lean back and bask in his nearness. "You own this place?" she asked, needing to fix her mind on something more concrete than the problems between them.

"Part owner. When Andre got the opportunity to buy the restaurant after the original owner died, I was more than happy to be an investor. Andre cooked those scallops and made that hot fudge sundae you loved so much, remember?"

She did. It was their wedding night. "He's the chef, here?"

"Yep, chef, owner, dishwasher. It's a small operation for now. He's only been open a few days. This is my first official visit."

Sarita remembered being impressed by Andre's culinary talents. The sundae had been the bomb. "Well, I'm looking forward to this."

He was pleased to hear her say that. What he wanted most though, was to see her smile again. He reached out and placed his hands over hers. "I don't want to fight, Sarita. We've been having a good time."

"Yes, we have, but that man scared me, Mykal. I don't like being kept in the dark."

"I know. Hopefully, I'll be able to answer all of your questions soon."

She looked into his eyes. Lord knows she wanted to trust him, but she'd always had her own back. It was hard to put her life in the hands of a man she didn't even know six months ago. "Okay. I'll *try* and be patient."

Myk heard the emphasis she'd put on the word. "Thanks. In the meantime, keep your eyes open."

He said it with all sincerity, and she whispered back, "I will."

"Tomorrow, we'll have you take a look at some perp books and see if we can't put a name to your afternoon caller."

"That sounds good."

He reached out and cupped her cheek. He'd finally discovered a woman who made his insides sing, and he'd be damned if he was going to let someone mess it up. If anything happened to her, he wouldn't be able to live with himself. "I'm sorry I wasn't there this afternoon."

She pressed her hand over his and savored the contact. "I'm okay."

Myk knew she wasn't; neither was he. He took her hand in his and squeezed it tenderly. When the waiter stepped over to take their order, they were still holding hands.

After they received their food and began to eat, Sarita said to him, "Tell me about that man with Faye. You were pretty icy to him."

"Last time I saw Nelson, the Honduran authorities were hauling him off to prison."

"What for?"

"Rape. The girl was fourteen, I believe."

"Oh, my. I wonder if Faye knows his story?"

Myk shrugged. "I wonder how much time he did. He looked pretty prosperous. Seems to have done well with himself since then."

"Legally or illegally? He looked me over like a pimp."

"Which is one of the reasons I was so icy."

"Well, thanks for not giving him my name. It's fine with me if he thinks I'm Shanika. Faye can have all of that."

The subject then turned to the budding romance going on between Walter McGhee and Jerome's mother, Shirley.

Myk asked, "How long has she been a widow?"

"About five years. Her husband was a fireman. He died in a big warehouse fire on the westside."

"Walter likes her a lot."

"She's sweet on him, too."

"You think so?"

"Yep, she told me so, but don't you dare tell Walter."

He mimicked locking his lips. "My lips are sealed."

Meanwhile, downstairs, the maître d' told the impatient, foot-tapping Faye that because she had no reservation, it would be at least another forty-minute wait before she and Clark could be served.

Clark said to Faye, "Let's go."

But Faye didn't want to leave. This was the newest place to be seen, and she wanted to be seen, even if it had to be with a man on a cane.

"Let's go, Faye," Clark repeated firmly. "We'll eat somewhere else."

Faye didn't like it, but she let him lead her out.

Once their driver got the limo under way, Faye flicked on the small opera lights, then pulled down the vanity mirror so she could check her makeup and hair.

Clark watched her primping. "So that was Chandler's new wife. What do you know about her, other than she's fine?" Clark already knew all he needed to know about the lovely Sarita Grayson Chandler. His people had hunted down the remaining members of Fletcher Harris's crew, and they'd sung like Mariah Carey before being sent to gangsta heaven. Clark simply wanted to hear Faye's take on the woman.

Faye didn't care to hear him singing her rival's praises. "She's some ghetto social worker he found. Rumor has it she runs a kids' center, in the hood."

Faye looked over at him. "Why are you interested in her?"

"I'm interested in everything about Chandler. Aren't you?"

"Not her, no." Thinking about the new Mrs. Chandler and what she'd done to Faye's future made the seething Faye so heavy-handed with her lipstick, she wound up looking back at a clown. Grabbing a tissue from the dispenser in the armrest beside her, she wiped off the big red lips and started over.

Clark watched her angry movements. Faye was such a plastic bitch. She didn't like sex much, but he'd taken her to bed anyway; taken her like the whore she was beneath all that paint and expensive clothing. Vain, greedy women like Faye would sell their souls to the devil as long as he gave them a no-limit charge card and paid the bill. Were she fifteen years younger, she could go far in Clark's underground world, but she was pushing thirty-five, far too old for the kind of trading she'd need to do to make the kind of money she wanted to have. He did know a few men overseas who'd be willing to pay a reasonably fair price for her aging goods, though, providing she did a better act in bed. Clark knew just the right coach. "How long she and Chandler been married?"

Faye swung around. "Why do you keep asking about that little slut?"

"Answer the question."

Under the low opera lights of the limo's cabin, the steel in his eyes shone bright, and it made her nervous. She flounced back to the mirror. "I don't know. Late October. The reception was a few days after Halloween."

Faye was warm in her new fur coat, so she took it off, then spent a few slow moments smoothing her black cashmere sweater over her ample breasts. She was certain she had Clark's eye the entire time, and it pleased her. *Some men are such fools*, she thought caustically.

"You know, Faye, for a woman your age, you're not too bad."

She cut him a stony look. "What do you mean, for a woman my age?"

"A woman your age. What are you, thirty-five, thirty-six?"

"Thirty-two, thank you very much."

He laughed.

She did not. "What's so funny?"

"You. I like you, though. Come here and give me some head before we get to the restaurant. Thinking about Chandler's woman has got me hard."

Faye was outraged. "I beg your pardon."

"You heard me," he whispered smiling. And so that there would be no misunderstanding, he undid his pants, grabbed her hand, and placed it on him.

The sight and feel of him hard, thick, and awaiting her oral ministrations made Faye scoff derisively, "You must be kidding." She tried to pull her hand back, but he forced her to keep it where it was.

"Now, Faye, I thought we were partners?"

His smile touched Faye with an iciness that made her shiver. His manner brought to mind visions of the serpent in the biblical garden. "We are partners," she allowed, her voice shaking.

"Good," he oozed, "and since I'm the partner paying the freight, I think I deserve a bit of added compensation, don't you? You asked for help getting revenge on Chandler, and I'm the only man equipped for the job."

Faye refused to acknowledge the double entendre and again tried to pull away, but his other hand painfully attached itself to her jaw.

Her gasp of pain made his eyes glow with sinister pleasure. "Do this real good, and I'll buy you the biggest diamond you've ever seen."

The next day, after two hours of looking at pictures in the perp books Myk had given to her, without explanation as to how he'd obtained them, Sarita fingered the man on her porch. His name was Big Tiny

Crane, a local, for-hire bodyguard. Armed with a name, Myk, Drake, and their Federal friends put out the word to find Crane and pick him up.

It was now the second week of December, and the city had already gotten its first dusting of snow. Sarita had heard no more from Big Tiny Crane, and for that she was thankful. Sarita also hadn't seem much of Myk since the dinner at Andre's. Helping his brother work on the city's budget was keeping him at the mayor's mansion until late every night.

However, the city was seeing more and more media reports on the drug house busts. People living near well-known crack outlets took to staying up late at night in hopes their local drug dens would be the next target on the list and they could catch a glimpse of the men whose campaign had everyone so excited. The police were calling the masked men vigilantes, the mayor came on TV urging calm; but the citizenry didn't care. They were openly supportive of the mysterious men and their success in accomplishing what thirty years, and millions in government money, hadn't. The dealers were on the run, and on Sundays in churches all over the city, congregations prayed the men in black would keep on keeping on.

Seventeen

Myk returned home from his night's work weary in both body and soul. They'd had to shoot two young dealers tonight, kids no older than Keta and Jerome. He slowly climbed the back stairs to his wing in the 3 A.M. darkness and replayed the confrontation in his mind. The men and women under his command always tried to take a house down with as little violence as possible; a canister or two of tear gas was all it usually took. Not tonight. Tonight the kids holed up in the abandoned house had busted out the plywood over the broken windows and, with their faces covered behind towels and T-shirts, came out blasting. Myk and his people scrambled for cover as semiautomatics barked bullets that sliced through cars, trees, and everything else that could hold lead. Myk took a bullet in the initial fray; and he'd cursed because it was the same shoulder Sarita had shot him in. Fear-ing innocent people in the neighboring houses might be struck next, Myk clutched at the burning in his shoulder and radioed one of his operatives to take the kids down. With the aid of a nightscope, the ill-trained dealers were picked off in quick succession, and ten minutes later, the street was quiet except for the faint wail of sirens.

The injured kids were taken to a safe house to get their wounds treated. They'd be held there until their hearing before the NIA magistrate who'd decide their fate—either the state's correctional system or the NIA rehab ranch in Wyoming.

With Drake driving, Myk had made a quick stop at the mansion to shower off the tear gas and get his wound taken care of, but it still hurt like hell.

Moving through the quiet house, Myk hoped Sarita was asleep. He hadn't really seen her since their dinner at Andre's two weeks earlier; there'd been NIA business to attend to every night since then. He'd attributed his absences to working at Drake's, but the more Myk lied to her, the more it gnawed at him. No matter how late he got home, though, he always took the time to swing by her room to check on her, and sometimes he would just sit and watch her sleep; but tonight, all he wanted to do was soak in a hot tub, climb into the sack, and not wake up until next year sometime.

Entering his room, Myk didn't bother with any lights. The moon pouring in through the open drapes provided more than enough illumination, and, besides, he didn't have the strength. Trying to take off his black sweatshirt turned out to be a lot more difficult than he'd anticipated. Raising his arm set off rocket fire in his bullet wound. He lowered the arm and waited for the pain to subside enough for him to catch his breath. Grimacing, he tried it again. More fire erupted, and sweat broke out on his brow. The sound of his labored breathing filled the silence.

"Need some help?"

Myk whirled. There in the moonlight sat Sarita, in one of the chairs by the cold fireplace. She was dressed in a nightgown and had her bare feet tucked beneath her legs. He watched her rise. The prim, high-collared flannel gown flowed to her toes. The gown was the ugliest damn thing he'd ever seen; she, on the other hand was a treasured sweet sight to his battle-weary eyes. "I didn't buy that gown, did I?"

"Nope. I did. The saleslady said it was guaranteed against dragons and big bad wolves."

"I'll bet."

Sarita could see pain in his face hovering beneath the banter.

He eased himself down onto the love seat and winced as the simple movement jarred the wound beneath the bandage. "What are you doing up?"

"Can I help?" she asked quietly.

His reply was a firm, "No. And you didn't answer my question."

"I couldn't sleep and I heard Walter moving around, then at the window I saw him helping you in . . ."

"Oh, you were up spying?"

"No," she protested. "I—" She stopped, realizing he was teasing by the light of humor in his eyes. "Well, I'll bet my evening was a lot more innocent than yours."

"Oh, really," he replied in answer to her challenge. "And what did my evening involve?"

Sarita hadn't meant to be goaded into airing her suspicions about his nocturnal activities. She had been pondering the issue all week, and when she added up his nightly comings and goings with the mysterious men in the black vans, she'd made the only connection that seemed possible.

"Well?" he asked.

His voice brought her back. "I think you're involved with the dope busters."

For a moment he didn't say a word, and she realized how ridiculous her conclusion probably sounded.

"Why?"

"For one, even though you smell like you just had a shower, I can still smell tear gas. You don't get tear gassed or shot going over the mayor's budget."

Myk knew he shouldn't be surprised she'd figured it out. "And if you're right, what do you plan on doing with that information?"

"Not a thing," she said honestly.

Sarita waited for him to say something in response, but when he didn't, she added, "I'm no different from anybody else. Like I said the other day, I want my city back. The drive-bys, the crack, the carjackings, it's a cancer. I'm all for radical surgery."

Still no response, so she said quietly, "I just hope the good guys will be careful."

Myk's melancholy smile was hidden by the shadows. She'd figured it out. He wanted to take her in his arms and soothe away her worries. "I'm sure *they* will, whoever they are. Now, turn on that lamp and look over in the drawer. There should be a pair of scissors inside somewhere. The only way I'm going to get out of this sweatshirt is to cut my way out."

The scissors made short work of the black sweatshirt. One long cut from hem to neck up the front and back enabled it to be gently pulled down his arms and off. Under the soft light of the lamp, the white bandage Drake had applied to his upper shoulder glowed against the darkness of his muscled torso and arm.

Sarita set the scissors aside. Even though his participation had been minimal in the removal of the shirt, sweat was beaded on his brow. His forced breathing and closed eyes indicated he was in a lot more pain than he seemed willing to admit. "Did Drake give you something for the pain?"

"Didn't want anything."

"Of course, not," she said sarcastically. "What a silly question."

He opened his eyes. "How'd you know Drake patched me up?"

"I didn't. Thanks."

Myk shook his head with amusement. He wished he knew how much she actually did know. Probably enough to terrify everybody involved. He looked over into her intelligent dark eyes. God, he wished this were all over. If it were, he'd give Ms. Everything a run for her money. *She'd have to ditch that gown, though,* he told himself, scanning the flannel monstrosity critically. "Don't ever wear that gown again."

She looked down at herself, wiggled her bare toes, then asked innocently, "Why not?"

"Because it's damn ugly." He preferred her in fabrics thin enough to slide over her skin so he could feel the heat of her response. It was strictly the male in him, and he felt no need to apologize.

She countered, "It's not ugly, and besides, it keeps me warm."

"Keeping you warm is now officially my job. If I had two good arms, I'd tear it off and feed it to the fireplace."

Sarita smiled. "Impossible. It's Big-Bad-Wolf-proof. Remember?"

He suddenly assumed the storybook role and growled at her playfully, snatching at the loose-fitting waist of her gown in an attempt to bring her closer. Shrieking with laughter, she tried to jump away, but he caught a trailing sleeve. "Come here, little girl," he demanded in his wolf's voice.

"Let go!" she howled. She instinctively pulled against his hold, stretching both the flannel sleeve and his injured shoulder. The fabric gave first, tearing away the cap of her sleeve. The whiplash forced him back against his seat. Pain exploded, and he cursed.

Sarita froze. "You dummy," she whispered in soft condemnation. Moving to him quickly, she slid between the breach in his thighs, then leaned down to check his bandage. "You're bleeding again."

"Don't doubt it. Hurts like hell, too."

A red stain was slowly seeping into the cloth. "I'm going to call your brother."

He grabbed her hand. "No. Let Hizzoner sleep. I'll be okay."

"Chandler, don't you think you're taking this hero stuff too far? You could bleed to death." He was stroking her fingers with his thumb.

"Not a chance."

She clicked her tongue, intimating her displeasure, and pulled her hand away. Men. "Then at least lie down. Are you working tomorrow?"

"Yep. Have to be in Philly by noon."

"I think Philly should wait."

"Board meeting. Can't."

"Or won't?" she asked. "You don't need to be running around playing CEO. You're hurt, Mykal."

He met her eyes.

She added, "It takes old guys longer to heal."

"Did I hear you say, 'old guys'?"

She grinned.

"I'll show you *old guys*, Miss Thing."

The Big Bad Wolf slid one large paw beneath her gown and found her lusciously bare. Her skin was warm, soft, and he took his time exploring the smooth contours of her silken limbs.

"Ooo, Grandma," she cooed, "What nice hands you have. . . ."

Myk chuckled. "The better to feel you with, my dear . . . and where may I ask are your panties?"

"I think I lost them in the woods."

His explorations discovered a particularly flushed and moist place between her thighs, and Little Red purred in response

The wolf asked softly, "Do you like that . . . ?"

She did and silently widened her stance to show him just how much. He moved her gown up around her waist, and she held it there. The pain in his arm be damned, he filled his hands with her hips. "You should come visit Grandma more often. . . ."

Holding on to her gown, Sarita's breath caught in her throat as he dallied at the lodestone between her thighs. The heat pooling there set off the tight swelling that signaled the beginnings of wolf-induced arousal. "If Grandma stayed home more, maybe I would. . . ."

She then reached down and gently captured the source of all that made him male. His eyes closed in reaction to the slow up-and-down movements of her possessive hand.

He whispered, "Doing that is going get you in trouble, Red."

"I hope so," came her husky reply, "but then again, you're an injured Big Bad Wolf. How dangerous can you be?"

He stopped the hand moving up and down his hard length. The heat in his eyes singed her in places that might have rattled her in the past, but not anymore. He'd seduced her into exploring the depths of her passion too many times and in too many places to be coy about expressing it now.

"You don't think wounded wolves are dangerous," he asked slyly. He slid a finger up over her nipple, boldly teasing it through the gown until it blossomed, and she sighed with pleasure. He transferred his caresses to the other breast, seducing and arousing it, until it, too, stood out from the flannel like a jewel. Only then did he bite each nipple with just enough pressure to raise shivers.

The hand beneath her gown resumed its luxurious traveling, sensitizing her skin to his touch. First one, then two fingers penetrated her slowly, boldy, and the Big Bad Wolf smiled like the alpha male that he was. "See how dangerous I can be . . . ?"

Sarita had trouble standing while his long fingers did their slow dance. "Unbutton your gown," she

heard him say. At first, she didn't move; couldn't.
His scandalous fingers were overriding her senses,
making her unable, but more importantly, unwill-
ing to concentrate on anything but the rise in her
temperature and the free-flowing proof of her need.

"Undo your gown, Red. The wolf's hungry."

Somehow her hands freed the buttons on the
gown's bodice, and the open halves fell apart uselessly.

Myk had never known such a sensual woman. The
passion-hard features of her face had him mesmerized. When her gown fell open, he moved his attention to the beautiful dark-tipped treasures now
bared. The urge to touch them flared strong, so he
withdrew from the honey-filled sanctuary between
her thighs. As the contact broke, he noted her soft cry
of disappointment. "Don't worry," he murmured,
rolling woman-dewed fingers over her throbbing
bare nipples. "You'll get more. I promise. . . ."

When he took her into his warm mouth, Little Red
surrendered willingly and let the wolf have his way.

Alone in the War Room, Myk looked through all the
reports he'd let lie for the past few days while recov-
ering under the stern eye of Little Red Riding Hood.
The wound was healing but still kicked up a fit if he
moved suddenly or reached too far. At the moment,
though, he was interested in one report in particular
and quickly rifled through the stack until he found
it. Pleased, he pulled it free, but reading it made him
scowl. Sarita's Mr. Fukiya wasn't on any database
anywhere in the world; no credit cards, no bank accounts; no social security number, no record with

INS. The researchers had checked the FBI, CIA, Interpol, Scotland Yard, and their equivalents around the globe. Nothing. Myk knew Sarita would have his head for running her friend's name through the system, but Myk was curious about the so-called Ninja, and now the curiosity had grown. Obviously, the name Fukiya was an alias, and Myk knew that people took on aliases for myriad reasons. What was Fukiya's? What had he meant by saying he'd come to Detroit for his health. Had that meant physical health, as in sick, or health as in needing to hide himself from someone who meant him harm? Too many questions and no answers. Myk penned a note to the researchers to keep digging.

A knock on the door made Myk look up. Walter called from the other side, and Myk called back.

When Walter came in, he said, "I delivered the general to her troops."

Myk smiled. "What's going on over there today?"

"A trip to the market to buy the food for all the Christmas baskets they're giving out. She is amazing."

"That she is."

Walter came over and picked up some of the reports. He began skimming them.

Myk asked, "Have you met Mr. Fukiya?"

Walter looked up. "The so-called Ninja? Yeah, I met him last week at the center. Watched him conduct his martial-arts class. Guy's good. You know what a fukiya is, don't you?"

Myk didn't.

"A hollow bamboo tube Ninjas supposedly use to blow darts through. Sorta like the blowguns you see the Amazon natives using in those nature programs sometimes."

"You're kidding, right?"

"No."

Myk ran his hands over his eyes. Lord. Was Fukiya really a trained assassin?

Walter smiled. "I know, but hey, at least he's on our side."

"Let's hope," Myk said, and tossed Walter the info on the man.

Walter read it through. "So, he doesn't exist. That's interesting, but if you think about it, we may be better off not knowing. No telling who he is, and we've got enough on our plate. You're just interested in him because you think he's sweet on your wife."

"No, I'm not," Myk denied.

Walter rolled his eyes and changed the subject. "I went downtown to see if our Fed friends had anything we might be interested in, and they gave me this. Info on Big Tiny Crane and the man he's working for, your friend, Clark Nelson."

Myk stilled. "That's who owns the diamonds?"

"Our friends weren't sure, but a few days ago they threatened to slap those Chicago bookies with Federal terrorism charges for trafficking in blood diamonds, and the Russians sang loud enough to be heard back in Moscow."

Myk whistled as he read Nelson's sheet. "Faye's new man has been busy since I saw him last."

"Yeah, he's a major player on everybody's list: DEA, Treasury, Justice. Supposedly, he runs a legit import export business. Everybody's sure he's importing big cocaine, but they can't prove it. They think he's here trying to find a lead on the diamonds."

Myk didn't like this. If the Feds were right about Nelson owning the diamonds. . . . Myk steepled his fingers and thought about what he needed to do to keep Sarita safe until Clark could be arrested. "See if you can find Saint. We may need him. Are our friends keeping tabs on Nelson?"

"They were, but lost track of him sometime yesterday. He's checked out of his hotel."

Myk was liking this less and less. "He's probably ready to make a move."

"They think so, too."

"I don't want Sarita moving around the city without one of us with her."

"I'm already spending nights with her, she's not going to want a sitter at the center, too."

"I'll just have to tell her what's going on. She'll understand."

"You're going to tell her about NIA?"

"No, just about Nelson and the diamonds." Myk had already told Drake that Sarita knew he was a member of the Dope Busters, but Myk hadn't told anyone else. She'd promised to keep the information to herself, and Myk knew her well enough now to trust her at her word. "Anything else?"

"No. It's enough, I think."

Myk agreed. "You get on the Saint matter, and I'll head over to the center."

Walter left.

Myk took the pictures of Nelson and Crane that

had been included in the report and fed them into the scanner. When the copies were ready, he placed them in an envelope and went to get his car.

Driving to the center, Myk used his cell phone to put in a call to Drake to give him an update on the latest developments. The answering secretary said the mayor was in a meeting, but she would have him return Myk's call as soon as he was free. Myk thanked her and clicked off.

Myk had a stop to make before going to the center. He parked the car, then took the steps up to the flat's porch two at a time. In answer to his knock, the curtain on the door was pulled back. Kerry Fukiya looked out at Myk for a moment, then opened up.

"Mr. Chandler, what brings you here?"

Myk walked in. He handed him the pictures. "Them."

Fukiya studied the faces of the two men. "Who are they?"

"Their names are Crane and Nelson. If you see them anywhere near the center, call me."

"Are they child predators?"

"No, Empress predators."

Fukiya looked up sharply. "Oh really." He scanned the faces again, then handed the pictures back.

Myk said, "Keep them."

"No need. They're not faces I'll forget."

Myk saw that Fukiya lived spartanly. The furnishings of his living room consisted of a futon, a small serviceable table, and a few Asian-inspired pictures on the wall. A small shrine of some sort stood on a short marble pedestal on the far side of the room. There was a kitchen and a room in the back where he probably slept, but Myk was sure they were no more fully furnished.

Fukiya regained Myk's attention by saying, "I live very simply."

Myk nodded. "I see."

When he and Fukiya first met, most of the man's frame had been hidden beneath his parka. Now, dressed in sweats and a T-shirt, the sleek power in his neck and arms were revealed. He looked to be in top physical shape.

"I will keep an eye out for the men," Fukiya promised.

"Thanks."

"May I ask you a question?"

"Sure."

"Why did you come to me?"

Myk told the truth, "Because I know you care about my wife."

Fukiya smiled softly and dropped his eyes, but when he raised them, they were steely with resolve. "I care enough to make this pledge. If Nelson gets through you, *I* will be waiting." Fukiya bowed. "Happy hunting, Mr. Chandler."

Myk bowed respectfully in return. "I'll keep in touch."

Back in the car, Myk drove to the center. It was only a few blocks away, but he picked up the phone to see if Sarita had already left for the market. He needed to talk to her about Nelson as soon as possible.

Her phone was still ringing when Myk pulled up to the curb. He spotted Shirley and some of the Army members piling into the van. He put the phone down and relaxed knowing they hadn't left yet. Getting out, he walked up expecting to see Sarita behind the wheel, but Silas was seated there instead. "Hey, grandson."

"Hey, Silas. Sarita around?"

"Nope, she went with a police fella. He said he had some pictures he wanted her to look at downtown. Something to do with that fool Fletcher's murder."

Myk went still. "How long ago did they leave?"

"Ten, fifteen minutes ago. Why? What's the matter?"

Myk wasn't sure, but the fact that she wasn't answering her phone coupled with the knowledge that the police didn't suddenly just show up and take citizens away without calling first, made him suspicious. "Silas, I want you to send the fastest kid you have over to Fukiya's right now. Tell him Sarita may be missing."

"Sure." Silas studied the emotion playing over Myk's face. "You think she may be in trouble?"

"Not sure. She's not answering her phone. Hand me a piece of paper."

Silas picked up an envelope on the seat. Myk snatched a pen out of his pocket and hastily scribbled his cell number. "This is my cell number, if she comes back, call me. If I find out anything, I'll call you."

Myk was already running to his car. Inside he grabbed up the mailer, shook out the pictures of Nelson and his bodyguard, then ran back to the tight-lipped Silas. "If you see these two, call me."

Silas studied the picture, but when he looked up to ask Myk for more details, Myk was already back in his car. A second later he roared away.

Myk got hold of Walter and quickly explained the

situation. They agreed to meet at the Fed offices to see if their friends could help. Myk kept calling Sarita's phone. It rang steadily, but no one answered.

Sitting in the passenger seat of the police car, Sarita could hear the phone ringing inside her purse. This was the third call since she'd left the center but because the officer had forbidden her to answer it, she had to let it ring. She knew by the ring tone—the first few notes of "Who's Afraid of the Big Bad Wolf" that it was Chandler calling. She wondered how long it would take him to figure out she was in trouble.

She sensed she *was* in trouble the moment the policeman walked into her office. She didn't know why, but the feeling was strong. She'd never seen him before. He said there'd been a break in Fletcher's murder case and asked would she, as a neighborhood leader, come down and look at some perp sheets to see if she recognized anyone. When she told him she couldn't do it that day, hoping she could put him off, he pulled a gun, and that was that. He promised not to shoot her or any of the children if she came along quietly.

Sarita had no choice but to cooperate. With him right behind her, she went downstairs and, careful to keep her manner even, told Shirley and the others she'd meet them at the market because of the pics the officer wanted her to review. They'd waved, and she and the policeman went on their way.

That had been about twenty minutes earlier, and now, she was being driven deep into westside, traveling on unfamiliar streets in an area devastated by blight, drugs, and neglect. "Where are we going?" Sarita asked him again.

"I can't tell you, Mrs. Chandler," he said impatiently, "so please, stop asking."

"Am I being kidnapped?"

Silence.

Sarita knew being afraid wouldn't help her, but she was scared to death because she was certain the cop was tied in with Big Tiny Crane and his employer.

The policeman turned down an alley, and the car bumped its way along the cracked pavement past overflowing Dumpsters, fence-charging pit bulls, and a bearded homeless man slumped in sleep against a listing garage.

At the end of the alley, the cap stopped the car in front of a square squat building with a large corrugated metal door on front. The building was brick, and tight wire mesh covered the two windows. The building reminded her of the old car repair places that had once been prevalent in the neighborhoods before the city's downward spiral.

The phone rang again.

The policeman said tersely, "Give me that."

Sarita reached in her purse, but as she fumbled for it, she pressed what she hoped was the SEND button before handing it over. He rolled down the window and tossed the phone out. *So much for that*, she said to herself. When the metal door on the building began to rise, she drew in a shuddering breath and began to pray.

The police car pulled forward into the interior of the unlit building. Once it was in, the door lowered again.

* * *

Myk's phone rang. He picked it up. Seeing Sarita's name on the display made his heart pound. "Sarita, where are you?"

Drake, Walter, and the Feds looked up quickly when Myk spoke her name.

"Sarita!" Myk shouted. Silence. Myk studied the display again. "It's sending, but no one's on the other end," he told the others.

The DEA agent peered over Myk's shoulder at the display for a moment, then said eagerly, "Let's see if the phone company can trace that signal before the battery dies."

Myk opened his mouth to agree but his words faded away at the sight of Saint striding angrily into the room, his green eyes flashing, the hem of his long coat flying.

Saint didn't mince words. He leaned down and barked in Myk's face. "How in the hell did she get snatched! Where were you?"

Myk stood and met his half brother's anger. "You and I can do this after we find her."

Drake stepped between them. "Saint, leave it alone. Myk's right. Face off later. Let's find her first."

Myk was seething. He'd already beaten himself up over this. No one felt worse. He cared deeply for her, and not knowing where she was or if she was still alive was scaring him to death. Saint's anger was nothing compared to the fury Myk had reserved for himself.

Saint demanded, "Did you at least let Kerry know she's missing?"

Myk nodded. "Yes."

Saint snapped back, "Finally, something right!"

Myk's eyes blazed.

Apparently Saint didn't care about his big brother's anger. He marched out, yelling back over his shoulder. "I'll be in touch."

And he was gone.

Myk and Drake shared a look. Myk growled, "Let's get that signal traced."

When Sarita's eyes adjusted to the dimness inside the building she saw two armed men. One of them, a thin brother in a lime green suit, opened her door and motioned her out. He then took her purse. The other man, dressed in Miami orange, just stood there looking menacing. Out of the shadows stepped Big Tiny Crane. He was dressed in preacher blue pinstripes, and his gun matched his girth.

"Let's go," he demanded.

Sarita moved forward. Discarded batteries, rusted tools, and car parts littered the oil-stained floor. A chop shop? She didn't know, but right now, the building's function was the least of her problems.

He gestured her up a flight of wire stairs, then around the railed catwalk. Below her, she saw the cop backing his car out of the building. She wondered who he was and, more importantly, who she was going to meet.

Sarita saw Faye first. The bruises spread across Faye's face made Sarita's steps slow. Faye met her eyes. Sarita saw fury in them. Before Sarita could react further the behemoth pushed her forward. "Keep walking," he said.

Sarita moved, but she couldn't help but look back at Faye with concern. Was she in line for the same kind of abuse? Only then did Sarita see Clark Nelson. He was dressed in all yellow and sitting in the middle of the room on a battered black leather recliner as if it were the throne of Ethiopia, and he, Haile Selassie.

He greeted her arrival with a deadly smile. "Well, well, well. Hello, Mrs. Chandler. Glad you could make it."

Sarita raised her chin. So, this was Crane's employer. "Why am I here?"

"To answer a question or two."

"About what?"

"The diamonds you took for Fletcher Harris the night he was killed."

Sarita stilled. Gathering herself she lied. "I don't know what you're talking about."

"Sure you do. The diamonds were in Room 1533. I found some of Fletcher's friends down in Alabama, and before they died, they said you were the one Fletcher sent to the hotel to pick them up."

Sarita shuddered at the implication but didn't respond.

He smiled again, but it was the smile of the devil. "Do you know what a whipping boy is, Mrs. Chandler?"

Not sure why he'd asked, Sarita answered warily, "Yes, they took the whippings for child kings and queens."

"Ah, you're intelligent, too. I like that. Yes, the little kings couldn't be spanked, so some poor kid from the village was brought in to be hit instead. Well, Faye here is going to be yours. Every time you tell me a lie, this is going to happen."

He snapped his fingers and the big man walked

over to Faye and slapped her face so hard the force caused to stumble and cry out.

"Hey!" Sarita screamed in outrage and started across the room but was stopped immediately by the gun the big bodyguard turned on her.

Faye had a hand to her face and was weeping softly, but her eyes were fiery with hate. She spat, "You're a real big man, aren't you Nelson?"

He shot her a look. "Shut the hell up before I give you back to Big Tiny. He said you called his name real loud last night."

Sarita shuddered. Had Nelson really given Faye to the bodyguard? Apparently so, because the big man was smiling, and Faye was staring back venomously.

Nelson told Faye, "Fix your face. You look a mess."

Faye walked stiffly over to the pink overnight bag sitting a few feet away and angrily yanked the case open.

Nelson said to Crane, "Find Mrs. Chandler a chair so we can tie her up. She's going to be staying with us a while."

Suddenly, two shots rang out, and everything seemed to go into slow motion. Sarita hit the floor. Big Tiny Crane stumbled back, and twin bursts of blood spurted up out of his chest like a fountain. An astonished Sarita looked up just in time to see Faye calmly turn the Luger in her hands on the wide-eyed, terrified Nelson. She pumped him once in the leg. He went down with a high-pitched scream.

Sarita scrambled up and ran for the stairs. "Come on, Faye!"

Faye aimed at Nelson again, higher this time, but the gun jammed.

"Run, girl! Come on!"

But Sarita had forgotten about the men down-stairs. They came charging into the room, guns drawn. One man grabbed Sarita and threw her against the wall so hard that she saw stars. The other trained his gun on Faye. Faye gave him a smug smile and let the gun drop slowly from her fingers to the floor.

The air was thick with the smell of gunfire. Sarita looked over at Crane's prone body. He was dead. Nelson was slowly dragging himself off the floor and into the chair. The bullet caught him in his bad leg. Much to the satisfaction of the pleased-looking Faye, he was bleeding profusely. "You bitch!" he screamed.

She snarled, "I got your bitch, you bastard! You gave me to that cretin like I was some whore on the street! Be glad I didn't kill you first."

Nelson barked at his rescuers, "Tie them up, then get me to a doctor!" He looked at Faye, and said, "When I get back, I'm going to kill you personally."

Faye tossed back, "I died the moment I let you put your filthy hands on me."

Two old office chairs were found and dragged into place. The thug in the lime green suit held his gun on Sarita and Faye, while Miami orange pushed Sarita and Faye onto the seats. Their arms were forced be-hind the chairs and their wrists bound. He then knelt and tied another length of rope around their ankles. He made sure both sets of knots were tight.

Once Nelson was satisfied the women would stay put, his henchmen helped him out of the room, leaving Faye and Sarita alone. A few moments later, the lights went out.

As the silence settled, Sarita looked over at Faye, and said. "You okay?"

"No, but, he'll never rape anyone ever again."

In spite of the way they'd met initial tension between them, Sarita's heart certainly went out to her. "If we ever get out of here, I'll testify for you."

"Thanks, and I'm sorry for—all of this. I was so mad at you and Myk—I, I'm just sorry, that's all."

Sarita nodded. "Where'd you learn to shoot?"

"My mother was a cop."

Sarita was surprised.

"Yeah. Back in the eighties, sharpshooting was my talent for the Miss Virginia pageant. Hit six bull's-eyes in a row."

"Did you win?"

"Nope. Came in second to a blond baton twirler."

Sarita smiled.

Faye added, "My sidearm is like the slogan for that credit card. I never leave home without it. Me having a gun and being able to use it never crossed Nelson's mind. He paid for underestimating me."

Nelson wasn't the only one, Sarita thought to herself.

With each passing hour, Sarita and Faye began to wonder if Nelson was coming back. They'd spent most of the afternoon trying to work their hands free of the rope, but had succeeded only in rubbing their wrists so raw that they stung and burned. Dusk could be seen falling through the wire-covered window across the room. It was getting dark, and because it was also December outside, cold. Sarita at least had on coat and jeans; Faye did not. Her pale blue cashmere sweater set and matching skirt were cute, but not designed to keep her warm. Her coat was in Nelson's limo.

"How're you doing, Faye?"

"Terrible," she said in a shivering voice. "I wouldn't mind dying here if I knew he was somewhere bleeding to death."

"Let's keep a good thought," Sarita drawled drolly. She knew Mykal was looking for her, probably moving heaven and earth in the process, but that wasn't much help to her and Faye at the moment.

The sound of a soft skittering broke the silence.

Sarita shot panicked eyes around the room. The sound came again.

Faye asked, "What is that sound?"

"Rats."

Faye uttered a one-word curse.

"Big Tiny is going to be dinner. We really need to get out of here, Faye."

Sure enough, Sarita could see the eyes of the scavengers glowing back at her in the settling darkness. She knew the rodents would wait for a while to see whether she and Faye were a threat, then, little by little, they'd approach the corpse. Sarita thought she might be sick.

As she and Faye watched tensely, the rats began to shed the shadows. First one, then two. They were your standard city rats; gray, ugly, big as pampered suburban house cats, with tails long as snakes. Sarita hated rats; everyone in the city did.

They were moving in a steady stream. A few brushed by Sarita's and Faye's ankles. Both women screamed with alarm and tried to move away, but they couldn't. Their only recourse was to sit there cringing, and yelling, hoping it would scare the creatures away. The awful feel of warm fur scraped Sarita's ankles again and again. She closed her eyes and prayed she wouldn't be bitten.

But the rats didn't seem interested in live prey, at least for the time being. With the feast awaiting them and the smell of blood in the air, they were drawn in ever-growing numbers. Soon the silence was filled with their snarls and squeaks as they fought and fed. Sarita could hear Faye crying softly. Tears were running down Sarita's cheeks, too.

Sarita had no idea how much time passed, or how many rats were convened over the corpse, but suddenly, the lights were on, and the sound of automatic gunfire sent the rats scrambling.

Sarita's eyes took a moment to adjust to the glare, but when they did, there sat Clark Nelson in a wheelchair. Flanking him were the two armed men from before.

Clark smiled. "Bet you're glad to see me."

Both women hated to admit it, but yes, they were.

Eighteen

The phone company wasn't able to give Myk an exact read on the signal from Sarita's phone, the technology wasn't that precise; however, they were able to narrow the location to a ten-block section on the westside. So, for the past several hours, Myk and his people, some city police officers and Federal agents, had been combing the area within the targeted grid. They went through abandoned homes, alleys, neighborhood garages, even Dumpsters, but found no trace of Sarita. They hadn't been able to find Nelson either since he'd checked out of his hotel. Faye was missing, too. They all seemed to have vanished into thin air.

Dark had fallen, and Myk was sick inside. *Where was she!* He'd talked to Saint about an hour earlier and although his half brother was still angry, the two of them had managed to discuss possible strate-

gies without jumping down each other's throats.
Saint and some FAA agents were at the airport
keeping Nelson's private plane under surveillance.

Now, standing outside of the van serving as their
command post, Myk didn't even feel the December
cold. What he did feel was helpless and powerless,
not something the CEO of Chandler Works was accustomed to. He was accustomed to being in control, on top, alpha male. At that moment, he was just
a man being torn apart. The prospect of not ever
seeing her again was one of the bleakest he'd ever
had to contemplate. He had to find her; he needed
to tell her how much he loved her, and he did love
her, he realized, deeply, completely. Nothing in life
would be the same if she was removed from his
world, so Myk focused himself inward and began
to pray.

While Myk was seeking strength and hope Walter
was inside the van monitoring police dispatches on
the radio scanner. When he heard a call for a mobile
unit to investigate reports of gunfire, he listened intently. He quickly wrote down the address, then
went over to the laptop and punched in the numbers. The address came up within the phone company's grid. He knew reports of gunfire were
twenty-four/seven in an urban environment like
Detroit, and maybe this particular incident had
nothing to do with Sarita at all, but Walter went to
the door and hollered for Myk and the others just
the same.

"So," Nelson purred malevolently. "Did you two
bond while I was away?"

For all of his smugness, Clark didn't look well.

There was a paleness beneath his color that hadn't been there before Faye's shooting.

When neither of the women answered, Nelson asked, "Rats got your tongues?" He laughed at his own wit.

The women did not.

Still chuckling, he said. "Okay, enough silliness, how about we get back to the diamonds, Mrs. Chandler? We've a plane to catch in a few hours, and I'd like for us to be friends when the time comes. The only way we can do that is for you to tell me the truth."

"Where are we going?" Faye asked warily.

"You aren't going anywhere, remember?" His eyes blazed. "But don't worry, I'll take care of you in a while. Right now, it's Mrs. Chandler's turn."

Sarita met his eyes but didn't back down.

Clark asked her, "Did your husband tell you how he and I met?"

"No, but he did say you went to prison for raping a fourteen-year-old girl."

"The little bitch deserved it, and your husband didn't do a damn thing to help me."

Clark pointed to his withered leg. "See this. He's responsible. Bastard. If he had helped me, I never would have had worms under my skin, or had to cut my leg open to get the damn things out."

Sarita and Faye stared at each other.

Clark saw their confusion, and said, "Ever heard of the bot fly, ladies?"

Neither had.

"It's a tropical insect. The larvae need a warm-blooded host, so the bot fly captures mosquitoes and places its eggs on the mosquitoes' legs. When the mosquito bites, the eggs fall into the wound, and the larvae form beneath the skin. They soon grow little hooks to anchor them to the flesh, and they eat at you as they grow."

Sarita shuddered.

Clark told them, "I thought I had a simple insect bite at first, but the spots kept getting larger and larger and the pain getting worse and worse. The warden wouldn't let me see a doctor. So you know what I did?"

Neither answered.

"I did the only thing I knew to do. I took a knife and cut one open."

He asked them, "Ever had to cut into your own flesh and have a living breathing organism ooze out of your skin like a night crawler wriggling out of a hole?"

Sarita closed her eyes and bile rose in her throat.

"It made me sick to my stomach, too, so I had to wait a few days before I could take care of the other two bites, but I did it," he said proudly. "I thought I was home free until my leg got so infected and made me so delirious with fever the warden had to send me to the hospital. Two weeks and two operations later, this is the leg I was left with."

Not a pretty story, Sarita said to herself, but she had no plans to offer him sympathy.

He told Sarita, "Chandler owes me. If it hadn't been for him, I wouldn't be crippled. What better revenge than to have his wife stretched out beneath me night after night after night."

A cold fear crept over her, but she hid it beneath the contempt on her face.

"Now," Nelson said, returning to the matter at

hand, "how did Fletcher know Fishbein had my diamonds?"

The sound of glass breaking interrupted the proceedings. Nelson head's swung around like a reptile's. The guards raised their guns, and their eyes began roaming the room.

Nelson said to one, "Go see what that is."

Before the man could move, the lights went out.

In the dark, Sarita didn't know what was happening, but since it didn't appear to be anything Nelson had planned, she hoped it was scaring the hell out of him. It was certainly scaring her.

"Find a flashlight!" she heard Nelson snap. He sounded rattled.

"Where?" one of the thugs asked. He didn't sound real confident either. Sarita wondered if he might be remembering the rats.

"Go look in the limo," Nelson ordered. "Try the glove box."

"Okay."

Although there was a bit of light coming in off the street through the window, it wasn't enough to do anything but lighten the shadows. Sarita looked around and wondered if something was happening downstairs. Windows certainly didn't break on their own. Was it related to the lights going out, or just a fluke, like a dead fuse, or a power outage?

In the half dark, minutes passed, but Nelson's man didn't return. The other guard asked, "You want me to go look for him?"

"Yes. Leave me the gun, though."

The henchman hesitated. Sarita couldn't see Miami Orange's face clearly, but by the nervous way he kept looking around, it was plain he wanted the gun for his own protection.

Nelson snapped, "Give me the damn gun and go see what's keeping Terrell."

Miami Orange finally handed over the weapon and went off to find his missing partner.

He came back only a few minute later, saying nervously, "The glass is broke out of the window downstairs, and the screen's gone."

Sarita felt hope rise for the first time. She could feel Faye straighten, too.

"Did you see Terrell?"

"No. When I saw the broken window I came right back here."

Sarita wondered what Nelson would do now? Broken windows, lights out. Something *was* going on. It didn't take him long to make a decision.

"Cut them free. We're getting out of here."

The thug hustled over and quickly began using his switchblade on the ropes. Sarita had learned a lot about self-defense in Fukiya's martial-arts class. The kneeling man was perfectly positioned to get the crap kicked out of him, but she doubted her feet would obey her after being tied up all afternoon. There was also the small problem of the gun in Nelson's lap, so she sat quietly instead.

With the ropes gone, Sarita could feel the stinging in her ankles and her arms signaling the return of normal circulation.

"Let's go," Nelson commanded, looking around suspiciously.

Sarita groused, "At least give us a minute to get the feeling back in our feet."

"We ain't got time for that," Miami Orange told

her. He dragged her up and pushed her forward. Her dead feet weren't ready; she stumbled and fell. Her wrist took the brunt of the fall, and she winced sharply. Lying there she thought she caught a glimpse of movement in the shadows off to her right. She quickly looked away to keep from drawing Nelson's attention.

"Get up!" Nelson barked. He quickly rolled the chair over.

"My wrist is broken!" she snapped, and from the pain radiating up her arm, she was pretty sure it was true.

Miami Orange suddenly grabbed his neck. "Ow! Something just bit me!" He pulled his hand away and looked down at his palm. "A dart?"

For a moment, they were all so stunned no one moved, then their eyes widened as he crumpled like a wet sheet to the floor.

Sarita wanted to cheer, but Nelson raised the gun and began firing indiscriminately into the shadows. Sarita hugged the floor while bullets exploded and ricocheted over her head. Then came silence.

Nelson yelled, "Show yourself, or I'll kill them both!"

Sarita saw that Faye was on the floor as well.

When no one answered, Nelson said to Faye and Sarita, "Get up. Let's go!"

Sarita's wrist was screaming, and she didn't want to go anywhere; but he was up out of the wheelchair, one hand leaning on the cane, the other holding the gun.

"Out the door and around to the steps. Slowly now!"

Sarita could see how much it was costing him

physically to have to move under his own power. He didn't look steady at all on the cane, and his breathing was loud and labored, but he had the gun. She wanted to run so badly, but she didn't want to get shot in the back.

With that in mind, Sarita walked with Faye, slowly, staying no more than a foot or so front of him. They moved out of the room and out onto the catwalk that circled around to the stairs. Because they were ahead of him, they reached the catwalk a few steps ahead of him. In that breath of a second, Sarita could see the dark outlines of figures moving around. Sarita didn't know whether the persons were friend or foe, but from the surprise in Faye's eyes when she looked at Sarita, Sarita surmised Faye had seen them, too. They kept walking.

Myk and his people were kneeling in the darkness on the main floor. When he saw Sarita and Faye come out onto the metal catwalk, his heart filled with joy. *She's alive!* He raised his hand for his men not to fire, the ladies were too close to Nelson, and Myk didn't want them hit in a cross fire.

Clark limped slowly behind them, the pain in his leg like fire. The doctor he'd seen earlier that day had extracted the bullet successfully, but he'd advised Clark to stay off the leg for a few days. Clark didn't have that luxury though. He had to get the women out of there, take care of them, then fly back to Chicago to heal up.

Clark was so focused on his pain and on keeping the women in his sight, he didn't see the men downstairs until it was too late.

Suddenly he was in a spotlight.

"Put down your weapon, Nelson!"

Chandler.

Clark yelled at the women. "Stop right there!" Adrenaline pumping, he looked around wildly for a way out. "Stop dammit!"

With Mykal so close there was no way Sarita was going to let this monster have her again, so she grabbed Faye's hand and screamed, "Run!"

Nelson could see they were trying to get away, taking with them the info on his diamonds and his chance for revenge on Chandler. Furious, he bellowed, "Nooo!" and opened fire on them, then turned the gun quickly on the figures downstairs, forcing them to dive for cover.

Heart pumping, her wrist throbbing, Sarita ran; Faye ran. Bullets flew around them like a deadly hail. They made it to the stairs and thought they were home free when Sarita felt her back explode. Filled with more pain than she'd ever felt in her life, she pitched forward and slowly tumbled down the stairs.

"Sarita!" Myk screamed in anguish. Not caring about his own safety, he started running.

Up on the catwalk, Clark had drawn himself back around the corner, out of the line of fire, and as he caught his breath, allowed himself a small smile of satisfaction. He hoped she was dead. Chandler deserved no less. Clark thought he heard a noise behind him, and he turned, intending to blast away, but stopped at the sight of the oddly dressed man facing him. He was totally shrouded in gray—hooded, masked. The only part of his body visible were his eyes, and in those eyes, even in the dark, Clark saw death. Panicked, he raised his gun again, but it was too late. Two short knives whistled across

the distance. One caught Clark in the shoulder and
the second one in the heart. The twin forces stag-
gered him backward out onto the catwalk. Lit by
the spotlight, he hit the rail and went over. He was
dead before he hit the ground.

Nineteen

Myk stood outside the operating room in clothes still covered with his wife's blood. Back at the warehouse, when he'd reached her at the bottom of the steps, she was lying so still he'd refused to wait for the ambulance. Instead, he'd gently scooped her up and held her in his arms while Walter drove like a bat out of hell to the hospital. Myk carried her into the ER demanding help. The doctors rushed to prep her for surgery, and Myk had followed, ignoring the staff's demand that he wait in the lobby.

The surgery had been going on for six hours. Drake had come out of the OR an hour or so ago to let Myk know that although Sarita was in serious condition, her vitals were strong. Drake was confident that between Sarita's inner strength and the skilled surgeons attending her, she would make it;

but Myk wouldn't be convinced until he saw her smile again.

Saint was also keeping vigil outside the operating room. Walter, Shirley, and Silas were anxiously waiting downstairs.

Saint looked at his big brother, and said, "Sorry I was such a jerk."

"No problem."

"She wouldn't want us fighting."

"No she wouldn't."

Myk looked back at Saint. "You were right though. I didn't keep her safe."

"Wasn't your fault. I know you think you created the world, but this was beyond even you. Had we known about Nelson earlier, maybe things would have turned out differently."

"If she dies . . ."

Saint met Myk's eyes. "You love her, don't you?"

"Very much."

"I love her, too. Have since the day her grandmother brought me home to live with them. Sarie was nine. I thought she was the prettiest and toughest girl I'd ever seen. Still do."

Myk studied his brother.

Saint said, "But she doesn't love me like that. I'm her brother. She's chosen you, so I have to respect that."

Myk now understood. "Truce, then?"

"Yeah. I just want her to be happy."

Myk smiled. "Me too."

Silence settled as they resumed their vigil.

A groggy Sarita awakened to a body that was hooked up to tubes and monitors, and hurt like hell whenever she tried to move so much as a toe. Pain etched her face as she looked around. She spied a sleeping Myk sprawled in a chair. His clothes were wrinkled and creased. His beard had grown out on his cheeks, and he was snoring loud enough to wake the dead. She smiled and drifted back to sleep.

Four days later, she was out of the woods. Her broken wrist would be in a cast for another six weeks, and she was still being closely monitored by her nurses, Drake, and her surgeon.

Myk was her first official visitor even though she knew from Drake and the nurses that he'd not left her side since the night he brought her in. When he walked in carrying what appeared to be fifty dozen roses, she laughed, then stopped because it hurt.

He came over and gave her a solemn kiss on the forehead. "How are you feeling?"

"Like I've been shot, but other than that—"

Myk was pleased to know she was turning back into her old spirited self.

He put the roses on the windowsill and pulled up a chair. "Just so you'll know, the roses came from every florist on the eastside."

She smiled. "Thank you."

"I'm saving the ones I ordered from Spain until you come home."

She shook her head, then asked, "How are you?"

"Now that you're better, so am I."

"Drake told me you had the hospital in an uproar when you brought me in—yelling, threatening, ordering the doctors around."

"They weren't moving fast enough for me."

And they weren't. Holding her in his arms while

her life's blood soaked through his jacket, all he could think about was how much he loved her and how deathly still she'd been. He never wanted to go through something like that again.

She wanted to touch his cheek, but her physical limitations made that impossible for now. "So what happened with Faye? Did I tell you she shot Big Tiny and plugged Nelson in the leg? She should be on somebody's SWAT team."

"She told me about it, and the rats."

Sarita shuddered. "The rats were awful, but she had Nelson screaming like Fay Wray in *King Kong*."

Myk smiled. "We all underestimated Faye."

"Especially Nelson." Sarita then said, sadly, "Crane raped her and beat her up. That's why she killed him."

"I know. The police aren't pressing charges. She's going home to Virginia. I doubt she'll ever come back here."

Sarita and Faye might have started off at odds, but Sarita wished Faye well. "So do you think Kerry actually killed Nelson?"

Myk shrugged. "No one saw anything before Nelson took his plunge. The FBI lab is analyzing the knives. So far all they know is that the wood is Asian."

She thought about her run to the stairs that night and realized she could be dead and how thankful she was to be alive. "Drake said they took four bullets out of my back."

"Yep. The surgeon said you were lucky your spinal column wasn't severed or that there wasn't more internal damage."

"I feel like a put-back-together Humpty-Dumpty."

"But it's over now, no more Nelson or Big Tiny, or hiding out. You can have your life back. And my lawyers can dissolve our agreement as soon as you want."

Sarita stared at him. "What do you mean?"

It was the hardest thing Myk ever had to do in his life. "I don't want you hurt again, Sarita." Giving her up was the wise thing to do. There were going to be more Nelsons and Cranes in his NIA life, and he didn't want her to be a target. He loved her too much.

"But you just said it was all over."

"The part with Nelson is over, but—"

Sarita understood. "But the other stuff you're mixed up in isn't."

"No."

She shook her head and sighed sadly; she was too tired to have this conversation. "Did it ever occur to you, Your Majesty, that I might want to have a say in this?"

He studied her face, not sure what she was getting at.

"You don't tell a woman on her deathbed—oh by the way, I'm divorcing you." She met his eyes. "Is this what you want, really?"

Myk knew it wasn't. He wanted to grow old with her—help her rebuild her center—make love to her in every country in the world; but more importantly, he wanted to love her until the day he died. "No, it isn't."

"Then now's the time to tell me all about this secret life, don't you think?" Sarita winced as a stitch pulled. "After that, I'll decide if I want to divorce *you*."

Myk shook his head, chuckled softly, then told her all.

When he was done, she was quiet for some time, then said, "That's a pretty ambitious job."

"I know."

"And NIA is just an experimental group for now?"

He nodded. "Yes. If it works here, the government may try and establish it in other cities. We're the test case. We're being funded for about eighteen months more."

Sarita mulled over all he'd said. She had nothing but admiration for the men and women he was working with and hoped they would be able to make a difference.

He then added, "I don't want anyone else coming after you because of me."

Sarita's heart swelled hearing his concern, but he didn't get to take all the blame. "This was my doing, too. If I hadn't made that deal with Fletcher—"

All they'd shared since the night they met in Room 1533 came back to her. She loved this man as much as she loved hot fudge sundaes. Was he really trying to break things off? "I thought we were getting along okay before all this happened."

"We were, in fact—" He paused, trying to find the words he wanted to use to relay the depths of his feelings.

"What?"

"I'm in love with you, Sarita. Plain and simple."

Sarita let his declaration feed her soul, then told the truth. "Plain and simple, I love you, too."

Myk couldn't believe it. He viewed her closely. "Are you sure?"

"Sure as I can be. You're one of a kind, Mykal Chandler."

"So, I can tear up the divorce papers?"

"Into tiny little pieces."

For the first time in his life, Mykal didn't know what to say or do. He wanted to climb to the hospital's roof and yell out his happiness so loud folks would hear him in Sault Ste. Marie. "Will you marry me, again? I want it to be at the center."

Sarita was stunned. "Why, Grandma, what a soft heart you have."

He leaned over and kissed her lips. "The better to love you with, my dear."

She grinned, and he grinned back.

Twenty

 Myk and Sarita were married again at the center on Valentine's Day. Drake was asked to officiate, and the the kids decorated the place like a wedding cake.

Standing up with Sarita were Shirley and the Army. Myk chose Walter, Keta, and Silas to be his supporting cast. He tried to get Saint to stand up with him, too, but Saint refused to put on a suit, so he stood off to the side to watch the happy proceedings with the rest of her friends. Kerry Fukiya came bearing a beautiful emerald silk stole that he presented to her as a gift. Sarita gave him a strong, grateful hug, and he bowed solemnly in response. He and Myk shook hands, then Kerry smiled and went to stand beside Saint.

Drake had just began the words when an elegantly dressed, elderly women draped in furs and diamonds swept into the center. Hurrying to keep up with her determined stride was a drop-dead-gorgeous young man dressed in chauffeur livery. Everyone turned to stare.

"Who's that?" Sarita asked.

Myk swallowed. "My grandmother and her latest chauffeur."

"Mykal Vachon Chandler!"

Myk winced. "Hey, Gram."

Sarita could see smiles on the faces of Drake and Saint.

"Don't you 'hey, Gram' me," she said, walking up. The crowd parted like the Red Sea. "I should take a switch to you for not letting me know you were getting married. I had to find out from Saint."

She then turned to Sarita, and said, "Hello, dear. I'm Eleanor Chandler. You sure you want to marry this lug?"

"Yes, ma'am."

Eleanor eyed Sarita closely. "You know he's arrogant and bullheaded?"

"Yes."

"Do you know he can't cook? Not even a boiled egg."

Sarita liked Eleanor on the spot. "Yes, ma'am."

"You still want to marry him?"

Sarita nodded.

Eleanor sighed, "Okay then. Go ahead, Drake. Hurry up and marry them before the girl changes her mind."

Everyone laughed.

After the ceremony, the party began. The buffet prepared by the Army was set out, and Myk popped the corks on the champagne he'd flown in from California for the adults. Shirley and a few mothers had to convince the kids to turn off the hip-hop so Myk and Sarita could take the traditional first dance, but once Myk and Sarita were done, the music went back to thumping and bumping.

When the dance ended, Walter, who'd had a bit too much champagne, stood up, and said, "Shirley Lee, I want your hand in marriage."

Shirley looked up from the cake she was eating, eyed him for a moment, then said, "If you still feel that way in the morning—we'll talk."

Once again laughter filled the room.

When Myk got finally Sarita home, he carried her upstairs and into his room.

Sarita was so happy. "I feel like I'm floating on air."

Myk chuckled, "I think you had too much champagne."

"Maybe, maybe not," she said, grinning.

He set her on her feet, looked down into her eyes, and said, "I love you very very much, Sarita Chandler."

"And I love you, too. So much so, that I got you something."

He grinned down. "What?"

She ran out of the room, and he thought to himself, *Yep, too much champagne,* so while he waited for her to return he stripped off his tie and thanked God for putting her in his life.

She was gone so long, he almost went to find her, but she returned wearing a flowing red kimono that was as transparent as a cloud. The open halves were bordered with a band of silk-topped lace that also edged the cuffs of the long filmy sleeves. It had no buttons or ties, it just hung open, tempting him with teasing flashes of her breasts, the nook of her navel, and her red hot thong.

Myk swore his eyes were going to burn out of his head. She must have taken a quick shower, too, because her body looked oiled, and he could smell her sexy perfume. "My, my, my," he said. She looked rich, scandalous, and ready for whatever pleasures he wanted to bestow.

In her hand she had a square thin package wrapped in gold paper. "For you."

Myk took it and gave her a soft passionate kiss in thanks. Tearing off the paper, he revealed the book inside. When he saw the title, he roared with laughter.

She winked at him, and he asked, arousal in his eyes. "Do you want a bedtime story?"

Desire rising, she nodded. "Yes."

He reached out and teased a nipple until it hardened just the way he liked it. "Have you been good?"

"Oh, yes," she breathed.

Myk slipped out of his clothes. A few moments later, he was beside her in his big bed and one light was turned up just bright enough for him to see the words. Opening to page one, he began to read: "Once upon a time, there was a little girl named Red Riding Hood. . . ."

A content Sarita snuggled closer and smiled.